"THERE ARE M
I'D RATHER BE . . .

"Many other men with whom I'd rather keep company."

"Then go to them, and with my blessing. Spread your ghostly thighs for as many bucks as you like."

Her mouth flattened. She seemed unaccustomed to having anyone tell her what to do. In her life, she must have been a woman of status. He'd seen the same upright posture in aristocratic women, the elegant hauteur that came from generations of selective marriage. Yet this ghost held more confidence in the set of her shoulders than any living female, a confidence born from innate power.

He frowned as desire flared through him. He couldn't desire a *ghost*, and certainly not *this* ghost.

Needing to be away from her, he walked on, until he found himself in the library.

Neither the fire nor the candles were lit. The only source of illumination came from the sickle of a moon throwing weak gray light upon the patterned rug and calf leather–bound books. Their impassive spines offered no comfort—but he'd never turned to books for solace.

As he stared at the shelves, the ghost took shape beside a heavy cabinet. She threw off her own light, a pearlescent gleam that softly touched the wooden carvings in a way that was almost beautiful.

He took another drink. "How impossibly dull you are."

Lifting her chin, she was haughty as an empress. "I'm not here by choice." She eyed him, her gaze lingering on his partially unlaced shirt, and how the fabric clung to his damp skin. Alive or dead, he understood women. And he was not mistaken in the flare of carnal interest in her eyes.

Books by Zoë Archer

The Blades of the Rose

Warrior
Scoundrel
Rebel
Stranger

The Hellraisers

Devil's Kiss
Demon's Bride

Published by Kensington Publishing Corporation

SINNER'S HEART

The Hellraisers

Zoë Archer

ZEBRA BOOKS
KENSINGTON PUBLISHING CORP.
http://www.kensingtonbooks.com

ZEBRA BOOKS are published by

Kensington Publishing Corp.
119 West 40th Street
New York, NY 10018

All Kensington titles, imprints, and distributed lines are available at special quantity discounts for bulk purchases for sales
promotion, premiums, fund-raising, educational, or institu-
tional use.

Special book excerpts or customized printings can also be
created to fit specific needs. For details, write or phone the office
of the Kensington Special Sales Manager: Attn.: Special Sales
Department. Kensington Publishing Corp., 119 West 40th
Street, New York, NY 10018. Phone: 1-800-221-2647.

Zebra and the Z logo Reg. U.S. Pat. & TM Off.

ISBN-13: 978-1-4201-2229-9
ISBN-10: 1-4201-2229-0

First Printing: April 2013

10 9 8 7 6 5 4 3 2 1

Printed in the United States of America

For Zack, and all we have survived together

Chapter 1

London, 1763

There was no pleasure in sinning when one sinned alone.
Not so long ago, Abraham Stirling, Lord Rothwell hadn't
been alone. When Bram would plunge into the night and its
pleasures, there had been others beside him to share the
wickedness. The five of them had done such acts as to make
the whole of London their stage and audience, the city held
rapt by scandal of the Hellraisers' making.

It was down to him, now. Whilst his friends had strayed,
he held tight to the wild paths. Sin and immorality and in-
dulgence at any cost. His one reliable means of forgetting.

Bram was alone tonight, but soon he wouldn't be.

Laughing, Lady Girard swayed down the corridor, away
from the crowded ballroom. She did not look back, but his
footfalls upon the polished floor deliberately announced his
pursuit. Bram made no secret of his hunt. Breaking her
studied insouciance, she cast him a deliberate glance over
her shoulder as she slipped into one of the small, empty
chambers, leaving the door open.

Behind him, sharp laughter rang out, the sounds of men
and women determined to enjoy themselves no matter the

price. Desperation edged their gaiety, as though by dancing, drinking, and flirting, they might beat back the specter of madness that haunted the city.

He wouldn't think of that. He would think of nothing but his own pleasure. Thus his aggressive pursuit this evening of Lady Girard, as her husband gambled away a fortune in the card room.

Whit never cared for the games of chance at assemblies. He had said they never played deep enough for his liking, the stakes far too low. More than a few nights with the Hell-raisers had been spent in gaming hells, immersed in risk, winning and losing staggering sums of money. Whit had his strategies, even before he'd been able to manipulate the odds. He'd tried to instruct Bram, but Bram hadn't the patience for calculation and cunning. Not at cards and dice.

Loss carved a hollow within his chest. No, he wouldn't think of Whit, either. Nor Leo nor Edmund. Not even John.

This night is mine. Lady Girard will be mine.

He stepped into the small chamber and closed the door behind him. The sounds of forced gaiety muted. The only noise within this sitting room was the ticking of a gilt clock on a mantel, and Lady Girard's heeled slippers tapping on the floor as she walked backward, watching him with a sly gaze.

Light from a single candelabra turned her yellow, low-necked gown lustrous and painted the tops of her breasts gold. She was beautiful, her powdered hair as pale as ivory, her lips bearing traces of artful paint. A glittering trinket of a woman.

Just enough sparkle to distract him for a few blessed moments.

"That daring gown flatters you, Lady Girard."

She leaned back against a small table, her hands resting on its edge. The position thrust up her chest so that the neckline of the gown dipped even lower, almost fully exposing her breasts.

"*You* flatter me, Lord Rothwell."

"Flattery is a means of deception, and I do not deceive." He stalked closer, feeling the hum of anticipation through his body, until he stood over her.

She chuckled. "I know all about you." She trailed a finger up the length of his chest, toying with the sparkling jet buttons of his waistcoat, and lingering in the spaces between the buttons. A hum of appreciation curled from her lips.

Lust, and only lust between them. So simple. The call of one body to another. Animal and basic, for all their sophisticated voices and urbane glances. The lush realm of the senses.

He stepped closer, the froth of her skirts about his legs.

"You claim to know all about me." He ran one finger over the curve of Lady Girard's collarbone, and her eyes drifted closed. "Yet here you are."

"I'm told that too much chocolate is detrimental to my health, and yet I crave its taste." She looked pleased by her wit, and he'd no doubt she would repeat the phrase again to another lover.

"We have circled one another for long enough."

"And here I was, despairing that I might ever draw your notice." She gazed up at him through the fan of her lashes, a coquette's practiced look. God knew that Bram had seen an abundance of that same calculated flirtation, and done his own share.

"You have it now."

She tossed her head. The sapphires at her ears danced. Another deliberate move. "What if I desire more than your notice?"

He was in no mood to indulge her need for flattery. Too much burned through him—loss, anger, despair. There was only one way he knew to gain solace. It might be temporary, but any relief was better than none.

"Do you want me to swive you, or not?"

Her eyes widened at his directness. "Well, yes, but—"

"Turn around and put your hands on the table."

For a moment, she just stared at him, as though shocked by his command. He stared back, and reached into himself, drawing upon the power within him. It was a pair of velvet shackles he might fasten wherever he desired. A single suggestion, and he felt her will bend, supine, to his.

Her eyes turned glassy and bright. He knew that look well.

"Of course," she murmured with a little smile. Her gown made a rustling sound as she turned and bent over the table. Over her shoulder, she sent him a sultry glance.

He gathered up her skirts, his hands filling with silk that felt like brittle, dead leaves. He did not look at her legs, though they were soft and satiny, but concentrated on the back of her neck, where a line of fallen hair powder had gathered and mixed with her sweat.

The need took hold of him, brutal and demanding. To fall into the torrent of lust, where only bodily pleasure existed, and he could forget the collapsing world.

He reached for the fastenings of his breeches.

Lady Girard stirred. "Are we to have an audience?"

Frowning, he said, "We're alone."

"Then who is that?" She nodded toward the farthest corner of the room, veiled in shadow. "And why is she in fancy dress?"

He stared. A woman stood in the corner, watching them with a mixture of bewilderment and fascination.

She wore the clothing of ancient Rome: draped tunic, diadem in her artfully curled hair, snake-shaped bracelet winding up her arm.

He cursed. He knew her. All too well. Valeria Livia Corva.

"Leave me the hell alone," he growled.

Livia started. She glanced down at Lady Girard, then back up at him. "You . . . see me?"

"Of course I bloody see you." Though Lady Girard shifted beneath him, he would not relinquish his hold on her skirts.

"I do not . . . how am I . . . ?" Livia drifted closer, out of the shadows.

"Oh, my God!" Lady Girard pushed away from the table and Bram with a scream.

For the light revealed that Livia was translucent. The details of the chamber could be seen through her softly glowing form, and she did not walk upon the floor but hovered. As she moved nearer, she passed through a chair as if she were made of vapor.

"A specter!" Lady Girard bolted toward the door. She did not look back as she tore it open, then ran out into the corridor, her slippers pattering like raindrops.

Bram wanted to call her back. Yet he had used his power upon her already. It worked only once for each person. And he doubted very much that even a man as skilled in seduction as he could woo her back. For most people, the sight of a genuine ghost was terrifying and strange.

He was overly familiar with the terrifying and strange. And it enraged him.

"Spare me from your invectives and lamentations, for I haven't the stomach for them tonight." His gaze raked her as he straightened his coat. Thwarted lust seethed beneath his skin. "At least you once had the good manners to appear to me in private."

She drifted closer, hand outstretched in demand. "You must—"

"None of this. I cannot abide hearing more of your dictates."

"But—"

"Enough," he snarled. "My pleasure here is ruined, so I must seek it elsewhere."

She scowled. "There's far more at stake than your *pleasure*."

As though he needed reminding. Edmund was dead. Whit and Leo were lost. And John . . . Bram didn't know who John was anymore. The five Hellraisers now scattered to the winds like ashes as the world burned. And they were the ones who lit the tinder.

He stared at the specter. "I don't bloody care."

Before she could speak again, he strode from the chamber. Returning to the ballroom, he saw Lady Girard being comforted by three swains. She turned her stunned gaze to him, but he didn't linger. Like everything in his life, tonight had been thrown to hell. He shouldered his way roughly through the sweaty, perfumed crowd, ignoring those that called to him or pulled at his sleeves.

Finally out of the ballroom, he sped from the house— Lord Dunfrey's place? Did it matter? His long stride took him away from the assembly, the voices, his hindered seduction, that damned *ghost*, and into the night. Into the darkness.

Night lay heavy over the city. The few lamps lining the avenues burned fitfully, trails of smoke curling toward the sky. Linkboys' torches barely penetrated the darkness. Even here in elegant St. James, shadows felt endless, choking.

He didn't know where his legs took him this night, only that he must move, and keep moving, as if the hounds of hell snapped at his heels.

Turning a corner, he heard the shouts before he saw the

men. Guttering lamplight revealed two figures locked in a fight. Knives gleamed in their hands and made metallic arcs in the air as they swung at each other. The men weren't beggars or drunkards. Their coats were clean and of fair quality. Both had lost their wigs in the scuffle, so the weak light turned their shaved heads to bare skulls.

He knew these men. Lesser nobility, and brothers. Their thrown punches and jabs with their knives revealed that they meant to hurt each other.

"Goddamn son of a whore," one snarled.

"You're a liar and a rogue," the other spat. "I'll spill your guts upon the ground."

In an instant, Bram stood between them, his sword drawn. His was no gentleman's decorative blade. The weapon had seen use.

"The both of you, stand down."

The two men stumbled backward, their gazes moving from his sword to his face and back again. He stood lightly, ready to fight.

"This isn't your business, my lord," one of the men panted.

"I don't like seeing corpses in the road." Only a week ago, Edmund had lay in the street, his blood pooling between the cobblestones. The sword that had pierced Edmund's chest had belonged to John. They had been as brothers not long before. Bram had seen it all unfold, stood in horror and watched as one of his good friends killed the other. Afterward, he envisioned the scene over and over, and every time, he was unable to prevent the outcome. Edmund dead at John's hand.

This, at least, he could stop.

"There's two of us," the other man said. "One of you. It could be *your* corpse in the street."

Bram stared at them, unblinking. He raised his sword. "One blade is all I need to spill your blood." If he couldn't stop these brothers from fighting, then by God he would make them sorry for challenging him.

The men's gazes moved to the scar that snaked down his throat. His daily reminder that he'd faced death, and survived. Bram was not easy prey.

Whatever the brothers saw in his face and stance, they didn't care for it. Eyes wide, cheeks ashen, they both dropped their knives, then turned and scuttled away like roaches.

He waited a moment. Sheathed his sword, and walked on. Yet the seething fury within him continued to burn, stoking him, his whole body alight.

Where Bram went, he didn't know. Only that all around him, the city seemed in chaos. Here, in genteel Mayfair, more fights churned on street corners. Glass from shattered shop windows glittered on the sidewalk and crunched beneath his heels. A night watchman ran from a mob.

This city is a runaway horse, careening toward disaster. As though something had been unleashed, something dark and wild, gnawing away at humanity, turning everything rancid and ugly.

You know the cause.

He stared at his jagged reflection in a broken window. Pieces of his face stared back. His eyes—when had they become so cold? His mouth—had it always been this cruel? Or had these changes come over him these past few months, ever since that night at the Roman ruin near his country estate?

It doesn't matter. Nothing matters.

He stalked on. His steps slowed when he discovered himself standing outside the Marquess of Colfax's mansion.

A smile curved his mouth. Several months ago Bram had challenged the other Hellraisers to a shooting contest, and they'd shot off the finials on the marble balustrade. Leo had been the winner, and they'd gone to celebrate his victory with a cadre of opera dancers and smuggled French brandy.

Bram now walked close and placed his hand on the chipped stone. The marble finials still had not been replaced. Neither had the memory.

The front door to Colfax's home opened. Bram stared as Colfax himself came charging down the steps. Uncharacteristic rage twisted the marquess's face. He'd always been the most genial of men—Bram had once accidentally spilled wine on Colfax's velvet waistcoat, and the marquess had actually apologized for being in Bram's way—yet now the older man barreled toward him with fury in his eyes.

"You think I didn't know? You think I didn't see?" Colfax jabbed his finger into Bram's chest. "The lot of you, despoiling my property and laughing. Laughing! I watched the whole thing, and I didn't do a damned thing to stop you. But I won't tolerate it, d'ye see? Not any longer. The five of you will pay!"

The shock that had held Bram immobile snapped. Anger surged. Here was another sign that the world had gone mad. The five Hellraisers were no more, their friendship razed, and lunacy gripped the city. He still woke, sweat-drenched, from dreams of past madness, the shouts of dying soldiers and Indian war-cries ringing in his ears. And here they were again, his old demons—death, chaos, brutality. No matter how fast he ran, he couldn't outpace them.

His hand shot out and wrapped around Colfax's throat. He didn't care that, as a baron, he was outranked by Colfax. All that mattered was the wrath that blistered within him.

The tirade abruptly stopped as Bram lifted the marquess up so that the older man's feet left the ground.

"We should've gone on as we had," Bram snarled. "But everything changed and fell to ruin. It didn't have to."

Colfax's eyes bulged as he clawed at Bram's hand. His gaze fixed on Bram's wrist, and clouded with confusion.

Following Colfax's gaze, Bram saw what appeared to be a drawing of flames tracing up his wrist and curling up his thumb. Yet it wasn't a drawing. It was the mark of the Devil.

What had begun as a small image of fire just above his heart now encompassed the whole of his left pectoral and down his arm. The flames even traced down toward his abdomen. They grew nightly, and some day, he suspected, they would cover him entirely.

Here then, the reason why everything changed. The Hellraisers had gained their name through their misdeeds, but one night, several months ago, they became Hellraisers in truth.

My fault, all of this.

Shouts sounded from the house as servants came running to aid their master.

With a snarl, Bram released Colfax, then stalked away. He heard the marquess coughing, and the worried murmurings of the servants, wondering if they should call the constable. But Bram put Colfax behind him, and sank back into the night.

He did not know if he chased something, or if he was the one being hunted. His body churned with restless energy, setting his every nerve aflame with no means of smothering the blaze.

His muttered curse startled a sweep scurrying home. The boy stopped, nearly dropping his brushes. Face blackened with soot, the sweep's round eyes appeared startlingly pure, the only part of him not coated with grime.

"You look like an imp," Bram said.

The boy frowned. "What's an imp?"

"A little demon that stokes the fires of hell."

Painfully thin, clad in rags and barefoot, the sweep believed enough in divine intervention to cross himself. "Preacher says we aren't to speak things like that. Tempts the Devil, he says."

"Did you know the Devil is real?"

"A gent with horns and a tail, what lives under the ground?" The boy scratched his head. "Sounds crooked to me. But I don't know nothing, so my master says."

Bram took a step toward the sweep. "What if I told you that the Devil had no horns, no tail? That he looked and dressed like a gentleman, a gentleman with crystal-white eyes, and he called himself Mr. Holliday."

"Funny name," the boy said.

"He's a whimsical creature, the Devil. Can grant you the means to have your deepest desire, but never tells you the cost. Not until it's too late."

Not so long ago, Bram would have disputed the existence of the Devil. Evil existed, yes. He'd seen it in the forests of America, heard it in the screams of the dying, smelled its rot as desecrated corpses decayed in the sun. But he'd believed that evil came from the hearts of men, not a creature that ruled a mythological underworld. He knew differently now.

Would this little child tempt the Devil? For all the harshness of his existence, he was still just a child, metaphorically unsoiled, even if coal soot covered him from head to toe. A precious, untouched soul. The Devil hungered for just such a meal.

"Way you speak," the boy said, eyes round, "it's like you know 'im."

Bram's mouth twisted into a kind of smile. "We're in business together." He tossed the sweep a thruppence.

The boy snatched the coin from the air, then clutched it close. "Thank'ee, my lord," he piped. "If you got a chimney what needs sweeping—"

"Go on home."

Immediately, the sweep scampered off, the darkness swallowing him. Perhaps Bram had deprived the Devil of one less soul tonight. He felt a perverse satisfaction in denying his patron.

Alone once more. Icy sweat filmed the back of Bram's neck, and the familiar chasm opened up within him. He pushed himself into motion, into action, his long stride eating up the streets.

Several sedan chairmen hailed him—"Take you wherever you wish, my lord. Your pleasure"—but he needed to feel the ground beneath him, the movement of his body, driving away thought.

The streets he traversed grew more crowded. People thronged, voices raised, mingling together in a wash of jagged sound. A crowd milled outside the opera house in degrees of finery, yet even here tension wove through the atmosphere, as though a brawl might begin at any moment. Strolling whores plucked at his sleeve and threw bold glances like discarded ribbons. He ignored them, losing himself in the city.

"My lord, welcome back!"

Bram started, realizing that he'd taken himself without thinking to the Snake and Sextant. Smoke choked the tavern, both from the fire blazing in the hearth as well as the numerous pipes of its patrons. It smelled of beef, tobacco, beer and horsehair—the scents of a man's haven. Customers crowded the heavy tables, bent over their chops and ale, jostling elbows, loud with the evening's attempt at cheer.

But the laughter now was harsh, forced, and the patrons eyed one another with mistrust over the rims of their tankards.

Once, this place had been his refuge. Even it had become corrupted.

The tavern keeper came forward, wiping his hands on his apron, his jowls folded up into an anxious, welcoming smile. "Been too long, my lord."

"Has it?" Bram's answer was distracted, his gaze moving over the tavern in restless perusal.

"Aye. At least a month. Mayhap more. Began to worry, I did. My most esteemed patrons all vanish, as if they'd been spirited away." The tavern keeper coerced a chuckle. "Folly, of course, and here you are now! There's some blokes in your usual table, but I can shoo 'em off like flies from a carcass."

Bram looked past the tavern keeper, toward the table where he and the other Hellraisers used to take their meals. The habit had been long-standing. A meal at the Snake, fortifying them for the night's exploits, and then the exploits themselves: the theater, pleasure gardens, gaming hells, bordellos. The Hellraisers indulged in every privilege, even Leo, who was of common birth. The five of them had been inseparable. *Had* been.

Other men crowded the Hellraisers' table tonight. Their clothing was less fine, their manners more coarse, yet, if Bram allowed the smoke to blur his sight, he could almost picture his friends seated there, and trick his ears into hearing them. John would be holding forth on some political invective, only to be calmed by even-tempered Edmund. Leo would divulge all the latest intelligence from the coffee houses—whose fortunes were up, whose were down—and Whit would lay bets on anything, even when a drop of ale might fall from the rim on one's mug. And Bram would try to coax all of them to join him for a night's debauch. It never took much to tempt them.

"I imagine your friends will be joining you shortly, my lord," the tavern keeper continued, "so I'll just clear those other lads out."

"Don't."

The tavern keeper raised his brows. "My lord? It is *your* table, after all—"

"They won't be joining me."

"Ah, well, gentlemen will have their quarrels." The man gave another forced laugh. "It will all set itself to rights, my lord. You wait and see. In the meantime, I've got a lovely place right here for you, all nice by the fire." He waved toward one of the settles nearest the hearth.

Bram felt like the wood burning in the fireplace—black and blistered on the outside, inside carved away by flame. His familiar haunt only reminded him of privation.

"My lord?"

The tavern keeper's voice followed Bram as he turned and left. Whit and Leo had disappeared from London, but Bram was the one in exile.

How did she come to this place? Valeria Livia Corva could not feel her body, was merely a shade, yet she was dragged through one man's consciousness, as if her foot had caught in the stirrup of a runaway horse. She was jostled, careening, his thoughts as vivid to her as her own memories.

Time held no meaning, nor notions of space. This was the swirling vortex of one history, and she spun through the currents, without means of fixing herself in place.

Even her own memories were fragments. Temples, rites. An ever-present hunger for more and more power. The summoning of a great and terrible evil. A frightful battle, and then . . .

A millennium of darkness, trapped in the nebulous boundary between life and death. Madness. That had been her punishment—she remembered that much.

But she was suddenly wrenched from her recollection of the shadow realms. Now she drifted in a room full of leather-bound books, with undulating green hills and mist outside the tall windows. Two men were here, one old, one young. The young one resembled the older, same hawkish profile, same piercing blue eyes. The older one wore a wig, powdered and long. The younger had tied his black hair back, and in the smooth lines of his face, the narrowness of his shoulders, she saw he was a youth just emerging into manhood. He looked familiar to her.

"The commission is a good one," the older man said. He sat behind a large, heavy desk, its legs carved into the forms of mythical beasts. "A lieutenant in the Royal Regiment of Foot."

"I wanted a captaincy." The youth crossed his arms over his chest, more a peevish child than a man.

"And you'll get it, but it must be earned."

The youth snorted.

"Two options are open to you." The older man planted his hands upon the desk and stood. He wore the confidence belonging to a man of consequence, the pride that arose from careful, selective breeding. The old, esteemed families of Rome carried themselves in just such a way—in her life, she had been one of their number.

"Join the clergy?" The youth affected a sneer, yet beneath his aggressive self-importance, he feared and loved the man who stood on the other side of the desk. She was both an observer of the scene, and *within* the youth, his emotions twined around her own heart. "I'll not rot away, trapped in a rural parish and delivering sermons to drunk farmers."

"Then you shall take the lieutenancy, and be glad of it. Perhaps you will surprise us all and find yourself suited for a soldier. You brawl well enough at school."

A bolt of hot shame coursed through the boy. "If the tutors taught us anything worthwhile, I mightn't resort to fighting. School is so deuced boring."

"No one ever thought you a scholar, Bram. Leave the thinking to Arthur."

The one with value. Bram had been conceived as a contingency, but that left him with greater freedom.

I know him, Livia thought. He was one of the five men who had freed the Dark One from his prison, liberating her, as well.

"Will I go to war, Father?" He might prove himself on the battlefield, show himself to be a great hero.

The older man came around the desk, hale and handsome in a settled, prosperous way, though he'd thickened with age. At one time, he had been a sportsman, and a portrait of him hung upstairs, showing him astride a sleek horse with an alert hound quivering at attention nearby. The youth hoped to emulate his father, even though he could never have the significance of his older brother.

"Oh, my boy, 'tis unlikely. But don't look so crestfallen. For you will cut a fine figure in your uniform, and ladies do enjoy the sight of a man in gold braid and scarlet."

The boy brightened. He did like ladies. Greatly. He tried to envision himself in the uniform, striding down a London street with the regard of everyone flung in his path like roses.

Won't Whit be jealous, when he sees me looking so fine?

Yes, she knew Whit. He'd been the first of the five men to turn away from the Dark One. She needed to reach him, and his woman. They were her allies.

Yet when she reached out, trying to pierce the mists between the living and the dead, she was flung back into Bram's memories. Time splintered again, scattering images.

She was in a field at the edge of a forest. All around the field were thick-trunked trees, bare limbs stretching up toward a metallic winter sky. Scents of rotting vegetation rose up from the mud. And the sharp smell of blood, which could not be dulled by the cold wind rattling the branches. Bodies lay in the bent, brown grasses, their red jackets garish. Men with dark copper skin advanced, heavy war clubs in their hands.

"Fall back!"

It was the youth, but not so young now. Bram had become a man, his shoulders filling the bright red coat, his legs sturdy in tall black boots. Mud spattered the uniform he had coveted years earlier, and grime coated his now angular face. He raised a sword and shouted again to the remaining troops.

"Make for the cover of the woods."

"But, sir, orders are—"

"Major Townsend is dead, Corporal, and if we stand and fight the Indians, we'll be joining the Major." *Now is not the time for fear. Don't think of the Major with half his head beaten in, and his brains showing.*

"Sir?"

"Now, Corporal."

The troops obeyed, and they slogged back through the sucking mud, finding shelter in the forest. They were not followed, and he led them over miles, his legs aching, his body weary. Yet he forced himself to walk upright, for he was their leader now, and must get them back to the safety of the fort.

So few of us now. Half the men killed, the other half sick and wounded. I cannot fail them. What if I do? I cannot. I am in command now.

Time fragmented again, jagged as strewn pottery shards, each with images of different moments, different places. She felt herself pulled through them, and they tore at her mind.

Now she saw ornately carved walls and a gleaming wooden floor. The chamber itself stretched out on every side, a vast chasm of a room. Music and heat saturated the air. Women in wide, silken skirts tittered behind fans, and men in equally bright silk postured and paraded before them.

Livia drifted amongst the people. Their powdered faces became the faces of her own past. Mother, father, shaking their heads over her machinations. The head priestess, who saw in Livia an unquenchable demand for greater power—a need that had taken her to the farthest reaches of the Empire. Yet these people did not wear *tunicas* and togas. They garbed themselves in stiff, glittering fashions, and instead of mosaics, gilded wood and polished mirrors covered the chamber in which they displayed themselves.

Conversation stilled as five men strode into the chamber, all gazes turning toward them like flowers following the sun's progress across the sky. These men shone with the absence of light, a brilliant darkness, and the possibility that they might do anything, and no one could stop them.

A murmur rose up from somewhere in the crowd. "Hell-raisers, the lot of them." Yet the words were spoken half in fear, half in admiration.

Bram stood at the front of the group, leading the charge. The intervening years had hardened him. He was carved obsidian. Evening clothes had replaced his grimy uniform, and the sword at his side was meant for show, not killing. Shadows haunted his eyes and thoughts. She heard them, felt them.

What shall I take this evening? The dreams won't leave me, but I can beat them back. Who will it be tonight?

Women swayed nearer. He might choose from any of them. More than a few had already filled his bed, if only for the night, but he sought something new, for his need never left him, nor did the black images that crept forward in quiet moments.

"Rothwell!"

A red-faced man stalked toward him. Collingwood. The guests stepped back to give him room, watching in scandalized fascination as he shoved closer. Then he stood before Bram, glaring up at him.

"You are a rogue and a villain," spat Collingwood.

The crowd gasped at this insult, thrown so publicly.

"I own to both titles," Bram answered.

"Have you no respect for the vows between a husband and wife?"

"*Your* wife does not, clearly. For she abandoned them with an extraordinary enthusiasm."

Gazes turned to the wife in question, who stood at the other end of the chamber. Her hands covered her mouth, and her eyes were perfect circles of mortification.

Collingwood purpled. "You will give me satisfaction at dawn."

Before Bram could speak, Whit drawled, "He already has his second."

"And third," added Leo.

"I advise you to spend the intervening hours with your fencing master," John said.

As Collingwood paled, Bram smiled, his hand resting lightly on the pommel of his sword. It wasn't properly balanced for dueling, but there would be enough time to return home and fetch his favorite Italian-made blade.

Collingwood stormed from the chamber. A cry rose up from the end of the room, and Collingwood's wife was borne away, hanging limply from supporting arms. Excited words filled the ballroom, everyone eager to spread the news of scandal.

"Should we also retire?" Edmund murmured.

"There is considerable time from now until the sun rises," said Bram. "And we've only just arrived."

Edmund shook his head, but his smile was wry. Together, the five men moved further into the assembly, wearing their wicked reputations like cloaks of scarlet. Yet none of the other guests turned away. Their smiles came wider, the women's glances more flirtatious.

Truly, we have whatever we desire. Yet it never satisfies.

The opulent chamber broke apart, and memories came so thick and fast that Livia could not separate them, lost in a tempest of one man's history. Images and emotions. Faces, voices. Anger. Sensuality. Despair.

Wasn't it torment enough that she must have her own memories of life? Now she was lost within the remembrances of a dissolute scoundrel, thick tendrils of sorrow knotted about his heart.

He prowled the streets now, troubled and restive, with Livia dragged along in his wake.

The Dark One had him in a stranglehold. Yet she felt Bram's heart as though it overlaid her own. He was damaged but surviving. Not lost, not yet.

Though if he gave himself fully to the Dark One, then evil's strength would grow a hundredfold. More. That could not happen.

She must fight the Dark One's hold on Bram. Every passing moment he stalked closer and closer to ruination. Once he crossed that boundary, he would be an unstoppable force of evil, tipping the balance into darkness.

His former friends might aid her. They could help pull him back from that chasm. She needed out of Bram's memories, needed to reach the few mortals who were her allies.

Furious, desperate, she clawed her way free. She had to disentangle herself from him, even if the price was a return to madness.

Chapter 2

He stood outside his own home. With no memory of how he got there.

"My lord?" The footman looked baffled at his appearance on the front step of his house on Cavendish Square.

Bram stepped into the foyer. The longcase clock revealed the time to be minutes after midnight. No wonder the footman appeared mystified. Bram had not been home at this hour in . . . he couldn't remember when. Likely he had still been in leading strings.

"Shall I fetch for a physician, my lord?"

"Fetch brandy," he answered. "Bring it to me in the music room."

"Yes, my lord."

As he strode down the corridor, he pulled at his stock, loosening it from around his throat. He cast off his coat along the way. Both stock and coat dropped to the ground as if he shed a carapace. He was not usually so careless with his clothing, but tonight he could not bring himself to care about spoiling the velvet or dirtying linen.

The music room had earned its name years prior, but the pianoforte was now covered with Holland cloth, and the chairs and harp were gone. Bram stalked to a press, the chamber's sole piece of furniture. Throwing open the press's doors, he found not silver, nor linens or clothing. Swords lined up in neat rows. He brushed his hand over their scabbards, then selected the curved hanger sword.

Stepping back, he gave the sword a few practice slashes through the air, loosening his shoulders. The sword was an extension of his arm, as natural as his own muscle and movement.

The footman came in with a decanter of brandy and a glass on a tray, unblinking at the sword in Bram's hand. He knew his master well enough not to falter at seeing Bram armed. Yet the footman approached slowly. Bram plucked the decanter from the tray, ignoring the glass. The servant bowed before leaving.

Taking a long drink directly from the decanter, Bram paced toward the chamber's only other occupant. He stalked to the figure, readying his sword. An expressionless face stared back at him. But he expected no response from the straw-stuffed dummy positioned in the middle of the chamber. He stared at its blank face and drank again.

The brandy burned on its way down. It wasn't enough. It would take far more than drink to ease this monstrous emptiness within him.

Prowling around the dummy, he assessed it as if it was an enemy. He feinted. Then swung his blade at the dummy. It hacked into the straw-filled canvas. Bodies felt different from straw—meaty and yielding, until you hit the resistance of bone. Dummies didn't bleed, either. But if you hit a man just so, his blood would spray across your clothing, your face. He had taken a coarse rag to his skin after one fierce battle near the Niagara River and not known whether the blood staining the water was his or if it belonged to the French soldiers he'd killed.

He'd come to learn the feeling of steel meeting flesh. Grew skilled enough to know where to strike a man so that he could no longer run, and how long it took to die from a wound to the stomach.

And how much of his own blood he could lose, and still stay alive.

The blank face of the dummy shifted, transforming in his sight to the Algonquin who'd cut his throat. Snarling, Bram now launched into an attack, chopping into the dummy as if he could kill the Algonquin all over again. He still sometimes woke, choking on imaginary blood, hand pressed to his throat. But instead of an open wound, a scar snaked across his flesh, its every contour familiar.

He thrust his sword deep into the dummy's chest. Its face changed again, and he found himself staring at Edmund— looking just as he did when he'd been stabbed. His mild brown eyes were wide with shock, his mouth forming soundless words. Only this time, Bram killed him, not John.

Perhaps he was responsible. He hadn't been able to stop it. He could have moved faster, blocked John's blade.

Rearing back, he pulled the sword from the dummy, and it clattered to the ground.

Bram hadn't called upon Rosalind, Edmund's widow, half afraid of what he might find. He didn't know if she even mourned her husband, or if she'd woken from the dream, and now embraced autonomy. With the Devil's magic no longer binding her to Edmund, she might do anything she pleased.

She'd better mourn. For Edmund had loved her, in a way Bram could barely fathom.

The same emotion was in Whit's eyes when he gazed upon his Gypsy woman. And Leo with his wife, Anne.

Bram had no knowledge of what it meant, how it felt.

He didn't want to know. Love was unreal. Or worse— perishable, fragile. Like everything else in this world. Once he believed friendship could outlast anything. Curse him for a damned fool.

After taking another deep drink, he paced back to the cabinet. His hand closed around the handle of a tomahawk. Holding it up, he studied its brutal, efficient lines. A memento he'd taken from the bastard who had cut his throat. Bram had torn it from the Algonquin's grasp and buried its blade in the Indian's skull. The weapon was his now.

He hefted the tomahawk and turned his attention to the thick logs leaning upright against the wall. Strange decoration for a room that still had gilt paneling and crystal chandeliers, but he'd insisted, and no one dared gainsay him.

Restless energy still tightened his muscles, so he strode to the logs. Raised up the tomahawk. Then brought it down, hacking into the wood. Over and over, using the tomahawk like the vicious weapon it was. He chopped away at the fury and despair within him, not stopping even when sweat slicked his body and his arm ached.

His own face stared back at him from the log. He redoubled his efforts—hacking himself down, the tomahawk's blade sinking into his flesh as he destroyed himself.

"Bastard," he snarled. "Deceiver. Betrayer. Villain."

He lifted his arm, preparing to strike again. Then froze.

Hovering between him and the log was the ghost.

"I made myself abundantly clear," he said through clenched teeth. "Hie yourself off to Tartarus, or wherever you dead Romans go."

The ghost glared at him. "I don't take commands. Certainly not from you."

He swung the tomahawk. She actually flinched as the blade passed through her torso and into the log.

After giving her a cold, contemptuous stare, he stalked away, leaving the tomahawk lodged in the wood. He took another drink as he strode into the corridor. The brandy was doing nothing.

The specter hovered in front of him, her expression murderous.

"Would've thought an axe to the chest sent a clear enough message." He narrowed his gaze. "Get out of my house. Leave me."

"There are many other places I'd rather be. Many other men with whom I'd rather keep company."

"Then go to them, and with my blessing. Spread your ghostly thighs for as many bucks as you like."

Her mouth flattened. She seemed unaccustomed to having anyone tell her what to do. In her life, she must have been a woman of status. He'd seen the same upright posture in aristocratic women, the elegant hauteur that came from generations of selective marriage. Yet this ghost held more confidence in the set of her shoulders than any living female, a confidence born from innate power.

He frowned as desire flared through him. He couldn't desire a *ghost*, and certainly not *this* ghost.

Needing to be away from her, he walked on, until he found himself in the library.

Neither the fire nor the candles were lit. The only source of illumination came from the sickle of a moon throwing weak gray light upon the patterned rug and calf leather–bound books. Their impassive spines offered no comfort—but he'd never turned to books for solace.

As he stared at the shelves, the ghost took shape beside a heavy cabinet. She threw off her own light, a pearlescent gleam that softly touched the wooden carvings in a way that was almost beautiful.

He took another drink. "How impossibly dull you are."

Lifting her chin, she was haughty as an empress. "I'm not here by choice." She eyed him, her gaze lingering on his partially unlaced shirt, and how the fabric clung to his damp skin. Alive or dead, he understood women. And he was not mistaken in the flare of carnal interest in her eyes.

Objectively, he recognized that she was wondrous to look upon, possessing a regal, dark beauty, even in this non-corporeal state. In the bold angles of her face, her full mouth and proud nose, there could be no mistaking her Roman origin. Knowledge and experience shone in her eyes, far more than possessed by even the mostly worldly English lady. Her thick dark hair was piled in artful arrangement and held back with a fillet. The pinned, draped tunic she wore revealed a lushly curved body. He was a man who knew the feel of many women's bodies, yet hers he would savor. Were she mortal.

But she was not mortal. He wanted no dealings with her. "You're dead. You have choice in abundance."

"Not in this I don't," she snapped. "Dragged around like a mule, tethered to an even bigger ass. A dissolute second son." She threw a dismissive glance toward the books. "Nothing has changed in here, not in decades. It's derelict."

He wheeled away, then strode up the stairs, until he found himself in the master's bedchamber. His room. In deference to current fashion, the walls were covered in silver paper imported from France, and silver tasseled silk hung from the canopy of the large bed. A gentleman's chamber, in which he had conducted himself in a most ungentlemanly manner. The servants knew better than to make remarks or even acknowledge the behavior of their master.

Restless, angry, he walked the length of the chamber. The clock on the mantel showed the time, so distressingly early he felt almost embarrassed. He could not recall the last time he was in this room, alone, at this hour.

Something gleamed beside the fireplace. A glowing shape that took the form of a woman.

Her.

"Hecate curse it." She said something else, something

that might have been Latin, but he'd retained nothing of his brief Classical education. He could infer her meaning, though.

"Most women are pleased to find themselves in this chamber," he felt compelled to say.

She eyed him, unamused. "I am not most women. And none of your trollops ever found themselves in my plight."

The firelight shone through her as she drifted closer. He saw the set of her mouth. Nights at the gaming hells with Whit had taught Bram something of how to read a face. This ghost held a bad hand of cards.

"You and I," she said, "we are now bound together."

She did not anticipate that he would greet this news with enthusiasm, and she was right. He looked appalled.

"More of your madness." He scowled, a look so fierce that, were she a living woman, she might be afraid.

"My mind is clear." Though it had been a struggle. Even now, she twisted between his memories, her own, and their shared present. "Unlike yours, addled by drink."

He threw the decanter. It smashed against a wall, spraying glass and amber liquid in glittering arcs. She threw up her arm to protect herself unnecessarily, then cursed her habits when he sneered at her.

"There. I'm sober as a Quaker. Yet you're still here."

"Against my will. Where you go, I'm forced to follow."

"Not because I've wished it."

"I'm well aware how little you desire my company." None of the Hellraisers had ever been pleased to see her. Neither had the two mortal women. Even in life, she would enter a chamber, and faces would shift into wariness.

Bram was a fortress walled with ice as he gazed at her. "This is one of your damned tricks."

"I don't play *tricks*. That's for the weak-willed." She had no feeling of the fire's warmth, and noted the chill black sky outside the windows yet possessed no sense of time. She knew only that the Dark One gained greater strength with every descent of the sun.

"And your character has been most admirable." Sarcasm all but dripped from his words to stain the carpet.

She had no blood to heat her cheeks. "This chamber holds two sinners. But *I* work to undo the wrongs I've caused."

"I am all esteem." He bowed, lean and elegant and venomous. "And you are as trustworthy as a spider. Catching Whit and Leo in your web was very clever, but I'm no foolish moth you can ensnare through deception."

"There is no deceit." She wished she had a physical body so she might strike him. "As you move from place to place, I'm dragged along with you. You and I are manacled together." It galled that she didn't know the how or why of it.

"And I'm to believe this passel of lies, with no proof." He crossed his arms over his chest, feet braced wide as if facing down a storm.

Frustration welled—curse him for having a will as strong as hers. "Do you think my knowing you were a second son was a fortunate guess? I was *there*. I saw it, in your memories. When your father bought you a commission. You and he stood in a room like the one downstairs, and you complained because it was not the rank you wanted."

His frown deepened. "There's no way you could know that."

"I know because I have been in your thoughts, your memories. I saw them, felt them."

Gaze and mouth hard as winter, he growled, "You had no *right*—"

"It wasn't by design," she shot back.

"My memories are *mine*." He stalked toward her, until a small distance separated them. She saw the ring of indigo that encircled the ice blue of his eyes, and the freezing anger within them. "You violated them."

"This, from the man who uses magic to get women into his bed. Isn't that a violation, too?"

His gaze dropped, briefly. "They're all well pleasured."

"Yet you take choice from those women, and no amount of pleasure ameliorates that." Was that regret tightening his jaw? Could she imagine that he felt remorse for his actions? She had tumbled through the tempest of his mind, and yet he remained opaque as steel. "I've memories enough of my own. I don't need yours, yet I saw them anyway, after I found myself in a chamber with you and one of your conquests."

"*Intended* conquest." His mouth twisted. "She didn't care for a spectral audience."

Livia would not feel contrite. She had no yearning to watch this virile, lean man make love, taunting her with what she had lost and would never have again. Though she could not stop images and thoughts from seeping in. In his sleek movement, he revealed his capability, his sensuality. He would be an expert in love play, turning an animal act into something creative and perhaps even brutally beautiful.

Stop this. Don't torment yourself.

"That wasn't by choice, either." She glanced away, then back. "Watching such scenes is a punishment."

His gaze narrowed at this, and moved over her, assessing and bold. "I can see how that might be so."

When she had been alive, few men had possessed the insolence to look at her so brashly. She'd been one of the first families of Rome, and a priestess of considerable power. Was it her spectral state that allowed Bram to stare at her, his gaze brazen, openly carnal? Or was it the man, himself?

"There's no deceit here," she said. "No guile. If this were my strategy, I'd choose a far less punitive one."

"Meaning I am *haunted*." His words cut like mirror shards. "By you."

She nodded.

"Tell me how long I have to endure your presence."

"Any moment is too long," she snapped. "And I have no answers."

He glared down at the floor as if it whispered calumny. "Another delightful turn of events." Turning to her suddenly, a hard, keen look crossed his face.

She felt a change in him, a gathering of power drawing around him like shadows.

"I urge you to leave." He spoke the words as if they were an incantation, then waited.

"Must we go over this again? We're *tied* to one another." She stared at him. "You just attempted to use your magic on me."

A scowl darkened his face. "It hasn't yet failed me."

"The power that lashes us together may be stronger than yours."

"Or it doesn't work on dead women."

"If you think to insult me with your bluntness, you will be sorely disappointed." She waved down at herself, the transparent luminosity of her form. "I've had a considerable amount of time to adjust to my circumstances."

He was a thundercloud of a man as he swung away. Easy to see him as a soldier in the lethal economy of his movement. "I'm not so inured to the presence of ghosts, let alone being chained to one."

"Witness my own joy at this state of affairs." Yet it need not be a wasted opportunity. This man was the linchpin in the fight. If she could turn him to the cause of defeating the Dark One, surely the chances of success must increase. He could be very powerful, if he so chose to be. But whether his power was for the Dark One or against him, that was yet in doubt.

He went to stand at the window, staring out at the darkness.

She drifted closer to him, until she was beside him. Women would be drawn to such a man, helpless as starving deer, craving a taste of him. Even without the magic given to him, he would pull them near. If he had a scent, it would be woodsmoke and clove. But she couldn't learn his scent, nor the warmth of his body or touch of his hands. She had only the memory of her senses. Everything else was ashes.

"The gifts given to you by the Dark One, they were but pretty trinkets in exchange for your soul."

He did not turn to her as he said without irony, "Didn't think I had a soul."

"All men do. But it was *yours* the Dark One craved."

"Then he's the bigger fool, for it has a negligible value."

She peered at him. "You truly believe that?"

"Once I had a fine, dazzling set of beliefs. They are all tarnished now. Or thrown onto the midden."

His bleakness made her frown. "The world is going up in flames."

"Let it burn." He sounded weary.

"It's not simply a matter of the world ending. It's not the blaze of the fire followed by cold nothingness. If the Dark One is victorious, it means suffering. Unending suffering for every living being."

He did turn to her then. "We're all suffering."

"Worse."

Shadows shifted across his face like clouds across the moon. Yet he remained as distant as the moon, as well, shuttering away doubt. "Cannot be stopped."

"It can—"

"You've denied me my night's pleasure, and the Devil

knows how long you'll keep me from my peace, but you won't keep me from my rest." He moved away from the window.

She glided forward to intercept him. He started to walk around her, then moved *through* her. She stiffened, anticipating sensation. None came. He went through her as if she were nothing, not even a vapor to leave a chill upon his skin.

Coming to stand beside the bed, he stared at her with that cold, ruthless look of his she was coming to recognize. It had been intentional, his walking through her. Proving a point. She could not impede him.

Slowly, his fingers moved to his waistcoat. The buttons sparkled and winked beneath his fingers as he undid them.

Once his waistcoat had been opened and he let it fall to the floor, there were more layers. His torso made a firm, broad shape under the fabric of his shirt.

He watched her the whole while. A thief's gaze. Canny and calculating.

By all the gods, he was undressing. Deliberately. Knowing that she watched him.

His laced shirt followed the waistcoat, making a soft white shape on the patterned carpet. His torso gleamed in the firelight, still slick with sweat from his combat practice. Scars marked him, not merely the one that twisted down his neck, but relics of other past wounds. She recognized the scars left behind from blades, but a strange circular one on his right shoulder puzzled her. There were odd new weapons now, weapons that exploded with fire and hurled balls of lead, piercing the body. *Guns*, she'd heard them called. A person could be *shot* by a gun.

He had. During his military service, perhaps. Such an injury must kill most men. Not him. Someone had shot him, and he had survived.

This collection of scars was not what made her stare, however.

He followed her gaze to his chest. They both studied the

markings winding across his flesh, over his heart, along his ribs and down his left arm.

She'd observed them on the other Hellraisers, these images of flame, promises of torments to come. Yet to see the markings upon Bram reminded her of all that hung in the balance.

"When it covers you, the Dark One owns you completely."

His mouth twisted. "I thought I was his already."

"Until your flesh is entirely engulfed by the markings, there's yet hope."

"To regain my soul." He stared at the images of flame a moment longer, his expression austere. "To become the man I once was." The way his words frosted, this prospect didn't seem to be much of a prize to him.

"The other Hellraisers, Whit and Leo, they found ways. They reclaimed their souls. It's not an impossible task." A current of dark energy rippled through the chamber, and she frowned, seeking its source. It hadn't come from Bram, but seemed to originate from somewhere in the house.

"They had something I don't—motivation." He toed off his buckled shoes and peeled off his stockings, and then began to unfasten the buttons of his breeches.

Thoughts of mysterious dark energy fled. She watched with breathless anticipation as his breeches slid down, revealing the sharp muscles angling toward his groin, and then his cock. He was not as indifferent to her as he affected, for he was thickening, rising, as he stripped with her gaze upon him.

"Cruel." Her voice was a rasp.

"If necessary, yes." He pulled off his breeches, uncovering sinewy thighs.

"I'm not your enemy. We might be allies in this fight."

"Having gone to war already, I've no desire to do so ever again." He flipped back the blanket, baring the mattress. He fixed her with a heavy-lidded look. "A pity you haven't a physical body. We might find intriguing ways of distracting one another while we're tied together."

She was glad she had no body, for it would have been easily misled by him. "Is that what you do? Distract yourself with bedsport?"

"As a strategy, it's very effective." He reached up and pulled the tie from his hair. Freed from its binding, his hair fell around his shoulders, ink black. It was probably silky to the touch.

"The Dark One looked into your soul and saw more need there. That's how he works—he offers us what we think we want."

"Now look at me." Nude, unashamed, he spread his arms. "A man fulfilled."

"You don't believe that."

"And you've no way of knowing what I do or do not believe."

She drifted nearer. She could be cruel, too. "I was inside your mind, your memories."

He dropped his arms, and for all his muscularity and strength, he seemed vulnerable. But it passed quickly, and he was beautiful and cynical once more. "I'm amazed boredom did not kill you all over again."

Frustration welled. "Bram—"

Someone scratched at the door. He turned away and paced to a wooden cabinet. He pulled out a long robe of dark green silk. After shrugging into it, he stalked to the chamber door and threw it open, revealing a servant.

A strange wave of shadows descended, and she felt herself pushed back into the in-between mist. Glancing down, she saw her image fading, her hands so translucent as to be almost invisible. Her consciousness remained in the room—she heard and saw everything, yet had no form.

"I'm not to be disturbed after I retire," Bram growled.

"Forgive me, my lord. He insisted that I wake you. It's most urgent, he says."

"Who?"

"Mr. John Godfrey, my lord. He's downstairs, and if I may say, most anxious to speak with you."

Had she a heart, it would have seized in her chest. Only two Hellraisers remained, Bram and John. It was *John's* dark energy she had felt moments earlier; the strength of his power enveloped the house and dimmed her own strength.

Though she had faded into invisibility, Bram turned and looked directly at her. The servant peered around his master, curious to see what had drawn his attention, and frowned when there was nothing but an empty room.

"Where is he?" Bram asked, turning back to the servant.

"In the Green Drawing Room, my lord."

"I'll be down directly."

Bowing, the servant withdrew.

She tried to reach out to Bram, tried to speak, but with John so near, she became an empty shell incapable of words. Damn and hell, she *had* to keep Bram away from John. The other man's poison would infect Bram.

"You're still here," he rumbled. "I can feel you."

Don't go to him, she tried to say. *There's still a chance.*

She had no mouth with which to speak. No hands to grab hold of him. Rage at her helplessness burned through her.

He turned and strode from the chamber.

Chapter 3

Bram strode through the darkened corridors of his home, with only a few lit candles flickering in the shadows. Stillness smothered the house, yet his heart beat loudly in his ears as he descended the stairs.

A lone footman stood outside the closed doors to the Green Drawing Room, candle in hand.

"No one disturbs us," Bram said.

Bowing, the footman backed away. Bram stood alone in the corridor, his hand upon the door, his muscles and thoughts taut. How to face the man he once considered one of his closest friends? The man was now a murderer. Was he here to kill Bram as well?

In a fight, John would be no match for Bram. Yet there were new measurements of a man's capabilities beyond physical strength. Bram himself had witnessed the Devil bestowing more power upon John, though what that power might entail was yet untried—upon Bram, at any rate. The Devil had tried to give Bram more power as well. The ghost had prevented it, however, stepping between him and the bolt of magic. Because of her, he possessed only his original gift.

She might be his savior. She might be his destruction.

He didn't want saving, and his destruction was assured.

Something brushed along his neck, cool and electric. It moved through him in volatile waves. *Her.* He knew the feel of her presence, her force and purposeful cunning. He knew no living woman like her, and that was a blessing, for of a certain such women were created to rule the world.

He stared into the shadows, waiting for her to manifest. Yet she did not. She remained a formless, invisible energy swirling through the dark. Agitation thrummed through her.

Don't go in there.

Her voice resounded in his mind, low and urgent.

"He's one of my best friends," he muttered.

Neither of us knows what John truly is anymore. Send him away.

"No." For if there were judgments to make, he'd make them himself, not at the command of a long-dead Roman with a siren's voice.

But—

He pushed open the double doors and stepped into the Green Drawing Room.

John whirled to face him. Aside from a slight disorder in his clothing, he seemed much as he always had, with his scholar's sharp face, his lanky height that he had never grown into, as if he had more important and worthwhile things to consider besides the thickening of his body.

"Bram," he said after a moment.

"John." They stared at one another. Of the five Hell-raisers, Bram and John were the most disparate, and had spent few hours alone together. Now they were all that remained, a strange irony. The rakehell and the man of letters. "How did you know to find me at home?"

"This is my final stop of the night. I tried all the familiar places first." John glanced at Bram's banyan. "You've been pulled from your bed. Are you alone?"

Livia's presence clung close, buzzing and unquiet. Yet Bram answered, "I am."

Frowning, John studied him, searching for something. "Certain? I might've sworn—"

"There's only me." He didn't know why he concealed Livia from John. These were perilous times—no one could be trusted.

Moving further into the chamber, he went to a side table and poured himself a brandy. He silently offered a glass to John, but his friend shook his head. The most abstemious of the Hellraisers, was John.

"What are you doing here? I would have thought you'd be sequestered in the corner of some assembly, engineering a political alliance."

"It is for that reason I've searched you out." He lowered his voice, confiding. "I've come for a favor."

Bram raised his brows. "You mistake me for one of your Whitehall power brokers."

"There are more ways to gain influence than direct channels." John offered a smile.

"I've never cared for subtlety."

John chuckled, though Bram did not share in the laughter. "Direct as the point of a blade, as always. Yet you've your own means of persuasion." He gave Bram a meaningful look, for he knew the specifics of Bram's magical gift. "In truth, that is why I am here tonight. I need your persuasive talents to get inside a certain gentleman's private study. Into a desk drawer in that study."

Where, no doubt, important and confidential documents were kept. "You want a housebreaker, not me."

The corner of John's mouth curved, the most he could provide for a smile. "Your way is so much more elegant. It's a simple matter of persuading one of the servants to let you into the study."

"Bribe one of them."

"All the servants in this household are nauseatingly virtuous. Come now, Bram, we're friends, you and I. There's no need to dissemble about your own virtue. I've seen you seduce married women right out from under the noses of their husbands."

"If a woman is under her husband's nose, he's got her in the wrong place."

Bram felt, rather than heard, Livia's amusement. Then her voice within him. *The worst kind of scoundrel.*

Oh, he answered silently, *but I'm very good at it.*

So I've witnessed. I myself found it far more entertaining to be wicked than respectable.

This intrigued him, but John's words brought his attention back to the room.

"Will you do it? It is a very small favor, but it would be an immeasurable assistance."

Bram only stared at John. "We've not seen one another since Edmund's burial."

The heavy velvet curtains suddenly became fascinating, for John fixed his attention on them. "A sorrowful day."

"As of now, I'm the only Hellraiser you haven't tried to kill." He took a drink. "That might change. I may wake up with your rapier in my heart."

Shaking his head, John said, "This is precisely what Leo and Whit want—division between us. But we two, together we're the strongest of all. So much power. We can have anything we desire, anything at all." He stepped closer, the light from the fireplace paring his face into sharp yellow planes. "Mr. Holliday's gifts were twofold—we were given power, and we also learned which of us were weakest."

"Whit and Leo weren't weak." Bram had known Whit for most of his life, long before either of them had seen the world's true face, full of ruin and loss. They had stalked the streets of London together, haunted its glittering ballrooms and smoke-shrouded gaming hells. When Bram had returned from the Colonies, unable to do much beyond drink and fuck, Whit had not judged him. He'd given Bram acceptance, when Bram could not accept himself.

"No?" John scoffed. "Even with the power they were given, both were misled by *women*. That Gypsy girl, and Leo's insipid wife. No man of strength could be so deluded by a woman." He smiled. "Not you, Bram. You know exactly what women are for—bedding, and nothing else."

Fool, Livia fumed in Bram's mind.

Bram took another swallow of brandy. "So my cock makes me strong."

John seemed to make the decision to be amused. "How marvelous that you are so little changed."

Was Bram the same as he'd been before? He barely recognized his reflection in the water of his washing basin. The face he knew, but what was beneath it, *that* had been irrevocably altered. Witnessing one friend murder another tended to do that.

"It's not usual," Bram said, "for a man to attend the funeral of the one he killed."

John's face tightened. "The damned fool stepped into the path of my blade."

Not enough regret, whispered Livia. *Not nearly enough.*

"The blade that was meant for Leo."

This, at the least, John did not dispute. "He'd turned against us, turned his back on the Hellraisers. He could not suffer to live." His voice was cold and hard as frost.

"This is *Leo* we're talking of. The man you once carried home on your back when he'd been too fuddled with drink to walk. You and he used to debate for hours about phenomenally dull finance policies."

"That was before." His mouth hardened. "We've learned valuable lessons since then."

"I was never much for education."

Stepping closer, John said, "Bram, *think.* Consider

everything we've been given. You and I aren't like the others. We won't fall to the wiles of females. We know how to use our gifts to our best advantage. With our abilities, anything we want can be ours, anything at all."

"I've already got what I desire."

"Yet you could have *more*." His eyes burned like coals. "Mr. Holliday's power is great in me. All thoughts are mine to read, from the limbless beggar to the mightiest lord."

"Tell me what I'm thinking now." In truth, Bram wished John would, for his own thoughts were tempestuous and made for rough navigation.

John made himself look rueful. "All minds but the Hell-raisers'. Those are illegible to me."

Perhaps that was for the best. He felt Livia close, agitated and angry.

"Inconvenient," answered Bram.

"But I don't need to worry about what you're thinking." John narrowed his eyes. "Do I, Bram?"

Bram did not answer. Nor did he look away. He only stared at John until the other man chuckled.

"The hour is late, so I'm for bed." John strode to the door of the chamber. "You won't forget that favor I've asked of you."

It didn't escape notice that this was a statement, not a question. "I won't forget."

But will you do *it?* Livia pressed.

He refused to respond, and stood in the middle of the room as John made a quick bow before leaving. The front door opened then shut. The wheels of John's carriage clattered down the street.

Studying the carpet beneath his feet, Bram followed the snaking pattern of vines. If plants such as the ones in the Savonnerie rug existed in real life, they would trap unwary animals and either choke the life out of the creatures or else consign them to a slow death by starvation.

Damn him, if only he had power over time. With that gift, he'd take the Hellraisers back to the moments before they had freed Mr. Holliday. He would keep them from journeying to the ruined temple where they had found the Devil's prison, distract them somehow, and they would go on just as they always had.

"You can't go back." Her voice did not come from within his mind. Glancing up, he watched a silver white glow appear in the gloom of the chamber. It coalesced into a form he was coming to recognize far too well.

"I'm aware of that," he snarled.

"All of that"—she waved her hand toward the door from which John had exited—"was a test. Asking for a favor serves to bind you to him. And the rest . . . he wants to know where your loyalties lay."

"What a habit you have of stating things I already know." He poured himself another drink and took a goodly swallow.

She shook her head, and he felt her displeasure down in his marrow. He tried to shake it off—he'd stopped courting anyone's opinion long ago. One imperious, assertive ghost meant nothing to him.

Yet she persisted, hovering nearer. "You'll have to make your choice. Sooner rather than later."

"I don't need to choose anything. Neither you nor John can force me to." He heard the petulant note in his voice and didn't care. He was a man grown, beholden to no one and nothing.

"What will it take to break the haze of debauchery that surrounds you? Another death? The earth splitting open and catching fire? Wait long enough, and all of that will come to pass. But by then, it will be too late."

He slammed his glass down onto a table. "I exorcised my conscience decades ago. The position doesn't need filling." He turned away.

Yet she now appeared right in front of him, her dark brows drawn down, her hands curled into fists.

"Stop running and listen to me—"

"No!" he roared. "Not another bloody word! I order it."

She stared at him coldly. "I'm not a soldier to be commanded. I'm not one of your empty-eyed strumpets, either."

"What you are is a goddamn plague. And I want you gone."

Her teeth clenched. "I. Can't. Leave. Whatever binds us together, it can't be broken."

"You haven't really tried."

Her eyes blazed and she whirled around the room. In her fury, she was something from ancient legend, awful and beautiful. "Don't you ever question me!"

"If you're no vacuous harlot," he drawled, "then I'm no fearful acolyte. This temper tantrum is wearisome. As you are." He tilted his head, considering. "But I've resources at my disposal. For enough coin, I could get a priest to exorcise you."

She snorted. "A feeble ritual with no true power. All the strength of that faith has been gutted. It's now nothing but blind devotion to empty ceremony. Not even the priests believe."

"I've another power to call upon." He smiled cruelly as her eyes widened.

"Don't—"

"Haven't we established that I never respond to commands?" His gaze holding hers, he spoke with deliberation. "*Veni, geminus.*"

The candles guttered, the fire dimmed. Shadows engulfed the chamber. Only Livia's illumination remained constant. The scent of burnt paper rose up to the ceiling, curling amongst the molded plasterwork.

From the darkness, a shape emerged. A man.

Bram relit the candle. He turned to the newcomer. The

man stepped nearer, revealing his elegant evening clothes of burgundy velvet, a baronial signet ring on his hand that rested on the pommel of a dress sword. He had Bram's height, his size and form, his dark, unpowdered hair, his bright blue eyes. In every respect, he looked exactly like Bram.

His twin.

Born from the darkest part of himself when he struck his bargain with the Devil. The other Hellraisers, Whit and Leo, had been stunned and appalled when they finally discovered that their *gemini* were their doubles. Doubles who did wicked deeds, all whilst wearing their faces. Whit had alluded to it when they had all met on St. George's Fields, and Leo had made his revelation clear when they had gathered outside his home weeks ago.

But Bram never shared in Leo and Whit's horror. He'd known all along exactly what the creature was, what it meant. And he hadn't cared.

"My lord," the *geminus* said, bowing. It was Bram's voice, Bram's bow. "How may I serve you this night?"

Bram pointed at Livia. "Get rid of her."

Livia spun to face the *geminus*, readying herself for battle. She had little desire to be bound to Bram, but the creature's method of removal was guaranteed to be unpleasant. She led the cause against the *geminus*'s master. Of a certain, it would try to destroy her.

She reached for her magic, an ancient spell stolen from the wild lands to north, preparing to fight the creature.

Yet, before she could summon her power, the *geminus* stared at her and stumbled back. It blanched, eyes round, its mouth open. It held its hands up, as if to ward her back.

The thing was *frightened*. Of her.

"No!" the *geminus* cried. "Keep her from me!"

Bram scowled. "I told you to get her out of here. You've magic of your own. Do it."

The creature only shook its head, scuttling backward until it collided with the wall. Livia stared at it, baffled by its fear. Stranger still was seeing Bram, or something that looked and sounded exactly like Bram, cringing in terror. So very unlike him.

"I command you—"

"No!" the *geminus* shouted again. "She is a danger! The greatest danger!" It glanced wildly between her and Bram.

And disappeared.

For a moment, she and Bram simply gazed at the spot where the *geminus* had cowered. Then they looked at one another.

"The hell?" he growled.

"Twice I've helped kill *gemini*. Doubtless that's earned me a reputation." She couldn't keep the smugness from her voice, but it had been far too long since she'd held an advantage over the Dark One. She needed to keep herself from complacency, however. This was a very minor victory in a much bigger war.

"Marvelous," Bram drawled. "I'm shackled to Devil's biggest adversary."

She whirled on him. "You rat-eating bastard! That creature might have destroyed me."

"Yet here you are. Safe as virgin in a library."

"But you didn't know that when you summoned it." Fury poured through her. "Is my presence such an inconvenience to your debauchery? Are you too concerned that I'll disrupt your pursuit of quim? Distract your cock just as it's about to spend?" She sneered. "Poor Bram. All he wants is to fuck himself into oblivion, but the fate of millions of souls keeps intruding. What a nuisance."

His face twisted with cold rage. "Quiet."

"I've never been quiet," she snapped. "Not in life, and

most assuredly not in death. And I vow to you, *vow*, that someday I'll make you pay."

"Why wait?" Bram planted his hands on his hips and tilted his chin. "Do your worst, Madam Ghost. For nothing can match the hell I'm in now."

Anger surged in hot waves, and she embraced it. She'd been trapped within this half state of being, without substance, without feeling, battling an enemy that was and always would be more powerful than she. Mighty men once trembled before her, kneeling in supplication, begging for her aid. Her, a daughter of Rome, a priestess of incalculable strength. Now brought to the lowest kind of existence, and lashed to a man of boundless self-interest.

It was intolerable. Galling. A wound that could never heal.

At that moment, she didn't care if Bram was crucial to the fight against the Dark One. All she wanted was to hurt him, as she hurt.

"That is one order I'm happy to obey," she spat. Energy swirled within her, magic she could wield like the fiercest weapon. Once, she had studied ancient scrolls to learn the proper incantations, but she no longer needed papyrus or words. The magic had imbued her very blood. Even in this spectral state, she had power few could match. She had given a Gypsy woman the means to control fire, and bestowed command over air to an English girl.

"I've razed buildings of stone," she snarled. "Torn demons apart with just a wave of my hand. I was the woman who first summoned the Dark One. You are nothing."

"Tear me to shreds, Madam Ghost." Challenge glinted in his glass-blue eyes. "The only people who'll mind are my servants, and simply because of the mess."

She raised her hands, gathering her power. An Egyptian killing spell, the Summoning of Seth. Bright energy poured from her palms and shot toward him. He did not move from where he stood, waiting.

Before the stream of energy could hit him, it veered away like a bird with a broken wing. It collided with a small table off to the side. The table shattered.

Livia stared down at her hands. Never had that happened before, not even when she was a girl newly learning the ways of magic, surrounded by clay tablets and papyri.

Bram grated out a laugh. "That happens to men sometimes. Not me, though. Not since I was a lad."

She bared her teeth at him. "It's only because I haven't tried to hurt a mortal yet. But my power will soon learn the way." She flung her hands out again, and another burst of energy rushed from them.

And once more, the energy went astray, digging a deep gouge in the floor.

His laughter was an ugly, taunting thing.

"You ought to visit a clockmaker," he said. "Get those gears back in alignment."

"I . . . can't understand it." Shame choked her as she once more gazed at her hands. It felt as though her arms had been severed from her body, something crucial missing. "Always, always magic was mine to control. What has happened?"

"Don't know whether I'm relieved or disappointed." He crouched next to the gouge in the floor and ran his fingers over it. "Too bad you haven't any money, for this will take a good bit of coin to repair. And you owe me a table."

She barely heard him. Instead, she turned her focus inward, searching, seeking. There had to be a reason why her magic had failed. It hadn't stopped entirely, so it still existed within her. But it was broken. Incomplete.

She inhaled sharply. *Incomplete. Half the power it once had.* Which meant that the other half of the power was in another place. Where?

Bram rose up from his crouch, sinuous in his movement. And then she understood.

"It's in *you*," she rasped. Drifting closer, she said, "My

magic . . . when we were bound together, part of my magic went into you. That's why my spells don't succeed."

His brow lowered. "I don't feel a damned thing."

"Because you aren't cognizant of anything above your waist. But it's there. I know it is." Gods, what an agonizing thought. Magic belonged to her and her alone. She shared it with no one, especially not Bram. It was as though she had to share her heart with him, or else the blood would cease to move through her veins.

But she needed her magic. Without it, she was simply another woman. Worse than an ordinary woman. She was a ghost with no strength, no power. As futile as a snake's dream of flight.

"We need to work a spell together." She forced the words out.

"You're jesting."

She shook her head. "I must have use of my magic. I *must.*"

"I've never performed a spell in my life."

"You use the Dark One's magic to get women into your bed."

He waved his hand dismissively. "Entirely different. I'm not a bloody sorcerer."

"If you just *try*—"

"No," he roared. He drew a breath, and dragged his hands through his hair. "I'm no one's pawn, damn it. Not yours, or John's, or Mr. Sodding Holliday's. I have one agenda. One."

"Your own," she surmised.

His mouth firmed. "Splendid, Madam Ghost. You *have* been paying attention."

"It doesn't matter if you maroon yourself on an island. The floodwaters continue to rise, and eventually even the most distant isle will be deluged. You'll drown."

"I know how to swim."

"No," she countered, "you know how to *float*. Swimming entails effort, and that's something you are determined to withhold. This selfishness will destroy more than yourself."

"If this is your technique for persuasion," he sneered, "it's no wonder you're on the losing end. Allies aren't won through insults."

"Forgive me. I hadn't realized you were weak enough to need flattery."

He spit out a vile curse and stalked toward the door.

"Where are you going?" she demanded.

"Doesn't matter if I tell you or not," he said over his shoulder. "You'll wind up there anyway." Pulling open the door, he then stormed from the chamber.

The moment he left the room, it began to dim around her, as though a heavy veil draped over her eyes. Resentment and anger were her most vivid sensations. She refused to follow him. She'd rather dwell in this half-world of mist and shadow than spend another minute in his company.

He possessed half her magic. When he wasn't in her presence, the world retreated. Without him, she was reduced to one of those pathetic specters who drifted aimlessly, frightening weak-minded mortals but capable of little else. Yet John's appearance this night proved to her that the Dark One's power waxed, and its poison had sunk deep within John's veins. He belonged to the one he called the Devil— no matter how much the mortal believed he acted in his own best interest, the ultimate victor would be the Dark One.

John planned something, something that would likely engulf the nearby territories of the earthly realm. Yet John had no idea that the Dark One would assume control, destroying everything, devouring the world entirely. She knew this from her own bitter experience. With her lashed to Bram, however, she could do nothing to stop this destruction from happening again.

She needed Bram. And she hated him for it.

* * *

There truly wasn't enough brandy in the world to solve this. Drink would not take any of it away.

But that didn't stop him from trying.

In his bedchamber, Bram sprawled in a chair by the fire, drinking steadily from the decanter. He stared at the flames. They shifted and danced, forming shapes that appeared then vanished. Nothing he could hold.

As a child, Arthur had been the one to watch the fire, entranced by its constant change. He would try to tug Bram down beside him, tell him stories about what he saw within the flames. But Bram had always wrested away, impatient. He had wanted to run, to splash through the creek that ran through the northern corner of the estate, to laugh and stage battles with the boys in the village.

It didn't matter how many times Father caught Bram sneaking back to the nursery, bruised and scraped, his clothes torn and dirty. Father whipped him to teach a sense of decorum, as would fit the child of a baron. None of the whippings made a bit of difference. Bram kept running through the brook, kept challenging village boys to fights.

"Obstinate barbarian," Father had called him.

Bram remembered standing in the corridor, listening to Father berate the latest tutor for Bram's execrable spelling and unmannerly penmanship.

"My lord," the tutor—Mr. Filton? Mr. Finmere?—objected, "the boy simply refuses to be taught. He will not be guided by anyone, even if what one suggests would directly benefit the boy. It must be done at his decision, or not at all."

Mr. Filton or Finmere had not lasted long. Soon after, Bram was sent away to school. Where he met Whit. They weren't immediate friends. In truth, they used to beat each other bloody, until mutual antipathy toward another boy became the foundation of their friendship.

Where was Whit now? Still in London? Or had he and his Gypsy woman fled the city in the wake of Edmund's death?

A furious, aching loneliness gathered in Bram's chest. He drank more brandy. It did nothing to relieve the sensation.

He wasn't truly alone. Livia, his own personal Fury, was close by. Not in his bedchamber at the moment, yet she remained near. She couldn't leave him even if she wanted to. And she wanted to.

Her words echoed. Accusing him of being selfish, concerned more with his own pleasure than the doom of countless souls.

"I *am* selfish," he said aloud. "Always have been." It formed a comfortable cloak, his aggressive egoism, keeping others' demands at a distance. He needn't worry about anything but making himself happy.

He laughed into the darkness. Happiness was ever elusive. But he knew its shadowed caricature: depravity. And for years after his return from the Colonies, that had been enough. Or so he'd believed. The Hellraisers had been good company, never asking questions, as intent on the pursuit of pleasure as he.

He didn't trust John. No reason why he should. And the hard, eager look in his eyes unsettled Bram deeply. Ambushers had the same eyes as they lay in wait. But what was John planning?

It didn't matter. Nothing mattered. All of them—Livia, John, the Hellraisers, Mr. Holliday—all of them could go rot. He was beholden to no one. No one relied upon him, either.

Watching the fire as it consumed the wood, he outlined

his own plan: Drink until he lost consciousness. When he woke, he would immerse himself in the realm of London's voluptuaries, and there he'd remain, importunate ghost or no ghost. And if the world burned down, he'd watch it burn, letting the flames engulf his own flesh.

Chapter 4

Bram awoke with a pounding head and a ghost in his bed. She hovered near the foot, her upper body emerging from the mattress. Her gaze was distant as she watched him.

Rubbing the heel of his hand in his eyes, he stared at her.

"Not a dream, then." His voice was a groggy rasp, as it always was upon rousing from sleep. He'd no love for the first hour after waking, a relationship made more complicated today by the ill-effects of too much brandy. And the fact that a Roman ghost was there to share the unpleasantness. "Damn."

"The enthusiasm is mutual." She glanced back toward the fireplace, where an upended chair and empty decanter gave evidence as to how he spent the rest of his night. "How much did you drink?"

"Not nearly enough." He raised up on his elbows, the blankets sliding down to his abdomen, and he didn't miss the way her gaze moved over his bare flesh. She looked at the mark of flame, but moved quickly on to the muscles of his chest, the ridges of his stomach. Her nostrils flared. This ghost was not unmoved by the sight of a nude man.

Neither, it seemed, was the man unmoved by her. The curtains were still drawn, the chamber swathed in shadow, and he could see how her tunic clung to the lush curves of her body. Full breasts, rounded hips. A sensualist's body. Her beauty was both patrician and earthy. The kind of woman who'd command her slaves to bring scented oils, but use her own hands to rub them on her lover.

Against his will, against his judgment, his own body responded to her. His cock stirred, eager as always for the pleasures of women. The damned thing had to suffer disappointment, however. *This* woman, for all her sensuality, had no substance. He might as well try to fuck the air.

Throwing back the covers, Bram rose from bed. He felt her gaze on him as he walked, naked, to the low cabinet where the chamber pot was kept. For a moment, he debated whether or not to go behind the screen in the corner of the room. Ridiculous. He wasn't going to affect modesty for this termagant. So, after his partial erection subsided, he relieved himself in full view of her. If she didn't like it, she could just . . . fade away.

Once finished, he strode to the washstand and cleaned himself. He splashed water on his face and torso, all the while watching her in the mirror that perched on the washstand.

Her gaze never left him, traversing the length of his body, lingering on his buttocks. Hunger gleamed in her eyes.

An image materialized in his mind: her stretched out beneath him, her ankles locked around his thighs and her fingernails digging into his arse as he thrust into her. She would be a fierce bed partner, the both of them struggling for dominance and enjoying the fight.

Oh, his cock liked that. But he didn't. He flung more cold water on his face and even onto his groin.

What he felt was only thwarted desire. He hadn't enjoyed Lady Girard last night, thanks to Livia. And it was a very short journey from anger to lust.

A scratch sounded at the door.

"Make yourself invisible," he growled at Livia. "Don't want you frightening my servants."

She scowled at him, but at least she did as he commanded, her form growing less and less substantial until only a vague outline of her shape remained. Unless one deliberately looked for her, she'd remain unseen.

Bram waited until his erection subsided, thinking of the most dull aspects of estate management such as irrigation and drainage, before calling out, "Enter."

The door opened and Cleeve, the valet, entered and bowed. "Good afternoon, my lord. Might I open the draperies?"

Bram grunted in assent. He squinted against the glare as Cleeve pulled back the curtains, revealing a patchy gray sky. The valet remained disinterested as he went about straightening the room, setting the chair back up on its feet, putting the empty decanter on a table, picking up the discarded banyan.

He held the banyan out. "A shave, my lord?"

Bram took the robe and donned it, then sat. The rich fragrance of sandalwood soap rose up as Cleeve used a boar bristle brush to stir up the foam for shaving. As he did this, a maid appeared in the door, a tray in her hands.

"Coffee and rolls, my lord?"

At his nod, she came in and set the tray down on the bedside table. He paid his servants well to remember his habits, and they did. The maid poured him a cup of coffee—no sugar, no milk, just as he preferred—and set it on the washstand so he might have it close by.

"You chuckle, my lord," said Cleeve, dabbing the foam on his cheeks and chin. "Something amusing at the theater?"

"This is all so damned ordinary."

"My lord?"

"All this." Bram waved at the shaving supplies laid out on

the washstand, and the maid tidying his bed. "Everything's changed, and nothing's changed."

Cleeve did his best to hide his confusion. Perhaps he thought his master still weathered the death of a close friend. Perhaps he believed his master showed the very first signs of madness. Whatever the valet thought, he simply answered, "Yes, my lord. Will you hold still, my lord?"

Bram remained motionless as Cleeve glided the razor down his cheeks, but his gaze flicked to the ghost's hazy outline hovering in the corner. What did she think of this, the daily rituals of an English nobleman? Were they different from how men of her time met the day?

Likely she thought him a selfish rogue, attending to his toilette instead of rampaging up and down the streets of London, seeking the Devil and preparing for battle.

"Please do not frown, my lord. It makes it more difficult for me to shave you."

He attempted to smooth out his scowl. But anger still seethed within him. He'd seen his share of battle and wanted nothing more to do with it.

Life would continue as it always had for him. Everything must remain the same. And if Livia or John objected to that, they could go hang.

"Lay out my fencing clothes," he said once Cleeve wiped the last of the shaving foam from him. The academy had a chamber for changing one's garments, but he did not want to go through the tedium of dressing, undressing, and dressing again.

The valet bowed and, after putting away the shaving supplies, moved to the clothes press. He pulled out a lightweight shirt and soft doeskin breeches, and a short padded jacket. Bram and Whit often practiced their swordsmanship first thing in the day. Bram had abandoned these regular training sessions after Whit deserted the Hellraisers—training at home rather than try to cling to what had been lost. Yet Bram would make everything return to normal.

Dressing for his practice, he felt Livia's continued stare. His jaw tightened. Yes, he'd go on as he always had, and there wasn't a damned thing the ghost could do about it.

The shouts and grunts of men echoed in the arched ceiling. Pale sunlight washed down through high windows, illuminating men moving back and forth across the scarred wooden floor. They lunged and danced, thin swords forming arcs and whistling as they cut through the air, and off to one side, a man vaulted up and over a wooden horse. Though she had no sense of smell, Livia imagined the large chamber reeked of sweat.

She hovered, unseen, beside Bram as he strode into the hall. Though the clothing and weapons differed from her own time, she recognized this place.

Men are always looking for an excuse to fight one another, she thought.

Because we're good at it, Bram answered.

And not much else. It's a marvel we women keep you around at all.

You like us between your thighs well enough.

She had no answer to that. Gods and goddesses, how she missed the pleasures of the flesh! So basic, so satisfying. The most essential element of life. She hadn't felt a man's touch for over a millennium. Was it any surprise that her thoughts kept straying toward the carnal, especially when Bram flaunted his delicious masculine form?

Easier to think of frustrated lust than the Dark One's strengthening power. She had been pulled behind Bram as he rode toward this fighting school, weaving her way through the streets. Even in daylight hours, a combustible tension lay heavy over the city, a thick, choking net of malevolence revealed in mistrustful glances and broken windows.

"Good day, Lord Rothwell." A red-faced man with close-cut hair stepped forward, a sword beneath his arm. He wiped his forehead on his sleeve. "It's been a spell since last we've seen you." He glanced past Bram, and for a moment, Livia thought the man might see her. But his gaze moved right through her. He was looking for someone. As though Bram usually arrived with company.

"Afternoon, Tranmere." Bram's voice was clipped. "I'm looking for a good, hard fight today."

Tranmere made a tsking sound. "You an' everyone else, my lord. Not so much practicing proper swordsmanship as it's a battle royale. Been like this for weeks, but today's especially fierce."

Turning her attention back to the rows of men, she noted their bared teeth, their wild swings at one another. As if they were truly battling, driven forward by a need for blood and pain.

She knew who was responsible.

"Perfect," said Bram. "Find me a partner."

Tranmere bowed before hurrying off.

Why do you come to this place? she asked Bram. *I would've thought you'd had enough of fighting.*

Anger coursed through him. He still didn't care for the fact that she'd experienced his memories.

Always need to be prepared, he answered.

Prepared for what?

Anything.

Tranmere trotted forward, a large man trailing behind him. He and Bram nodded to one another.

"Mr. Worton will be happy to spar with you, my lord. I believe his fighting style matches well with yours."

"I don't care for pretty forms and dainty foot positions," Worton said. "Just a good, tough fight." The sword he carried wasn't as thin as those used by the other men, looking more like a weapon of war than a genteel sport.

"Then I'm your man." Bram hefted his own sword, and it was equally brutal.

Without another word, Bram and Worton paced off toward an unoccupied portion of the chamber. Unseen, Livia drifted through the fencers as they leapt and attacked. Intriguing, how the techniques had changed over the millennia. Though Tranmere had bemoaned the lack of finesse the fighters showed today, they were still quite different from the soldiers and gladiators she'd seen practicing or in actual combat.

She'd always had a fondness for soldiers and gladiators. They made for very good company in bed. Their calloused hands, their uncomplicated need. Subtle and nuanced? No. But she seldom wanted subtlety in lovemaking. *Had* wanted. Never again would she feel the sweat of a lover's body on her own skin, or the vibrations of their groans against her flesh.

She *must* stop thinking these tormenting thoughts. Yet it was difficult when surrounded by young, hale men in their prime, all gleaming with perspiration as they vigorously used their bodies.

The tie that bound her to Bram drew her through the chamber and close to where he and Worton stood. They each took a few practice swings through the air, loosening their muscles, until, satisfied, they faced one another. After a terse bow, they took up ready stances, swords upraised.

Worton swung. His blade only tapped Bram's sword. Once, twice. Getting a sense of Bram's readiness. Bram held his position, not allowing Worton to drive him back. Yet he wasn't content to let his opponent do all the testing. He, too, took a handful of investigative swings, as though sounding the depths of a shore. The men held themselves loosely, but the casualness belied a tension even Livia could sense.

Bram and Worton circled one another. Their strikes grew harder, more direct. A swing, a block.

The tension suddenly broke as Worton lunged. Bram countered with quick, fluid motion. And then the fight truly began.

She had seen combat. In the gladiatorial ring. In a few skirmishes as she had journeyed from Rome to Britannia. Like any good Roman, she admired fine fighting skill, for it revealed not merely a strong body, but also a quick mind. She could claim no expertise in the techniques of armed battle, only knowing talent when she saw it.

Her gaze held fast to Bram. She could not look away even if the Dark One appeared right beside her. This—Bram in combat—this was beautiful.

Bram and Worton traded strikes. They circled, struck, lunged and darted back. Worton had the advantage of height and reach, yet Bram had speed and vicious accuracy. Their swords rang as they exchanged blows. A furious exchange.

She was rapt. This was not a genteel sparring exercise. These men seemed gripped by a need to hurt one another. They grunted as their padded jackets absorbed the sword point's force—though the points were dulled, the strikes still would have wounded were it not for the jackets' protection. Worton fought hard, relentlessly, yet he could not match Bram for ability.

In truth, Bram seemed *made* for this. He had a fluidity of motion that enthralled her. Each strike from Worton he blocked with the speed of a serpent, and his own attacks were brutally, savagely beguiling. She had seen him practice his combat, but with a true opponent, he transformed into another man. A man well-versed in the art of killing.

Had he been this adept, or did soldiering shape him into an expert fighter? Whatever the origin, it came to full fruition here. Men would gladly lose years off their lives if they could wield a blade with half of Bram's ability.

Murmurs distracted her enough to pull her gaze away from Bram for a moment. The other swordsmen had stopped their practice in order to watch Bram and Worton fight, as though drawn by the force of Bram's skill.

"A guinea says Rothwell takes it," someone said.

"Only a damned fool would bet against him," came the answer.

Worton must have heard this pronouncement, for his attacks increased, growing stronger, more aggressive. Yet Bram continually beat him back. He fought with targeted hostility, as though far more than a gentleman's reputation with the sword was at stake. She wondered if, when Bram looked upon Worton, he saw someone else, some*thing* else. The Hellraisers? The Dark One? Perhaps even himself?

The light of fury rose in Bram's eyes. Sweat glossed his forehead. As soon as Worton began his retreat, Bram pressed forward, giving no quarter. Worton backed away, until he couldn't go any further, the wall behind him. He tried to block a strike—too late. The point of Bram's sword struck him right in the heart. A fatal blow without the padded jacket and dulled tip.

Worton lowered his blade. "I yield," he panted.

Yet Bram advanced, his expression hard and merciless. His sword point hovered close to Worton's right eye. The bigger man sucked in a breath as he pressed against the wall. He dropped his sword, and the sound reverberated metallically through the chamber.

Would Bram actually drive his blade into Worton's skull? He truly might. Even with the tip of the sword blunted, it could pierce an eye—and, wielded with strength, go even further.

"I say, Rothwell," someone called. "The man's yielded."

"My lord," added Tranmere nervously, hovering near, "you've won."

Bram showed no signs of hearing them. A demand to kill seemed to have him, unrelenting. He kept his sword close to Worton's eye. The bigger man screwed his eyes shut, as though something as flimsy as an eyelid could stop a blade.

This must not happen.

She drifted close, keeping herself unseen, and spoke directly into Bram's thoughts.

Fine warrior you are, to slay an unarmed man.

He's the enemy, Bram answered.

Of what? Hygiene? I'm sure the sweat of his fear stinks like rancid meat.

I have to kill him.

Go ahead. Yet it takes a special variety of coward to kill a man with no weapon.

I'm not a damned coward!

Then put your sword down.

Bram blinked, as though awakening from a daze. He stared at the cringing Worton, then down at the blade in his hand. Slowly, he looked around at the faces of the gathered men, their eyes wide and expressions cautious.

"My lord?" Tranmere took a wary step forward.

The tip of Bram's sword lowered, then he dropped his hand, so the point scraped against the floor. Worton and everyone else within the chamber exhaled. Even Livia, who had no need of breath, eased out a sigh.

Bram glared around the room, almost in challenge. No one accepted. Without a word, he strode from the room.

He stormed down the winding, narrow stairwell. Men ascending the stairs pressed into the wall, careful to avoid his gaze and angry scowl. Bound as she was to him, Livia hovered at his side, his rage and confusion twisting beneath the surface of her own phantasmal skin.

This has happened before, she said.

Not to me. His voice in her mind was a snarl. *Not since I left soldiering.*

When I freed the Dark One, she amended. *A madness gripped everyone, a need for blood. I saw a respected citizen, a merchant, stab the proprietor of a bathhouse for having the water too hot. There were riots in the market-place. The army mutinied.*

So I'm a symptom of a greater illness, he answered.

Not an illness. A plague.

She and Bram reached the street. Clouds obscured the sun, throwing the remaining daylight into early shadow. A servant hurried to open the door to the waiting carriage, but Bram was faster, and he threw the door open himself. He flung himself into the vehicle. It rocked with the force of his body against the upholstered seat.

"Home," he snapped to the servant.

The servant closed the door and hopped onto the back of the carriage.

She hovered at the sidewalk, invisible, watching the carriage drive away. A woman crouched by the side of the street, a child in the crook of her arm. The woman stretched her hand out to all the fine gentlemen walking past. No one threw her any coin. The child—girl or boy, Livia could not tell—stared directly at Livia.

"Strange lady," it chirped. Yet its mother paid no attention, busy wheedling and beseeching the passersby.

Someone walking quickly knocked the woman to the ground. They did not stop to help her up. Nobody did, and the child began to cry.

A sharp tug yanked Livia from where she hovered. She was dragged behind Bram's carriage like a tattered ribbon. Helpless to stop herself, she could only follow, unseen by everyone she passed. She had never felt so alone.

Not quite alone. Down the length of the connection binding her to Bram, she heard his thoughts.

*I don't know myself anymore. I don't know a damned
thing. I'm lost.*

She had been lost too, not so long ago. Yet Bram had an
advantage that she had not: a guide. Would he accept her
guidance, or continue to fall headlong into the dark unknown? Once, she might have cast an augury spell taken
from the arcane wisdom of the Etruscans. Her magic had
been split apart since then, and as to what the future held,
in that she was as lost as Bram.

In the glass, Bram surveyed his appearance, a soldier
readying himself for battle. The night and its pleasures *were*
a battle, one from which he always emerged victorious.
Nothing would change that.

He studied his reflection as his valet made final adjust-
ments to his ensemble. The deep red velvet of his slim coat
appeared almost black until candlelight turned it the hue of
spilled blood. Complex embroidery worked its way down
the front of his bronze satin waistcoat and at the very cuff
of his matching breeches. The black silk solitaire around his
neck could not fully hide his scar—nothing did. He'd grown
almost used to the fact by now.

With his hair pulled back into a simple queue and bagged
in silk, his stockings faultlessly white, his buckled shoes
gleaming, and the jeweled shortsword at his side, he appeared every inch the aristocrat, a man who expected and
would receive entrance anywhere he chose. No one would
suspect that only hours earlier, he'd nearly killed a man for
no reason. All that had prevented him from taking Worton's
eye—and life—had been the scornful words of a ghost.

A tremor worked through him. God, he'd almost *mur-
dered* someone. And he had *wanted* to, to see Worton
sprawled upon the ground at his feet. Bram hadn't thought
of him as simply a fellow swordsman engaged in training,

as Bram himself was. A red-edged fever had taken hold of him. Worton had transformed into the Algonquin, into a French soldier, into a creature with a twisted face and a mouth full of fangs.

Insanity. Yet he'd been driven by a need to kill this enemy. Was this the madness of which Livia spoke? The one that had gripped her own time after she had freed the Devil? He tried to picture what London would be like if its streets teemed with men and women eager for blood—and shoved the image from his mind. The hell he'd experienced in the Colonies would resemble a May Day fete by comparison.

No—it wouldn't come to that. It *couldn't*, no matter what the ghost claimed.

He felt her near, somewhere at the edges of his bed-chamber. She was never far. Strange—he thought he'd find her presence an anathema, but there was a curious . . . comfort in having her close.

As if one took comfort from the millstone around one's neck.

Cleeve tugged gently at the lace at Bram's wrists, ensuring that just the proper amount showed. It was easier to prepare for actual warfare. A check to make sure the weapons were all sharp enough and ready to fire, and then into the heat of battle. A French grenadier didn't care if Bram's stock lay perfectly snug against his throat. He only wanted Bram dead.

The fine hairs on the back of Bram's neck rose. Livia was drawing closer, hovering near. He couldn't see her, but he sensed her, his body growing alarmingly attuned to her presence. If he let his eyes almost close, he could nearly see her, the soft outline of her curved form.

What might she look like if she truly walked upon the ground? All women had their own innate rhythm and move-ment, unique to each female. He had made a considerable study of it. Some moved with intrinsic sensuality, others with deliberate provocation as if throwing down a gauntlet. Both intrigued him, for he did enjoy challenges. There were women who moved with the rigidity of automatons, uncomfortable in their bodies. He avoided them.

How might this Roman ghost move, had she a corporeal body? She might carry herself with patrician stiffness, a queen descending from her throne to unwillingly mingle with the rabble. No. She'd be a seductive thing, those rounded hips canting from side to side with each step, a lure no living man could resist.

He was alive, but she wasn't. She was also a virago, a presence to be endured only because he hadn't any choice.

Splendid attire. Her words drifted through his thoughts, laced with slight hints of admiration. *Not suitable, I think, for a quiet evening at home.*

I haven't spent a quiet evening at home since I was fifteen, he answered. *Tonight won't see me break that tradition.*

Where will you go?

Anywhere I can have female company.

He felt her sardonic smile. *But you'll have an audience.*

Don't sodding care.

Fighting at the fencing academy had done nothing to quell the restless, dark energy burning within him. Only one thing offered him any kind of respite. He needed the gentle voices and soft hands of women, their beguiling smiles and silken sighs. The peace he achieved never lasted long enough, but he'd take whatever he could get. A parched man would rather have a drop of water upon his tongue than nothing at all.

If the world was truly going to hell, as Livia claimed, then he would seize his pleasure wherever and whenever he could.

He expected Livia to object to his plan for the night, yet when he turned to leave, she only drifted beside him.

If you must *go out tonight,* she said as they made their

way down the corridor, *be careful. It gets worse after dark. I remember that, as well.*

This sword isn't merely decorative.

Use it if you have to.

He stopped walking, then said aloud, "That's not what you said this afternoon."

A nearby footman glanced toward Bram. "My lord?"

Bram was about to snap that servants weren't supposed to intrude upon the master's private conversations, before realizing that, to the footman's eyes, Bram was alone, conversing with no one. He walked quickly on. The servants would talk about the master's strange behavior, but this was the least of Bram's concerns.

You were about to kill an unarmed man who presented no threat to you, Livia continued. *That's not the same as protecting yourself in a dangerous situation.*

I know the difference.

This afternoon you didn't.

He had no riposte, and her words sunk into him like a blade. Again he thought of a London clutched in the frenzy of bloodlust, hundreds of thousands transformed into riotous beasts. No safety. No peace. Only chaos and death.

It will come, she said, seeming to know his thoughts. *It's already here.*

You're wrong. He had to believe that.

Reaching the foyer, a footman handed him his tricorn hat and cloak, then opened the door once he'd donned them. The carriage waited, ready to speed him off into the night and his ceaseless quest for pleasure.

Go then, she said coldly. *Go and see.*

Everything appeared exactly as it ought. Hundreds of expensive beeswax candles threw blazing light from atop massive crystal chandeliers. The parquet floors gleamed.

Musicians stationed in the corner filled the chamber with the very latest from the Continent. Talk and jewels packed the room, both sharp and calculated to dazzle. Footmen circulated with trays bearing glasses of wine. Someone had organized a card game in an adjoining chamber, and shouts of the players mingled with the music and voices.

By most standards, the assembly at Lord Millom's would be considered a success.

But something was wrong.

Standing in the doorway, with an invisible Livia beside him, Bram surveyed the chamber. He knew most of these men—aristocrats and nobly born gentlemen, and a handful of wealthy burghers who had bought their way into the ranks of the elite. And they knew him, offering him polite bows or nods as his gaze moved past them. Distracted, he barely returned the gesture.

Despite the smiles, the attempts at cheer and insistently ebullient music, a wrongness hovered over the assembly like an invisible pestilence.

Then he understood.

He snared the arm of the Marquess of Lapley, affecting a careless stroll past him.

"Where are the ladies?" Bram demanded.

Lapley grimaced. "Damned strange, ain't it? Aside from Lady Millom"—he nodded toward the woman in question, a tense middle-aged lady laced tightly into yellow satin—"there ain't another female here. No one's dancing."

The space normally occupied by dancers going through their intricate steps stood empty, a lacuna of parquetry. No bright silk or fluttering fans circled the chamber. The low drone of masculine voices was unrelieved by female chatter. Not a giggle or trill. Gallants awaited the arrival of fair maidens, eager to prove themselves by fetching glasses of negus or offer up sparkling compliments in the continuous ritual of courtship.

Every man at the assembly wore a baffled smile as false as pasteboard marble.

"It's like someone's blotted out the stars," Bram muttered.

Lapley snorted. "Aye. What's the use of coming to these bloody assemblies if there ain't no ladies to flirt with?"

"Your wife isn't here." Bram looked pointedly at the empty space beside Lapley.

"Wouldn't come. Said she felt nervous and out of sorts. With all the peculiarity going on around town, I was glad of her choice. Ain't been safe after dark. Last night, five different gentlemen were almost shot in their own carriages. Covingham barely escaped with his life."

All this was news to Bram, but without Whit and Leo to meet him at the coffee house for the day's intelligence, he hadn't gone and heard the latest reports.

"What of the other ladies?" Bram pressed. The Season was at its height. No woman of social standing missed an assembly. At the least, they needed to parade their daughters before eligible bachelors.

Lapley shrugged. "The same, I'd wager. Makes for a sodding dull assembly. Unless," he added, brightening, "you brought some females with you."

I don't believe I count, Livia said, her voice wry in Bram's mind.

"I'm alone," Bram answered.

With a disappointed mutter about wasted opportunity, Lapley drifted away.

Bram continued to stand in the doorway, surveying the assembly that was not truly an assembly. The men in the chamber continued to circulate and affect conversation, but it felt like a sham. Or there had been a Biblical purge, and instead of slaying first born sons, the Angel of Death had killed every last woman, save one.

Citizens' wives wouldn't come out after dark, Livia said.

They hid in their homes, cowering in corners with their arms around their children. Only female slaves forced to venture out of doors did so. I walked the streets disguised so no one knew my sex.

Powerful witch like you, he retorted. *You've nothing to fear.*

All *women share the same fear, magic or no magic. And their fear is well-founded. I saw what happened when the mobs caught women out after sunset.*

He felt her shudder, and his own blood iced.

It isn't like that now.

You've looked out the window of your carriage. You've seen.

Maybe he hadn't wanted to see, for, at the time, it made no impression on him. But thinking on it now, he remembered the protectively hunched forms of women scurrying inside. Only the women forced to earn their livings on the street remained—whores, orange sellers, beggars—and their eyes had been wide with fear.

In the span of a single night, the world had changed. He felt the whole of society, both high and low, clinging to a precipice, the rocks crumbling beneath their fingers. Soon the whole cliff would collapse. All that remained was the fall into darkness.

But his hands were strong, and he'd hold on for as long as he could. The darkness wouldn't claim him just yet.

From the exterior, the building appeared like any other home in this fashionable part of town. Tidy and reserved, its modern brick façade looked out onto the street with perfect respectability, proportioned according to the most classical standards.

Bram ascended the short flight of steps, hearing the clatter of his carriage pulling discretely into the mews. Livia drifted behind him. Her curiosity was a flame at his back.

What's at this place? Another gathering?

Without answering, he tapped at the door, and it opened immediately. They knew him here. Inside was just as tasteful as the exterior, done up in the latest style, with cream colored paneling, and paintings of serene landscapes upon the walls. A liveried footman took his hat and cloak.

"They are gathered in the drawing room, my lord," the servant murmured. "Shall I show you in?"

"I know the way." He strode down the corridor, Livia just behind him. Along the way, he passed a maid in cap and apron, and she curtsied, her eyes upon the ground.

Female voices drifted into the hallway from behind the drawing room's closed doors.

Wherever we are, Livia mused, *fear hasn't kept the women away.*

We'll assuredly find women here, he answered.

He opened the doors of the drawing room. Settees and couches were arranged throughout the chamber. Upon them lounged young women in filmy gowns, and they all turned their gazes toward him as he entered the room. Some attempted to smile enticingly, but their attempts failed—the smiles withered like hothouse flowers.

"My lord, you are most warmly welcomed." An older woman came forward, her hands outstretched to take his. She wore artful amounts of powder and rouge, a patch applied to just below the corner of her mouth.

"Mrs. Able." Bram bowed, pressing a kiss to the back of her hand. "Like always, lovely as the evening star."

"La," trilled Mrs. Able, "pretty words from a pretty knave."

"I save all my pretty words for you alone."

"Then you must have a very short supply, my lord."

"More than Dr. Johnson's dictionary, ma'am."

Mrs. Able laughed. "Such a charming rogue! 'Tis no wonder you're the girls' favorite."

She says that to all the customers, Livia said, her voice sour. *You might've told me you were going to a brothel.*

And ruin the discovery?

He sensed her move away, straining against the bonds that tethered them together. Her presence left the chamber, and he couldn't decide how he felt about that.

"Pick any girl, my lord," Mrs. Able said, gesturing to the women upon the settees. "Almost all are at liberty tonight."

It was then he realized that the brothel suffered from the inverse of Lord Millom's assembly. Normally, men crowded Mrs. Able's establishment. But aside from one morose gentleman with an anxious girl upon his knee, Bram was the only man in the drawing room.

"Slow this evening," he murmured.

"Aye," agreed the madam, and she made a sound of displeasure. "Patrons haven't been coming round much these past weeks, and those that do want the kind of services we usually don't provide. Not our usual sort of client. And when we *do* get regulars, the girls don't want to go with 'em." She tightened her painted mouth. "Uneasy, they are. Scared."

So they were. Even the most veteran of Mrs. Able's girls had a pinched, nervous mien, twisting their hands in their laps and casting fretful glances around the normally cheerful drawing room.

If he sought solace and peace, they wouldn't be found here. Acid churned in Bram's stomach. Piece by piece, the world rotted away, leaving decayed flesh and pallid bones.

Mrs. Able seemed to recollect herself, and to whom she spoke. "Of course, my lord," she beamed, "any of my ladies will be more than happy to entertain *you*. Let me arrange it for you. Kitty, Cynthia!" She clapped her hands.

Two girls rose up from a couch, one fair, one with hair

tinted a vivid shade of red. Though they were dressed in audaciously transparent robes, they approached slowly, timorously. The redhead took hold of the blonde's hand. It wasn't a flirtatious gesture designed to stoke a patron's lust, but one that sought reassurance.

He'd believed that he had no heart left, that his time in the Colonies and since then had cut it from him. But, to his surprise, he now felt it withering in his chest, watching these two whores approach him like martyrs going to the lions. He could use his power, say something persuasive to both women so that they would eagerly take him to their bed. The idea tasted rancid.

He turned away, and Mrs. Able peered at him, a worried frown creasing lines in her face powder.

"Some other girls, my lord? You might enjoy Rosabel. A very sophisticated one, Rosabel. She can—"

"No. I don't want any of the girls." The words came of their own will, and it stunned him to realize he meant every one. He'd become a stranger to himself.

Mrs. Able's mouth dropped open. "But—"

Bram did not hear her objections as he felt Livia's presence come rushing into the chamber. Though she kept herself unseen, he sensed her distress. Candles flickered and the fire guttered. Shivering, several of the girls wrapped their arms around themselves and huddled close to one another.

"What is it?" Bram demanded.

The madam glanced around. "Are you speaking to me, my lord?"

He paid her no heed. Instead, he heard only Livia's voice in his mind.

Go upstairs. Go upstairs right now.

"Why?"

Hurry.

He stalked from the chamber, leaving a room full of

baffled women behind. One hand on the hilt of his sword, he took the stairs two at a time. Livia's faint outline drifted at his side.

Reaching the next floor, he saw nearly all the doors lining the corridor standing open—a testament to the brothel's lack of business. Two doors, however, were closed.

"Behind the door on the left." Livia spoke aloud, not attempting to hide her presence.

He hesitated outside the door. The sound of a woman weeping forced him into action. Trying the door and finding it locked, he pounded his fist on the wood.

"Let me in," he shouted through the door.

The woman inside only cried harder.

Cursing, Bram backed up then kicked the door's latch. Several girls peered fearfully from open chambers, but none tried to stop him. With another kick, the door to the locked room flew open.

Bram strode inside, then stopped abruptly. A nude woman huddled in the corner, her head on her knees. Sobs shook her. Sprawled on the bed lay a man, partially dressed. A stiletto stuck up from the side of his chest. His eyes stared vacantly at the ceiling. Judging by the amount of blood soaked into the mattress, he'd been dead for several minutes.

Throat tight, Bram moved toward the bed and stared down at the dead man's face.

"Thomas Auden," he said quietly. "Poor bastard." He'd been a genial man, always quick to laugh.

"He attacked me!" cried the woman in the corner. Her paint ran down her face in watery streaks. She tilted up her chin, revealing a necklace of bruises around her throat. "Just started throttling me, calling me filthy names. He would've killed me if I hadn't—" She glanced at the knife protruding from Auden's ribs and burst into tears again.

Bram backed from the room, his gaze riveted to the stiletto. Not so long ago, he'd seen a sword plunged into

Edmund's heart. They buried Edmund last week. Auden's family would bury him, too. But the chain of death would continue. On and on, until the dead outnumbered the living and the cobbles were slick with blood.

Heedless of who might see her, Livia appeared before him, her face tight and grave.

"This is how it will be," she said. "I've seen all of it before. I know what will follow. Whether you believe it or no, this world is truly going to hell."

Chapter 5

She was coming to know his bedchamber very well. The tall windows that looked out upon a narrow, well-tended but never used garden. The heavy furniture, carved from dark wood. The silver paper-covered walls, sparsely adorned. The bed, large and canopied also in silver. The man slumbering in that bed.

Livia stared down at Bram as he slept. A restless, active sleeper, he'd twisted the covers around him as he shifted his long body, sometimes muttering faintly in the half-coherent language of dreams. At that moment, he'd turned onto his back and flung one arm overhead. Both his hands were knotted into fists.

A sliver of light worked its way between the drawn canopy curtains, tracing the contours of his body, its planes and ridges. The light caught along the sharp lines of his face, no softer, even in sleep. Already stubble darkened his chin, despite shaving earlier in the day. She placed her palm against his jaw, wanting to feel its roughness, and silently cursed when she felt exactly what she always did—nothing.

He muttered again, his muscles tightening, and she moved away. Spending the long hours whilst he slept in a study of him offered no distraction, only emphasized what she couldn't have. Enough slack existed in the bond between them that she might go elsewhere in the house. So she had, invisibly exploring its numerous floors, the narrow chambers where the servants slept, the countless unused but elegantly furnished rooms. Yet she had returned here, to the bed-chamber, and its sleeping occupant.

She could loosen her hold on the mortal plane, drift back to the in-between place where time dissolved and the world retreated. But she'd spent too long there already. The realm of mists and shadow held no appeal. She wanted to be in the world, and of it. Which left her here, spending the hours alone and keeping watch over a restively slumbering man.

An empty decanter of wine lolled on the floor just beside the bed. He'd drained it in order to sleep. He didn't say as much, but she knew that the murder in the brothel shook him, deeply. Bram had lingered as men of the law were summoned, the body carted off, the girl who had killed him also taken away. Livia had not seen the murder itself, coming upon the girl moments after it had happened. To the men of the law, the girl had tearfully explained her self-defense, but whether the law would show her mercy, that was uncertain. Even when Livia had been alive, whores hadn't received much in the way of justice. This modern era didn't seem so different.

Too much was familiar. Over and over again, she witnessed echoes of her own time. Everything reminded her of her own folly, and the chaos that had followed.

She drifted to a window to watch the smoke-veiled stars, but her gaze saw a clearer, older sky. The night sky over a distant outpost of the Empire. Londinium. Much smaller than it was now. But large enough to become a living hell.

She saw not the tall brick and plaster buildings of London, but the courtyards and villas of her time, ablaze, smoke churning up into the night. Livia had stood upon the roof of her own villa and watched as the city destroyed itself. Screams and shouts rose up, as choking as the smoke. The cries of children. The shrieks of a blood-crazed mob.

Through the haze of time, she still felt the tears dampening her cheeks.

This isn't what I wanted.

The thrill she had felt in summoning the Dark One turned fetid. A sick cavern had opened in her stomach, watching from up high as the Dark One's wicked influence transformed the people of Londinium into vicious animals. Yet it wasn't only mortals who tore the city down. Vile creatures from the depths of the underworld had clawed their way to the surface, mixing with the humans, urging them on to greater brutality. Or tearing the mortals apart, their human blood splattering on frescoed walls and mosaic-covered floors.

This is my doing. I'm to blame for all this death.

"Can't you think of something peaceful?" Bram's voice growled out from behind the canopy. "My dreams are full of blood."

He shoved back the silver silk of the canopy with one arm as he sat up in bed.

She glided closer. "What did you see?"

"A Roman city on fire. Demons in the streets. Nothing pretty."

"My memories."

He pressed the heel of one hand into his eye. "We seem to share them now."

"Then you know that mine are as pleasant as yours."

A humorless smile curved his mouth. "A shame you didn't spend your life tending flower gardens or making love to beautiful women."

She couldn't stop her laugh. It caught them both by surprise, and they stared at one another for a moment, uncertain.

"It's damned cold with the canopy open." He jerked his

head in a summoning motion. "Come and sit or hover or whatever it is you do."

She raised a brow. "I'm to join you in bed?"

"If you're going to keep me awake with your memories, I'd rather be awake someplace warm. So either come here or stop thinking."

She wavered. Sharing a bed with him seemed far too . . . intimate. Ridiculous. He was mortal. She was spirit. There would be no shared intimacies.

Drifting forward, she moved through the canopy. Her torso emerged from the mattress, near the foot of the bed.

He frowned. "Can't you *sit* on the bed? I don't think I can talk with someone who's poking up from the mattress."

"But I don't need to sit."

"Just . . . do it."

"For a man of such esteemed breeding, you've terrible manners."

"A benefit of privilege." Seeing that she wouldn't comply without a little more finessing on his part, he said, grudgingly, "Please."

She decided to be amenable. Concentrating, she hovered higher, until her body fully emerged from the mattress, then lowered herself back down, tucking her legs under her. She focused her thoughts on creating a solid surface beneath her, and exclaimed in surprise when she actually found herself sitting atop the bed.

"Sitting," she murmured. "How novel."

"Many people seem to enjoy it." He let the canopy fall back, enclosing the bed in soft shadow. She heard more than saw him edge back until he sat upright, propped against the headboard. "Even myself, on occasion."

"What a rich and varied life you lead."

"I used to think so."

"And now?"

He rubbed his palms against his face. "Now I'm rethinking my original assessment."

"That seems to be the way of it," she said quietly. "We see the past so much more clearly than the present."

For a moment, he was silent. She studied the pattern on the blanket rather than look at him, for he was a man, beautiful to look upon, and she felt clutched by a surge of loneliness, cut off forever from the company and comfort of the flesh.

"The Hellraisers," he said, breaking the silence. "We didn't know what we were doing. When we opened that box in the underground temple, none of us knew who or what was kept within it. I remember seeing the box in that Roman skeleton's hands, and all I could understand was that I *had* to open it. A voice in my head, an urge in my muscles. Everything shouted at me to open that box."

"The Dark One's doing. Even within his prison, he wasn't without influence." She stared at the images of flame that marked Bram's skin. Within the span of a day, they had grown, spreading down his abdomen. She forced her gaze up. "He sensed the power within you, within all of you. He coveted that power, and lured you to him."

Bram made a soft, scoffing noise. "We had titles. Leo had wealth. But we spent our hours chasing diversions and pleasure. Nothing powerful about any of us."

"Your power was latent, unused, but it was there. It dwells within you now." She felt it coursing through her like lightning, and her form glowed brighter. "Such a banquet of strength—the Dark One couldn't resist."

"And we were the fools who blundered right into his trap." Then he stared right at her, and the shadows within the bed couldn't hide the hard, sharp blue of his eyes. "What's your excuse?"

"No excuse," she answered. "What I did, I did with full knowledge. I spent months ferreting out the secret of how to call upon the Dark One. Burned through amphoras of lamp oil as I stayed up late into the night, pouring over ancient texts in the temple libraries. I searched this wild land of Britannia to find the power I'd need to perform the summoning. I found what I was looking for in an Indian slave and a Druid priestess. They became my prisoners, and I understood full well what I intended to do with them. I combined spells of Hecate with the primitive power I uncovered here to steal the women's magic. There was no blundering." She shook her head. "Not at all."

"A calculated strategy. The same way an officer plans his attack."

"I'd have made a good soldier. Had I been born male."

He lifted a brow. "If you'd wanted to become a soldier, you would've done so. Sex had nothing to do with it."

She almost smiled. Already he knew her better than any of her kin. They had been statesmen, her family, but without real ambition to better the Empire. Other families dedicated themselves to the shaping of Rome. Not her father, her uncles and brothers. Content with their roles as minor players, they couldn't understand her ambition.

"Rome's first female general," she mused. "Perhaps. Though Roman people worshipped in temples, they did not believe in magic. It was hidden from the eyes of ordinary mortals. I was ever careful to keep my power veiled. Even so, wielded with cunning, magic had always been my weapon of choice, not the sword."

"That's why you summoned the Devil. To gain more magic, more power."

"Would it surprise you to learn that once, my motives had been altruistic?" At his skeptical look, she amended, "Not altruistic, perchance, but not entirely selfish, either. I loved Rome. She was a shambling mess, beset by strife, but I thought somehow I might make it better. For its citizens, for the peace of its empire. Stabilize it, in a fashion."

"Lofty aspirations."

"I've never been lacking in determination. If there's something I want, nothing keeps me from pursuing it."

"So I've learned," he said, dry.

"Everyone learns it, sooner or later." To her family, she'd been an enigma, a wolf amongst lapdogs. "That's why I journeyed from Rome all the way to these distant shores. There was only so much I could learn at home—and Britannia was rich with untapped magic. I had gained enough power to find new sources, and track it to this land. Yet this knowledge was mine alone."

She remembered her first steps off the ship, how power seemed to flow in the very water and course just beneath the surface of earth. The forests of sycamore and chestnut and oak sang with magic, and that song repeated in her blood.

Half to herself, she murmured, "There are people who, when they see a beautiful bird in flight, simply watch its progress across the sky, delighting in the creature for its living energy, its liberty. But there are others who catch the bird. They cage it, clip its wings so it can't fly away. They must possess it, revel in owning something that was never meant to be owned."

"You caged it," he said, "the magic you found here."

"My intent had been so different. I wanted to claim just a little, just enough to make me stronger so I might do more to make Rome stronger. But . . . I couldn't stop at just a little. I took as much as I could. With spells I had learned in Rome, I stole magic from every source I could find. Stripped it from each sacred stone, wrung it from the holy lakes and chopped it from the hallowed forests." Hot shame choked her words, as she recalled with cutting clarity her desecration of shrines and theft of revered objects—a stone crudely carved into the likeness of a goddess, an iron dagger.

She forced herself to continue. "My ambition to help Rome crumbled away. I wanted only to help myself. The more power I gained, the more I desired. My soul blackened and charred. What did I care? Mine was a hunger that couldn't be sated. Then . . . a revelation. If it was power I wanted, where best to find it? None other than its origin."

"The Devil."

"That wasn't the name I knew him by, but yes. How clever I thought I was, discovering the secret to summoning him, opening the door between his realm and ours." She forced out a brittle laugh. "Whenever we think ourselves clever, it's a clear sign that we're actually being fools."

The bedclothes rustled as Bram shifted. "But you learned your mistake. I saw it, felt it, in my dream. My dream of your past."

Sharing memories felt impossibly intimate, another's presence in the carefully guarded palace of her psyche. She didn't know if she liked the sensation. But she'd had the same access to his thoughts, his past, lacing tighter the connection between them—whether they wanted it or not.

"Too late," she said. "I learned it too late. The Dark One gave me just what I wanted—I was drunk with power. Knowing I would serve him well, he directed his ambition to the rest of the mortal realm. So exciting to me, seeing how wild men and women truly were at heart. But it degenerated. Mobs, madness. Death. It spread like a wind-borne fever, to the walls of Londinium and beyond. I was angry, sick."

She wanted to cover her face, but wouldn't allow herself the escape. Unblinking, she met Bram's gaze. "I had brought the Dark One to this realm, and I had to send him away again."

"At the cost of your own life."

"The price of wisdom is very dear." She would go on paying it for eternity.

Bram grunted. "All the lecturing, all the berating and reprimands to turn from the path of wickedness, you dared all this, and yet it was *your* greed that started the whole bloody mess in the first place."

She did not flinch at the recrimination that hardened his voice. "Which means it's up to *me* to stop it."

"Couldn't you have been content with a few little spells? Straw into gold or men into pigs?"

"Men smell better than pigs. Marginally."

He only stared at her.

She exhaled. "No. I couldn't be content. Greedy, just as you said. But that's how sin works—the more we consume, the hungrier we become, until we devour ourselves."

"Oh," he muttered, "I know a lot about sin."

Images from his past tumbled through her mind, scenes of unbridled dissipation and debauchery. If she still possessed a body, such visions would have heated her, the blood coursing through her becoming thick and hot. Yet she had only her recollection of fevered, shocked arousal to stir her. He had applied himself to licentiousness with the same single-minded purpose he had toward combat. In both, he was an expert.

"We're of a kind," she said softly, "you and I. Left to our own devices, we're wicked creatures indeed. But it wasn't always so."

After a long moment, he answered, "Not always."

She had felt the bond he'd shared with the other Hell-raisers. Such friendship and trust was alien to her, but the echoes of his loss reverberated through her own insubstantial body.

"Did it frighten you?" he asked in the darkness. "Knowing that you'd have to sacrifice your life?"

"Most grievously." She had not gone into battle with the Dark One with this knowledge, but as she had fought, it became clear that in order to put an end to his destruction, those moments would be her last. "The pleasures of life were sweet. There was so much left undone, so much I hadn't experienced. Sensations I wanted to have again. All of it would be lost. Yet what choice did I have? If I clung to life, the world would become a hell, and then life wouldn't be worth living anyway."

"Sounds like you were damned rational about dying."

She shook her head. "These thoughts were but momentary grains of insight, falling through my fingers. I understood what I had to do, and I did it." She peered at him through the shadows. "You've been to war. It's much the same, is it not?"

His exhalation came from deep within his chest, and he lifted his hands to grasp the headboard behind him. He was shadows and sleekness.

"It's a dawning horror. We're fed stories of valor, and the great good we perform for our grateful nation. I'd hold it with both hands, that heroism, praying for it when all around was carnage." Bitterness laced his voice. "I wanted to run."

"Yet you did not. You stayed, and fought."

He snorted. "Because I was a dolt."

"Not a dolt. Courageous."

In a blur of moment, he rose quickly from the bed. She had the impression of long, hewn limbs, and then he threw on a robe. A tinder hissed, then light flared as he lit a candle. His eyes were glacial in the flickering light.

"I'll show you proof of my courage." He strode from the chamber.

Even had she not been tethered to him, she would have followed. She floated from the bed and went after him, into the shadow-strewn house. At the end of the corridor, she glimpsed the silk of his robe. He stalked the house like a hunter, silent and intent, the candle he carried casting transitory light.

She trailed him as he pushed open a door at the end of the passageway and went inside. In her solitary haunting in the depths of night, she had made a cursory examination of this chamber—it seemed to serve no other purpose beside superfluity. This house, with its many rooms, far surpassed even the most luxurious villa. Wealth, it seemed, always strove to be impressive, regardless of the era.

Bram stared up at a large gilt-framed painting upon the wall, and she joined him in his contemplation. Holding the candle up, the painted surface of the canvas gleamed, revealing the artist's minute brushstrokes. She had seen the painting but not paid it much attention, the chamber too dim for anything but the most perfunctory study. Now both she and Bram looked at it.

A dark-haired youth stared back at them. He wore a uniform of scarlet, white and gold, a polished gorget at his throat. A scarlet sash crossed his narrow chest—he hadn't yet broadened into a man. The youth leaned against a column, one hand on his hip, the other holding a braid-trimmed hat. Unlike some of the other somber portraits she had seen in these modern homes, in this painting, the sitter smiled. So much pride and excitement in that smile, so much eagerness for the world and its chances for glory, a certainty that the glory would be his; it made the nonexistent heart in her chest ache.

"Behold, Madam Ghost," Bram said, his voice cold and cutting as a shard of ice. "I call this *Portrait of Folly.*"

She continued to stare at this other Bram, this inchoate form. He held himself with such confidence, assured that whatever he desired would be his. His eyes were bright and clear, looking into a future of gallantry and daring, a boy dreaming of tomorrow. He had seen nothing of the world. Not yet.

No scar marred his throat. He was unmarked.

"Not folly," she said. "Hope."

"Ridiculous hopes. Other younger sons went into the

military, and in that, I was no different. But I was singular in that I truly believed I'd do some good. I didn't want to spend my military career doing useless drills and showing off my uniform in town. When they told us we'd be going to the Colonies to defend our people, I was *happy*." He spit out the word. "Thought I would make a difference."

"You did. I have seen it. Those people on the frontier, you defended their homes. There are scores of lives you saved."

He made a dismissive wave with his free hand. "Token gestures. Nothing could keep pace with the spill of blood."

"All of it meant something."

Turning to her, his mouth twisted in a sneer. "Ned Davies would argue otherwise."

"Ned . . . ?"

"He's here." He tapped his forehead.

Memories began to engulf her, swirling around her in a misty vortex. The chamber receded, fading, transforming into a muddy hill. The scent of gunpowder hung thick in the air, as did the groans of dying men and horses. Atop the hill stood a military fortress, its walls made of felled trees as though hastily constructed. Part of the walls had been blasted away. The yard within the fortress held more wounded men and bodies.

Outside the fortress, soldiers in red picked their way through the fallen.

"Find all the wounded," said a blood and smoke-streaked Bram to the soldiers. "Bring them to the surgeon."

"He looks fair gone." One soldier lifted the shoulders of a man upon the ground, his head lolling back to reveal an ugly wound in his shoulder. If he lived, the injured soldier would of a certain lose his arm.

"Does he breathe?" Bram demanded.

The soldier bent close to the wounded man. "Aye, sir."

"Then there's a chance for him. Get him to Dr. Balfour."

After signaling for some assistance, the soldier and one of his comrades bore the wounded man away, toward the fortress. Bram continued to move through the bent and contorted shapes of fallen men, his face ashen, lips pressed tight. Yet he appeared familiar with the aftermath of battle and the sight of the dead. He waved away clouds of flies from the face of a dead boy holding a drum.

"What of this one, sir?"

Bram turned at Sergeant Davies's question. Bram outranked the Cornishman, not only in rank but station. Back in England, they would have had little to do with one another, Bram being the second son of a baron, Davies being the fifth son of a farmer, yet in the strange methods of war, they had become unlikely friends. They told one another stories of home and laughed raucously at remembered childhood exploits. He'd had no idea that a farmer's boy could be just as reckless and foolish as a baron's supplementary heir.

The other officers did not care for Bram's fraternization with an enlisted man, but it seemed even war could not dim his insistence for doing whatever he damn well wanted.

Now Davies stood over a fallen French soldier, the enemy moaning weakly. One of his legs was nothing but tatters, taken off inelegantly by cannon fire.

The battle had been a rough one, with losses heavy on both sides. Bram had witnessed many of his brothers in arms killed, including men with families, and men who weren't men, but boys who hadn't grown a single whisker or been between the thighs of a woman. These were the fellow soldiers who, only the day before, talked longingly of their mother's elderberry preserves, or cleaned their muskets and whistled. Now they were carcasses.

"The Frenchman goes to Dr. Balfour, too," said Bram.

Davies looked hesitant. "You sure? I saw 'im gut Fitzhugh

with a bayonet. Just tore 'im open, innards spilling out. Made me lose my tea and hardtack, it did."

A wave of nausea threatened Bram's struggle for composure. Evisceration was no way to die, slow and brutal. "We won't leave him out here to be picked at by crows." He'd seen too many men, still breathing, torn apart by scavengers.

Davies shrugged. "You're the officer."

The sergeant bent down to pick up the wounded enemy soldier. As he did, the Frenchman lifted his hand. He held a pistol. And aimed it at Davies's face.

"Davies!" Bram shouted. He ran toward them.

Too late. The French soldier pulled the trigger. A flash and bang, and the pistol fired directly between an astonished Davies's eyes. Most of his face blew apart.

Bram was there in an instant, his sword drawn and ready to run the Frenchman through. But the soldier denied him the pleasure, toppling back to the mud, dead.

Davies also lay in the mud, his arms outflung, his one remaining eye staring at the cloud-smeared sky. What was left of his face held a look of almost comic surprise. As other soldiers came running, Bram sank down to the sodden earth and could not look away from the fallen Davies, burning the image into his mind and heart.

The field covered with the dead vanished. As did the overcast sky, the ravaged fortress. Livia found herself once more in the elegant but unused chamber in Bram's home, the bodies of the soldiers now pieces of furniture, the muddy ground turned to patterned carpets. Bram wore a robe instead of his uniform, but the expression on his face was the same. As though he'd torn the heart from his own chest and stared at it, clutched in his hand.

"For nothing," Bram growled. "Ned Davies died for naught. The battle was over, the Frenchman was to have been given medical attention. Ned got his brains blown out anyway."

Hollowed by his grief, she looked away. "I cannot pretend to know the whys and wherefores of combat. In my time, men fought and died simply for the amusement of the crowd."

"In my time, men fight and die for many reasons, none of them worthwhile. There's only death, and more death. That stupid boy"—he nodded toward the portrait of himself—"was an ignorant child. The only thing he achieved was the fashioning of the man standing here. And that's a piss-poor accomplishment."

"Nothing has been decided," she fired back. "For over a millennium, I have seen this world change, constantly remaking itself. Until our bodies become the food of worms, we've the means of transforming ourselves. We might be anything we want. Anything at all."

His jaw tightened. "Including those that would take up a futile fight against the Devil."

"Winnable, unwinnable—all that matters is the fight." She drifted closer, wishing she could touch him, though she didn't know if she wanted to gently stroke his face or strike him. Any means of reaching him within the depths of his self-constructed crypt.

Gaze bleak, he turned away. "No."

She darted through him, passing through his body, to stand in his line of sight. She pointed to the painting. "That boy was ignorant, yes, but he *believed*. That belief still dwells within you."

"Don't you understand?" He bared his teeth like an animal. "Men went to war. Some were killed. Others maimed. And others returned home and took up their lives. Not me. I was never strong enough. I came back broken."

He stepped nearer so only a few inches separated them. Though she could feel nothing, some vestige of his heat penetrated the mists surrounding her, the first hint of sensation she'd had in over a thousand years.

"I see the world going to hell all around me," he rumbled. "I know what will come. But I cannot fight anymore. If I ever possessed honor and virtue—which I doubt—they are long gone."

"Wrong. You are wrong." She flicked her gaze to his scar, dull and raised in the candlelight. It had to have bled copiously, covering him in scarlet, his clothes, his hands, smelling of metal as it poured upon the ground. "It's *because* you have a good heart that the war damaged you so badly. You cannot go back to being that boy. He's unneeded. But you can move forward and become someone wiser, someone stronger."

"Damn you." His voice was barely human. "Why can't you leave me in peace?"

Moving away from him, she hovered beside the window. So little was this chamber used that the servants had not closed the curtains for the night. The fog-choked city appeared beyond the glass, and the muted sounds of men and women plummeting deeper into an unrelenting nightmare speared through the heavy silence.

"There is no peace, Bram," she said over her shoulder. "This night has proven it. You can close your eyes and cover your ears, but it makes no difference. Bit by bit, piece by piece, the world is crumbling away. All we can do—all we *must* do—is fight."

"None of this was my doing."

She whirled around. "Tell yourself that, but you know otherwise. I did summon the Dark One, so the original blame is mine. Yet deep in your heart, no matter your protestations, you understood *exactly* what your bargain with the Devil meant. The burden falls to both of us."

When he only scowled at her, she spread her hands wide. For the first time ever, she had to supplicate herself, show . . . humility. *I was wrong. We have the means of transforming ourselves even after death, because I am not the woman I once was.*

"Please, Bram." Her voice was a bare whisper, raw as a scraped knuckle. "I cannot do this alone. I need your help."

The entreaty in her eyes and words must have shaken him, for he looked away. "This cause deserves a better champion than me."

"Perhaps it does." She felt a flare of exultation as he whirled to glare at her. He wasn't immune from pride, and she needed that. A humble man made for a poor warrior. "But you are all we have."

Chapter 6

He could not recall being awake at this hour, not having already seen his bed. Usually if Bram watched the sun crest the spires and rooftops, he was on his way home after a night's revelry, experiencing the waking city as a visitor from a distant land. Men of trade bustling to their offices. Farmers walking beside their drays laden for market. Crossing sweeps, housemaids, bankers, merchants, costermongers. Here was the realm of business, ambition, subsistence—concepts as alien to him as breathing underwater or flight.

Yet now he rode his chestnut mare through the glare of a daytime London, and though oppressive clouds draped low in the sky, he squinted against the brightness. He had the oddest feeling that the good, industrious citizens would stand and point accusing fingers at him as he wended through the streets, demanding the intruder be driven from the gates and there to pass his days in exile.

But rest had been in short supply as of late. He'd barely dipped below the surface of sleep before his eyes had opened, sticky and hot, to stare at the bed canopy overhead. Livia's words had dug beneath his skin like burrs, banishing peace. He'd risen from bed no more replenished than he had been hours earlier. Almost on principle, he'd thought to lie abed until his usual hour, but disquiet churned like a rising storm. After nearly murdering an innocent man, he doubted he'd be welcome at the fencing academy. How then, to quell the cagey energy that goaded him into motion?

His grooms had been startled by his appearance in the stable and demand for a horse to be saddled. They had complied, as they were paid to do, and minutes later he trotted toward the park. Impatience burned him. A full gallop was the only pace that could give any measure of release, yet traffic demanded that he keep himself at a sedate gait. At the least, it allowed him the rare experience of seeing London at the height of its bustle, the innumerable people jostling and hurrying from one end of the city to the other on important—or unimportant—business.

All was not order and civility, however. The streets were littered with broken glass, shattered pieces of masonry, and charred wood. An overturned carriage lay on the cobblestones like a carcass, picked clean by carrion feeders. Broken windows reflected back the cloudy sky in shards. And the people moved as though chased by resolute assassins, their heads down, shouldering aside whomever crossed their path, snarling in anger should anyone prove a slow-moving obstacle.

The disease advances, Livia's voice murmured in his mind.

If a limb is infected, he answered, *it's amputated.*

Too late for that. The sickness is in the blood, and our own hearts spread its decay.

He had no answer to that. Everywhere around him was proof. As he progressed toward the park, he felt Livia's presence, always near, always close. Impossible to feel truly alone when she never left him, like a second heartbeat.

The greater irony? Only days ago, he considered her the

greatest punishment. Now . . . the piercing loneliness he had felt, even sometimes in the company of the other Hell-raisers, kept itself in abeyance. She was opinionated, obstinate, maddeningly headstrong. And the only person—if a ghost could be called a person—who gave him no quarter. Whit, his closest friend, never knew him as thoroughly as Livia did. Whit never had access to Bram's most closely-kept self. Livia was everywhere within him.

Guiding his horse around two women arguing in the road, Bram thought, *Last night was a first for me.*

Visiting a brothel without partaking of its merchandise? Her voice was wry.

That was *novel. But I've never had so much conversation with a woman in my bed.*

Technically, I was on *your bed. And I'm not truly a woman.*

Most assuredly you're a woman. When sleep had come, his dreams had alternated between scenes of chaos and fevered images of Livia, fully flesh, fully nude, her dark hair tumbling over her shoulders, her olive-hued limbs entwined with a man's. Sometimes the man had a stranger's face, sometimes the face was Bram's. A mingling of her memories and his. He'd awakened with an uneasy heart and an aching cock.

Did he desire her? Resent her? *Like* her? Or was it an uncomfortable alloy of all these feelings?

You must have spoken to the women you took to bed, she answered.

Not certain if 'Spread your legs,' counts as legitimate discourse.

Her low chuckle was that of a goddess, pagan and earthy. *I was never one for an exchange of confidences either. There were more important matters to attend to once a mattress was in the vicinity.*

I'd no idea Roman women were so . . . unconstrained, he thought. *Aside from Messalina.*

She was too stupid to conduct her affairs with discretion, Livia scoffed. *But my freedom was my own doing. I didn't want to suffer the confining virtue of being a wife. And honored daughters resigned themselves to respectable, stultifying chastity. A priestess of Hecate, however, and one with my wealth of knowledge about magic, the years of study and natural ability . . . if there was something, someone I wanted, I could have them.*

You sound like a Hellraiser.

Had there been such a thing when I lived, I surely would have been one.

You would've been fearsome indeed. He seethed with restlessness, but thinking of bedsport was a continuous drumbeat, like an ancient slave ship urging its captives to greater speed on the oars, lest they suffer the wrath of the lash.

At last, Hyde Park came into view, its treetops and wide swaths of field a welcome respite after the tight press of buildings and people.

A relief to see that it wasn't a hanging day at Tyburn. Massive crowds would gather around the triangular gallows, with wealthy spectators in Mother Proctor's Pews to get the better view of the condemned's last few moments alive. People of every stripe and class all assembled—shopkeepers, apprentices, gentlemen, ruffians. All hoped for a good show; displays of bravery were applauded, but fear received boos. Gingerbread sellers and people hawking copies of the condemned's last words—before they had even uttered them—worked the crowd. Pickpockets found ample prey, an irony given that many of those about to be executed were thieves. The din and bloodlust could make one's head pound.

Only once after his return from the Colonies had he gone to see a hanging. He had comported himself with reserve, watching the criminals dance at the ends of their ropes with a façade of disinterest, but the moment he had returned to his private chambers, he'd emptied the contents of his stomach. Thereafter he found ways to occupy himself far from Tyburn Tree on hanging days.

He avoided Rotten Row and the early risers sedately parading their horses up and down. What he wanted was a good, hard gallop.

Reaching an open expanse of grass, he kicked his horse into greater speed, and his heart gave its own kick to feel the animal bolt into motion.

The wind in his face, his greatcoat flapping behind him, the horse tearing across the field, he smiled.

He felt Livia gather close around him like a mantle, and together, they rode like demons through the park. Bent low over the neck of his horse, he gave the mare full rein. The animal was bred for speed, and it took the open space with ground-eating strides. Its hoof beats became the beat of his heart, fast and heedless, the world turning to a blur of gray and green. He lost himself in the velocity, his muscles attuned to the horse's, his thoughts naught but motion.

Faster, urged Livia.

His mouth pulled into a grin, and he pushed the mare into greater speed.

Above the rush of wind and the pound of the hooves, he heard Livia laugh. He couldn't stop his answering laughter, both of them caught in the heady taste of freedom, where nothing existed but speed. As if they could outrun the coming catastrophe. For a few moments, they could pretend.

Yet the horse could not sustain its pace for too long. It would run itself to death, if he so desired. He had no wish to have the mare collapse beneath him, and so he was forced to slow, gallop to canter, canter to trot, and finally, a docile walk. The horse snorted and steamed, pleased with itself.

That was . . . a marvel, Livia said. Pleasure sparkled through her voice, and he felt her smile like a caress.

Her pleasure gleamed beside his own, and that gave him a curious sense of . . . satisfaction. Strange, to gain that feeling from something out of bed.

And the time with Livia *in* bed had been just as strange. He had never spoken to a woman, in bed or out, with such depth, such intimacy. Some women had pressed him for details of his time fighting in the Colonies, their gazes and hands continually drifting to his scar. He would push their hands away, make their eyes close in pleasure, and kept his history to himself. A few facile anecdotes for the more insistent females.

None of the Hellraisers were aware of the details of what Bram had seen and done in the Colonies. Not even Whit knew about Ned Davies. Only Livia.

He waited for his mind to rebel, to recoil in horror at letting anyone learn the brutality of his existence in the army. All that he found was an odd, unfamiliar loosening within his chest. As if binding chains at last fell away, leaving him to test the scope of his newfound freedom.

So long had he dwelt with those chains—he almost missed them. Almost, but not quite.

I used to race with Whit and Edmund here. Edmund never could beat us, but he surely tried. We used to terrify the people out for a peaceful stroll.

Leaving a swath of sighing maidens in your wake.

Never cared for maidens, he answered. *Inexperience makes for tedious flirtation.*

Inexperience makes most everything tedious. But a jaded eye takes the luster off the most glittering diamond.

Bram guided his horse back toward the more populated section of the park, where men and women paraded themselves and made conspicuous their leisure. When he was a boy, he loved coming to the park, watching the dashing bucks and flower-hued girls engage in the complicated, arcane maneuvers of the adult world. He loved to see the gentlemen on their prime horses, both with twitching flanks and proud miens. He used to stand on the banks of the Serpentine and send off armadas of twigs, creating vast naval battles in his imagination.

Now all he saw were vainglorious attempts at consequence, another generation of fools chasing dross, and a large, muddy artificial river.

But there was a young girl crouched at the edge of the Serpentine, dropping leaves onto the surface of the water and watching them drift. Her inattentive nurse gossiped with a fellow servant. Meanwhile, the child most likely saw not leaves but fairy barges gliding upon the river. Her pleasure, and dreams, were real. For a few years more, she would have the privilege of dreams. Their loss was inevitable, but for now, they were hers.

If she survived.

Something moved in the river. An unidentifiable shape, more like a shadow, and it headed for the girl. He strained to get a better look, then jolted in shock.

A creature. He could barely discern its outline—its skin seemed to mimic the appearance of the water.

Gods preserve us, Livia cried in his mind. *A demon.*

He'd only glimpsed a few of those beasts, as they'd fled Leo's burning home. They had run by too quickly for him to truly see them, but he'd had fast, vague impressions of claws, teeth, yellow eyes. This thing seemed another species entirely.

Whatever variety of demon it was, the thing moved toward the girl playing on the riverbank, its outstretched claws reaching for her. And no one noticed. Except him.

It will pull her into the water, Livia said, horrified. *Drown her.*

Bram acted without thinking. He spurred his horse into a

hard gallop and raced toward the child. Pedestrians leapt out of his way, some crying out, but he paid them no heed. His focus was solely on the girl and the demon that stalked her.

The child looked up in shock as he rode right to her. Without slowing his horse, he leaned down and scooped her up into his arms. She squirmed in his grasp, but he held on tightly. Riding up to the stunned nursemaid, he handed the child over.

"She was about to fall into the water," he explained tersely.

Cradling the child, the nurse stammered her thanks, but Bram was already riding away.

The brief peace he'd obtained moments earlier rusted and flaked away.

Such events grow more common the longer the Dark One is at liberty, Livia murmured.

Needing a distraction, he turned his horse toward Rotten Row. The hour was far too early for true men and women of fashion to be out, but that did not prevent a goodly throng from assembling.

Bram nodded at passing acquaintances. Conversation barely stirred. People rode on horseback or carriage as though impelled by the last vestiges of societal imperative, their gazes chary, their words hoarded.

His bones heavy as iron, he urged his horse forward. A small collection of elegant but soberly dressed men stood at the base of a tree, their heads bent together, their brows furrowed in the way only men of importance could frown.

One of them glanced up as he passed. Lord Maxwell. An earl who took his Parliamentary duties with extreme gravity. Maxwell recognized Bram, and waved him over. Bram mentally groaned. He only wanted to go home and retreat into the welcoming recesses of a brandy decanter. But, Hellraiser or no, he couldn't outright ignore Maxwell.

Slowly, Bram guided his horse toward the group of men. They all stared up at him as he neared. All of them were known for their political authority—even a disinterested nobleman like Bram had knowledge of them.

After terse civilities were exchanged, Maxwell spoke. "We beg a moment of your time, Rothwell." He eyed Bram's horse. "Perhaps you might deign to lower yourself."

The impulse to kick his horse into another gallop and ride away seized him.

These men may have vital intelligence, Livia said. *If they are as influential as you believe, we cannot afford to ignore them. Not in these dark hours.*

I've made no pledges to any cause, Bram reminded her acerbically. Yet he dismounted and edged his way into the circle. He counted amongst the five men two senior cabinet officials and one of the king's closest advisors. Anxiety deepened the lines on their faces and formed bags beneath their eyes. Bram wasn't alone in his insomnia.

"Unusual to see you about at this hour," Maxwell noted.

"I need coffee or brandy, or perhaps both," Bram said. "So let's keep this brief."

Maxwell cleared his throat and exchanged glances with the other men. "You are an intimate of John Godfrey, are you not?"

At the mention of John's name, the hair on the back of Bram's neck rose. Livia, too, tensed. "We have been friendly, yes."

"*Have* been," pressed one of the cabinet officials, "but are no longer?"

"My time is my own, just as John's is his. Tell me what you want."

"Can we trust you?" This, from the king's advisor, his knuckles whitening on his ivory-topped walking stick.

"I wouldn't trust anyone," Bram answered.

"He's useless," the cabinet official growled at Maxwell. "Either he's deliberately being obtuse, or he's Godfrey's man."

"I'm *no one's*," Bram said through clenched teeth.

"What choice have we?" Maxwell looked helplessly at the other men in the circle. "Godfrey keeps his intentions to himself and everyone else at a distance. Rothwell is our only option. He's the closest thing Godfrey has to a friend."

The advisor let out a heavy sigh. "Go ahead, then."

"Nothing has been agreed to," Bram interjected hotly. The lingering remnants of his temper unraveled. "And if you talk of me like a dumb animal, then I'm getting back on my horse and you can all go to hell."

Stop growling like a wounded bear, Livia snapped, *and listen. John is the Dark One's closest, most powerful ally. Surely whatever these powdered wigs are speaking of must have significance.*

Though Bram's anger continued to roil, he forced out, "Just say what you want of me."

"Godfrey's becoming more aggressive in Parliament," Maxwell said after a pause. "Creating alliances, breaking apart old confederations. Brokering deals and ensuring that other pacts collapse. 'Tis clear that some greater scheme is afoot, but none of our efforts have been able to determine precisely *what* he intends."

"I'm to play the role of spy." Bram's voice was flat.

Several of the men grimaced. Typical that they would cringe away from plain speaking—the only means Bram had available to him.

Not so, corrected Livia. *You are remarkably subtle and insinuating when dealing with women.*

Except you.

I am always the exception. Pride laced her words. He could imagine her tossing her head, regal as an empress.

He fought a smile. Damn, but it was difficult to engage in two conversations simultaneously, especially if one of them was with a ghost that had invaded his consciousness.

"If you might gain Godfrey's confidence," Maxwell said. "Learn more about his objectives, and the means he intends to use to gain those objectives."

"Then pass this intelligence on to you and this distinguished company." Bram stared at each of the men in turn. "Thus the reason why I keep my involvement with politics to a minimum. I like not this business of cunning and guile." Strategy was reserved for the battlefield—yet to these men, Whitehall *was* the battlefield.

"Will you do it?" pressed the king's advisor.

"Why should I?" Bram fired back.

All of the men began speaking at once, throwing out words like *duty, honor,* and *greater good.* The crown itself was endangered, and England would fall with it. Their voices battered against him as waves against a cliff. It took hundreds if not thousands of years for those waves to carve away at the stone.

Cease your reflexive obstinacy, Livia snapped in his mind. *Whether you will do as they ask or no, nothing's harmed by saying yes.*

He held up his hand, silencing the cabal. "If it will quiet your infernal nattering, then I agree." His words were meant for the gathered men as well as Livia.

The men exhaled in a communal sigh of relief. The ghost, however, had some choice Latin curses for him.

"Come to my home tomorrow at ten in the evening," said Maxwell. "We shall discuss your findings then."

Bram mounted his horse. He looked down at these powerful men of England, their worn, weary faces, the lines of strain around their mouths. They dressed in the finest in tailoring, and their wigs were immaculately dressed. For all that, they were but a collection of bones and flesh, as vulnerable as a pauper begging for alms, subject to the same inevitability of death and obscurity. They controlled the fate of the nation, but there would come a time when every one of them would be laid out in a box of pine and lowered into the ground.

"When I decide I have something to recount," he said to them, "I shall let you know. We'll discuss it at a time and place of *my* choosing." Before anyone could speak or argue, he urged his horse into motion.

What will you do? Livia asked as he rode away.

Dance on the edge of a blade, he answered. *As I always do.*

Books and papers lay in riotous profusion upon every available surface, including the floor. Maps draped over chairs, and the abundance of broken quills on the carpet resembled the massacre of flocks of birds. Unlike Bram's study, John's saw much use, and John himself unfolded from behind a massive desk as Bram entered the chamber.

A look of wariness passed briefly over John's face when the footman announced Bram, but he smoothed it into a welcoming smile, his hand outstretched in greeting.

"A most agreeable surprise," John murmured, shaking Bram's hand.

"You seem well-engaged." Bram released John's grip and glanced at the mountains of paper on the desk.

"Never too occupied for an old friend and fellow Hell-raiser." Stepping back, he asked, "Can I offer you some tea? Wine?"

"Brandy."

John's brow rose, yet he picked his way through the stacks of books and debris toward the sideboard. He poured two glasses.

Bram. Livia spoke with tight urgency. *His arms. His hands.*

I see them.

For his work at home, John had discarded his coat, and the sleeves of his shirt had been rolled back. Markings of flame covered every inch of exposed skin. His forearms. His hands—from fingers to palm. Bram's gaze rose higher. Without his stock, the neck of John's shirt hung open. More flames wound around up from his chest, creeping up his neck like a choking weed.

It's spread much faster on him than it did on any of the others, Livia said. *Fertile ground.*

John wended his way back to Bram, navigating the clutter and bearing two full glasses. "'Tis a veritable labyrinth in here. The fault is mine, not my servants, for I forbid any of them from cleaning."

"And keep them out with a locked door when you aren't around." Bram took the offered glass.

John patted a pocket of his waistcoat. "At all times the key is on my person. There are so few who can be trusted."

Livia snorted. *How he enjoys this.*

"Yet I can trust you, can I not?" John held Bram's gaze with his own. Neither of them were fooled by his smile.

"As much as you can trust yourself," answered Bram. He did not wait for John to offer a toast, but drank down his brandy in one swallow.

More leisurely, John sipped at his drink. "We ought to arrange an excursion, you and I. It has been far too long since we kept company. Perhaps an assembly, or the theater. You were ever an enthusiast of the theater."

"Actresses and opera dancers," Bram said. "The plays themselves bored me."

Refined as always, sighed Livia.

"It was Edmund who actually watched the plays," added Bram.

John studied the bottom of his glass as if it held a miniature marvel. "If not the theater, then some other diversion."

"Of late, the city has become less diverting. Had to find other means of occupying myself." After setting down his glass on a small table, Bram pulled folded pieces of paper from his coat's inside pocket. Mutely, he held them out to John.

John took the papers, frowning, and unfolded them. His frown dissolved as he read their contents. "But this is marvelous." He grinned. "I trust you received no trouble for your efforts."

"None."

In truth, the only trouble he had experienced came from that long-disused machine of his conscience. Rusty and corroded, it had groaned as he had used his Devil's gift of persuasion to gain entrance into a minister's home and private study. The papers were easily secured, just as easily spirited away, with Livia acting as sentinel.

He hadn't wanted to pilfer the documents. Outright theft was not one of his many crimes. Only Livia had convinced him to act.

Sin is often required to ensure success, she had argued.

Ruthless, that's what you are, he had answered.

In everything. There had been no shame in her voice. It verged on admirable, her merciless resolve. She would permit no obstacle to subvert her will.

Now he had handed over a packet of stolen documents to John. It seemed to have the desired effect.

John continued to scan the papers, his gaze sharp and rapacious. "With this information in my possession, I shall be much closer to my goal." He glanced up at Bram. "You've my gratitude."

"Is that all?"

"What do you mean?"

"I'd want suitable compensations."

This isn't what we agreed upon, Livia interjected with alarm.

Rather than look hurt or angry at Bram's demand, John smiled. He seemed to approve of Bram's greed. "Name something you desire, and it shall be yours."

Bram's eyebrow arched. "Far-reaching claim."

John held out his hands, brandishing the marks of flame on his skin. "It is a claim I can make with all assurance. If I can rely upon your support, the pleasures and privileges you have enjoyed will seem miniscule in comparison."

With disinterest, Bram examined the title page of a nearby book. The frontispiece promised a long and phenomenally dull treatise on methods of governance, written by a gentleman with far too much education. He thumbed through the pages and found not a single illustration, only an abundance of long words and foreign phrases. Carelessly, he tossed the book over his shoulder. It landed with a thud and John winced.

"Give me your word," Bram said, "that I shall have precisely what you promise."

We were only going to draw him out, Livia protested, her voice turning strident.

"Give me yours," came John's immediate answer. "Betrayal is thick around us, and I've only use for those I can trust."

"You have it," Bram replied after a moment.

No! Livia's shout echoed in Bram's head, and he struggled to keep from scowling.

Still, John looked dubious.

With a sigh, Bram bent and pulled a poniard from his boot. John stepped back, yet a pistol suddenly appeared in his hand, retrieved from somewhere on the desk.

Livia's cursing nearly drowned out Bram's own thoughts. Her frustration at being powerless seethed through him.

"A gun's damned prosaic for a man with the Devil's mark on his flesh," Bram drawled.

"The gifts he has bestowed upon me are elegant and subtle."

"Elegant and subtle can't rip a hole in a man's chest. Thus, the pistol. But it's unnecessary, at least where I'm concerned. If it's a blood oath you require . . ." He drew the tip of the poniard across his hand. Bright crimson welled. "Here it is."

Smiling, John tucked the pistol into the back waistband of his breeches. He took the offered blade from Bram and made a cut across his own palm. Their hands clasped.

Stop, stop, stop! This is the wrong choice! Did nothing penetrate your obstinate skull? We have to fight John, fight the Dark One! You cannot—

"There's proof," Bram said, and John started. Bram had not realized he had all but shouted his words, trying to drown out Livia's excoriation.

Satisfied, John stepped away. He took a kerchief from a pocket in his waistcoat and wrapped it around his cut hand.

"The gesture is appreciated," he murmured. "And if you knew my intent, you would understand such an action's necessity."

"I cannot know your intent unless you tell me. The reading of thoughts is *your* bailiwick."

"That night outside Leo's home, Mr. Holliday gave me another gift." John's words were laden with boasting. "I've but to look upon a man, or woman, and I know how they might benefit or harm me. As if a parchment scroll of their attributes appeared in my hands, visible only to me."

"So this," Bram raised his cut hand, "was unnecessary."

John smiled, rueful. "As with my other gift, it does not apply to Hellraisers." He narrowed his eyes. "What of you? Did not our patron bestow some further power to you that night?"

I stepped between you and the Dark One's magic, Livia murmured. *That may be why we are anchored to one another. His power had an unforeseen consequence—it bound us together.*

But John didn't know that. He had no idea about Livia's whereabouts, particularly that she haunted Bram.

"All my falsehoods are believed," Bram improvised. "Like yours, this ability doesn't extend to Hellraisers."

"What a wondrous creature, is Mr. Holliday." John's smirk faded quickly. "Have you any word of Whit or Leo?"

"None."

"That's as it should be. I've made arrangements."

Bram's blood iced. "What sort of arrangements?"

"Nothing you need worry about. Even so, we'll stay vigilant. I do not want them interfering with my plans."

"The plans you still haven't disclosed to me."

"'Tis quite simple, truly. The key to supremacy in England is in Parliament."

"I thought the king ruled the country."

John scoffed. "He's made too many concessions. Piece by piece, the royal authority has fallen away. The king is barely more than a figurehead. No, the cornerstone is Parliament." He spoke like a scholar explaining a simple fact to a very dense pupil. "All that is required of me is to seize control of the entire body, and place myself in the central position of power."

"Sounds difficult. And time consuming."

"For an ordinary man. I am not ordinary."

He's the Dark One's pawn, Livia spat. *And now, so are you.*

Bram clenched his hand into a fist, stemming the flow of blood, though it continued to well through his fingers. "To what end?"

"To every end. The country will belong to *me*. Every part of it will be mine, including its military." Anticipation sharpened his words and his gaze. "I shall lay claim on other nations' territories, their commodities. Russian timber. Hanoverian silver mines."

"And if they protest these proposed acquisitions?"

John shrugged. "Then I shall make war upon them."

Bram kept his posture loose, leaning back against a bookshelf and folding his arms across his chest. "I've been part of England's military. We barely beat the French in the Colonies. What's to say that these already overburdened and poorly paid soldiers and sailors could take on the armies and navies of France, the Hapsburgs, and everyone else?"

John's face stretched into a grin. "There will be a wealth of assistance."

"Given that you mean to make war upon the entire world, I doubt much support from other nations will be offered."

"There is one realm whose collaboration is guaranteed."

Goddesses and gods, Livia hissed. *He cannot mean . . .*

John's gaze dropped to the ground. Then back up to Bram. His grin widened.

Numb cold crept through Bram's chest and limbs. "The underworld."

From a pile of books on his desk, John selected one large tome bound in black morocco. No decorations adorned its spine, nor its cover. The book seemed to draw in all the light in the chamber. John flipped through the pages until he stopped on one in particular. He held it up for Bram's inspection.

It showed a cavern of fire, with wretched naked humans writhing in misery as their bodies endlessly burned. Hosts of misshapen creatures dwelt amidst the flames, some of them presiding eagerly over the suffering people. Set in the cavern's stone ceiling was a gate. Directly above the gate stretched the surface of the mortal world, complete with houses and churches.

I recognize that image, Livia whispered. *I saw an earlier version of it when I delved into summoning the Dark One.*

"The boundary between the two realms is surprisingly slight," John said. "One only needs a sufficient supply of power, and the gate that divides our world from Hell can be opened. Once it is opened . . ." John's lips quirked. "Let us say that I shan't want for soldiers."

For a moment, Bram could only stare at John. The cut across his hand began to throb, a delayed pain that radiated up his arm.

"Demons," he said at last. "Fighting for England."

"Fighting for *me*," John corrected. He closed the book and set it back on his desk. "And, Bram, when the time comes to lead this army, there is only one man I want in command." He stared levelly at Bram.

Despite his intention to appear impassive, Bram couldn't stop his startled frown. "Me? At the head of a demonic army?"

"Who better?" John spread his hands. "Your military skill is unparalleled. You've a surfeit of expertise—and there is no one I trust more."

"I resigned from the army. I'm done with war."

"Ah, but think," John said, persuasive, insinuating, "this war will be fought under *your* command. Every wrong you saw on the Colonial battlefields, every error in judgment, every misguided order, you can correct them all. You shall have thousands, nay, *millions* of soldiers—human and demonic—at your command. Combining your ability with such might guarantees clean, unequivocal victory."

The end, Livia whispered. *The end of everything.*

Bram said, "You promise me an army of demons, but that illustration is likely the work of a bedlamite. It can't be taken literally. There's no gate between Hell and our world."

A condescending look crossed John's face. "You do not know what I know, Bram."

"And you know how to open this gate."

"I do."

"Tell me."

John narrowed his eyes. "That knowledge shall remain mine. For a while longer, at least."

Bram felt his mouth thin. "I'm to be your general, but already we've reached the limits of your trust."

"I simply do not want to confuse the issue." John paced around his desk. "For now, I only want you to stay alert. Let me know if, in your nocturnal ramblings, you hear anyone speak of me. And if you can use your gifts of persuasion and dissembling to gain more information, all the better."

Bracing his hands on the desk, John leaned forward. A sliver of afternoon light pierced the curtains, drawing a line down the middle of John's face, burning white.

"There are only two real Hellraisers now, Bram. You and I. That means a greater share for each of us."

"Share of what?"

John placed his hand upon the black book, as though taking an oath. "Everything."

The sexton at St. Paul's usually did not allow visitors in the upper galleries after dark, but Bram slipped him a shilling, and so by the light of a single taper, he made his solitary way upward. The stairs climbed ever higher, and he ascended like a fallen angel arduously trying to return home from banishment. He half expected to be barred entrance, a clap of thunder or streak of lightning hurling him the hundreds of feet down, to smash his body upon the checkered quire floor and stain the marble with his blood.

Livia continued in her silence. Not a word or thought from her since Bram had left John's study. She said nothing, even as Bram wound his way into the soaring dome of the cathedral. Candles flickered far below, distant as dreams, but the stairs and upper galleries remained dark. She expressed no awe in the gold and white walls, nor in the towering height. Her silence felt like a constricting band of iron. Yet he forced himself upward, from the Whispering Gallery to the Stone Gallery encircling the dome. Until, at last, he reached the Golden Gallery at the very top.

Stepping out from the cupola, Bram walked to the railing. He blew out the candle and set it at his feet. There, spread out on all sides, was the whole of London.

"A god's prospect," he murmured.

Livia shimmered into view, the light of her form coalescing. She had been so long in his mind, to actually see her again produced a strange, resonant thrill. Though an icy wind blew, causing Bram's coat to billow, her robes remained still and her hair kept its intricate arrangement. She stared out at the city, giving Bram the clean elegance of her Italianate profile.

Still, she remained mute. They looked at the city together, yet separate, choked in silence.

"I've been up here a few times." He spoke into the darkness. "Always during the day. Hard to see much of anything at night."

The shard of moon threw enough light to see the twisting, sluggish Thames snaking its way toward the sea. Tiled roofs reflected back the illumination, but the streets themselves were all in shadow, broken fitfully here and there by link and lamp. Despite the darkness, the city was not quiet. Shouts and screams rose up from all corners, harsh laughter and cries. A fire burned in Whitechapel. A clot of flame revealed a mob moving through the lanes of Smithfield. Only the distant hills of Hampstead were peaceful. Yet it wouldn't be long before the madness infecting London spread outward and into the country.

Words spilled from him, as if he could build a barrier with them, holding back the rising flood. "I often thought it would be exciting to have a woman up here. She could grip the railing as I lifted her skirts. We'd see the entire city as we took our pleasure."

"And if the height frightened her?"

He started. He hadn't expected Livia to speak, or perhaps the first words from her would be a bitter condemnation.

He nodded toward the stone cupola behind them. "We'd make use of that wall. If she was very afraid, she could close her eyes." He raised a brow. "Are you frightened by heights?"

"They mean nothing to me now."

Again, smothering silence descended. Bram's hand continued to pain him, though the wound was superficial. He glanced down at his palm. Within a few days, the cut would vanish, his body obliterating evidence of his actions.

"I've failed." Her voice was flat, devoid of life. She still would not look at him. "For the first time, I did not accomplish what I set out to do. The others, Whit and Leo, and their women, they could not have defeated the Dark One without me. And this—turning you from him—was my most important task."

"There's been no failure."

She gazed at his hand, where dried blood formed an arrow across his skin. "You have taken a blood oath. With *him*."

"I cut myself. He cut himself. We shook hands. Nothing else happened."

"How can you say that?" Disbelief edged her words. "The taking of a blood oath is sacred, inviolate—"

"Perhaps you've noticed," he drawled, "that I don't hold much respect for anything, especially the sacred and inviolate."

She stared at him. "It was . . ."

"A ruse." He crossed his arms over his chest. "John had to trust me. The meaningless spilling of blood seemed a ready means of gaining that trust."

"And everything else, all the claims you made about joining his cause—more deceit?"

"John's a chary bastard. He'd reveal nothing without securing my support."

He thought she might smile, or sob her relief. Instead, her scowl was fierce, her gaze hot. "You said nothing! Played your part and kept me in ignorance!"

"Is that why you're angry? Don't like being in the dark?"

"Damn you," she spat. "You might've given me the smallest hint what you were about."

He shook his head. "John cannot read the minds of the Hellraisers, but he's sodding perspicacious. If I let even a trace of duplicity enter my thoughts, he'd have read it on my face. So I kept quiet." He stared at her. "You believed I meant everything I said to him."

"Taking a blood oath is usually reserved for the sincere."

"That, I am not."

At last, her hands came up, covering her face. Her shoulders sank. He suppressed the urge to touch her, comfort her. She had no body to touch, and would rebuff his efforts, even had she flesh to touch. But her moment of vulnerability ended quickly.

"You are," she said, lowering her hands, "a devious *bastard*." She made this sound like a compliment.

"I wasn't always so. Perhaps you've been influencing me."

Bracing his forearms on the railing, he looked out over the rooftops of London. From this vantage, it was a collection of miniatures, tiny structures that could be scattered by a strong wind. Less than a hundred years earlier, half the city burned to the ground, and thousands of corpses littered the streets, felled by plague. It rose up again, but not much stronger. The city could burn once more. It did already.

His ride from John's home to St. Paul's had been fraught with horrors. More brawls, more destruction. Thrice he had beaten savagely men in the middle of assaulting women. Everywhere across the city, scenes were enacted. Atop the cathedral's dome, he saw and heard all.

"In the Colonies," he said, "I saw hell on earth. Acts of barbarism I never would've believed, had not I witnessed them with my own eyes. My father died of a fever whilst I was fighting, and all I could think was that he'd been given a clean, merciful death. Soon after I returned, my brother got a miniscule cut on his leg that turned septic. It killed him and I inherited a title I never thought to possess. All I sought to do with its privilege was staunch the memories with as much pleasure as I could grasp. Not precisely the heir my father had intended. But I didn't care. The only thing that mattered was ensuring I never experienced that hell again."

Livia did not watch the city as it slithered toward pandemonium. Her dark gaze rested solely on him, and he felt it in every bone, every breath. He hadn't known that a man could feel both ancient and restive, exhausted and spurred to action. The process of living, and nearly dying, brought him far more education than university ever could.

"But hell is here." He gestured toward the spires and roofs. "You might have brought it forth originally, but the Hellraisers and I . . . we gave it fertile fields. Watered it with our sins. It grows, and if nothing is done, the harvest will be plentiful."

"A reaper of souls, is the Dark One."

"Including mine." He rubbed at his shoulder, the markings' phantom heat spreading out in waves. "For me, hell is a guarantee. Yet I can stop it from consuming the world."

Livia straightened, then drifted closer, slowly, as if afraid he might bolt away like a stag flushed from the bracken. He thought he might feel numb, or fearful. Instead, tumblers within him clicked into place. Unlocking a certitude he hadn't anticipated.

"Speak plainly," Livia urged, "for there cannot be uncertainty. Not in this."

He gazed at the moon, then at her. They shared a timeless radiance, and she worked her will upon the tides of his intention. Yet no one could make him do anything. He alone dictated his actions. When words formed on his lips, they were *his* words, fraught and unsparing.

"I've been in hiding, but I can hide no longer." He inhaled, smoke from the burning city clouding his lungs, then breathed out. "The time to fight is now."

Chapter 7

It was an odd sensation—wanting something for so long, and then finally gaining the objective you desired. The feeling mystified Livia. She merely stared at Bram as they stood high above the city atop this immense building, aware of the vast blanket of night and the rooftops and the river and a thousand other things. Yet she was hardly able to understand the meaning of his words.

"I refuse to be toyed with," she said. "I must know where you stand."

"I've stood in shadow," he answered, his voice low but resolved. "I won't be accepted into the light—I'm too far gone for that—but I won't turn away, either." He rested his broad hand upon the hilt of his sword. "Since I've come back from war, I've done nothing with this blade but practice or battle imagined foes. But my strength is in the fight. In the killing of my enemies. That's my true purpose." His gaze burned in the darkness. "I'll fight at your side."

This thing welling inside of her . . . she struggled to identify it. A hard, luminous rising. She pressed her hand between her breasts, though she could feel no heartbeat, no flesh beneath her palm. Something was there, however, alive and emergent. The feeling grew the more she looked upon him.

The radiance from her spectral form cast silver light upon him, illuminating the sharp contours of his face and the gem-bright blue of his eyes. The veil of apathy had fallen away. Here was the man who had been a soldier. Was a soldier once more.

She moved closer, lifting her hands. He held himself still as she neared. The moment was fraught, an infinity of time within the span of a second. Once, he had looked at her with hatred. Now, tense anticipation honed his expression, as though he wanted her touch.

He would be solid beneath her hands, a powerful weapon of a man, taut with muscle. The beat of his heart would resonate against her. He was purpose and intent. She would feel all this in only a touch, and craved it as a bird craved flight.

When she placed her palms on his chest, disappointment stabbed her. She felt nothing. Her hands actually moved through him.

They both looked down at the sight. Until she pulled away. Her insubstantial body served as reminder—she could never again have the comfort and pleasure of touch. Especially not his.

This was not the moment for thinking of what she had lost. There were greater battles ahead.

Her thwarted touch seemed to turn the heat in his gaze to something harder, shadowed, as though a bonfire could be made of darkness rather than light.

"I'll cut them down," he said, jaw tight. "John and Mr. Holliday might know the way of magic, but I know war."

At that moment, standing high above the city, sword at the ready and eyes ablaze, he *was* war. Merciless and inexorable. It stirred a primal fear and fascination within her, and she could not look away.

"You're a different soldier now," she said.

"Stronger."

"In body, yes. In humanity, as well."

His mouth twisted. "I've none of that." He tilted his head back, showing her the length of his throat and the scar that ran along it. "The pulse you see there beating quickly—it's not the chance to do good that speeds my heart. I want to feel the bite of flesh against my steel. I want to smell blood again." He lowered his chin. "It's the fight I hunger for. Humanity has been ripped from me."

"You say that to convince yourself," she answered. "I know differently. The Dark One may have your soul, but it exists. And we *shall* reclaim it, no matter the challenge."

"We can't."

"There are vaults, all *gemini* keep them. The souls of their prey are kept there. The vaults weren't as impregnable as the Dark One and his minions believed." She smiled cruelly. "That was my doing. Two Hellraisers' souls I've helped to free. Doubtless your Mr. Holliday has learned hard lessons, and the vault where your soul is kept is surely more protected than the others, but heed me, we *will* find a means of stealing back your soul."

He pressed his knuckles against his chest. "Doing so would reveal to Mr. Holliday and John that I'm no longer their ally. No, the tactical thing to do is leave my blighted soul exactly where it is—in the Devil's possession."

"Simply *abandon* it?" She scowled. "That leaves you imperiled. If you should die before we retrieve your soul, your eternity shall be torment and suffering, like all the other damned."

"If I die and am sent to Hell, it's what I deserve." He spoke over her objections. "We cannot let either Mr. Holliday or John know that I'm not of their number. My soul has to stay where it is. For now."

Curse him, he was right. Yet, the thought of him trapped

in eternal agony was a cage of burning iron around her heart. "When the time is right, your soul shall be liberated."

He seemed disinterested, as though they discussed the retrieval of a pair of boots. "Issues of my withered soul aside, I own that I'm unfamiliar with battling the Devil. Military strategies won't apply when facing demons and the powers of hell."

"Not so. For the first matter of business is assessing strengths and weaknesses, and gathering allies."

"Whit and Leo," he said. "And their women, the Gypsy and the lady."

"I've no way to use my own magic now, but the women can, and their men are strong." She nodded. "We need them here."

"The last I saw of them was outside Leo's home, weeks ago. Just after—" His jaw tightened; he had to be thinking of his friend's death. "They've likely made a temporary retreat from London as they regroup."

"They must be found, and summoned back."

He made a soft scoffing noise. "Neither Whit nor Leo are the kind of men who take well to *summoning*."

Tilting up her chin, she answered, "Their masculine pride must suffer in these circumstances." She had fought beside them before. Both men had proven themselves as willing and capable warriors. As had their women.

"We weren't on affable terms when we parted." His laughter was hollow, resonant with loss. "They'll do nothing to aid me, and with good cause."

"Much has altered between then and now," she said. "That won't escape them."

"They need to be found before any of this can be tested. Once we lived in each others' pockets. Now I've no idea where they are. Dozens or hundreds of miles could separate us. Nowhere to send a letter, and even if I had their direction, it could take weeks for any communication to reach them."

Now it was her turn to scoff. "Your thoughts are too prosaic. Magic can shorten the distance between us."

"At one time, yours might have. Conditions have changed since then." His voice was surprisingly gentle.

"That fact is never forgotten." She felt like a sculptor whose hands had been chopped off.

Hot anger constricted her throat. She had crossed the boundary between the living and the dead, exhausted herself time and again channeling magic into mortals and using her own power to fight. And the last, strongest Hellraiser had finally stepped into the fray. She could not allow herself to fall short, not now.

"If you had all of your magic," he said, "would such a thing be possible? Locating Whit and Leo, mustering them to London?"

"Yes. The work of a few minutes."

"Then we'll make use of that magic."

She scowled. "Already you've forgotten that I possess no magic."

"You have half. The other half resides . . . in me."

Her mouth dropped open. "The two of us, working magic together." She could hardly believe him. "You said you would not attempt such a thing."

"The last time you made that request, you were attempting to kill me with your magic. The poles have shifted since then."

The wind gathered in strength, his long coat catching against his legs and billowing behind him. Strands of his hair came loose from his queue. A fierce living energy radiated from him, as though he had emerged from dormancy, his strength greater than before.

Perhaps this war against the Dark One was not as futile as she had feared.

Yet she had to tell Bram everything. She couldn't lead him ignorantly toward danger. "The working of magic together has its own perils. So many ways it could go wrong, the damage it could wreak . . ."

"The Devil doesn't frighten me. This doesn't, either."

She shook her head. "With a single stray thought, we could become trapped between the mortal world and the realm of magic."

"Every tactic has its risks."

She saw he would not be dissuaded. "We shouldn't attempt anything here." Though they were high above the city, impossible to see from the streets below, they were still exposed. To the elements. To the possibility of the Dark One's watchful spies taking notice. Bram was new to working magic, as well. She suspected the task would need silence, privacy, and some measure of security.

"Home, then."

He said the word as if it was *their* home, not his. A remnant of warmth filtered through her—in her life, she had led a peripatetic existence, hunting magic, searching for power. She never sought such a place. Too confining.

It did not feel so now.

He motioned for her to proceed him through the doorway in the cupola. She shook her head at the gesture but glided past him. A ghost required neither courtesy nor decorum. He certainly hadn't shown her much before, and she did not expect it.

Small though the gesture was, however, its deliberate use gave her another pulse of warmth. As though she was not a specter, but a woman. A woman who deserved respect.

What man might believe this? Against all probability, the man turned out to be an inveterate sinner.

* * *

They sequestered themselves in the chamber that Bram used for combat practice. Even without her magic, Livia sensed his strength imbuing the room. They needed all of his resilience for the forthcoming task, and here he was confident, focused. He paced through the chamber, pushing all the furniture and practice targets against the walls. His movements were assured and unhesitating. If he held any trepidation about attempting to work magic, none showed.

The same could not be said for her. Outwardly, she kept herself composed, directing him to give them as much space as possible—with unknown variables, anything might happen—but inwardly, she was uneasy. She'd spoken truly. Should either of them let their concentration waver, she and Bram might become prisoners of the *Ambitus*. As she had been for over a millennium. A terrifying thought to be trapped there again.

She had helped Whit cure Zora of a demon's poison, but Whit hadn't any magic of his own. He'd been her corporeal hands. There, the danger had been only the loss of Zora's life. So much more hung in the balance with what she and Bram would attempt.

It was not his skill or unfamiliarity that troubled her. The unknown was *her*. During her life, she had been a student of magic, always learning, continually acquiring. She had never been a teacher, nor given to sharing. Powerful families had brought their daughters to her, hoping she would impart her knowledge, yet she hoarded everything—her power, her learning.

The seeds of her avarice now bore fruit. She was an untried teacher, utterly green.

Even if she could teach Bram how to invoke and use magic, the dangers were rife. How might she accomplish this? What if her own greed was their undoing?

"Stop worrying." He shoved a large musical instrument against the wall, its legs scraping on the floor.

"I am not," she shot back.

He gave her a look that said her protestation failed to convince him.

"This will be challenging," she finally acknowledged. "Not only the perils of using magic. As a teacher, I'm . . . unpracticed."

"Good to know you're inexperienced with something." He had removed his coat to move aside the furnishings, and he wiped his forehead on the full white sleeve of his shirt. "Mind, experience in a woman is an excellent thing."

"Thank the gods I have your approval." Yet his teasing strangely lessened her apprehension.

"What else will we need?" Hands on hips like a captain surveying his troops, he glanced around the chamber. "Black candles? The blood of a goat?"

She shuddered in distaste. "Props are for amateurs."

The grin he gave her would have made a mortal woman tremble with want. Fortunately, she had no pulse to race, no breath to sigh. No wonder so many females leapt into his bed. Between his smoldering gazes and raffish smiles, only a dead woman could remain immune.

He had never smiled for her. Not until that moment.

"Again," he said, "I give thanks for your experience."

"Between the two of us, there is not a speck of innocence." She steadied herself. "Let us begin."

He moved toward her, unhesitating, the black of his unbound hair as dark as the shadows. They faced one another. She did not miss the way his gaze moved over her in swift, appreciative perusal, lingering briefly on her breasts. A man could not resist looking at a woman, regardless of whether the woman was alive or dead.

She fought the impulse to preen. After all, when she had

been alive, many words praising her beauty had been spoken. She was no stranger to a man's approving stare.

But it was *this* man's gaze that filled her cheeks with the echo of warmth.

What she needed now was focus, not the silly flutterings of a female craving masculine attention.

"When I had full possession of my magic," she said, "locating someone was a simple matter. All living things have their own distinctive energy. A kind of light and sound unique to them alone. To find them, I searched for the flame of their psyche, followed it much as a ship is guided by a beacon."

"Sounds abstruse."

"Only in the telling. The doing becomes a matter of instinct."

He frowned. "In this, I have no instinct."

"We'll create it." She struggled to determine what she ought to do next, how to go about the utterly foreign process of developing someone else's magic. Some people, women especially, made for gifted teachers. She was not one of them. To teach was to steal from herself, or so she'd believed. Even now, the compulsion to hoard gripped her. She had to mentally pry her fingers from their vise, clutching knowledge close.

"To work magic, one must first find one's own power." She hoped her voice sounded far more confident than she felt. "Close your eyes. Let your gaze fall inward."

He hesitated for a brief moment, then did as she asked. She also closed her eyes. Before, her magic had always been close to the surface. She could call upon it without thought or effort. One did not tell one's heart to beat. Now, she had to recall what it was like when she had been a young priestess in training, learning how to harness the native magic within herself, and fan the spark into a flame.

"Deep within you resides magic," she continued. "It's

strange, and foreign, but you oughtn't fear it. Allow yourself to reach for it. Allow it to come into being."

He exhaled through his nose. "No damned soldier ever followed such a strange command."

"This damned soldier had better," she growled.

"I ought to call you Madam General rather than Madam Ghost."

"Concentration," she snapped. "Do not make this more difficult than it already is."

"Apologies, Madam Ghost General."

She clenched her teeth. "Just be quiet and still your mind. Search for the gleam of magic within. It is unique to each being."

"Not me."

"Most especially you. Think of the talents you possess, the skills distinctively yours. Leading men into battle. Beguiling women into your bed. Your art with a sword. You see them now, don't you? These gifts?"

A pause. And then he rumbled, "I see them."

"Follow them. Use them to guide you toward the magic inside you. It resembles a key, shining deep within you, as though at the bottom of a well. Look for that."

She must guide him toward his magic as she searched for her own. Thank the goddess, he obeyed, falling silent.

Now she had to heed her own directive. Finding one's magic meant utilizing magic, a painful irony. At the least, she possessed enough power for that. When she had been a girl first learning the mysteries of serving in the temple, the head priestess had revealed to her the existence of true magic. It was a secret hidden from most of the world. But the true magic dwelt within her, and she must train herself to find it, calling upon her native power to guide the magic within her to greater strength. She summoned that power now.

There—just as she had said to Bram. A gleaming key. It

didn't possess the same strength as it had before, however, its radiance dimmed.

"I see it." Surprise threaded through Bram's voice.

"Hold onto it," she said, urgent. "Hold it tight." She must combine their energy, something she had never truly attempted before. The Druid priestess and Egyptian slave had been her victims, their magic stripped away forcibly, and by her greater power. Now she must find another way, a gentler means.

Gentle was foreign to her. Yet she reached out to Bram with softer, searching hands. A careful coaxing forward. She wanted to touch his flesh, but could not. His psyche, his energy, these she could touch. A strange hesitancy danced through her, slowing her movement. Never had she shared such a communion. Always, she had been solitary, proud. This would not leave her unaffected.

She almost recoiled when she came up against the shimmering edge of his psyche—they had shared memories, thoughts, but this was even more intimate.

He hissed in a breath.

"Am I hurting you?"

"No, only . . . it feels . . . strange."

"For me, as well." She pressed onward, delving within him. His psyche held a dark edge, yet it glimmered, like a mirror made of black glass, taking in light and reflecting it back with its own illumination. She felt him everywhere within her, a closeness greater than sex. She could lose herself within him. A purpose brought her here, however.

Ah, now she found it. The key of his own magic. Of *her* magic, broken apart and residing in him.

She utilized a Thracian joining spell, softly chanting as she brought the two halves of their magic together. It flared brightly, light and sensation flooding her.

Both she and Bram gasped.

"Thought I'd felt damned near everything," he murmured. "But this is . . . new."

"It's . . ."

". . . Good."

Radiance and strength. An expanding. Of power. Of self. Even greater than she had ever experienced before. How could it be thus? She'd been such a powerful sorceress, capable of the greatest magic. This, though, was stronger.

Because of him.

It was an intoxication. She had been so long without magic, having it again made her head spin and the shade of her heart pound. Together, they were equal to anything. Any spell, any show of force. Her old hunger returned, its lupine teeth bright in the moonlight. Where to start? They could set the whole of London afire. They might turn the river Thames to ice. The possibilities spread out like a banquet.

"Madam Ghost," he murmured, summoning back her spiraling mind. "Livia. We've an objective."

She huffed out a startled laugh. "Now you become the voice of reason?"

"More proof that the world's turned upside down."

"You feel this, though. The power. The possibility."

"I assuredly do." Husky and low, his voice stroked through her.

They could be capable of a great many things together— powerful things, devastating things. Fortunate that her ghostly state created an impediment, for had she flesh, even his reasoning and gravity would not restrain her.

"Leo and Whit," he said.

Yes—she and Bram must find them. "Say these words with me: *kidbará kunu satu de*. A locating spell from vast deserts of Sumer."

He repeated the words, stumbling over the pronunciation. He said them again, the words smoothing out, and together, they began to chant. Their voices blended together, harmonizing in the darkness. The chant threaded around them, spinning outward, dissolving the walls of the chamber. The huge house faded, the street outside melted away, and the city itself dissipated like smoke in the rain.

Bram cursed.

She opened her eyes to find him staring at the bright mists now surrounding them. "This is the place of *Ambitus*, the In Between. The sphere through which all magic travels. The realm between life and death." She gave a rueful laugh. "So long I've been in this place, but I'd forgotten that you are a stranger here."

The *Ambitus* crackled with energy and potential. An eddying conduit of magic. Abstruse yet quick. That energy had been all that had sustained her during her long imprisonment. Yet it hadn't been enough to keep her from madness.

He gazed around, wonder vivid in his lapidary eyes. "Are we still in London?"

"We are everywhere. The In Between encircles and permeates the world. It was here I existed after trapping the Dark One." She couldn't keep the tightness from her voice. Her old madness seemed to call to her from the haze.

He gazed at the mists surrounding them. "A thousand years here? But I thought this was the space through which one traveled."

"Incantations break down the walls that divide one realm from the other. When one becomes adept at magic, the time spent here dwindles to nothing. It is merely a channel. But, in the beginning, it becomes a way station between the will to magic and its realization. And for me, it became my prison. Imprisoned between the worlds. Alone."

He looked grim. "I'd not wish that on anyone."

"It was a fitting punishment."

"Let's be gone from here," he said, "and quickly."

She struggled to calm herself and push back memories

of her long captivity. "The spell has to continue. Keep chanting. As you do, think of Whit. Picture him in your mind. His face. His voice. Memories of him. Use them, link between you. Do not let go of this—if either of us becomes abstracted during this part of the spell, we'll be trapped here." She nodded toward the swirling mist. "You see them? The blighted and unwary. I was one of their number."

He swore as flickering shapes in rough human form spun through the haze.

"There must be a way to free them from this place."

"The *Ambitus* has no walls to demolish, no battlements to breach. Once trapped, there is nothing to be done, you remain here forever. Only my connection to you pulled me fully from its grasp. But with you here, I'd have no such anchor. We'd both be imprisoned."

His expression darkened. "Then we'd bloody well better concentrate." He closed his eyes tightly and resumed the chant.

She followed suit, allowing the words to infuse with power as she conjured Whit and the Gypsy woman, Zora, in her thoughts. Whit had no magic of his own, but Zora did— fire magic which Livia had bestowed upon her. Given the strength of the bond between Whit and Zora, they would be together. If Livia could locate Zora, Whit would surely be close by. She held fast to this, keeping the oblivion of the *Ambitus* at bay.

"There—you feel it?" A spark in the mists. The dancing flame of Zora, the steel resilience of Whit.

"It's them," Bram said.

"Focus on them. Your mind as sharp and direct as your sword."

Feeling Bram's energy surging through her, she guided them through the mists of the In Between. Fleeting impressions of fields, trees, twisting rivers, all rolling past, remote. A vertiginous sensation as distance collapsed in on itself. Bram hissed in another breath.

The folding of distance abruptly stopped. No longer did she and Bram stand in a chamber in his home, nor were they in the In Between. Now they stood upon the bank of a chattering stream, stands of alders beside the water. Moonlight sieved down through the branches. It touched upon the forms of a man and woman lying a small distance from the stream, and two horses hobbled nearby.

Relief coursed through Livia. They had done it—crossed the *Ambitus* without being trapped.

The man and woman lay upon a woolen blanket, another blanket draped over them, the woman on her side, the man snug behind her. His arm wrapped around her waist. One could not fit a coin between them, for they were pressed close to one another, as close as two could be shy of making love.

A hot, startling dart of longing pierced Livia. This was a union of hearts, of bodies, and utterly unknown to her.

Bram, too, stared down at the sleeping man and woman. His expression sharpened, his lips pressed together, forming a taut line.

When had he spent the whole night with a woman? Did he have any memories of sleeping beside his bed partner, holding her close? Waking with her? Was that even something he desired?

Only days ago, Livia would have said no. But seeing the flare in his eyes, the searching, she might have to reconsider.

But they weren't here—wherever *here* was—to ponder the obscurities of intimacy.

"Whit," she said.

Though she spoke barely above a whisper, Whit came instantly awake, his hand going straight to the curved sword beside the blanket. He sat up and unsheathed the sword with a single movement. Barely a moment later, Zora also wakened. She raised up, and the flames that sprang to life around her hands threw flickering light upon the trunks of the trees and the grassy riverbank. Both the nobleman and the Gypsy wore vigilant, fierce expressions.

Vigilance gave way to recognition as they both saw Livia. Yet wariness returned when they beheld Bram.

Whit stood and faced them. He was fully dressed, down to his boots. Ready to move at a moment's notice. He did not lower his sword.

"Put your blade down," Bram growled.

Whit fired back, "And be skewered on yours?"

"Take note." Bram opened his hands. "I've no weapon on me."

"Nor the means to use it, if you had one," added Livia. "We're not truly here."

Stepping forward gingerly, Zora cursed softly in her language. She and Whit finally noticed that not only was Livia translucent, Bram was, as well.

"Are you dead, too?" Zora asked.

"Not yet," answered Bram.

"This is simple magic." Though it had not truly been simple. She still felt the quicksilver energy of Bram's psyche, resonant within her. "A means to find you."

Caution continued to hone Whit's expression. When Livia first encountered this mortal man, he had been swaddled in privilege, entrenched in the constant need to gamble, dissatisfied. Intelligent but unchallenged, possessing unrealized potential.

Much had changed between then and now. Like a sword upon the blacksmith's anvil, Whit had been forged by fire into something sharp and strong. And the woman beside him, with fire dancing in her hands, held just as much strength.

Thank the gods and goddesses they were Livia's allies.

"What do you want?" Whit's gaze stayed fixed on Bram.

Mistrust whetted the air between them. "Out reconnoitering for your master, Mr. Holliday?"

"He isn't my master," Bram clipped. "Never was."

"I don't know why I ought to believe you. Last we met, Edmund's body lay between us."

"That was John's doing."

"Yet you didn't lift your sword against him."

"Things have changed."

"Why should I believe you?"

"Because I say so."

"Faultless reasoning."

"Enough," Livia snapped. Men would ever grapple for dominance, fighting to push one another off the hill. Former friends seemed the greatest challenge. "Bram is here now. With me. It's clear his allegiance has shifted."

The wariness in Whit's gaze shifted, a glint of tentative hope emerging. Yet he did not lower his sword. "Might be a trick." He glanced at Zora. "Perhaps Livia has been gulled."

"I spent my life cozening *gorgios*," Zora answered. "Livia isn't someone who can be tricked."

"The Dark One fooled me," Livia noted. "Once." She tipped her head toward a frowning Bram. "I know the truth of his heart. He is our ally."

Whit peered at Bram intently, searching. And Bram held himself still under his friend's close scrutiny, his jaw tight, shoulders back.

Finally, Whit let the tip of his sword drop. He took a step toward Bram, and then another. As he did, suspicion fell away like plates of armor.

The two men reached out to clasp hands. But Whit's hand passed right through Bram's. They both started.

"We're not here physically," Livia explained. "Our bodies—*your* body," she corrected, since she had no body, "is still in London. Transporting flesh takes far greater magic than we possess."

Bram stared ruefully at his hand. "Beginning to understand your frustrations," he muttered.

"Try spending a millennium thusly."

"No wonder you went mad."

Livia scowled at him. "We did not journey here to discuss my previous mental turmoil." The scene—riverbank, trees, moonlight—flickered, and both she and Bram swore. "This magic cannot hold for long. We must speak to our purpose."

"Something has happened," said Zora. The flames gloving her hands vanished as she stepped close to Whit.

Bram nodded. "John. After Edmund's death, John's fallen even further." Succinctly, he told of everything that had transpired since last Whit and Bram had met. John's hunger for more power, and his plans to place himself in control. His scheme to summon a demon army to aid him in his conquest. The more he spoke, the bleaker Whit and Zora looked, Whit muttering curses in English, while Zora used her native tongue.

"Can he do such a thing?" Zora pressed. "Seize command of Parliament? Make himself the leader of the whole nation?"

"He's made allies," Bram answered, "and more enemies. Yet his power keeps growing."

"But to completely overthrow the existing government," protested Whit. "And then conquer the entire world? He's only one man."

Livia said, "A man who has the magic and patronage of the Dark One. Should he open the gate between this realm and the underworld and raise a demonic army—" She shook her head. "Even he does not realize what disaster he brings upon us all."

"If he's as powerful as you say," Zora said, "what can be done to stop this?"

"I, *we*, need you both in London," answered Livia. "At once."

"Leo, too. And his wife."

Whit's expression turned even more grim. "That's an impossibility."

"You're an earl," Bram pointed out. "Hire faster horses. Or a carriage."

"It's not a matter of cost. Nor distance." Whit tilted his chin toward the nearby stream. "Mark you well that little brook. Now observe." He walked toward the water.

Zora's hand on his arm stopped him. "Whit, don't."

"They need to see." Before Livia could press for an explanation, Whit sprinted in the direction of the stream.

A sound like a thunderclap splintered the air as Whit was flung backward by an unseen force. He landed on his back ten feet away. Zora was at his side immediately, kneeling in the grass as she held his shoulders.

"What the hell was that?" Bram demanded.

Zora said, "As of two days ago, we cannot cross water. Any water. Stream, river, lake or pond. Whenever we've attempted it . . . you've seen what happens." She brushed hair from Whit's forehead as his dazed look faded.

"John's doing," Livia said tightly.

"The wily bastard." Bram growled. "That's what he meant back in his study. You should see the books piled up. It's not just the Devil's power, but his own. He's used some magic to keep Whit and Zora from coming back into London."

"Doubtless he's worked the same spell on Leo and Anne," Whit said, his voice strained and breathless.

"It can be broken. Can't it?" Bram turned to Livia.

She exhaled. "Such a spell is a powerful thing. Even had I full possession of my magic, this insubstantial form couldn't engender enough strength. I would require a corporeal body."

"We can get your body back," Zora said at once.

Livia could not stop her embittered laugh. "Impossible." She waved down at her translucent form. "This is how I shall spend eternity."

"No," Bram said, his gaze dark. "There's a way. I've only to find it."

Silence fell, weighted with leaden thoughts. Despite Bram's claim, no one seemed to have a solution, the battles ahead already lost.

Whit said, "How can we—"

The scene became a blur of shape and color, a painting left in the rain. Whit's voice was lost in a haze of sound.

Livia struggled to grasp to magic that held her and Bram to this place. It slipped away, and she felt herself torn from the fabric of the world.

Chapter 8

Bram felt the world shudder around him, a breaking apart, and then a swift tug backward. His head reeled, his stomach pitched. For half an instant, he thought he might be sick—he who could endure any manner of rough sea crossings and the lurch of an unsprung carriage down a furrowed road. This motion was unlike anything he'd experienced before, permeating his every sense. The clearing with Whit and Zora spun away, and he plunged through formless infinity.

At last, stability. The whirligig in his head stopped its twirl, and he discovered himself standing in the middle of his practice room, just as he'd been before. He ran the back of his hand across his clammy forehead, and tasted dry metal in his mouth.

He was alone.

He waited for a moment. She would reappear from that *Ambitus* place. They had worked magic together—his mind still lurched at the thought of creating magic beyond what Mr. Holliday had provided him—and they were bound to one another. She would return. Then they could discuss their next move, formulate strategies. He had been very good at devising tactics and lines of attack.

The few candles in the chamber dripped wax and sent thin

coils of smoke toward the ceiling. No other movement in the chamber. Not even Bram, holding himself still, attentive.

Minutes passed, judging by the chime of a clock in the hallway. Still no Livia.

He called her name. His voice echoed in the room.

When no answer came, he reached into his thoughts. Never had he spent this much time in his mind as he did now. He searched for her presence, her haughty flame.

Unfamiliar panic welled when he found only himself within. Her presence was gone. She was trapped in the *Ambitus*. Again. Fury and despair clutched at him—he couldn't find the means to draw breath.

Then—there came dim flicker in the recesses of his self. Relief almost made his legs give way beneath him.

Livia, he thought.

She gave a murmur, but did not speak.

He thought her name again, adding urgency. She stirred, the flicker growing faintly brighter.

Are you ailing? he pressed. *Injured?*

. . . tired . . .

Her weakness disturbed him. Never had he felt her so fragile, so enervated. Always, she held the strength of a dozen storms, leveling anything in her path—including him.

Can you make yourself visible?

. . . will try . . .

His awareness returned to the chamber. A moment later, she appeared on her knees, the unsteady flame of a lamp. She cradled her head in her hands.

He crouched beside her. Acting on instinct, he brought up his arm to wrap around her shoulders, then cursed when all he met was shimmering air.

"The spell took its toll on you." He made his voice sound calm and straightforward.

She made a murmur of assent. "Never . . . tried it before . . . with another."

"Practice shall make us stronger."

Lifting her head, her limitless dark eyes met his. "Perhaps . . . even so, it might not . . . be enough."

He frowned. "It will."

"John is so strong. He can hold back . . . the Hellraisers. No simple magic. And I'm . . ." She held up her hand as if to block the candle's illumination. The light shined through her. She provided no barrier. "All I will ever be."

Bram surged to his feet. "The hell kind of nonsense are you spouting? You're a priestess, and a damned powerful one."

"So powerful I can barely take form." Her mouth twisted. "A spell that once cost me nothing reduces me to a trembling shade. I will never have flesh—which means I can never break the curse that keeps the Hellraisers from coming to our aid. I achieved this much, but shall go no further. The war is already lost." She lay her head down once more.

"I wish you did have a body." He growled. "Because if you did, I'd give you a hell of a shaking. Rattle some sense into you. For you're acting like a sullen, self-pitying child." The irony was not lost on him—she had made a similar accusation against him not so long ago.

She lifted her head, eyes ablaze. "Recant your words."

"Or what? You'll moan me to death?"

Expression thunderous, she bolted to her feet. "I will find a way—"

"Exactly." He stalked to her. "You *will* find a way."

She glared at him a moment longer before her scowl eased. "Is that how you rallied your troops? By insulting them?"

"Whatever means succeeded. I tried them all. Some

wanted kind words. Others fared better with sternness—especially the strong, stubborn ones."

She exhaled. Had she been flesh, he would have felt her breath warm against his face, and he wanted that with a sudden, fierce severity. To breathe her in. To taste her.

"I hate this," she growled. "Not knowing what to do, or how to do it. I hate that all I see before me is uncertainty."

"No war's outcome is ever certain."

"But there are means by which success is more readily secured. We have none of them."

Damn, how he wanted to touch her. To place the tips of his fingers beneath the proud line of her chin, feeling her pulse, and tilt her face up to his. To test the texture of her skin, and learn if she was as soft yet resilient as he imagined.

"You recruited me to this war," he said. "Not because you believed it to be easily won, but because you knew it had to be fought."

He captured her gaze with his own. "We may win, we may lose. But swinging a sword is better than digging a grave."

After a moment, she smiled. Or bared her teeth. He could not quite tell the difference. Yet he'd rather she snarl her defiance than extinguish her own flame.

Deep in the hours of night, when Bram might have once caroused and earned himself the name of Hellraiser, he now planned war. A war of stratagems and subterfuge, but war nonetheless. To consider an all-out frontal assault was as foolish as it was perilous. Much as Bram wanted to charge through the front door of John's home, sword in hand, he would be dead before he made it halfway to the study.

Poisons and planned assassinations would fare no better. Of a certain, John had safeguards in place. Their only recourse, then—ferret out precisely what Bram's erstwhile friend intended, and prevent those schemes from happening.

Thus, the war council of two: Bram and Livia.

She circled the bedchamber, counter to him standing immobile in the middle of the room. "From every angle, I cannot see a way in."

"Simple enough," he said. "I grab one of John's cohorts and wring the plan out of him. Or use my gift of persuasion, though," he added, cracking his knuckles, "it won't be as satisfying as a fine old interrogation."

"Then that cohort goes running back to John. And thus our subterfuge is ended."

He scowled. "Hell and damnation. How's a man to make war against the Devil if he can't break some jaws?"

"The shattering of bones must wait, much as it must pain you." She tilted her head, deep in contemplation. "These aren't the right strategies. We need more guile."

Frustration formed a red wall in his mind and spread tension through his body. "I only know the battlefield."

"Not so," she corrected. "You also know the bedchamber."

He dipped his head in acknowledgement. She had seen his most prurient memories, and they were abundant.

She continued, "If you wanted to seduce a woman without letting her know she was being seduced, how might you do that?"

Here was a subject he knew well. "The direct approach must be discarded. She has to think that mere chance has put me in her path. A chain of circumstance rather than deliberate intent."

"Forces outside of your control," she said.

"Yet now that she and I have been brought together, I find it most agreeable." He gazed at her. "Pleasurable, even."

"Pleasurable?" She raised a brow. "From her presence alone?"

"Is that so difficult for her to believe?"

She pursed her lips. "Given what she knows of your history, it is."

"Therein lies the wonder and truth of it." He stepped nearer. "I hadn't gone looking for such a bond, yet it found me. I need her guidance in this unfamiliar territory."

Livia did not back away, but tilted her chin up to meet his gaze without blinking. "She might be as inexperienced as you, and have no guidance to offer."

"Then," he said, lowering his eyelids, "we'll feel our way together."

After a long moment, she said softly, "Yes, I can see the efficacy of your strategy."

He was tense all over, tense in the way a predator readied itself before leaping onto its prey. In this instance, though, there were two predators, and the struggle would be all the more delicious as they each fought for dominance. How they'd claw and tear at one another. He never wanted anything more.

From beneath this onslaught of need, a revelation emerged. The best strategies for tracking bore striking similarities to a seduction.

"We've been busy checking the weapon," he said, "but not the target. *That* is where we should look."

She blinked, returning to herself, and it flattered him no small amount that she'd been just as ensnared as he. "John's enemies. They are the men who occupy *his* thoughts."

"He'll want to know what *they* intend, make his next move based on that."

"Those men in the park. Surely he knows about them."

She wasn't in his bed, yet he liked having her here, in this chamber. The two of them together, talking. Plotting. He had never planned strategy with women. He had thought up tactics to get them on their backs, but not this . . . this exchange of ideas and cunning that made his heart beat a little faster, his breath come a little quicker.

"They're the ones we need to attend to," he said. "For whatever Maxwell and the others mean to do, John will find out, and seek to prevent it."

"Go to Maxwell. Ask him what he and the others plan."

Bram laughed, rueful. "I may not know much about politics, but I know that nothing within it is straightforward. If I ask Maxwell directly, or use my persuasive ability on him, he might suspect me of double dealing. And then you and I shall have opposition from every angle."

Scowling in frustration, Livia took up her pacing. It was more of a continual glide, around and around the chamber, moving through any object in her path.

She radiated so much energy, even in this non-corporeal state. When she had been alive . . . she must have filled every room with her presence, all eyes drawn to her. God knew *he* couldn't look away.

"Servants, perhaps," she said after a moment. "They're the keepers of secrets, and easily bribed into silence."

"Servants know some secrets, but not all. They're more interested in domestic scandal than governmental machinations." He rubbed at his jaw as the seedling of an idea began to take root. "But there are a select few who learn all the hidden truths of a man's heart. Who learn his darkest thoughts, and private ambitions."

"Priests?"

He smiled. "Wives."

The mantua maker's establishment fronted the Strand, clear evidence of its fashionable status. Prints from France, displaying the latest styles, adorned the modern bow window, alongside a ready-made gown of white and green printed Colonial cotton. Within, bolts of heavy brocade lined up beside gleaming satin, fine messaline silk. Ribbons were arranged on spools, and trays bearing embroidered kidskin gloves and velvet flowers lined up on the counter. Rosewater and talc scented the air.

Bram gazed around the shop. He inhaled deeply, smiling. The realm of patrician women, soft, purposefully delicate and removed.

Yet even here, in this stronghold of gentility, dwelled darkness. Ladies swayed anxiously through the room, trailed by their wary-eyed abigails. Their fingers brushed over sumptuous fabrics, and they spoke in musical murmurs about cuts of a polonaise or the silver embroidery on a stomacher. Yet their voices were distracted, talking of assemblies none planned to attend. Several of the mantua maker's assistants kept throwing apprehensive gazes toward the watery gray light drifting in through the window, as though marking the hour, and when the last protective rays of the sun might disappear.

Catching sight of Bram in the doorway, the mantua maker herself danced over to him. "My lord, an honor. I am Madame De Jardin." Her French accent came direct to London by way of Ipswich. "How might I assist you this lovely day?"

"Merely perusing your fine shop, Madame." He affected a casual glance, his gaze never resting anywhere for too long, though he sought something, some*one* in particular. Ah—there she was. "When I need your assistance, I shall assuredly let you know."

Effectively dismissed, the mantua maker dropped into a curtsy then slipped away to help a dowager choose between black bombazine and black tabinet.

He ambled over to shelves holding more bolts of fabric, and feigned interest in studying their colors and patterns.

Is she here? Livia asked.

Toward the back. She's the one in bronze jacquard.

I've no idea what jacquard is, was the tart reply. *Clearly, you've learned much from undressing women.*

It helps to know many languages.

Livia made a soft noise of scorn. *Don't tarry. Go to her.*

Remember what I said before? Too much eagerness won't yield results. We take our time, and reap the benefits of our patience.

The veteran seducer's wisdom.

We know it has its uses.

He studied a bolt of pale blue sarcenet, lightly touching its lustrous surface. Despite Livia's impatience, she hummed with feminine approval. Bram tucked his smile away. For all her forcefulness and imperious declarations, she was still a woman.

You approve? he asked.

The silk shines well enough, but the color is too mild.

This, I think, is more to your tastes. He ran his finger down a length of deep gold charmeuse. Her skin would feel the same, silken and lithe.

Oh, she breathed. *That is . . .* Her words trailed away, and his mind suddenly filled with images of her, draped in a gold silk tunic. They were her own envisioning, yet they became his, and the vision made his mouth water. In her thoughts, she wasn't a translucent form, but a woman of solid flesh, her skin olive-hued and burnished, the charmeuse embracing her curves like a lover.

There was silk, too, when I lived, she said, regaining her voice. *It wasn't half as fine. The wonders of this modern era.*

They are abundant. But this modern era would be in awe of you.

He felt the warmth of her pleasure. Yet she said crisply, *Your flattery isn't necessary. There's nothing to be gained by it.*

A compliment needn't serve a purpose. It can simply exist.

Ah. A long pause. *Thank you.*

Those were not words she seemed familiar with speaking, but they were sincere.

He moved slowly through the shop, smiling politely when an assistant or client tried to catch his eye. The assistants, barely more than girls, blushed and curtsied, though their shy smiles faltered when they espied his scar.

Does it pain you? Livia asked quietly.

It healed long ago.

Not the wound. But the response it engenders.

I used to hate it. Wore my stock so high it choked me, just to cover it. Then I deliberately left my neckcloths undone—flaunting it, I suppose.

Surely that brought you more than a few female admirers. Few things are as appealing to a woman than scars.

One of the customers, a nobleman's young wife he dimly remembered from a card party, angled herself in his path. She wore an expectant smile.

He nodded, and stepped around her. The sound of her insulted huff bounced off his back.

I was a novelty. A tame monster. They wanted to boast to their friends about taking me to their beds and surviving.

Then everyone benefitted from the arrangement.

Was it a benefit? The single-minded way he hunted pleasure—from one bed to the next, one encounter following another—stripped it down to a basic, animal need, absent of true enjoyment. Barely had he risen from the tangled sheets, discarding the used lambskin sheaths he employed to keep himself in reasonably sound health, before he planned his subsequent conquests.

The grimness of this prospect looted any cheer from

the shop. Bright silks dulled, and the curlicue voices of the women flattened into toneless drones.

I . . . Livia sounded oddly contrite. *It wasn't my intent to lower you.*

I've been low, he answered. *Dwelt there for years. Whether I can climb upward is yet to be determined.*

He carefully maneuvered himself near his intended target. She idly toyed with a length of lace—Spanish, judging by the pattern. But her rouged lips were pressed tight, and she seemed little interested in the scrap of expensive fabric she fingered.

Something pressed upon Lady Maxwell's mind.

Though Bram was the only man in the shop, it was a measure of her distractedness that she did not notice him until he stood beside her. Only when her maid coughed politely to gain her attention did Lady Maxwell glance up. She nearly looked twice, her lips making an O of surprise. Of all the people she must have considered meeting at a fashionable dressmaker's shop, Bram must have been low on that list.

"Lord Rothwell."

"Lady Maxwell."

They offered each other decorous bows and curtsies.

"This is an unexpected delight," he said. He had, in fact, followed her from her home in St. James, careful to keep his horse out of sight from her carriage.

"I was unaware that you patronized Madame De Jardin's establishment." She glanced past Bram's shoulder. "You are here with . . ."

He watched her mentally run through the possibilities. He had no living female relations, and certainly no wife.

". . . A friend?" she finished. Beneath her powder, her cheeks colored. Mistresses might well be accepted fact amongst the elite, but ladies seldom discussed them with gentlemen in mantua makers' shops.

"I am alone," Bram answered.

Except for the ghost, added Livia.

Can't very well say that to her.

Lady Maxwell frowned in puzzlement. "This seems an odd place for you."

He shrugged. "I own that such establishments are not my usual domain. Yet of late I find myself greatly missing feminine company. Thus my presence here."

"Fie, Lord Rothwell." Lady Maxwell tapped his sleeve with her fan. "You never want for female companionship." Though she was some eight years his senior, Lady Maxwell was yet a handsome woman, well-maintained, and not above fashionable flirtation.

"Perhaps it is particular female companionship I seek."

Her brows rose. "You are roguish, sir." Yet she sounded breathless, intrigued. He knew that tone well.

"No offense was intended, ma'am." He bowed, noting how her gaze lingered on his calf, then rose higher up his leg. "Might I apologize more profoundly—in private?" He tipped his chin toward the back of the shop, where curtained rooms awaited women for changing and fittings.

Lady Maxwell hesitated. She glanced at him, then at the other patrons. Her maid studiously looked blank.

Is she so corruptible? Livia asked.

Almost everyone is. Especially amongst our set.

Finally, Lady Maxwell said in a theatric tone, "I believe my garter needs retying. Do excuse me." She hurried to one of the changing rooms, stepped inside, and then, with a pointed glance at Bram, drew the curtain.

She's rather maladroit at this assignation business, Livia said.

Her usual lover is away on the Continent. She's out of practice.

Fortunately, she has you as a tutor.

I'm here for a purpose. Bram slipped back toward the curtained room. *And it is not Lady Maxwell's charms, seasoned though they might be.*

He stepped through the curtain, and the sounds of the shop grew muffled. The lady in question whirled around from readjusting the small velvet patch on her cheek in the mirror. She took a step toward him, then stopped and narrowed her eyes.

"You've never shown an interest before, Rothwell."

"Always your affections had been engaged elsewhere. With Mr. Sedgwick absent, I thought I might press my advantage." He narrowed the distance between them, and took her hand.

She gasped, whilst Livia snickered.

"Lady Maxwell. Mary. Expecting you to accept my sudden suit would be a gross insult. If any offense was taken, I beg forgiveness. 'Tis my hot blood, I fear, that makes me importunate."

With her free hand, Lady Maxwell opened her fan and began to cool her face. "I might pardon you. Perhaps."

"Let me come to you," he continued, still clasping her hand. "Allow me to plead my case."

"Where might you do such a thing?" Her pupils were wide, her breath quick. Mr. Sedgwick was twenty years older than Bram, and Lady Maxwell's longtime lover. His heated protestations and avowals likely ended over a decade past.

A handsome young suitor such as you? What woman could remain indifferent?

No need for ridicule, Madam Ghost.

I'm not being sarcastic, was Livia's intriguing reply.

Bram realized Lady Maxwell waited on his answer. "At your home. When your husband is out during the night. I'll come to you then."

"Lord Maxwell seldom attends evening amusements."

"He's a man of no little influence in Parliament. Surely he has meetings at night."

A pleat of worry formed between Lady Maxwell's brows. "He might . . . I don't know . . ." Her gaze darted to the side, precisely the sort of movement Whit would call a *tell*.

"Mary." Bram moved to catch her gaze, and he gave her a long, slow smile. "How can I come to you if I don't know the particulars of his schedule? I'd hate to spoil our pleasures before they had even begun." He stroked his thumb across her wrist, back and forth. "Tell me when and where his next political gathering is to be."

At last, she said, "Tonight. A gathering at Camden House in Wimbledon."

The country estate of the king's advisor. Surely that meant that Maxwell and the others in the cabal planned on meeting there to discuss and strategize against John. Wimbledon lay ten miles from the heart of London.

Far away indeed for any sort of business. It had to be a secret council.

So secret that John won't know of it?

He'll know.

Having gained the information he sought, Bram wanted nothing more than to bolt from the little curtained room, out of the mantua maker's, and out into action. But he had a role to perform, and so adhered to the script.

"Tonight, then."

"But—"

He bowed over Lady Maxwell's hand and pressed a kiss there. "Until then."

Before she could say anything further, he strode from the dressing chamber. He gave just a hint of knowing smile response to the curious looks he received.

She might yet tell her husband that you asked about the meeting, Livia pointed out.

Donning his hat, he stepped out into the street. Though the day was at its height, the Strand remained eerily quiet, the numbers of men and women out shopping dramatically thinned. He paced quickly to where a crossing sweep held his horse and threw the boy a coin.

Swinging up into the saddle, he thought, *She won't. To do so would mean admitting to her husband that she was planning an assignation.* He kicked his horse into motion.

For a soldier, Livia said, *you're quite adept at subterfuge.*

There are many ways to win a war, he answered.

Locating John was their goal—and Lady Maxwell had been gracious enough in her infidelity to provide the details of where Bram would find her husband. Where Lord Maxwell was, John would be, as well. A gathering of his enemies made a perfect target.

John would act against them, though the how of it was yet unknown.

But we will be there to stop him, Bram thought, urging his horse to greater speed as he headed for Wimbledon.

Day faded to twilight, color leeching from the world as the sun dipped below the horizon. He crossed the river at Putney Bridge, and the Thames made a dark, slick shape beneath, empty of watermen ferrying passengers in their skiffs. The land felt emptied, derelict, as he pushed further south of London. Hardly any lights burned in the windows of scattered homes. The village of Putney was deserted, its streets dark, and so it went, the further Bram rode into the night, passing few people in the gloom of night.

Full darkness enveloped the countryside. At last, the stately form of Camden House appeared out of the shadows. It stood in the middle of a sprawling park. Crisply modern, it rose up two stories, proudly displaying rows of symmetrical windows in its brick and pale stone façade. In contrast to the darkness, lights blazed from the windows, an announcement that more than servants occupied the house.

Not especially discrete, Livia noted.

No one within believes they have anything to fear. Not tonight.

Where is John?

No bloody idea. But he'll show.

Weary though his horse was, the mare responded to his urging for more speed. It galloped across the wide, open parkland. Camden House drew closer. Men's sober voices drifted in muted waves across the park. No signs of disturbance or trouble.

He could be in hiding nearby, Livia said above the pounding hoof beats.

Movement in the darkness snared his attention. He turned his head, every sense on alert.

Bram, Livia cautioned.

Shapes detached from the shadows. Large forms, nearly the size of his horse. They moved with a loping shuffle, drawing nearer. They made hoarse, guttural sounds.

Something huge and heavy collided with Bram.

He flew off his horse, landing hard on the ground. He lost his breath and his head collided with the earth. But he couldn't pause to catch his wind or settle his spinning head. A beast was on top of him, its skin reeking of sulfur, and as it shrieked, hot, rotten air poured over him.

Dimly, he heard his horse's panicked whinny, and its hooves beating a retreat.

A cloud peeled away from the moon to reveal the creature.

It had eyes as huge as saucers, glassy and yellow, and slits for nostrils. Three mouths ringed its head, all of them full of serrated black teeth. Its humanoid body was covered in greasy amphibious skin that flung off slime.

Never had he beheld anything as foul. The other Hell-raisers had talked of battling demons, and John had promised armies of them, yet this was the first Bram ever saw such a creature at such close range. Sickness coiled in his belly. If this thing was a harbinger of what was to come . . .

The beast recoiled suddenly, leaping off Bram and scuttling back. Slowly, cautiously, Bram got to his feet.

The demon stared at him and hunched low. Its posture reminded him of a dog ceding dominance, and when it whined at him, he understood.

It doesn't know I've turned against the Devil. It thinks I'm still an ally.

The rest of them hesitate.

I still do not see John.

Bram glared into the darkness. *Nor do I. He sent these creatures to do his filthy work.*

Other demons massed, yet they hung back, watching him with vitreous eyes. The creature that had leapt upon Bram gazed at him, then at the house, tilting its head in question.

Even if John wasn't there, at the least, Bram could try to avert an attack on the cabal.

"Go," Bram commanded. He pointed away from Camden House.

The demon did not move.

"Away from this place!"

His commands were met only with more rasping sounds, and taloned feet shuffling in the dirt. The beast glanced toward the house and growled.

Cursed things won't listen to me.

We'll have to keep going. If John sent these things, then we must get to the men inside and protect them.

Bram took a step in the direction of Camden House. Then another.

The demon moved as he moved, keeping pace. It scraped out a questioning sound.

He kept walking, his stride lengthening. As he did, the other creatures loped along, keeping a distance between themselves and Bram. If demons could look baffled, these beasts did. They could not understand what he intended.

The creatures growled in agitation the closer he got to the house. Only a hundred feet to go.

He felt the demons' rising anger. They snarled as he quickened his pace.

Time to run, Livia urged.

He did.

A demon attacked. It launched itself at him, throwing its arms around his torso and dragging him to the ground.

He grappled with the heavy beast, battling to keep its long claws from tearing open his face. Snarling, he gripped its wrists, and fought to wedge his boot against the thing's abdomen. At last, he managed to plant his heel in the creature's stomach, and, letting go of its wrists, shoved.

The monster stumbled back. Bram leapt to his feet and drew his sword with one motion. He didn't give the demon a chance to rush him. He ran his sword straight through the beast's throat. Its shriek turned to a wet gurgle as he pulled the blade free. Dark, sticky blood shot from the demon's neck and into the dirt.

Bram waited just long enough to watch it fall to the ground before whirling around. A dozen of the creatures bounded toward the manor house.

He charged in pursuit.

Livia flickered into being beside him. She glared at the demons, then at her hands.

"I haven't enough power to fight them. We'll need to join magic so I can work spells."

"Can't really help you right now," he said through gritted teeth. The demons were not very fast, and he shortened the distance between them. Less than a hundred feet stood between the creatures and the house.

"You can't take those things on completely alone!"

"No choice but to try."

The demons shrieked at his approach. With a burst of speed, he flung himself into battle.

Chapter 9

Livia seethed with frustration as she could only watch Bram throw himself into the fight. Her magic was barely a flicker within, and her body was aught but vapor. No threat to these minions of the Dark One. All she could do was dart in between the creatures, distracting them, as Bram launched his attack.

She struggled to do her part, but her attention continually turned to Bram. She had witnessed him practice and spar, had seen his memories of combat, but not until now did she truly behold him in the midst of battle.

He moved like lightning, like death and beauty. Swift and lethal. He spun and wove around the demons, his blade forming arcs of silver, whistling through the air and cleaving into the creatures' flesh. His long coat flew out behind him like dark wings. No hesitation in his movement, no fear or moments of indecision. He was war itself.

The demons massed around him and fell back as he struck. They hissed in fury, eyes and claws gleaming in the moonlight.

Livia swirled herself around them, deflecting their attention. "Come and kill me, you toads," she taunted in her own language.

She did not flinch as their talons raked through her, nor when they shrilled with frustration that she could not be wounded. These demons were not especially intelligent, but she knew them to be relentless. She continued her distraction, hoping to keep their awareness divided between her and Bram. Able soldier he might be, but he was one man, far outnumbered.

Yet, as Bram fought, she felt a strange energy gathering within her. An expanding brightness, as though her magic grew, coalescing into the form of the key. What was its origin? Its strength filled her in glimmering waves. She became stronger, potent, her translucent figure gaining in brilliance.

A demon rushed at her. She spun, throwing out one of her hands in the instinctive gesture of attack. White energy shot from her palm. The demon was thrown backward. It landed on its back, sprawled, a smoking crater in the center of its chest. Huge glassy eyes stared up at the night sky, unblinking. The beast was dead.

Livia stared at her hand. She had used the Lightning Strike of Jove—an attack she had employed countless times in the past. Her magic had been cleaved apart since she and Bram were bound together. Yet now she felt the full strength of it. How?

More gleaming light drew her attention. The demons? No—Bram. As he battled the creatures, energy gathered around him in a bright mantle. Each strike of his sword, each parry and counter-offensive, the energy glowed brighter. She stared in amazement.

His expertise as a warrior roused the magic within him, building it to greater strength. Its power surged in their shared connection. Like a tide of fire, it rose within her.

It had been centuries since she felt such power. A grin stretched her mouth. Oh, she would enjoy this.

Seeing one of their number fallen, two more demons

broke away from Bram and charged her. She fired twin bolts of energy, one from each hand. One of the creatures took the hit right to the head, leaving its neck nothing but a smoldering stump. The other dodged the blow, but caught the edge of the energy across its thigh. It stumbled, but kept coming.

She held her position as the demon neared. It could do naught to harm her. Yet when its claw swiped along her shoulder, she hissed in pain and her energy flickered. She was stunned to feel pain for the first time in so long. It traveled in throbbing red waves through her.

How could it be? The demon had some magic of its own that allowed it to hurt a ghost. Or the charge of her power made her vulnerable to attack.

The reason for it did not matter. A change of strategy was needed. She could not fight as though invulnerable. Keeping herself as fleet as possible, she evaded more strikes from the demon, and threw hot flares of energy at the attacking beast.

One bolt of energy hit the demon in the stomach. It collapsed, shuddered, and went still.

"The hell?" Bram's surprised voice sounded above the demons' shrieks and the rush of his blade. Though his gaze was on her, he continued his attacks against the creatures.

"Don't question it," she threw back. "It strengthens both of us."

Only then did he notice the incandescent energy surrounding him. He started, then gave a feral smile. "Damned useful."

They plunged back into the fray, Bram felling demons with his sword, Livia cutting them down with her magic. The creatures seemed unprepared for such a show of aggression and resistance. They fought back, yet their numbers continued to thin. At last, only two of the demons remained. One of the pair shrieked at the other. They turned and fled into the darkness.

Both Livia and Bram attempted to pursue, but the demons abruptly disappeared. One moment, they scuttled across the field, and the next, they vanished, leaving behind the smell of sulfur.

"A portal," Livia said. "How they arrived here."

Sword in hand, panting, Bram said, "We give chase."

She shook her head. "Vitalized as I am, I've not the power to open a portal once it has been shut. Even if I did, we'd face legions of demons on the other side."

"I'm ready." He bared his teeth, savage.

She stared at him. He'd taken a few cuts during the fight, a thin line of blood crossing his cheek, and there were tears in his coat. Yet he stood like a warrior born, fierce and literally shining with martial power, gripping his blood-streaked sword.

The thrumming that resounded within her came only partially from the battle she and Bram had just fought.

The swell of her strength began to fade, its brightness receding like a tide. She swayed.

He was beside her instantly. "Hurt?"

"The demon somehow managed to wound me." She shook her head. "A minor injury."

He cursed, his expression lethal. The brightness around him also began to dim, leaving behind afterimages. "Don't know how to tend to a ghost's wounds."

"Truly, it will pass."

His gaze gentled. "I'd no idea Roman priestesses could fight like Spartans."

"I did not precisely follow the prescribed course of prayer and study."

"*Praying* against an enemy is never an effective strategy." He gave a crooked smile. "And I'm glad you weren't an ideal priestess."

During her lifetime, courting someone's good opinion had not been her ambition. Her ruthlessness earned her more than a few enemies. It did not trouble her. Only one opinion mattered: her own.

Yet Bram's words warmed her, far more than she thought a dead woman could feel.

She turned back toward the manor house. "You need to warn the men. There will be more attacks."

After wiping his blade on the grass, he sheathed his sword. "That is going to be an interesting conversation. 'Your political opponent is literally in league with the Devil. Time to invest in a few hundred bodyguards. Preferably ones with magic.'"

"They need to go into hiding—say whatever you must." She glanced at the demon bodies strewn across the grass. Already, their corpses were liquefying, the process of decomposition working faster on creatures of the underworld. "There is one certainty, however."

She gazed at Bram, the moonlight upon the breadth of his shoulders and ebony of his hair. Resonant energy turned his eyes to pale crystal, ringed with sapphire.

"John and the Dark One know, now. They know that you have chosen a side—and it isn't theirs."

Returning home was no longer an option. Livia was well aware of the consequences once a Hellraiser turned his back on the Dark One.

He's threatened by you, she said as Bram rode toward the city. *Which means he will try to destroy you.*

He can try, Bram answered.

I haven't the strength now to battle hordes of demons.

I'll take them on myself.

She snorted. *Arrogance gets men killed. Whilst your soul is in the Dark One's grasp, we cannot take that chance.*

Have you someplace safe, someplace John doesn't know about?

A small house in Spitalfields. My father bought it for his mistress. She died a few years after my brother inherited, and Arthur kept the place. Rented it out, but when I acceded to the title, I stopped taking tenants. It's been empty ever since.

Go there. You can rest in safety, then we can plan how we can draw John out.

Yes, ma'am, he answered, his voice sardonic. Yet he did as she directed, and she thought of the tumultuous minutes after the battle.

Bram had gone to Camden House first. The men within had all exclaimed in shock when they had beheld him, bloody and disheveled. In terse words, Bram had told them they were the intended targets of assassins and needed to go into hiding immediately. Some of the men had protested— half had wanted proof of his allegations, the others had wanted to summon the law and bring official charges against John.

"The law cannot help you," Bram had answered. "And I didn't fabricate these wounds. All of you need to go. To your country estates. Abroad. It doesn't sodding matter. If you value your lives and the lives of your families, you'll do as I say. *Now.*"

The men had seen the hard blue fire of Bram's gaze, and heard the steel of his voice, and had meekly obeyed.

Now she and Bram rode through the night-shrouded city, through quarters she little recognized. They passed mobs of men, some of whom lunged for Bram or the reins of his horse. Bram's sword made fast appearances, and the assailants retreated. Thereafter, he kept one hand on the reins, the other around the hilt of his unsheathed sword.

At last, he slowed outside a narrow house, with a lower story and two floors. The surrounding homes were genteel, if a little shabby, their façades cracked like porcelain, an occasional weed sprouting up from crevices in the plaster. The streets here were dark and empty, not a single light in the windows. A thin dog trotted down the middle of the cobbles. It did not stop or look at them, its nails clicking on the stones as it passed, in search of food.

Bram dismounted and led his horse around to the mews. The stable behind the house held only rotten straw and a rusted trough. After securing his horse and cleaning out the stall, Bram slipped into a neighbor's stable and gathered supplies—a bucket of water, some feed.

Don't your commandments forbid you from stealing?

Requisitioning, I prefer to call it. That's not a sin.

A large orange tabby cat ambled through the stable. Judging by the size of its belly, it had more than an ample supply of mice.

Bram tended to his horse. He murmured to the animal, patting its flank and nose. Briefly, he rubbed his cheek against the horse's face as he stroked its sleek neck. The mare snorted with pleasure.

Livia discovered she was jealous of a horse.

Once the animal had been taken care of, Bram approached his house's back door. Unsurprisingly, it was locked. He moved to a window and slipped off his coat. With one hand, he held the coat up to the glass, as the other drew back and curled into a fist.

Wait, she said. *No need to break into your own house. Lend me some of your magic.*

My way's more satisfying.

And noisier. Even if you muffle the sound.

Grumbling, he donned his coat, then closed his eyes. She did the same, and felt the gleam of her power rising. His own magic reached toward hers, its heat filling her, sifting through her body. She ought to be used to the sensation by now, this intimate merging. Ought to be, but was not.

Once she had gathered enough power, she directed the energy toward the keyhole. She shaped it, guiding it to match the tumblers, seeking the perfect fit.

This reminds me of something, he said, wry.

She didn't bother with a reply, though a different kind of heat suffused her. Instead, she made sure the key fit precisely, then turned it.

The door opened. Its hinges complained, but it was still quieter than smashing a window.

Bram stepped inside. As he did, Livia allowed herself to materialize just behind him. They moved through what appeared to be the kitchen. A cold, ash-strewn hearth was set into one wall, and a few earthenware bowls squatted on shelves. A desiccated lump of meat lay in the middle of the single table—once it must have been a roast. Now it was grayish brown stone.

"Don't need to light a lamp." Bram glanced at her. "You illuminate."

"I always have important knowledge to convey." She smiled, however, seeing how her ghostly radiance bathed the room. "Think of all the lamp oil that can be saved."

"Very economical."

They drifted from the kitchen, down a cramped corridor. An empty storeroom and an even more cramped closet lay off the passage. Judging by the cot and battered chest in the closet, it once served as a servant's chamber. They ascended a staircase to the main floor. One room was empty of everything but a broken mirror leaning against the wall and a dented metal serving platter. At some point, the room might have served as a place for dining. Now, one would receive a mouthful of grime for a meal. The other, larger room still had furniture, but dust filmed everything. Bram discovered a nest of mice within a chair's stuffing, a mother and her wriggling pink young. Pellets were scattered across the floor, evidence that other creatures called this place home, and spiders presided in the corners.

"The world goes wild so easily," Bram murmured. To her surprise, he did not disturb the spiderwebs, nor toss out the mice. He left them as they were. At Livia's questioning glance, he said, "I'd be a terrible landlord if I threw out the only occupants with nary a warning of eviction."

She shook her head, and glided up the narrow stairs. He followed, the steps groaning beneath his weight. Shadows were thick here, scarcely pushed back by her glow. More cracks threaded up the plastered walls. Something scuttled across the floorboards as Bram reached the top of the stairs. Two doors led off the hallway.

Before he could open the first door, Livia glided straight through it. Bram made a soft snort of amusement. He entered the chamber in a more customary fashion. They didn't linger in the chamber—moth-eaten curtains covered the windows, and more broken bits of furniture were scattered around like the bones of slow-moving herd animals.

The front-facing room revealed its purpose by the presence of a canopied bed. The canopy itself had been removed, leaving behind the bare wooden posts like trees in winter. No blankets covered the mattress. Bits of horsehair poked through the ticking. Bram gave the mattress a shove. Apart from a cloud of dust that made him cough, nothing else came out.

"Don't want to share my bed with rats," he said.

Aside from the bare bed, the chamber's only other furnishing was a small table that listed on a splintered leg and a few piles of debris huddled in the corners. Bram toed through the debris, shoving aside rags and broken ceramics, but seemed to find nothing of value.

"A poor protector, your father," Livia murmured, peering through the grime-streaked window. It looked out onto the street. After the chaos and noise of the earlier fight with the demons, the utter absence of sound and movement here felt yet more ominous, as though in suspension, awaiting a greater threat.

"This place has fallen into disrepair since Mrs. Dance's time. He kept her in fine style. A live-in servant, and a maid. A line of credit at the mantua maker's. She never complained." He stared at the sagging bed. "She may have even cared for him. Arthur said she went into mourning after Father died, and didn't live much longer beyond that."

"You might've installed your own woman here, when the house became available."

"I never had a mistress. As well you know."

That, she did. She did not know what humor provoked her to make such a comment. Untrue. She knew precisely why she had mentioned his nonexistent concubine. They were in a small bedchamber, utterly alone in this narrow house, and had fought side-by-side this night. Were she flesh, she would have pushed him back to the bed—though she suspected he would *allow* her to push him to the bed—and put her hips to his hips, her mouth to his mouth. Felt him. Tasted him.

Impossibilities.

Her desire understood nothing of what was impossible. It—*she*—wanted, without thought, without considering realities.

He must have seen the hunger in her gaze, for his own blazed hotter, and he took a step toward her.

She could not feel the warmth of his body, nor could he span the distance between them and take hold of her. Yet she moved away. An instinctively protective act.

"I've never known such frustration." She could not look away from him, though she kept herself as far from him as she could. They faced one another across the bare expanse of floor. "I thought that over a thousand years trapped with the Dark One was the greatest torment I'd ever known. To watch the world slip past, all the experiences of life that I could never have. Condemned to be a pair of eyes only." She now shut her eyes. "It *was* agony. Cost me my reason. But, in time, I regained my sense. I believed myself entirely sane."

"And now?" His voice was a rumble.

She forced her eyes to open. "Now I verge on madness again. So many things I want and cannot have. Because of this." She glided toward the bed and passed her hand through the post. "Without my flesh, my magic is only a shadow of what it needs to be. But I want more than my magic." She turned her gaze to his.

Hunger shaped the contours of his face, honing him to impossible sharpness. "You can have whatever you desire."

He strode to her. There was no thief's silence or cunning. His step was bold, direct. Only a few inches separated them, and she imagined what his heat must be like, the scent of his skin. Yet those few inches may as well have been miles, for it was a distance that couldn't be breached.

"You can have me," he said, husky and low. "Because, of a certain, I want you."

"More of your cruelty." She pressed her lips tightly together to keep from kissing him—ludicrous.

"The truth. I've never wanted a woman more."

His words were an agonizing caress. "Because you have not—what is the word you used—*swived* anyone in days."

"It's not desperation that makes me want you. It's *you*." He smiled, faintly mocking himself. "The first woman I cannot touch is the one that I need to have. It's not your body I desire, though," he added, with an appreciative glance, "that has its temptations."

He shook his head. "I thought I was finished with firsts, that I'd done everything and all things. Yet it turns out that there are still unknowns for me. A woman I want for herself."

Aside from the wound she'd sustained in the battle, she

thought herself incapable of physical pain. As he spoke, however, she felt a bodily ache of loss. "Look at me, Bram." Staring down at herself, she noted that the floorboards were plainly visible through her translucent body. "I've no way to touch you, no means of feeling."

"If that is your challenge," he said, "I accept."

She deliberately moved through him. "Enough. We'll speak of other things. We should—"

"Get on the bed."

Turning to face him, she raised her brows. "What?"

"I said"—he drew off his coat and tossed it to the floor— "get on the bed."

For a moment, she did not move. Instinct and self-preservation made her want to disobey his direct command. She bent her will to no one.

They stared at one another. She felt the tug and pull between them, the continuous will and desire. Neither of them obeyed readily or ceded control.

Yet she would do this for him now. He would be hers to command another time.

With deliberate concentration, she made herself sit on the bed.

"Lie down." His throat was revealed as his neckcloth joined the coat upon the floor. The angry line of his scar ran beside the fast beat of his pulse.

Using more concentration, she stretched out on the bed. It felt odd, mimicking of a quotidian action. How long had it been since she had lain upon a bed—both for sleep and for sex? Her memories were both too vivid and shrouded in lost time.

His gaze still holding hers, Bram pulled off his boots. The movement tugged his fine shirt tight along his shoulders, his arms, the supple doeskin of his breeches snug along his thighs and the thick outline of his arousal.

He prowled to the bed, then stretched out long beside

her. The ropes beneath the mattress creaked with his weight.
But they held.

Propping himself up on his elbow, he stared down at her.
"Take off your tunic."

She did not move, another instinctive fighting of command. Yet deliberate acquiescence took nothing from her.
She was unbroken, even in obedience.

She worked the clasps at her shoulders. Yet they grasped
at nothing. The tunic was just as formless as she, and part
of her, as well. "I can't."

"Doesn't matter. That's not where I would start. No," he
murmured, half to himself, "the first thing I would do is
take those ornaments from your hair. I'd unpin them, and
then I'd coil a lock of your hair around my finger. It must
feel like coarse silk, your hair. Heavy, soft. And it has a
fragrance. Spice and temple smoke. I'd breathe that in,
touching only your hair, watching it move as it falls over
your shoulders."

"I used to scent my bathwater with cassia," she whispered.

A corner of his mouth tilted. "Ah, I was right. Spice. But
I'd touch your hair for only so long before I'd need to feel
your skin. Here, and here." He moved his finger to right beneath her ear, at the juncture of her neck, then down her
throat to tarry at the hollow between her collarbones. "Like
velvet, your skin, and warm."

She could not feel his touch, yet his words stroked her,
drawing forth silken ribbons of sensation. It stunned her. She
could not feel, and yet she did.

"I'd feel the beat of your heart," he said, relentless.
"You'd respond to me. That wouldn't be enough, though. I'd
want your mouth. To feel it against mine. To taste you. I'd
start slowly, just little sips, the brush of my mouth against
yours. How silky your lips are, so full and ripe. Your lips are
made for kissing—did you know? You might think they
were for shaping the words for spells, or issuing commands

to your trembling underlings, and they do those things very well, but their true purpose is in kissing me. I'd show you that. I'd kiss you deeper. You'd taste of spice, too." He licked his lips and gave a small hum of pleasure.

By the gods, she could almost *feel* his kiss.

"There was a time when I loved nothing more than kissing," he continued, almost conversational but for the depth of his voice and the blue fire in his eyes. "Could do it for hours, and be satisfied. Perhaps I'll do that with you. Kiss you until you melt in my mouth and I drink you in." His nostrils flared. "Another time. *This* kiss is a prelude. I'd take my lips from yours and then I'd run them down your neck. I'd bite you there, too. My teeth just here." He circled the convergence of her neck and shoulder. "Hard enough to leave a mark, so anyone who saw you would know exactly what happened. They'd know that I bit you like a wolf claiming his mate. The mighty priestess marked. By me."

An involuntary moan crept up her throat. She could well imagine it—the gleaming flare of pleasure and pain, his hot breath upon her, the red indentations left by his teeth. His audacious, animalistic marking.

"What if I threatened to turn you into an actual wolf?" she breathed. "Transform you into a beast? Would you be so impudent?"

He grinned savagely. "I'd bite you harder. Until you give in."

"I never submit."

"Then this will be a delightful challenge. For, you see, as I'm biting you, I'd unfasten your tunic and slide it down to your waist. Cup your bared breasts in my hands. You've full breasts, but my hands are large. Nothing would go unattended. I'd stroke and caress them. They'd feel like . . . like paradise. So soft. Lush." His hands hovered over her breasts, and he stared with open need.

She arched up, even though she could not feel his palms against her.

"Your nipples would harden. I'd run the tip of my fingers back and forth over them, and you'd feel it all through your body. Then I'd take your nipples between my fingers and pinch."

She couldn't stop the gasp that formed on her lips. His words burned her, banishing the chill of her cold nullity.

"I'd take my fingers away and put my mouth in their place. Lick you. Have your nipple between my lips and tug. I'd make your breasts glisten from my tongue. Until you'd writhe beneath me, begging me not to stop."

She *did* want him to stop. This was a torment, a tease, and could end only in frustration. Yet if he stopped, she would tear the walls down with her scream.

"The tunic would come off, all of it. I'd push it past your hips, until you'd stand completely naked, wearing only the ripe curves of your hips and the dark gloss of your maiden-hair." He moved a hand down to hover above the junction of her thighs. She instinctively widened her legs.

"We'd have a bed nearby. Not this one. A better bed, with a good, firm mattress, and silk sheets. I'd urge you back to the bed and lay you down, your hips right at the edge, your feet on the floor."

"And where would you be?" she asked, breathless.

"Kneeling between your legs, of course. My hands would grip your thighs. They're sleek, your thighs, and I'd feel the tension in them, the muscles beneath your skin as you'd hold yourself in readiness. Waiting. Waiting. You'd jump a little at the first touch of my breath on you. A sigh, that breath, and a breathing in. This close, I'd smell how much you want me there. I'd see it, too. That gleam of wetness. Can you picture that? Can you see how your body would demand me?"

"Yes."

"But I'd be a hungry man, standing at the banquet. I'd not be able to wait for long before feasting. A few gentle licks at first, learning how you taste, feeling your impossible softness. You'd be so wet my face would be glistening. And you'd get even wetter. I'd suck on you, consume you. I'd thrust my tongue inside of you. God, you'd be delicious."

He groaned. "I'd take your bud between my lips, swirl my tongue around it. Back and forth. Inside you, over you. I'd fill you with pleasure. And you'd scream when you came, your fingers in my hair, pulling me tight against you."

She wanted to close her eyes, stop her ears, but he had her in his thrall, and she truly did writhe, gasping even though she'd no need for air.

"You'd think we were done," he went on, inexorable, "but I'd continue. I wouldn't stop. Not until you came so many times you'd go limp and had screamed yourself voiceless."

The dark tapestry he wove with words ensnared her. She fell, farther, farther, tangled in fantasy, craving what he offered, needing to give him what he gave her.

"That wouldn't be all," she breathed. "You'd be hard, and aching. Wanting inside me."

His lids lowered, and he dragged in a breath. "Yes."

"I'd undress you. This time fast, but there will come a time when I'd go slowly, peeling away layer after layer to bare your skin and your body. But for this moment, I'd be swift, because I would not be able to wait. I'd have you naked before ten grains of sand hit the bottom of the hourglass."

She had already seen him unclothed, but picturing it now within the illusion they shaped made her tight and ravenous. The moonlight would be silver upon the wide expanse of his shoulders, tracing the solid arcs of his muscles, disappearing into dips and hollows.

"And I would see how hard you'd be," she continued.

"Curving up, as if made to fit precisely within me. The head pulling upward. There'd be a small drop weeping from the slit, because you'd want inside me so badly."

His breath came raggedly, and he pressed his hand against the hard ridge of his cock. "Yes—just there."

"But not yet. I wouldn't let you between my legs right away. I'd stay on the bed, just where I lay, and make you kneel on the mattress beside my head. Your cock would be so close to my lips. I'd lift up, like this." She raised herself onto her elbows. "My mouth would open. You'd put one hand behind my head. And then . . . I'd take you into my mouth."

Bram gave another groan. His groin pressed into his hand. Yet he held himself back.

"Go on," she urged. "Let me see you."

His fingers flew over the fastenings of his breeches. With a hiss of relief, he freed his erection, his hand wrapping around its thickness.

Never had a crude piece of flesh been so tempting. His cock was dark, flushed with blood, and just as she had predicted, fluid glistened at the top of the round head. She wanted him within her so badly. But she was only spirit, so she gave him what she could with words.

"I'd lick you to start. Run my tongue around the top, and just beneath the ridge. There'd be a bit of salt on my tongue from your own need, and I'd lap that up. Then I'd draw you deeper into my mouth. Slowly. Inch by inch, stopping along the way to taste you. But I would take more and more of you within me, until I could go no further. And that's when I'd begin to suck."

His hand slid up and down his shaft as she spoke, yet she saw how he kept his strokes slow, light, as if trying to prolong the pleasure. No hurried release for him. He was a voluptuary, taking delight from sensation even more than the release.

"You'd feel my tongue on the underside of your cock. I'd run it all over you as I moved up and down. Every so often, I'd lightly scrape my teeth along the shaft, just enough to remind you that I'm a woman who is always in command, even with your cock in my mouth."

"And when you'd do that," he breathed, "I'd push a little harder on your head. Making you swallow more of me."

"*Both* of us could not be in charge. Someone has to follow."

"Neither of us are followers. We'll make it succeed. That I don't doubt. See, as you'd be sucking me, I'd reach over to stroke your sweet quim. You'd already be hot and wet from your climaxes, and I'd slip easily between your lips and inside you. Two fingers, I think." His fingers tightened around his shaft. "See? The two of us in command."

It would be a wondrous thing—the pull and push of each other, yielding and obdurate at the same time.

"But this wouldn't last," he went on. "Only so much I'd be able to endure before I had to have my cock truly inside you. I'd pull from your mouth—"

"And I would stay on the bed, my hips at the edge of the bed—"

"I'd stand between your legs and hold tight to your hips—"

"My breath would hold, and I'd watch you—"

"As I slid my cock into you."

She felt a bright radiance gathering within, coalescing. Trying to look away from Bram stroking himself was impossible. His hand moved faster, his grip tense, and his shirt clung as sweat filmed his body.

"You wouldn't move," she whispered. "We'd allow ourselves a moment to just feel one another, you thick and hard in me—"

"Your tight softness all around me. God." A rough animal sound reverberated from his chest. "Then I'd move.

I'd pull back, only a little, then thrust forward. A few slow strokes as we'd learn each other."

"Then you'd move faster, and I'd push to meet you."

"I'd watch your breasts shake with each thrust. I'd watch my cock as it slid in and out of you, wet with you. I'd watch your face as I filled you, watch the pleasure build, watch your eyes close, your mouth open."

"My hands would grip the blankets. I'd see you, the tension in your neck as you'd clench your teeth, the flex of your muscles as you'd move."

"I'd not be able to be gentle. I'd take you, hard, so hard, you'd be pushed further back onto the bed, and the bed itself would shudder and groan."

The brightness continued to build as she envisioned and felt him. She had always liked her lovemaking to be tempestuous, and Bram promised precisely that.

His touch upon himself was brutal, fascinating. "Release would call to you. It would demand your surrender."

"I don't surrender."

"To this, you would. I'd fuck you so powerfully, you'd have no choice. You'd come. So hard you'd lose your breath, lose your name, lose everything but the pleasure I'd give you. Come, Livia. Come *now*."

Sensation tore through her. It was a magnificent devastation, molten and unstoppable. Impossible. She had no body, no way to feel or experience release. And yet she did. Through his words alone, he tore down the barriers between the spirit and the flesh.

Oh, gods, it had been an eternity.

Her climax rolled on in endless waves. As she bowed up with release, she heard his guttural moan. She managed to pry her eyes open enough to watch him spend, his head thrown back, face carved sharp. Beautiful agony.

Had she been flesh, his semen would have coated her

belly and run down her thighs. But she had no body, and the droplets passed through her and onto the mattress.

He sprawled onto his back, chest heaving. After a few moments, he tucked himself back into his breeches and fastened them. He lay back, a man wrung dry.

"I never thought . . ." She struggled to find words, to gather her shattered mind. "To comprehend such marvels . . . *How* was that possible?"

"Because we are meant to be lovers," he said.

Such a simple explanation, yet it felt exactly right.

He gazed at her, and she could not stop her hand from stroking along his bristled cheek, as if she could truly feel him. His eyes slowly closed. Being mortal, and a man, Bram's breathing soon deepened and slowed. Livia lay beside him, listening to the sounds of his sleep. The blood on his face had dried. There would be more blood—his, countless others'. That was certain.

Tonight had been revelatory. Her magic drew strength when Bram fought; she was not as powerless as she had believed. And the pleasure he had given her afterward, here, in this derelict home that once housed his father's mistress, on a bed that was shabby and worn . . . that pleasure had been a wonder. It still was, echoing through her in golden reverberations.

More than physical release. An unexpected connection as intimate as two spirits might know. What was this man? Sinner, soldier. Lover.

Her lover—for now. Each hour that passed meant another hour lost, never to be regained. She could not rely on the future. It was a fragile web, and the impending storm would tear everything to tatters.

Chapter 10

From his vantage at the window, Bram watched the street. Christ Church's bell chimed the nine o'clock hour. The hour of business and industry—or so he'd been told, possessing neither the need to do business nor the impulse to industry. Good people walked the streets of London during the daylight hours. Silk weavers concentrated their shops here in Spitalfields, and, as the price of imported silk was exorbitant, the weavers were never idle. After all, England needed its finery.

But this morning, almost no one was on the street, walking to or from their workshops. A few men hurried past, gazes fixed on the ground, and one woman darted between two buildings, her shawl pulled over her head. Bram couldn't hear the clicking of looms. A child cried and was quickly stifled.

Bracing his hands on either side of the cracked casement, he stared down at the avenue and felt the frown shaping a pleat between his brows.

"Something's wrong," he muttered.

"It often is," answered Livia behind him.

A corner of his mouth turned up. Her mordant wit remained unchanged—yet he expected no less. A night's pleasure would not alter the heart of her, no matter how searing that pleasure had been.

If anyone would have told him that his most intense sexual experience would involve a woman he couldn't touch and who could not touch him, he would have laughed in disbelief and told his informant to keep drinking.

But last night . . . Nothing in the whole of his wicked, wayward life had ever equaled what he and Livia had shared. Even the thought of it now turned him molten. Sex had always been a purely physical action. With Livia, it had transformed into something far beyond himself, beyond the needs of the body, or the temporary cessation of sorrow.

Yet that pleasure couldn't hold back the evil he could sense growing.

"It's getting worse," he said.

"John and the Dark One know you are no longer their ally." Livia came to hover beside him, her radiance pale in the cold gray morning. "Of a certain, the balance continues to tip."

His stomach growled. Smirking, he laid a hand atop his empty stomach. "The doom of the world may hang in the balance, but I need breakfast."

She rolled her eyes. "Mortals and your appetites."

"You enjoyed those appetites last night."

"Most assuredly."

"There will be more." Moving away from the window, he stepped close to her. If she had been flesh, at this nearness he would have felt the heat of her body, smelled the fragrance of her skin. "I will give you pleasure to rival the gods."

"An audacious boast," she said, tipping up her chin. Yet her eyes darkened further and she ran her tongue over her bottom lip.

He'd happily burn down half of London just to kiss her.

"Not a boast, but the truth," he answered. "Whatever you experienced in your mortal life, any other lovers you may have had—I'll make you forget them all. You'll know only me."

She stared at him for a moment, her lips parted. "I want nothing more."

He reached for her, yet his hand passed through the curve of her neck. Acrid frustration welled.

Unconcerned with the demands of his heart, his stomach gave another complaining rumble. The last meal he had eaten had been a hastily bolted chop sometime yesterday afternoon.

"Go," Livia said, smiling. "Attend to your quotidian needs."

A thorough inspection revealed that nothing edible remained in the pantry. He'd have to go out to obtain something to eat.

"If I step out of doors in this," he said, plucking at his torn and bloody clothes, "I'll be dragged to Newgate as a suspected murderer."

"The law may show leniency if you tell them you only killed demons."

"Never mind Newgate. I'll be hauled to Bedlam and be lucky if the visitors pelt me only with rotten vegetables."

A search revealed a large chest shoved into the corner of a tiny room adjoining the bedchamber. Bram hefted the chest out of this small room. Setting the trunk on the floor of the bedchamber, he rattled the lid, and discovered it was locked tight.

"Could be empty," he muttered, "or simply hold bedclothes. Though I could wear a sheet as a toga."

Livia sniffed. "It takes more than a length of linen to wear a toga. However," she added with an appreciative leer, "if you strip down to your smallclothes, you'd make a fine gladiator."

He discovered he rather enjoyed being ogled. A thread of shadow worked its way through him, however. Once, he'd been a kind of gladiator, and gained scars both visible and unseen.

"I've a way to discover what's inside," she continued, kneeling down beside the chest. Seeing her on her knees brought to mind far too many distracting ideas and images—none of which could ever come to pass.

As he watched, Livia stuck her head inside the heavy wooden box, disappearing up to her shoulders. She re-emerged a second later. "Clothing," she announced.

"If I were a housebreaker," he said, "you would be extremely useful. I'd avoid all the empty coffers and plunder only those replete with treasure."

She started when he rammed the heel of his boot against the lock. After a few solid kicks, the metal broke apart.

"Magic could have opened the lock more readily," she said dryly.

"My way is more satisfying." He lifted the lid of the chest then pulled out its contents. A man's velvet coat and waistcoat, both musty, the embroidery along the cuffs and lapels frayed. Holding up the coat, he studied it with a frown.

"This was my father's."

"You and he were of a size," Livia noted.

"He always seemed so big to me." Yet, after Bram slipped off his torn coat and waistcoat and donned his father's clothing, he discovered they fit. He strode into the other chamber, Livia right behind him. There, in the cracked mirror propped against the wall, he considered his shattered reflection.

"He'd wear this to church," Bram said, staring at himself. "Baron Rothwell always made an impressive figure, even when supposedly honoring a higher power. I'd look back and forth between him and my brother as we sat in our pew. Arthur seemed so small next to Father." Bram shook his head. "That poor sod—I never envied him."

"But Arthur was the heir, the favored one."

He snorted. "Even better for me. I didn't want to have to wear the responsibility and decorum of the title. All I wanted was to pursue my own desires." He tugged on the sleeve of the coat. "Now *I'm* Baron Rothwell. Not the heir my father had wanted."

The coat was of an old-fashioned style, its skirt fuller than the current mode, its cuffs wider, and the waistcoat was longer than modern fashion dictated. Aside from an odor of must and cedar and the unraveling embroidery, the coat remained in decent condition. His father had always demanded the finest quality.

"There's a resemblance, as well," said Livia. "Between you and your sire."

"I don't see it." Father had been a formidable man who expected utter filial obedience. Bram remembered how cold his father's blue eyes could look when he was defied—and Bram had seen them cold many times. In the rare moments when Bram had seen Father without a wig, his close-shorn hair had been black as night. Black as Bram's own hair.

The mirror reflected him in jagged shards, a piecemeal man. A broken distortion of his father's successor.

He turned away from the mirror.

"My belly is empty," he said.

When he ventured out into the street, with Livia an invisible presence beside him, he realized it did not matter what he wore. No one looked at him, too busy hurrying to their destinations. An abrasive cold covered the city, the cobblestones treacherous and slick, people's breath coming in white puffs as they hurried in and out of buildings.

Bram himself walked quickly down the street, making sure that no suspicious characters lurked in alleys or trailed behind him.

Is it possible John would know where you might be? Livia asked.

Doubtful. Even I've never been to the Spitalfields house until yesterday. Just knew its direction from correspondence. Can't be too cautious, however.

Not anymore, she answered.

At a pie shop, Bram purchased two meat pies purported to be made of mutton. The pinch-faced shopkeeper wrapped up Bram's food in old broadsheets, looking nervously at the street all the while.

The pies weren't quite the fare Bram was accustomed to, but he'd eaten meat laced with maggots during a long siege in the Colonies. Suspect pie hardly bothered him.

"You're my first customer today, my lord," the pieman said. "Thinking of closing up shop after you."

"Not a soul?" Bram asked.

The shopkeeper shook his head. "Hardly anyone out these days. Been an ill feeling in the city for a long while, but it gets worse by the hour."

Bram muttered something inconsequential to the shopkeeper and set a handful of coins down on the counter. After buying a flagon of cider from a nearly empty tavern, he hurried back to the vacant house. Possibly John had eyes throughout the city, keeping watch, and Bram didn't want to risk being seen in public.

In the bare parlor, he ate his meal quickly, crouched on the floor like a scavenger. Livia made troubled circles as she drifted around the chamber.

"John's power grows," she said, voice taut. "I feel it like a web spreading over the city, and beyond. The barrier between the underworld and this realm weakens. He'll open the gate, and soon."

His food consumed, Bram crumpled the grease-stained papers and threw them into the corner. A rat emerged from a hole in the baseboard, sniffing, then grabbed the paper and scuttled back into its den.

"We tried to find him at Wimbledon, but he sent his minions instead. Perhaps a more direct assault is necessary. I'll go to his home." Bram rose to standing. "Persuade my way inside. Then put this"—he gripped the hilt of his sword—"into his heart."

Livia drifted close, her lips pressed tight. "We saw what John sent to dispatch his rivals. Imagine what guards his own home. Should you make it past his front steps, a host of demons will bar you further entrance. Your own gift won't work against them." She clenched her hands into fists. "Our joined magic isn't reliable enough to take on someone as strong as John."

"If you were flesh—"

"I'm not and never will be again."

"But if you were," he pressed, "would you have enough power to break John's curse, bring the other Hellraisers to London? You had the power to raise the Devil when you were flesh—this should be nothing to you."

"My magic draws its strength from living energy. Of which I have none." She growled in frustration. "These are meaningless pursuits, these hypothetical questions. My body is lost to me, and so is the full strength of my magic. There's nothing to be done. The task is impossible."

"A dangerous word to say to me, *impossible*." He stalked the chamber, keeping pace with his racing thoughts. "Where is your physical body?"

"Long since turned to dust."

He wheeled back to face her. "I saw your memories. When you imprisoned the Devil, you stepped on the other side of the door to close it. You didn't leave behind a corpse. The only bones the Hellraisers found in the temple belonged to a Roman soldier. But *your* body is out there, trapped somewhere. Between the realm of the living and the dead."

"A place beyond the *Ambitus*," she said, "making it irretrievable."

"You don't know that for certain."

"I know that one cannot jaunt back and forth between this mortal world and the underworld. To regain my body, to bring it back—that is hopeless."

A thought had begun to grow, spreading its roots through his mind, his heart. The very idea of it whetted him to a knife's point. He felt sharp and thin as a blade, but expansive as imagination itself.

"There's no hope for our fight if you stay this way." He waved at the translucency of her form.

"We might battle," she admitted with a scowl, "but never win."

"And the world would go up in flames."

Tense, silent, she nodded.

He understood now. What had been the smallest granules of possibility became tempered steel. He thought he might feel fear, or doubt. Yet the more he considered it, the more he understood its rightness.

This was who he had been before going to war. When he'd had purpose, and a belief in something larger than himself. Only now, he had lost his infantile optimism. He knew the world, now. It was a merciless place. Only savagery thrived.

He could be brutal. Brutality was part of him—he embraced it now.

Calm and purpose enveloped him. He felt a peace hitherto unknown.

Everything in his life had been leading him to this point. "I can secure our victory." He took several steps back. His gaze never leaving hers, he said, *"Veni, geminus."*

* * *

"You cannot," Livia cried, but she spoke too late. The words had been said.

The smell of burning paper thickened the air. The light within the derelict chamber dimmed, as though a bank of clouds obscured the sun. Shadows congealed and then—

There stood the *geminus*. Bram's double.

"What a hideous bastard," Bram said.

The *geminus* glowered at him. "My master is displeased by your perfidy."

"I don't care," Bram answered.

The creature opened its mouth to speak, then espied Livia. Its features tightened, fearful and angry. "*Her*. She has poisoned you, turned you against us."

"Leave the ghost out of this," said Bram before Livia could snap back a reply. "Disappear if you want, go slinking back to your master with tales of my whereabouts. But, stay, only a moment. I've a theory I want to test."

In a movement too quick to see, Bram drew his sword and cut it across the *geminus*'s face.

The creature shouted, bringing its hand up to cover its wounded cheek. At the same time, Bram gave a small hiss. A slash of red had appeared on his face, precisely where he'd injured the *geminus*.

"It's true, then," Bram said with a grim smile. "Any wound you sustain also injures me."

The *geminus* sneered. "Your Hellraiser friends learned the same. There is no harm that befalls me that will not also hurt you. A scratch, a bruise. To wound me is to wound yourself, whilst my master possesses your soul. Which he most assuredly does."

"Excellent," said Bram, baring his teeth.

He plunged his sword right into the *geminus*'s heart.

Livia stared in horror. No sound came from her mouth. She could not move, could do nothing but look on, appalled and terror-struck, as Bram sank his blade deeper into the *geminus*'s chest. The moment his sword had pierced the creature's flesh, both he and the *geminus* gasped aloud. A wound immediately appeared on Bram's chest, directly over his heart. It spread crimson and dark, staining the velvet of his waistcoat.

The creature gaped at the sword deep in its breast. It turned wide, stunned eyes up at Bram. "What . . . ? But you . . ."

"Yes," said Bram tightly.

He hissed as he withdrew his sword from the *geminus*. Blood seeped faster, both from him and his double. Ashen, the *geminus* stumbled, then sank to its knees. It pressed its hands to its chest. More blood oozed from between its fingers. A mortal wound.

Bram swayed on his feet. His chest was bathed in scarlet, yet he wore a fierce look of triumph.

Livia rushed to him and tried to place her hands against the wound, but they passed right through him. She fought to locate her magic, seeking its radiance within that she might work some spell, any spell, to help. Yet the more she searched, the less she found, only a growing darkness. Fear unlike any she had ever known shredded her.

"Gods, what have you done?" she cried.

"What I . . . had to." His face white, he listed, then went down hard on one knee.

Rage against her phantom stage threatened to choke her. She could do nothing, not even hold him up or touch him, comfort him. All she could do was watch as his leg gave out beneath him, and he toppled to the ground.

Dimly, she heard the *geminus* collapse onto the bare floorboards, as well. Yet her attention, and terror, held fast to Bram. She sank down, stroking her spectral hands over his pale forehead. His gaze never left her face.

"I can't . . . I can't stop this," she choked.

"Don't . . . want you . . . to stop it."

"No." She had no tears to shed. She had nothing but fury and sorrow. "There's a way to save you. I'll fetch a healer."

He shook his head, a faint movement. "No leeches. Can't be . . . saved. I have to . . . die." Already, the brilliant blue luster of his eyes faded.

"Why?" she demanded.

"For you and . . . for me. Livia . . ." He reached for her, his hand cupping her face, yet contacting only air. "I . . ."

His hand dropped to the floor. His eyes stared up, glassy and vacant.

"Bram! Bram!"

He did not answer her. He was dead.

Livia screamed. A scream of rage and grief and helplessness. She did not care if any mortal on the street could hear her. She did not care if the heavens collapsed and crushed the world. She cared for nothing. All she felt was anguish.

Whatever loss she had experienced in the whole of her existence—watching the destruction of Londinium, the sacrifice of her life to trap the Dark One—these were but motes of dust compared to this devastating agony.

All the power she had ruthlessly hoarded, for what? She couldn't help Bram, could not bring him back from death. She was as weak and useless as any mortal.

Her scream continued. It had no beginning, no end.

The walls rattled. Creatures that dwelled within them ran, scurrying for safety. And then—the windows exploded inward. Glass flew in every direction. It sprayed in glittering arcs.

Mortal voices exclaimed outside. Fleeing footsteps clattered over the paving stones.

Livia had no breath to catch. No need for air. She would scream and scream for all eternity, crouched beside Bram's body, until the house crumbled, until he was nothing but bones, until time itself became ash.

The darkness of the *Ambitus* was absolute. Not merely the absence of light, but the absence of everything. Heat, cold, time, distance. Bram plunged through this emptiness, or it enveloped him, or he was part of it. He had no sense of anything but oblivion.

No—not true. He knew one thing: Livia. Her face, beautiful and hollow with mystified grief, as she looked down at him. He knew regret, too. For he would have done anything to keep her from such agony. Yet there had been one choice, one path.

Or so he hoped. This fathomless shadow, he had not anticipated it. This place was very different without Livia's guiding magic and presence. He sensed a difference, too, for his body had died, severing him from the realm of the living

Was this it? Would there be no more? Had he thrown everything away for a chance that would never materialize?

I won't allow it.

Immersed in the darkness of the *Ambitus*, he felt a sharp tug. Drawing him downward. It felt like talons on his legs, trying to sink into his flesh and drag him away. He sensed something's immense hunger, a ravenous demanding of more and more, and the promise of pain. It waited for him, wanted him. The time had come for the bargain to be fulfilled. What had begun months ago in a ruined temple now saw its realization. For such a man as he, there was no alternative.

He was being dragged down into Hell.

Fury and fear tore through him. Not fear of punishment, but that he wouldn't succeed in his goal. He'd killed himself for a reason.

He had to break free of this relentless pull. Had to reach her. Everything would be lost if he failed.

He fought. Using his every ounce of strength and will, he fought. He kicked free of the grasping claws, grappling with the clinging shadows. Scaled arms thrashed against him, and he battled back, straining his power to its utmost. Yet it would take more than this to break away from the covetous grip of Hell.

Livia. He must get to her. It was for her that he ran a blade through his heart.

Summoning her face in his mind, he recalled her voice, her very essence. The unstoppable force that was her. It was a wonder he had resisted her for as long as he had, for she had a will as unbending as his own. More so, in truth. Yet even if he could not match her for resolve, his own was formidable, and he used it to shove back at Hell clutching at his heels.

The grip on him loosened. A howl of outrage sounded as he pushed away.

The amorphous darkness receded. Not fully—he was still mired in shadow, but shapes began to emerge, distinct forms. Form and distance solidified, including his own.

Shadows shaped themselves into rolling hills steeped in dusk. A continuous wind swept across the hills, smelling of loam and freshly dug graves. Isolated stands of trees dotted the hills. Shapes crouched upon their branches, larger than birds. Yet it was too dark for Bram to distinguish what, exactly, the crouched things were. A lace of rivers threaded through the landscape, glinting dully beneath a mist-shrouded evening sky. As he watched, the rivers shifted like snakes, and the hills undulated as if they were waves. They made soft groaning sounds.

Human figures roamed over the rippling hills, searching, directionless. Shadows and distance hid their faces. But everywhere he looked he saw these restless forms, and heard their voices upon the wind, speaking words without meaning, the rise and fall of human yearning tumbling over the knolls.

This was humanity's deepest mystery and greatest fear. The realm of the dead. The place no one could avoid.

Yet he sensed that these shadowed, unstable hills were but one aspect of the hereafter. He could sense its enormity, far beyond the limits of mortal understanding. He had already felt the tug of Hell—felt it now—and this place held a fraught tension, as though in a perpetual state of uncertainty. Neither the reward of Heaven, nor the torment of Hell.

Torment which awaited him. He had pushed back Hell's claws, but they wouldn't be held in abeyance forever. They would find him again. Not a matter of *if* but *when*.

One thought propelled him forward—*find her.*

Dried grass crackled under his feet as he ran. The tree branches were bare as bones. Nothing lived here, nothing thrived or grew. The sky overhead remained empty and without the possibility of light. No sun would ever rise. No stars would emerge, and the moon would never climb over the shifting horizon. The things in the tree branches muttered from their perches.

The ground shifted beneath him as he ran. He struggled to keep his footing, staggering like a drunkard but always moving forward, impelled by his need to find Livia. He held her image fixedly within his mind and heart—thoughts of her had helped free him briefly from Hell's grasp. He must use her as a beacon now, her light guiding him in this vast wasteland.

As he ran and the hills moved, faces emerged from the shadows, people pressing forward. They glowed as they neared. Upon their bodies they wore clothing from every era, from his own time back to coarse tunics and woad. Upon their faces they wore expressions of loss and bewilderment.

He shuddered inwardly. To be trapped for eternity in this half existence, neither rewarded nor punished, but perpetually adrift, stripped of hope. Not unlike the life he had been leading since his return from war. A shade of a man in eternal suspension.

He had purpose now.

Bram did not linger. He sped on, holding fast to thoughts of Livia, sensing the hungering presence of Hell at his back.

He willed the moving hills, commanding them with his determination. *I shall find her.*

As though responding to his thoughts, the hills buckled, forming an even darker vale where the shadows thickened and a twisting stream ran along the valley.

"Bring her to me, damn it," he growled.

"Bram—?"

He swung around. There, breaking free from the gloom on the other side of the stream, a woman in a saffron tunic appeared. She stepped nearer.

Her form . . . was solid.

It was her. He had willed her to him. And there she stood. Livia.

Bram stared, seeing Livia for the first time as an actual woman. Not a ghost or the hazy shape of her memories, but alive, and entire.

Her skin was olive-hued and burnished, her hair an opulent brown. And her eyes. Dark and sparkling and wise beyond measure. Wicked, too. Hers was a wisdom not limited solely to the mind.

When he saw grass flatten beneath her sandaled feet as she approached, his heart pounded. She did not glide or hover, but *walked*, her lush hips hypnotic beneath the silk of her gown. They stared at each other, he on one bank of the stream, she on the other. The stream itself was less than six feet across, so that, when he looked upon her, he could see the rise and fall of her chest, the wonderment that parted her lips.

"You are truly here?" Disbelief and hope tightened her voice.

She sounded different, as well. Her words came from actual breath, and were far richer and more potent than he could have believed.

"I've come for you."

"No one leaves this place."

"You will." He held out a hand for her.

He could only reach as far as the middle of the stream, his arm outstretched, his hand open and waiting.

For a moment, her gaze moved back and forth between his hand and his face. Then, slowly, she reached for him.

His breath refused to come as he watched her stretch out her hand. For so long he had wanted to touch her. To feel her skin against his. He'd never wanted anything more.

And then, at last, her fingers touched his.

The contact of skin to skin roared through him like a lightning storm. Only the brush of her fingers against his, and the pleasure was so acute he fought to remain standing.

Her fingers moved down the length of his, until their palms met, and they clasped each other's wrists.

He felt her pulse beneath his fingertips, and his throat ached. He tore his gaze away from the sight to look up at her face. Her eyes glistened.

Yet this was not enough. Still holding tight to her wrist, he stepped into the stream. Icy water flowed around his boots, and the rocky bed was slick, but he barely noticed. He pulled her toward him.

She gasped as she plunged forward, splashing into the water. And gasped again when their bodies met.

The stream twisted away, leaving them standing upon the

ground. This, too, shifted beneath them like a restless animal.

He didn't notice. He felt her, touched her. His mind stilled. His heart raced.

The length of her body pressed against his, warm and firm and living. Her arms were around his shoulders, pressing him tightly to her, and all he could do was simply *feel* her. In this vale of death, he knew only the sensation of Livia touching him and her in his arms. Made all the more wondrous and agonizing because it was their first and last time they would ever feel one another.

She pulled back enough to gaze up at him. "There is only one way to reach this place—death."

"You did not die to come here."

"But you did."

He nodded once, brief and clipped.

She clenched his shoulders. "Gods. Why?" Her throat worked. "Why would you doom yourself?"

"If one of us needs to be alive, it must be you."

"Don't you understand," she cried. "They will come for you. The demons. They'll drag you to Hades. There's no escaping them."

"I've already felt them at my heels. If I can outrun them a little longer, long enough to get you back to the realm of the living"—he smiled faintly—"then everything is as it should be." He threaded his fingers with hers. "It was my intent to find you and bring you back. I've accomplished one of those goals. Now it's time to realize the other."

"Nobody has ever returned."

"You will."

"But you shall not."

He remained silent.

"Damn you," she choked, pressing her face against his chest.

He held her close, cupping the back of her head. If they

could only stay like this. If only they had more than this moment. It would have to sustain him for what was to come.

And so it would.

Bram tensed as screams like rusty knives punctured the quiet. Even the creatures perched in nearby trees muttered in fear at the sound.

"Flee," Livia urged. She held up her hand, and glowing energy danced between her fingers. "I'll attempt to hold the demons back. You might conceal yourself, find some other realm in which to hide. Please. I cannot watch them drag you away."

He stepped back, her fingers still threaded with his. "I'll run, but I'm taking you with me. I will see you back amongst the living. And then . . ." He made himself grin. "Hell will have to contend itself with a true Hellraiser."

Chapter 11

Bram didn't know what the creatures were that intended to haul him to Hell—whatever they were, they'd be damned unpleasant, and he had no intention of letting them succeed in their goal—not until he'd gotten her safely to the other side. With Livia's hand clasped in his, he raced over the twilight hills.

Shadows and gloom spread over the landscape, oppressive in their absoluteness. This was a place in which the sun never rose. The ground radiated no lingering warmth, the grass and trees were fed by darkness.

Even with the creatures in pursuit, there was a physical tug within himself, pulling him down into the underworld. He gritted his teeth, fighting that demand.

Yet as Bram's heart pounded, he felt the heat of Livia's skin. And he heard the enraged pursuit of large, leather-skinned creatures. Their shrieks echoed over the hills, their fury a palpable thing.

Dark shapes gathered at the corners of his vision, and then he saw them. It would have been better to have remained ignorant of their appearance. They stood eight feet tall, and resembled putrefying corpses, their flesh hanging from their bones or else pulled tight in a decaying bloat. Some had patchy hair, but others' skulls gleamed through a web of skin, and their eyes were burning green orbs stuck into the sockets. Claws and serrated teeth ensured their prey would not escape.

Livia *would* be free. And then he'd contend with the demons.

"Where are we headed?" she gasped.

He did not break stride. "To find a way out."

"If this *can* happen, it will require an actual door."

"Know of any doors?" All he saw were hills and more hills.

"No," she panted. "Hold—the *gemini* use doors in the vault where they keep souls. The vault lies just beyond the *Ambitus*."

"Then we need to find that vault." He helped steady her when the ground buckled. The demons' growls sounded as they too fought against the unstable ground.

"Your soul is in it," Livia said. "But when the demons get hold of you, your soul's also pulled into Hell."

"Going there, anyway."

"Not yet," she shot back. "We can use your soul as a beacon, have it lead us to the vault. Use our thoughts to find them both." She chanced a quick look behind her. "Concentration's difficult."

"Has to be now." Bram kept his body moving, fighting to stay ahead of the demons as well as stay upright whilst the ground continued to reform itself beneath him. His mind and purpose, however, worked to find his soul's presence.

Everything was chaos and darkness. The Devil had possession of his soul, yet Bram almost doubted it existed. But he felt Livia's certainty, her belief in him, and, as they ran, he joined his thoughts with hers. Her presence filled him.

To his shock, he began to sense something. What was it?

"Yes," she encouraged. "More."

There—a gleaming warmth he instinctively recognized.

His soul. A shock to feel it, when he'd been so sure it didn't exist. But she'd brought him to it.

"Cleave to it, hold fast," Livia urged.

Following the beacon of his soul, he pushed through the layers separating the worlds. The dead landscape around them drifted away like smoke. He sensed Livia's own will, joining with his as they struggled upward, to the *Ambitus*.

Triumph surged when, just ahead of them, stone walls began to materialize from the darkness. Whatever it was, he and Livia had willed it into being.

And then they were inside.

Glancing around, he took in the chamber in which he and Livia stood. Calling it a *chamber* seemed too defined a word, for the heavy stone walls appeared to dissolve into twilight as they rose upward. Overhead, men and women drifted like autumn leaves. They skated across the surface of a too-large moon, their gazes searching, but vacant.

Bram turned his attention away from these shades and back to the nebulous chamber. The visible walls appeared thick, and large flagstones covered the floor. Along the walls were heavy wooden shelves. Upon the shelves, spherical objects rested. They glowed, these objects, brilliant, radiant. Replete with life. Simply to look upon them filled him with a bittersweet pleasure.

Souls.

"The vault of souls," Livia murmured. "Where your *geminus* keeps its plunder. It steals them from unknowing or foolhardy mortals."

"Stole," Bram corrected. "The thing's dead now. It can't thieve anymore."

The shelves were crowded with souls, some brighter than others, yet all of them painfully beautiful to look upon. The *geminus* had been busy, the foul bastard.

"There," Livia said, pointing to the far end of the vault, where a heavy wooden door marked the only way out.

They hurried toward it. Passing the numerous souls upon the shelves, he felt their life and vitality reaching out to him, warm where everything else in this terrible place was cold. The souls promised strength, power, the living essence of humanity. Intoxicating.

As they hastened farther into the vault, they came upon a large, thick table. A silver salver rested atop the table. An object lay upon the salver. Its golden radiance bathed the table, surprising in its intensity.

His soul.

Bram approached it warily, with Livia trailing behind him. He scowled in disbelief when his eyes grew hot. His soul should have been a cold black slab of rock, or a sickly, viscous lump that oozed acid. But he never anticipated this . . . this lambent beauty.

Anger scoured him. Didn't his soul understand that there was no beauty in him? Nothing good? How dare this thing shine like a little sun, insisting through its luminosity that he could be capable of decency and honor?

He was seized by impulse to grab his soul and throw it to the ground, crush it beneath the heel of his boot.

Livia neared the table with his soul, face alight with wonder. "This is yours," she whispered.

He did not question how she knew. "Yes."

An unfamiliar sheen gathered in her eyes as she stared at his soul. "You disputed its existence, but look how it shines." She turned to him with an unexpected scowl. "Curse you for throwing it away so easily."

The soul's brilliance still felt like an indictment. He took no pleasure in it, only knew the chasm between what he might have been and what he was.

The stone walls of the vault rattled. They shook with a noise like thunder, and over this came the demon's screams. They were trying to get inside.

"Come," he said, "it's time to get you from this place." He tore himself away from his soul, pulling her behind him.

At last, they reached the door. He pulled on its handle. It refused to move. "Damned thing's locked."

He backed up enough to give himself room, then kicked hard at the door. It rattled, but did not open. Again and again, he slammed his boot against the door. The bloody thing must open—he had to get her free. As he did, he felt the glow of magical energy growing within him, fed by his fury.

"Yes," she cried. "I can join our power." Chanting, she lifted her hands. Between her palms grew a swirling eddy of light. It gained in size, growing larger and larger, until it spun around her, then twisted toward the door.

The walls began to buckle. Demon shrieks grew louder as their fists pounded against the stone. Soon, they would be inside.

"Damn it," Bram shouted at Livia as he continued to kick at the door, "use all the magic we've got to get out of here."

"I've not worked a spell like this before," she said through clenched teeth. "It takes time."

"Which we haven't got." The demons would never let her open the door. Bram turned from the door and drew his sword. "Finish what we started. Get yourself through. I'll hold them off."

Livia's gaze locked with his. He saw she understood that this would be the moment of their parting. She started to reach for him, yet as she did, the spell weakened.

He moved back. They had touched for the last time. A sharp ache spread through his chest as he turned away to face the demons' onslaught. They had shattered large fractures in the vault's wall, and their long, cadaverous arms reached through to rake the air with their claws.

Bram readied himself for combat. He could never win

against these demons. They were death itself. But he could gain Livia time.

Something gripped his arm, and he spun around in an instinctive attack. It was Livia. He stopped his blade an inch above her throat.

"Finish the bloody spell and go," he snarled.

"I cannot work it on my own," she fired back. "It needs more of your magic for completion."

Cursing, he turned back to the doorway, yet he kept his sword unsheathed. "Tell me what I need to do."

"Say with me," she panted. A string of strange-sounding words curled from her mouth. "It's the only way I might have a chance of breaking the door open. Both of us, working the spell together."

He repeated the words, forcing himself to concentrate. Bloody hard to do when a horde of demons threatened, his every instinct to fight them rather than turn away. But even as he and Livia spoke in unison, the door glowed, and strained on its hinges.

Reaching for the power within himself, he chanted. Hers was there, as well, in him. Bright as a fire on a winter night. Stronger than ever before.

With a groan, the door swung open. Fathomless darkness lay beyond. At the same time, the far wall of the vault collapsed. The demons rushed in.

Immediately, the door began to close, as though the very act of opening was unnatural. Bram leapt forward and braced his free hand on it, still chanting, fighting against its tremendous weight. It wanted to shut, and he struggled to keep it propped open enough for Livia to slide through. His muscles burned at the excruciating strain, but he would release it.

"Go, damn you," he shouted when she hesitated, worriedly looking between him and the nearing demons.

Livia ducked under his arms, edging through the door.

He felt the pressure suddenly lessen. Looking down, he saw her hands gripping the door, pushing against it to keep it open. She hadn't run on to safety, to the realm of the living. She stayed behind for him.

"Leave," he growled. The demons were almost on them.

"Not without you." She wrapped one hand around his wrist, and with unexpected strength, pulled.

He tumbled through the doorway. It scraped against him as it began to swing closed. A demon's claw raked his shoulder. The door slammed shut.

And then, abruptly, he was swallowed by complete darkness.

Livia's scream abruptly stopped. Her throat felt raw. Her throat *felt*.

The floor was hard beneath her legs where she knelt. She was aware of the weight of her body, a mass of bones and muscles and solidity. Staring down at her hands, she saw they were opaque, and when she pressed them to the floor, she felt its dust and the grain of the wooden floorboards, the bite from miniscule pieces of glass.

Immortal Hecate, I'm alive. But how?

Her gaze flew to Bram. He lay upon the ground, his eyes open and sightless. Blood pooled upon the floor. His face was waxen and pale.

Across the room sprawled the body of the *geminus*. She barely glanced at it. All her attention was fixed on Bram.

Reaching out with a trembling hand, Livia placed her palm upon his chest. She gasped at the touch, but the gasp broke apart and turned jagged when she felt his stillness. He had brought her back—at the cost of his own life.

She could not marvel at her corporality, not when he lay dead on the floor of this crumbling building. She could only feel the renewal of sorrow. It was like the world being made then suddenly destroyed a moment later, the ember of life crushed out by an indifferent creator. She stood on a barren plain of loss, a howling nothingness on every side.

Something moved beneath her palm.

She snatched her hand back, then, tentatively, lay it down on his chest once more. There. Another pulse. Stronger this time.

Her breath caught as she felt his heart. Beating.

He suddenly arched up, gasping.

Livia stumbled back, falling onto her behind, as she stared at him.

He sat upright. His eyes widened as he saw the blood all around, his hands moving over his chest. He pulled at his shirt to uncover his skin. No wound pierced his heart. As color returned to his cheeks, he looked at her.

"You're . . ." His voice was hoarse. ". . . Here."

"As are you." Words, real *words*, came from her mouth. Everything was astounding, from the feel of her heartbeat to Bram, alive, gazing at her.

Slowly, they reached toward each other. Their hands paused as bright orbs of light streamed from the partially-open chamber door. Power permeated the chamber, imbuing it with tangible life and potential.

"Souls," Bram said, wondering. "From the vault. They must have fled with us."

She saw herself, in a vast stone-walled room, and the gleaming souls within. Including Bram's soul.

Other souls swirled around the room, yet her gaze went to Bram's immediately. It shined brighter than the others—not a pristine light, not pure, but replete with strength, and edged. It and the other souls spun through the chamber, borne upon the wave of magic she must have created within the realm of the dead.

The other souls veered out of the room, flying through the shattered windows and beyond, into freedom. They streaked away, seeking their owners. Watching the souls wing free, the space within herself became expansive, weightless. Some of the Dark One's wickedness had been undone, her own misdeeds set right.

Bram's soul remained. It circled the chamber as though wary.

Movements stiff, Bram got to his feet. She did the same, dimly aware that she stood for the first time in over a thousand years on solid legs, her own strength keeping her upright.

Both she and Bram watched, unspeaking, as his soul neared. He eyed it guardedly.

"It doesn't want me," he said, bleak.

"You belong together," she answered.

He raised his chin, the line of his jaw hard as he stared at it. Belligerent, challenging. "Stay or go," he said. "Make your choice."

Livia held her breath as the soul hovered at a distance, as if deliberating. Aware of time at last, she felt another thousand years pass as both she and Bram waited for the soul to make a decision.

Her breath left her as the soul began to drift forward. She chanced a look at Bram—his eyes briefly closed, his only admission of relief, then opened again.

Only a few feet separated Bram from his soul. In a moment, they would be united after so long apart.

She staggered as the house suddenly quaked, and Bram braced his legs wide to absorb the shock waves. They both glanced around, alarmed, looking for the source of the tremor.

A man appeared in the chamber. The Dark One.

Before she or Bram could move, the Devil reached out. He snatched Bram's soul from the air. As if he were stealing an apple.

His long white fingers gripped the soul, and he brought

it against his chest, cradling his prize. He drawled, "This is mine."

Nausea rolled through her to see the Dark One touching Bram's soul.

"Return it," Livia spat.

Bram raised his sword, his face dark with fury. "Thieving bastard."

The Dark One lifted his brows. "To the contrary, we made a fair exchange. It is you who undermines the terms of our agreement." He made a sound of disapproval. "And look," he continued, glancing toward the body of the *geminus*, "you've gone and cost me one of my best servants. Quite ungentlemanly."

Indeed, he looked a gentleman. He wore a suit of embroidered silver satin, expertly tailored to his lean form, and in his hand he carried an ivory-tipped ebony walking stick. He was ageless, his skin unlined, yet his pulled back hair shone a pure white that did not come from powder. His eyes were as glass, the pupils vivid black dots in the middle of colorless irises. He might have been a handsome man of fashion but for the color of his hair and eyes—and the unmitigated malevolence pouring off of him in poisoned waves.

"This isn't gentlemanly, either," said Bram, and he lunged with his sword at the Dark One.

The Devil merely waved his hand, and the sword in Bram's grip transformed into a snake. Instead of stabbing the Dark One, the serpent reared back, hissing. Bram threw the snake across the chamber before it could strike him. It coiled in the corner.

"Don't need a blade to make you hurt," Bram growled. In a blur of movement, he darted forward, fists swinging.

The Dark One merely waved his hand again, and Bram flew backward, slamming into the wall. Chunks of plaster rained down as he groaned and slid to the ground, conscious but dazed.

Red-limned fury boiled through Livia. She sensed her magic within her, whole now. Yet difficult to wield—this physical body of hers felt ungainly after the lightness of being a phantom.

She imagined the shapes of ancient symbols, simplest writing from the earliest time of desert and flood. With them called forth the most powerful spell she knew, a killing curse. Burning power poured through her, singeing her within—she had forgotten how visceral magic could be. It fed her rage. With a snarl, she flung the spell at the Dark One, and it shot from her hands like lightning.

Smirking, the Devil simply flicked his fingers, and the spell turned to a clot of harmless black flies. They flitted away into the dust of the house.

"Truly, Valeria Livia Corva," he sniffed, "have you learned nothing from our long association? None of your magic, nor your flimsy mortal weapons, can harm me."

Livia only glared at him as she hurried to Bram's side. He was already rising to his feet, despite the hard blow he'd been given. Still, he looked a little unsteady, and she wrapped her arm around his waist, supporting him as he stood.

Despite the Dark One's presence, she yet marveled at the feel of Bram, at her own solidity and the heat and sensation of his body.

"You've cost me a great many souls," the Devil continued. He held up Bram's soul, admiring it the way one would a prized bauble. "This one I shall keep." He turned his pale, cold gaze on Bram. "The promise you held—all wasted."

"If I get to slice that smirk off your face," Bram answered, "then nothing's wasted."

The Dark One pressed his lips together into a white line. "Your mistake is a costly one. There shall be no safety. No peace. Killing you will be merely the commencement of your suffering."

He did not snap his fingers nor wave his hand. The Devil simply disappeared like a candle winking out. Yet he left behind a miasma of evil, choking the air with its malevolence. Livia's stomach roiled from it—and she started at the unfamiliar sensation.

Rage followed on its heels. "If I could rip him into bloody scraps, I'd do it."

Bram laughed humorlessly. "Damned once more."

"We'll get it back," she said, heated.

"Love, I never thought to get my soul back at all."

She stared at him, and her throat tightened. "If the Dark One hadn't already done so, I'd curse you a thousand times." The urge to strike out was so strong, she clenched her hands into fists.

He raised his brows. "You've an odd way to show gratitude."

"Gratitude!" She stalked to him. "How am I to feel *grateful* to you for killing yourself? With my own eyes I watched your blood pool on the floor, I saw the life leave your body." Her voice was a rough rasp. "And there was nothing, not one accursed thing, I could do to help."

His gaze darkened. "I'd never willingly pain you. I wish it hadn't been so, but there it is."

"So insouciant about your own death. *Knowing* that you were to face eternal suffering. Why? Why would do such a thing?"

Quietly he said, "You know why."

Her breath left her in a hiss. A shock to feel her eyes heat.

"In war, there were so many I couldn't save," he said. "Even my death couldn't have helped them. Yet I had a chance to save you, and, by hell's fire, I had to take it."

"I'll not allow you to make such a sacrifice again."

A corner of his mouth turned up. "Allow? Last I noted, my will was my own."

"And almost suffered everlasting agony as a result."

"No—*you* kept that from happening. Were it not for you, at this moment some demon would be ripping out my entrails. You risked your own eternity for me. So, enough of your rebuke."

"Swear that you will not take such a chance again," she insisted.

"Like hell. I'll do it over and over if I have to. And you'd do the same."

She could not deny it. Gods, he knew her too well. A terrifying, humbling feeling. "We cannot linger here." She looked at the snake in the corner. Its jet eyes watching her and Bram, it uncoiled and slithered into a gap in the baseboard. "The Dark One's power is flawed. He needs others to complete his work. Either he will send demons, or tell John where we are, and finish the job."

"A shame my father only kept one mistress." Despite the nonchalance of his words, Bram's voice was tight with pain as he rubbed the back of his head. "Running out of places to take shelter." He looked down at her, and his eyes blazed vivid blue. "My God, *look* at you." His fingers stroked along her throat, lingering on the flutter of her pulse. "I can touch you. Wherever I want. As long as I want."

She fought to keep her eyes open, but it was a struggle. She wanted nothing more than to sink into his touch, into this new realm of sensation. Yet—"We must leave," she said, regretful. "Time runs away from us, and we're in poor condition to fight."

He took his hand away, though his movement was reluctant. "There's a warehouse not far from here, in Wapping. It belongs to Leo. Should be empty."

"Does John know of it?"

"Unlikely. He had little concern for Leo's financial

endeavors. And I only know of it because Leo tricked me into going. Said there'd be some female company to meet us, yet there wasn't anything but a shipment of India cotton he wanted to gloat over. I left right away. Found it dull as church."

Of course he did. "Can you walk?"

He straightened, testing the strength of his legs. "Enough to get to the stable out back."

"Let us hence," she said. The corporeal weight of her body felt heavy, and her magic dimmed with her exhaustion. Each moment they tarried in this house meant John or some other demonic creature could be drawing closer, and with them, bringing a fight that neither she nor Bram could win. Not now.

Together, his arm around her shoulders and hers clasped around his waist, they made their way back through the house. They did not get far out of the chamber and into the corridor before he halted their progress.

"Careful," he said, "there's broken glass all over the floor." He frowned at the empty windows. "The Devil's doing, I'd gather."

"Mine." When he glanced down at her questioningly, she explained, "Your . . . death. Distressed me." Even speaking of it now, when he was beside her and clearly not dead, felt like a fresh wound.

His arm still around her shoulders, Bram turned her to face him. His face seemed carved from stone, harsh and beautiful. The heat of his gaze scorched her, alight with hunger. She had seen his face many times, of course, in memory and in truth. Yet now she gazed upon him with mortal eyes, from within a mortal body, and the difference was potent, both drugging and quickening. She could feel the waves of need coming from him, and the answering demands of her own body.

He released his hold on her shoulder, moving his hands

to cup the back of her head. The sensation of his rough fingertips sliding through her hair and against her scalp traveled the length of her body. He walked them backward until she met the wall. It felt as solid and hard as Bram himself. The whole while, his gaze never left hers.

Both weakness and strength surged through her. What he had willingly surrendered, for her . . . she could hardly comprehend it. And to have all of him, solid and true, pressed to her, to have sensation after so long without—it was too much, and she wanted more.

"Your hair, your skin," he growled. "Everything. I tried so damned hard to imagine what you'd feel like."

"Have I surpassed your imagining?"

"The difference between a candle and a conflagration. You demolish me."

Her heart was laid bare. The things she had seen and done in her life, and the centuries that followed, wicked and cruel woman that she was, she'd thought herself inured to emotions such as these. Feelings were for the young and credulous, those who hadn't gained experience or sense to protect themselves. Here she was, past youth, past innocence, and with his words and gaze and touch, she felt as raw and open as if she had been torn, squalling, from the flesh of the world.

She wanted to touch him everywhere, run her hands over his body, his face. Draw him into her completely. She stretched up on her toes. As she did, her hands and breasts slid along his chest, and she moaned at the contact. The need she felt for him was a palpable thing, an ache.

He tipped her head back. His mouth lowered to hers.

Her breath caught, anticipatory. Their lips touched. She exhaled.

The gods protect her. His kiss . . .

He knew this art. He knew her. But they had never done this together. And it was the dawning of everything.

His lips were firm against hers, yet supple. They traced her mouth, learning the shape and feel in measured exploration. Control did not last—for either of them. For with only a few touches of lips to lips, hunger erupted from its cage, tearing through her. She opened her mouth and stroked her tongue against his.

An animal sound rumbled deep within him. His tongue met hers, and they loosed themselves upon each other. A greedy consuming. He tasted of autumn apples and masculine spice. The first thing she had tasted since made flesh. Over a thousand years, she had known no flavor, and now—him. If she tasted nothing else for the rest of her days, she would be content.

He pressed her tight between the wall and his body. She pushed back into him, straining. She felt his kiss everywhere. She learned her own body all over again, discovering it as his kiss drew awareness from her and filled her with sensation. It was a revelation of the soft and needy places in her body, in the thick beat of her heart. Her hands drifted from his chest to roam all over him, at last knowing the hewn hardness of his form, taut and muscled and living.

She gasped against his mouth when he grabbed her wrists and pinned them to the wall.

"The final thread of my sanity will snap if you keep touching me," he rumbled.

"I've been mad," she said, breathless. "We can lose our minds together."

Yet he did not release her. Finally she knew his true strength, unrelenting, as he held her fast to the wall. He trailed his mouth along her jaw, then lower, down the curve of her neck, until he reached the hollow at the base of her throat. He licked her there, and made a growling sound of appreciation.

"Succulent," he murmured. "All of you."

Her body had fully wakened. She knew what she was

capable of, and wanted it with him. "Kiss me again," she demanded. "Just one."

Yet he stepped back. "We both know it can't stop at one kiss. And we both know that we have to get the hell out of here. Now."

Every part of her protested. She also knew he spoke the truth, much as it pained her.

She pushed away from the wall. "How far is it to this . . . Wapping?"

His gaze raked her. "Too far." Yet he held out his hand to her.

After drawing a shuddering breath, she laced her fingers with his.

He moved to rest his free hand on the hilt of his sword, then scowled when he discovered there was no sword. "I've a bloody armory at home. But home isn't a possibility."

With a quick incantation, she conjured up a small crackle of lightning that sparked from the tips of her fingers. "We aren't entirely without defense." Her magic, however, hadn't its normal strength, tapped as it was by the trying events of the day.

Bram walked along the corridor and down the stairs leading to the basement, towing Livia behind him. They passed through the kitchen, and then stepped out into ashen day. Pale as the sunlight was, she still blinked and squinted, adjusting herself to the new phenomenon.

He glanced at her, and she knew he saw her for the first time in true daylight. She even cast a small shadow, watery though it was in the weak, diffused sunshine.

"A force beyond nature, that's what you are. Yet you're mortal, too." He stared at the place in her wrist where her pulse beat. "Vulnerable. The Devil knows it. And to hurt you, he'll go to any lengths."

"I won't hide. You voyaged to the realm of the dead to ensure I'd fight."

"So I did. And I wouldn't be here if it hadn't been for you. We fight together." He placed a fingertip beneath her chin. "I'll arm myself. Then God help who or whatever stands against us."

She said nothing. Brave, his words were, but the Dark One was an enemy few could defeat. Whatever had enabled her to trap him once before, she doubted such miracles occurred twice in a lifetime.

Chapter 12

Though the streets were nearly empty, Livia felt herself ablaze with awareness and power. She perceived everything—the wash of light over the cobbles, the feel of clammy air rippling over her skin, the stink of refuse rotting in the gutter. Voices and sounds were louder, sharper, and she drew everything into herself, feeding upon sensation.

Bram rode through the city, with her sitting behind him, her arms clasped about his waist. She held onto him as a means to restrain herself. Now that she possessed form and flesh, she wanted to devastate, to devour everything. The greed she had felt once was miniscule by comparison. She had been denied for a millennium. No longer. Magic and power hummed through her veins. She felt herself capable of anything.

Valeria Livia Corva had returned.

Pushing down her avarice taxed her. It felt as though she struggled to chain a starved lioness. And everywhere was meat, fresh and bloody.

Bram drew up beside a shop and dismounted. After helping her down, they went inside, his hand a continual assuring presence as it clasped hers.

A bell rang when they entered. Merchandise of every

description filled the small shop—chairs and desks, baskets brimming with clothing, porcelain, framed paintings, even stringed musical instruments. Light barely penetrated the crowded window.

A dark-haired woman emerged from the dusty shadows. Livia whirled to face her, then saw herself. She stared at her reflection in a mirror. Tentative, she approached, studying herself. She had not truly seen herself in over a thousand years. The mirrors of this era were far better than the ones of her time, revealing every nuance and detail in their polished surfaces.

"How may I be of assistance, my lord?" A shopkeeper appeared, her gray hair pinned beneath a cap. She paused when she saw the bloodstains on Bram's clothing.

"I've need of several items," answered Bram.

The shopkeeper recovered. "There is nothing you cannot find in my establishment."

"Swords."

"I keep them in the back," she replied.

"Bring them out. Quickly, for we've not much time."

"Yes, my lord." There came a soft clatter as the woman picked her way to the back of her shop.

Livia barely heard their conversation. Her attention held on the image of herself in the mirror. There—she could see the rise and fall of her chest as she breathed, and she could just make out the faintest crease in the corner of each eye. And a few silver strands interwove with her dark hair. At the time of her death, she had not been a girl, but a woman grown. Nothing had changed. Everything had changed.

Bram's image appeared behind hers in the mirror. Dark, lean, his jaw and cheeks covered with stubble but his eyes sharp as cut sapphires, he was as feral as she.

"Are you as you remembered yourself?" he asked.

"That woman was greedy and vain." She traced her

finger around the outline of her face in the glass. "A wicked creature."

"Transformation is better than reformation."

She exhaled a small laugh. "If I'm to keep myself in check, you'll need to offer me more restraint than that."

"The last thing I can offer you is restraint." Raw hunger gleamed in his eyes.

A throb of need resounded low in her belly. What they had started back in the abandoned house truly was the beginning of something ravenous, something that could consume them both in its heat and immensity.

They both seemed to understand that they hadn't the luxury of time to explore their desire. Their gazes broke apart, an act of mutual self-preservation.

"Here you are, sir," the shopkeeper said, returning. She cleared off a section of the cluttered counter and set several long wooden cases atop it. "All legitimately acquired, I can assure you. From gentlemen who have found themselves in impecunious circumstances."

Both Livia and Bram turned to examine the cases as the shopkeeper opened the lids. Rust-colored velvet cradled half a dozen swords of different sizes and shapes, some thin-bladed, others heavier and curved. Knowing little of weaponry, Livia watched Bram as his trained and critical gaze moved over the various swords.

He picked up one weapon and frowned at it, turning it this way and that, running his finger along its edge. Whatever he saw there did not meet his standards, and he returned it to the case. He took another sword and did the same inspection. Moving into the center of the shop, he took several practice swings, his movements precise and fluid.

As many times as Livia had seen Bram in combat or even practicing his swordplay, she continued to be enthralled by the sight of him in motion. The shopkeeper thought so, as well.

"This will do," Bram said, setting the sword on the counter. "A pistol, too, if you have one."

"I do," the woman answered. "I also have some fine garments that might interest you, my lord. And you, my . . . er . . . lady," she added, glancing at Livia. Her gaze moved over Livia's tunic and sandals.

"Bring those, as well," said Bram.

"My tunic is made of silk from Seres," Livia insisted when the shopkeeper bustled off again. "Carried thousands of miles upon the backs of camels, over treacherous mountains and scorching deserts."

"Lovely, to be sure. But a beautiful woman dressed in the style of Ancient Rome invites attention. And we don't want attention."

He was right. Too many dangers lurked close. When the shopkeeper returned, her arms full of rustling dresses, Livia selected one that seemed closest to her size and preference—a gown of apricot-hued silk, trimmed with blue ribbon. The ribbon was frayed, and some of the stitches along the sleeves gaped. Livia eyed this evidence of wear with distaste. She had never worn second hand garments.

"I'll take you back to Madame De Jardin's," Bram said. "A whole new wardrobe, made for you alone."

Neither voiced the question as to when they would have the gowns made. It spoke of a future that she nor Bram could vouch for.

"I also brought some, ahem, undergarments." The shopkeeper surreptitiously uncovered a snug-looking white article that appeared as though it encircled the torso.

Livia poked the garment. It was rigid. Like a cage. "I'm to *wear* this?"

"Begging your pardon, my lady, but have you not worn stays before?"

"She's from Italy," said Bram.

The shopkeeper nodded sagely. "I see you have no maid with you today, my lady. If you'll follow me, I can help dress you."

Livia was no stranger to being clothed by a servant. From the time she had been a small child and all through adulthood, she'd had slaves and later temple acolytes who had served her. With a regal nod, she let herself be led to the back of the shop, to a cramped, curtained nook.

Dressing was an exercise in constraint as she was squeezed into the stays and draped in layer after layer of garments. Several minutes of this and then she emerged from the nook, the older woman trailing behind her.

Bram had been peering out the window, scowling as he surveyed the street, yet when he caught sight of her, his scowl lifted. He prowled toward her, gaze hot and lingering on her exposed chest.

"These modern clothes suit you very well," he murmured, eyeing the low neck of her gown.

"The stays are an appalling contrivance," she answered. "Even worse that women of this time submit to them. And no Roman woman of virtue reveals herself so boldly."

"The sacrifices we must make for the sake of modernity."

"I note *you* aren't the one with a cage of metal around your ribs." She glanced down critically at the garment. "My own clothing was better."

"You flatter whatever you wear." Bram swore in frustration. "Damn John and the Devil. If they weren't threatening to tear London apart, I'd show you my appreciation."

Her cheeks heated, and the shopkeeper coughed. Livia reveled in the warmth flooding her face—it meant she was alive, and earthly. Yet she could do nothing to explore her carnality. Not with such meager time and safety. Like Bram, she cursed circumstance.

She made a sweep of the shop, gathering up a few items. "I'll want these," she told the shopkeeper.

"Yes, madam." The older woman could not fully hide her curiosity at Livia's selections, but Livia had neither the time nor interest in explaining the intricacies of spellcasting.

They concluded the rest of their business quickly. Bram purchased a pistol, a lantern, and a shirt that was threadbare but clean. He declined to barter his coat and waistcoat. When the shopkeeper offered him actual money for Livia's silk tunic and gold ornaments, he looked to Livia for the answer.

Livia considered the muslin-wrapped bundle she now carried. In this world, she had no wealth, only the things wrapped in a bolt of coarse fabric. Doubtless she could fetch a considerable amount for her jewelry, at the least. And she had been trapped in the same garments for over a thousand years. Easy to grow tired of them after so long.

"I purchased the bracelets from a Greek artisan," she murmured. "He had a shop in Trajan's Market." The artisan long ago had turned to dust, and the market itself likely was a ruin. Her jewelry and clothing were relics—like her.

"I'll keep them," she said.

The shopkeeper looked disappointed, yet, seeing Livia's resolve, acquiesced. A large handful of coins on the counter helped silence the older woman's objections.

Glancing toward the window, Livia saw that the sky darkened. "Darkness is falling." Which meant that the danger increased. The Devil preferred to carry out his work under cover of night. Though soon, if he went unopposed, day or night would no longer matter. All of it would be darkness, and every moment would be misery.

She felt it even stronger now that she had been given flesh—the Dark One's growing strength. It choked the streets and wove its way between the smallest crevices in the buildings. Unseen but palpable.

The shopkeeper now seemed eager to have Livia and Bram leave. She scooped up the coins into a pocket in her apron, and all but shoved her and Bram out the door.

Dusk cloaked the street, and figures scuttled in the shadows. Livia pressed the bundle of her clothing to her chest and shivered from the cold. In a swirl of velvet, Bram draped his coat over her shoulders. His warmth and scent enveloping her gave some comfort, yet for all his strength and determination, he was still mortal. As was she. They could both be hurt. Or worse.

Silently, he paid the boy holding the reins of his horse. The boy scurried off the moment the coin touched his palm.

Bram mounted his horse, secured her bundle of old clothes, then held out a hand for her. She seated herself behind him, struggling a little with the mass of her cumbersome gown, then clasped her arms around his waist. Warily vigilance tightened his body. The night held a venomous chill, as though it had been honed to a cutting edge.

"And now?" she asked, her words barely a whisper.

"We seek shelter where we can." He pressed his heels into the horse's side, setting it in motion. "But whatever safety we find won't last."

Bram seethed with frustration. None of the circumstances were as he wanted them. Here was Livia, no longer a spirit but a woman of flesh, and he wished to take her back to his home, settle her upon a fireside couch strewn with silk pillows, feed her scalloped oysters, sweetmeats, the tender leaves of artichokes glazed in butter. There would be glasses of full-bodied Chambertin gleaming like rubies. He wanted a soaking tub filled with warm water perfumed by jasmine blossoms. He desired gowns of crimson damask, emerald faille—bright, rich hues to flatter her olive skin. He would surround her in luxury, in comfort, in sensuous pleasure.

Instead, they crouched on a coarse woolen blanket on the dusty floor of an empty dockside warehouse, gnawing on stale bread and tough lumps of mutton, trading sips from a bottle of dubious wine—the only food he'd been able to procure.

Riverside chill seeped between the cracks in the walls. Noisome vapor, smelling of rot and sludge, curled amongst the few crates left behind from the last shipment. It was so quiet Bram heard the water slapping against the pilings. Yet the other sounds of river traffic and life, the ferrymen and mudlarks and stevedores loading and unloading ships, those were absent.

The whole of London seemed suspended, waiting, an animal crouched in anticipation of a coming attack.

But he was no toothless, shivering dog rolling onto its back. Watching Livia consume her first meal in over a thousand years, her expression carefully neutral though he knew the stale food was a disappointment, he vowed to fight whoever and whatever threatened. As soon as her strength was restored, she would cast a spell to release the other Hellraisers. And then the fight would truly begin.

Despite the middling quality of the food, Livia devoured everything. Bram gave her the remainder of his meal over her objections.

"It'll do me good to get back to army rations," he said. "A man with an overfull belly makes for a poor soldier. Besides," he added, "my last meal was only hours ago. A whole millennium has passed since you ate."

"Spiced wine," she mused. "Oysters, partridge with figs and walnuts, boar in *garum*. Pears from my own villa's orchard and honey from my apiary."

"Not half as fine," he said, glancing down at the remainder of the food, "but it's all we have, and you need it far more than I."

Before she could object further, he stood and moved through the warehouse. He had already made an initial reconnaissance, but there was no such thing as being too aware of one's surroundings. The structure had a high ceiling, and was large enough to hold cargo from several ships. Aside from a few crates and a dusty bolt of cotton, the warehouse stood empty. A battered desk and three-legged stool huddled in the corner. Searching the desk drawers yielded only scraps of paper, the ink faded to nigh illegibility. Tucked into the very back of the top drawer, however, he found a slim-bladed knife, which he tucked into his boot.

Two large doors could be used for bringing goods in and out of the warehouse, but a stout padlock kept out all would-be thieves and squatters. He and Livia had gained entrance through a smaller door, also locked, but easily breached through her use of a quick spell.

The slight effort had cost her. She had moved listlessly into the warehouse, and sank down onto the blanket he had spread on the ground. It seemed the simple act of being within her body again took a toll. Thus, he gladly went without a full supper, no matter his own demanding appetite.

He gazed back through the gloom shading the warehouse. They had taken a small chance and brought the lantern purchased at the shop to dispel some of the darkness. In contrast to her surprisingly delicate shape, outlined against the lantern's glow as she continued to eat, she radiated power. Despite everything that had taxed her, she remained an unstoppable storm.

I'm awed by her.

He expected an answer to his thoughts. She had been within his mind for, what, days? Weeks? Whatever the span of time, it now felt perfectly natural to have her thoughts interwoven with his own, her voice nestled into the recesses of his mind. Gone, now. They were separate entities once again.

He turned away to continue his patrol, primed pistol at the ready, his hand upon the hilt of his sword.

She might no longer haunt him, yet he was aware of her at all times. The quiet rustle of her skirts as she shifted. Her very presence like an ember in the darkness.

His body tightened in response. It knew she had flesh now, that she could be touched, and both his heart and his body demanded the same thing—her.

Yet she was hungry, tired, overwhelmed by the world and the immensity of the enemy they faced. The curse barring the Hellraisers from coming to their aid needed to be broken. She had to cast the spell to break that curse. He had to keep a harsh rein on his needs, painful though it was.

She rose up from the blanket, took the lantern, and moved toward him. Her footsteps echoed softly through the warehouse, and this simple sound made his blood race as she approached.

The lamplight gilded her skin, the underside of her jaw, and nestled in the shadows of her hair. She had a rolling, sensuous walk, full-hipped.

Her gaze was troubled as she came to stand before him. "This place is ill-omened."

"Not an amiable part of the city, Wapping. Sailors live here."

"It's not a mortal evil I sense."

His sword was drawn before she finished speaking. He glared into the darkness. "Damn—thought we'd be safe here."

"For now, we are," she amended. "But our safety won't last. The realm below is a kettle on the verge of boiling over, their world erupting into ours."

"And John's the bastard throwing fuel on the fire." Bram sheathed his sword. "The time to move against him is now."

"The time is *soon*," she corrected. "When this"—she set the lantern upon the floor and twin spheres of light appeared in her palms, gleaming with power—"grows stronger."

"I've weapons of my own." He glanced at his sword and pistol.

"And more." One of the spheres of light blinked away, and she touched the tips of her fingers to the center of his chest. Yet when she touched him, another gleam appeared—and he was its origin. Its warmth spread through him.

"How?" he wondered.

"Because I helped you unlock your magic." She took her fingers away, and the light continued to shine. "Years of study and training were needed before I could truly access my power. For you, it's merely the work of a few moments."

"Never thought I was gifted with magic."

"On your own—no. You had a benefit I did not." She smiled at him. "Me."

They both watched as the light slowly faded, a lambent warmth lingering within him.

She said, "Now you wield your power the way a priestess might."

"A priest, not a priestess. And I refuse to take a vow of chastity."

"I may as well ask the fire not to burn." Her smile dimmed. "You and I aren't enough to win this war."

He saw what she meant to do. "You aren't strong enough yet."

"There isn't time to wait. It must be done now. Tonight."

"At what risk to you?"

"Impossible to know."

"Damn it," he growled, "I didn't stick a blade into my own chest just to lose you again."

Her dark gaze held his. "No one is more aware of what

you sacrificed. This is the reason you made that choice. The peril is greater now. My magic is, too."

She spoke the truth. He did not like it. "I'll lend my power to yours."

"All I ask of you is vigilance whilst I work the spell."

He gave a clipped nod.

"Come back with me to the blanket," she said, nodding toward their makeshift accommodations. "The spell requires I should kneel, and I've no desire to test the fortitude of my new flesh upon this . . ." She eyed the grimy floor. ". . . This surface."

They returned to where the woolen blanket was spread upon the ground. She set the lantern down, then arranged several objects upon the blanket—things she'd gathered from the chandler's. The feather, the stub of a candle, a pearl.

When she'd positioned them to her liking, she kicked off her slippers, revealing glimpses of slim feet and curved ankles. Need built as she knelt upon the blanket, her movements economical yet elegant, her skirts billowing around her like faded petals upon water.

"Have you a blade?"

Frowning, he handed her the knife he had found in the desk. His jaw clenched when she dragged the blade across her thumb, a bright line of crimson appearing in its wake.

She dripped blood upon the objects, staining the feather, candle and pearl with red. Then she trickled her blood on the ground, murmuring softly as she did so. It looked obscene, the red purity of her blood mixing with the filth coating the floor. A desecration of her body. Yet her expression remained composed, removed, as blood fell in ruby droplets.

His hand upon his sword, senses attuned to the slightest movement or sound, he watched her eyes close. Her dark lashes were lacy against the upper curve of her cheek. The arcane words she murmured grew in strength and volume.

They seemed to fill the cavernous space of the warehouse with their intricacy, complex as labyrinths.

Light gathered around her, gold and lambent. It covered her, its radiance like a cascade sweeping across her in waves. An unseen wind pulled her hair from its pins so it blew about her shoulders. Though Bram remained alert to any signs of intrusion, he could not look away from her, shining like a goddess. Her magic turned the air electric. He could feel it in the reticulation of his veins and sponge of his lungs. When he breathed, he breathed her power.

The glow surrounding her grew, spreading outward until it formed a sphere that encompassed them both. Energy skittered across his skin.

The light abruptly flickered, dimming. Livia swayed and her voice weakened. She looked suddenly haggard. Alarmed, he darted forward. Something was awry. Yet before he could touch her, her eyes opened. They glowed. Her irises and pupils were no longer visible, replaced by more golden light.

He halted, his hand hovering over her shoulder. She stared directly at him, but did not see him at all. She chanted louder. With a flare, the glow surrounding her returned, stronger now, so that it stretched out in a radius that engulfed half the warehouse.

A gust of wind pushed Bram back. He struggled to keep standing as Livia's voice increased in volume and the tempest battered at him.

The unknown language she spoke shifted, and she cried in English, "Return—there are no barriers! Hellraisers, the time to undo your wickedness is at hand. *Revertimini!*"

The light around her flared, blinding him, and the warehouse shook. Small pieces of wood shook down from the ceiling and struck the floor. Abruptly, the wind died, the light was quenched, and stillness enfolded the building.

Bram blinked, clearing his vision from its dull red

glow. He rushed forward when he saw Livia supine upon the blanket.

Falling to his knees, he gathered her up. She lay listless and unmoving in his arms. But for the slight rise and fall of her chest, she was utterly still. He stroked her hair, her cheeks, his heart pounding fierce enough to rip from the cage of his ribs. She felt altogether too slight, too fragile. Her cheeks were pale, the beat of her pulse barely fluttering against the fine skin of her throat.

He brushed his lips against hers. Light as thistledown, her breath, and shallow. He drew upon it, as though he could pull it from her and drag her back to consciousness.

"Livia, love," he urged, his voice a rasp, "you aren't to go anywhere. Is that understood?"

There was no response from her. Not a word spoken, nor even a flutter of an eyelash.

"I'm a wastrel," he continued, "but I'm a soldier, and a bloody officer. I won't be gainsaid. Disobeying me is a whipping offense. You obey me now, damn you."

The softest movement of her lips. She struggled to form words.

His throat burned as it constricted. "What is it, love?"

"I obey . . ." She drew in a thready breath. ". . . No one."

"Just this one time, do what you're told." His heart was a leaping animal when her eyes opened, dark and rich, and focused on him. He could not stop touching her face.

"Only this once," she whispered. "I caution you, however . . . do not get . . . accustomed to such behavior."

"I am duly warned." He glanced down at the rough woolen blanket spread upon the ground. "Damn. You need to rest, but I don't want you touching this coarse thing."

She lifted her head enough to glance around the warehouse. "Take me to the desk."

He gathered her up in his arms and carried her the

distance. The feel of her nestled against him, her soft, sleek weight, coursed like fire.

She instructed, "Say the following." She spoke series of words in a tongue he'd never heard before.

He repeated the words as best he could. Nothing happened.

"The second syllable of the fourth word needs to be drawn out," she said, and repeated the spell.

He fought for patience. A damned linguistics lesson when she needed rest. But he mimicked her pronunciation of the words. To his surprise, a glow spread out from his chest. It flowed from him to surround the desk.

When light dissipated, the desk had transformed into a low, Roman-style couch. It had curved wooden legs, elaborately carved and gilded, and was covered by a long silk-wrapped cushion. More bright silk pillows were strewn about the couch, tasseled with gold. A small brazier at the foot of the couch sent spice-fragrant smoke curling up toward the beams of the ceiling.

"A useful spell," he murmured. "We could've used this when first we arrived here."

"The outcome of my spellcasting was unknown. I was uncertain if we would need your magic for something else. Healing, or retrieval. But now . . ."

Carefully, he arranged her on the couch. Her skirts rustled as she settled back, combining with her sigh in an intimate caress of sound.

After retrieving the bottle, he discovered a few swallows of wine left in the bottom. He put the bottle to her lips, and she took a sip. A droplet of wine clung to her bottom lip. Rather than lick it off, he drank from the bottle. It did nothing to quench his thirst, especially after the tip of her tongue darted out and caught the droplet.

"The spell is broken?" He needed to occupy his thoughts with the looming danger, or else he would stretch himself out beside her, or cover her body with his own, seeking out her hot and yielding places.

"The other Hellraisers may cross water now. I have summoned them to us. The matter of getting here, and how quickly, that is theirs to determine." She let out a long exhale. "Bram?"

"What is it, love?"

"I feel strange."

"How?"

"Heavy and lethargic, and my eyes keep trying to close."

He leaned over her, running the backs of his fingers over her cheek. "You're simply falling asleep. Nothing to give you concern."

"I haven't slept in so long. I don't remember what it's like."

"It can be very pleasant. Peaceful. You may even have dreams."

"What if . . ." She swallowed hard. "What if I do not wake up?"

"You will. I vow to you that you shall awaken." She still looked uncertain, rare vulnerability in her gaze. "I'll watch over you."

Already, her lashes fluttered as sleepiness overtook her, and her words faintly slurred as she said, "Thank you."

"Rest now, love. I'm here. And I will be here when you wake."

As he watched, she dozed off, her breath becoming even and slow. This was the first time he had ever seen her asleep, or anything other than vigilant and aware. Her beauty at all times pierced him, and in repose she had an unguarded softness, a pliancy.

An illusion. She was steel and fire, her will as indomitable as his own. Precisely as he desired. Yet in her weakened, sleeping state, she needed protecting. He would watch over her—for as long as she needed.

* * *

He kept his vigil, leaving her side in brief intervals to patrol the building. Restlessness gnawed at him, the need to move, to take action, yet there was little to do except wait.

Some hours later, as he made another sweep of the warehouse, he was alerted by the sound of her gown rustling. By the time she blinked open her eyes, he sat beside her, brushing loose strands of hair from her forehead.

"There, you see," he murmured. "Still amongst the living."

"And you are still at my side."

"No sign of trouble while you rested," he said. "We're safe."

"For now."

He was well aware of the impermanent nature of their safety. "And how do you feel?"

"Restored." She stretched, pulling her arms overhead and arching her back. The action had the effect of pressing her breasts tighter against her bodice. The gown's previous owner must have been a woman with a smaller bosom, for Livia all but spilled from the neckline, a vision of dusky golden flesh. He inwardly groaned when he caught sight of the barest edge of her nipple, a lush tawny brown.

He gave a hoarse laugh.

She glanced at him questioningly.

"God, Livia." He held up a hand. "This is what wanting you has done to me."

"You're shaking."

"Like a damned boy with his first woman."

Her puzzled expression shifted into a smile of pure feminine allurement. "It's been over a millennium since I've had a lover. But we'll not speak of anyone else."

"There's only us." He'd never known this kind of need before, not in all his years of sensual experience. Here she was, stretched out upon this bed, answering desire in her gaze.

Her pupils were fathomless and wide, her cheeks flushed. She reached up and curved her fingers over the back of his neck. Her gaze was flame.

Bram slowly exhaled. The moment he'd wanted for so long had finally arrived, and he would not rush. He did not care what it cost him to go slow. Every second with her needed to be savored.

He braced his hands on either side of her and brought his mouth down onto hers. Lust and need and fire blazed through him, yet he took her lips in deep, searching strokes. Her fingers tightened against the back of his neck as she pulled him closer. He tasted the wine, and her, and the sensations expanded within him in hot, heavy pulses.

He felt her other hand tugging open his coat, her fingers slipping beneath his waistcoat to grip his shoulder through the thin fabric of his shirt. She, too, shook, and it unnerved him a little to know how much they wanted each other. No veneer of sophistication, no cultivated distance. They revealed themselves with every touch and exhalation.

It took forcible effort to break the kiss long enough to lean back and pull off his coat. As he did, Livia helped by undoing his waistcoat buttons.

For all the heat in her gaze, she took her time, slowly tugging open his waistcoat, allowing her nails to scrape against his torso. Each scratch shivered through him.

"Witch," he murmured.

"More powerful than a witch," she answered. With his coat and waistcoat tossed aside, she bent forward and bit him through his shirt, just beneath his collarbone. "*This* is the feast I want."

He moved away long enough to tug off his boots and disarm himself. Yet he kept both his pistol and sword close, both of them just beside the couch.

No sooner had he divested himself of these cumbersome obstructions than he lay fully on the bed, stretching out atop her. She purred as he settled himself between her legs, one arm wrapped around her shoulder, the other moving in heated exploration of her clothed body. She held his shoulders, stroked down his arms and back—all the while they kissed with a building, insistent hunger.

He learned anew her mouth, her flavor, her need as covetous as his own. She whispered against him, words that could have been a prayer or incantation or demand. Whatever it was she asked for, he was more than eager to give it to her. As her hands shaped over his straining back, he slipped from her mouth to graze his teeth along her jaw and down her neck. He inhaled her scent and warmth, and when he bit lightly at her collarbone, she arched up, moaning.

"Need to feel you," he muttered thickly. He pulled at the fastenings of her gown, hands clumsy with desire. He knew his way around women's clothing, yet suddenly everything became a mystery, an obstacle to her flesh.

She tried to help, though she knew the way of these garments far less than he. "Curse these modern fashions. Sewn by fiends." She tugged at the ties beneath her stomacher, and the hooks attaching the skirt to the bodice.

"Let me." He urged her up. With single-minded purpose, he stripped her from her gown and threw the whole thing aside in a flurry of peach fabric.

He allowed himself a moment to admire her in her stays and chemise, delighting in the contrast between the white cotton and the olive shade of her skin. Yet he could only admire for so long before he needed more.

He turned her around. Rather than immediately unlace her stays, he ran his mouth down the length of her neck, and lower, between the wings of her shoulder blades. The stays prevented him from moving farther down, so he traced the exposed flesh of her back with his lips, murmuring formless words against her skin.

"Please," she gasped. "Free me from this cage."

Quickly, he unlaced the stays, the stiffened material spreading apart until he was able to pull it off and cast it onto the discarded gown. She tugged off the chemise, dropping it to the ground, and turned back to him.

Thought fled. He could only stare at her as she sat upon the bed, nude, dark hair loose about her shoulders. She was lushly formed, narrow of waist, long of leg. Her generous breasts, full and round, had large coffee-colored nipples drawn into hard points. Between her thighs, her curls were ebony black. He drew his heated gaze up her body, lingering over her curves, to her face. She wore a look of changeless female power as she gazed back at him.

"In all my cursed life," he rasped, "I've never seen anyone or anything as beautiful."

She tipped her head in acknowledgment, and he smiled to himself, for she accepted his compliment as her due. This was a woman who understood her own strength and allure.

"I demand the same privilege," she murmured.

He obeyed at once, throwing off his clothes with a lad's haste. He no longer was the veteran seducer, who had divested himself of his garments with a seasoned and practiced air. All he desired at this moment was to remove all barriers between them.

Their clothing made twin piles upon the ground. The dust would stain everything. He didn't care. He concerned himself only with the longing and desire in her gaze as she watched him disrobe. When he was naked, standing beside the bed, she sighed with pleasure.

"I could not conjure a man half so wondrous," she breathed. Her gaze moved over him, seeming to take pleasure in all his hard surfaces, the body he had meticulously maintained as a weapon. Even his scars seemed to excite her. Yet when she looked upon the marks of flame on his chest, her eyes darkened, and her lips compressed. The markings had grown, dipping down all the way to his hipbone. Consuming him.

She appeared to deliberately move her gaze away from his markings, and her attention centered precisely where he showed his need for her most. His cock grew even harder under her scrutiny, pulling high and curved up toward his navel. A look of purest lust crossed her face.

"We've looked long enough," he growled. He lay down upon the bed.

Then, finally, their nude bodies touched, and he understood that, of all his transformations, this one would be his last.

Chapter 13

The future kept itself swathed in shadow. If they had only this night, Bram would luxuriate in every experience.

His body partially atop hers, he touched her everywhere. Arms, legs, the soft curvature of her belly, the roundness of her hips, elegant and earthy. He felt a moment's regret for the roughness of his calloused hands—practicing his swordplay without gloves had left him with hands far from aristocratic. Yet she writhed beneath his touch and seemed to draw further pleasure from the rasp of his rough palms against her glossy skin. He smoothed his palms over her breasts and growled.

God and damn and hell. She overflowed his hands, abundant, pagan. He teased her nipples to yet greater tightness, and then, when he had her gasping, he covered one with his mouth.

She moaned. Her fingers wove into his hair and pressed him closer. As he licked and sucked one nipple, he continued to toy with the other with his fingers. She was luscious beneath his tongue, vibrantly hot. And the sounds she made, throaty and unbound, traveled through his body and straight to his cock.

He moved his mouth to her other nipple, and his hand

traveled along the architecture of her ribs, down her stomach. Until he found her soaking quim.

He growled against her flesh to feel her like this. Liquid, silken heat. He willed himself to a blind man's sensitivity, discovering her most intimate place through his fingertips. The folds of her sex, the pearl that made her gasp and twist beneath him.

This is what he had been born to do, this was his purpose upon the blighted earth—to stroke and caress Livia, taste her skin, bring her pleasure upon pleasure by any means.

He touched her folds and moved lower, to circle her opening. Two fingers he sank into her, feeling all that clinging, tight heat.

Sounds of abandoned ecstasy tumbled from her throat, and he brought his mouth back to hers in a deep, demanding kiss, his fingers flowing in and out of her.

A rumble of surprise resonated in his chest when he felt her fingers wrap around his cock. Again, he wrestled with his control, needing to last even as the sensation of her hand on him pushed him perilously close to madness.

"You've magic in your hands, sorceress," he managed to gasp as she stroked him.

"This is a spell only we can create."

It seemed unreal, that the woman he caressed and kissed, and who caressed and kissed him back, was *Livia*, the woman for whom he burned but could not have. Now they were here together, in this conjured bed, making one another moan and sigh with pleasure. Carnal need built, testing his resolve to go slowly.

"Need my mouth on you," he said, hoarse. "Need to drink you up, swallow you whole."

"My appetite is far from sated." She arched her eyebrow, the wickedest woman beneath the stars, and he the lucky bastard sharing her bed. "Lay back."

He responded to her command, stretching out his long

body. When she positioned herself above him, her hips over his mouth while she faced toward his feet, he couldn't draw enough air into his lungs. His hands gripped her hips, lowering her to his mouth. At the same time, he felt her breath upon his cock. The first stroke of his tongue against her was the culmination of every desire.

Yes yes yes yes.

Her flavor was exquisite, the feel of her on his tongue sublime. And the way she tasted him, drawing his cock in and out of her clever mouth . . . perhaps he had stayed in the realm of the dead. Perhaps he had been forgiven and this was the promised reward of perfect bliss.

He heard and felt her scream in release, his cock in her mouth, his lips drawing pleasure from her quim. He had brought her a kind of pleasure when she had been trapped in her ghostly form, but this was real, her shudders and cries were real. *He* had given this to her, him and no other.

They made this together, their shared selves creating pleasure.

For the first time in his life, he wanted to brand himself upon another. Mark her as his. Only one man upon the face of the earth would ever bestow this pleasure upon her. Him.

His possessiveness—unexpected, unfamiliar—shook him. Yet he was too far immersed in sensation. He could only obey the increasingly primal demands of his heart and body. So he continued to lap at her, thrusting his tongue inside her, and she cried out and trembled. Over and over, he brought her to climax. And all the while, she sucked at him, bands of fiery sensation radiating outward through his body.

Yet it still was not enough. He wanted all of her.

"More," he demanded, pulling away. He moved quickly, flipping her onto her back. He knelt between her legs, hands gripping her taut thighs, gazing down at her. She looked up at him, eyes dark as mystery, skin flushed and lightly glistening with sweat, her arms stretched overhead to grip the edge of the couch. She was so vividly *alive* his eyes burned and his throat ached.

"Everything, Bram," she said with her siren's voice. "I've been without for over a thousand years. Give me everything."

He lifted her hips, raising them up from the cushion. Then, in one stroke, sank into her.

He sounded like a beast, like an animal, the wordless growls he made, but he didn't care and he couldn't stop.

Her hands clasped the edge of the couch, the sleek muscles of her arms tight as she pushed herself closer. Lamplight touched the rounds and hollows of her body. Her eyes closed. She threw back her head, exposing the curve of her throat, and cried out.

Much as he wanted to move and lose himself in the primal demands of his body, he held still, reveling in the sensation of her all around him, of him as deep within her as he could be. They had shared thoughts, and while that connection had been severed, they could share this profound closeness, their bodies joined so intimately.

He drew back his hips, then slid forward. His thrusts were deliberate, measured, for all that he wanted to simply pound into her. But this slow drag and plunge gave such boundless pleasure he refused to go any faster. This had to last forever. He would make their sex into the whole of the world.

"Yes, Bram, yes, you are so . . . yes . . ." Her words ran together, and he adored her, this cunning, ruthless woman who gave herself and took from him immoderately.

His thrusts grew stronger, deeper. Her breasts shook with the force of their bodies moving together.

"This is what you wanted," he growled. "What we needed."

Her only response was to moan and urge her hips closer to his.

With one hand on her hip, he brought the other between her legs. He stroked and rubbed at her pearl, feeling its readiness beneath his fingers. She arched up with a cry, contracting around him.

Seeing her in the throes of her climax, he could not stop his own response. His release poured forth, incendiary. He lost himself in the pleasure, in her, as it surged on and on. His body shook, his heart opened, he was ablaze with sensation. Only when the very last tremors wracked him did he sink down, spent and devastated and vast as the sun, to lay beside her.

They were quiet together, bodies slick with sweat, the only sounds their breath slowly returning to normal. He ran his hand along the length of her thigh and discovered goose bumps, and only then did he realize how chilled it was within the warehouse. He found a woven blanket draped at the other end of the couch, and drew it over them both.

She wrapped her body around him. Here was another sensation he'd never known—not merely the fulfillment of his own needs, nor the smug acknowledgment that he'd given his lover pleasure, but that they had created ecstasy together, a selfless giving and taking.

"A thousand years is a small price to pay." Her voice was a sleepy murmur, gratifyingly satisfied. Her fingers traced shapes on his chest.

"Not if you know what you're missing." He waited for the sense of restlessness that usually arrived after he'd concluded his bedsport. It never materialized. There was nowhere he wanted to be more than here, in this drafty warehouse by the river, the gloom barely held back by the lantern, the scent of sluggish water and layers of dust heavy in the air. These were not a voluptuary's ideal conditions. But having Livia nestled in his arms, both slack and languorous from what surely was the most intense lovemaking he had ever experienced—he could think of nothing finer.

He felt none of the clinging darkness within himself, the shadowed thoughts that invariably crept in. From bed to bed he had leapt, finding relief from that pall during moments of base pleasure. The darkness always quickly returned, however.

For once, his demons were silent.

The actual demons were still a danger, the war with them and the forces of the underworld looming like a storm. Success was uncertain. Yet for now, here were beasts he could defeat.

He felt Livia's limbs relax against him, and he indulged himself by stroking her shoulder, her arm, and the curve of her waist.

"You should have been a priestess of Venus," he murmured.

She made a soft scoffing noise. "I'd no interest in advancing the cause of love. That was for girls with no ambition. Choosing the path of magic brought us here."

"All roads lead to this moment."

Her shoulders rose and fell. "The other priestesses, they said that everyone's fates were already inscribed. The three deathless sisters spun, measured and cut the threads of our life. What could any mortal do but let their thread be severed? Myself, I believe the gods merely watch, and do nothing. The thread is ours to spin. Whether it is to be knotted or straight, short or long, that's for us to decide."

"Not a very priestess-like stance."

"When it came to the devotional aspects of my duties, I did not excel." Yet she smiled as she said this, and he smiled with her.

His smile faded as he stared up at the shadow-shrouded beams. "A baron's son, well-favored, rich. Obliged to no one, as a second son. The world bent to my will. So I thought. The Colonies taught me otherwise. Nothing but chaos and destruction there. A good man or a sinner, scrupulous plans or adrift on the current—none of it mattered. Everything resulted in death."

Her arms tightened around him, and he realized how bleak his voice sounded.

"Only one end to this journey of life," he said. "None of us can avoid it."

"You did," she noted. "Only today."

He needed no reminder. That shade would chill him the rest of his days. "I'll have to make that voyage again, with no coming back. It's inevitable. However," he added, seeing her solemn expression, "what we do with the intervening years, that is *our* decision, and the measure of our consequence."

She levered herself up, leaning on his chest. Cupping his face with her hands, she bent forward and kissed him, a kiss of unexpected sweetness. She pulled back enough to look into his eyes.

"We aren't paragons, you and I," she whispered. "The way of goodness does not come easily to us. Perhaps therein lies the secret. To see the more difficult course, and to choose it, anyway."

"Sage counsel." He brushed back a few clinging strands of hair from her forehead.

Her smile was wry. "I had over a thousand years to reflect on my shortcomings. Given enough time, and with a proper amount of boredom, anyone can become a philosopher."

He pulled her back for another kiss. Her mouth was supple and eager against his, and he felt himself stirring again, wanting her.

The kiss ended in sensuous increments, until they broke apart and she settled against him with a sigh. He loved the feel of her hands on him, her breath soft against his flesh as she fell asleep.

Gathering her close, he continued to stare into the

darkness. He'd no knowledge what the following day would bring. More revelations. More danger. The hazard of death all over again. Worse, the possibility of literal hell on earth.

As she slept in his embrace, he remained awake, in vigil, refusing to grant himself slumber's oblivion.

He'd died today. And his single thought, as he lay dying on the floor of his father's deserted house, had not been for the Hellraisers, nor the fight against the Devil. He'd only thought of Livia. This same thought came to him now.

I'm lost without her.

Livia started awake. She had heard something, the faintest noise, yet it had penetrated the depths of her sleep. Sitting up, she felt Bram's arm warm and heavy across her waist. It surprised her that, with his keen senses, he continued to slumber. There it was again, that sound. As if someone walked back and forth, sandals rasping against the stone floor.

The room in which she had awakened was not the warehouse. Glancing around, she saw elegant marble columns, frescoes of pastoral scenes, and mosaics inlaid upon the floor. Light from oil lamps painted the chamber in flickering gold. Platters of apricots, almonds, and spiced cake sat atop a low table. Someone in another chamber played upon a flute, the notes low and coaxing.

A bronze silk tunic lay across the end of the couch, and Livia slipped it on as she rose to investigate. Bram did not stir.

She walked from the chamber, down a corridor lined with burning torches. This was no warehouse, but a villa, precisely the sort she had known in Rome, and Londinium. Everything she passed sparked pained recognition, from the braziers perfuming the air to the pots of rosemary placed between supporting columns. Through the narrow windows, the night sky sparkled, free of coal smoke and choking fog. It had been an age since she had seen a truly clean sky.

The villa stretched on, and she followed the sound of footsteps. Yet as she walked, she passed no one. No other inhabitants, no servants, no slaves. Wariness marked her steps, but she did not stop. She needed to know who was pacing back and forth, and what they wanted.

Turning a corner, she found herself in an open courtyard. Here grew carefully trimmed Cyprus trees, and a fountain trickled in the center of the courtyard, a bronze sculpture of a nymph bearing an amphora standing atop the fountain. More torches burned here, and a feast had been set up, with roasted partridge, oranges, and goblets of wine.

She stepped into the courtyard. The footsteps grew louder, and she bit down an oath when a man emerged from the shadows beneath the arcade. He wore a nobleman's silk tunic and robe, a large ruby-studded pin fastening the robe at his shoulder, and more gold and rubies adorned his fingers. His snow-white hair was short but brushed forward in the popular fashion. The irises of his eyes were also the color of ice, and just as cold.

The Dark One, appearing to her as he did when she first summoned him.

Livia raised her hands, readying a Minoan spell.

"That is a poor way to greet my hospitality." He spoke the language she had not heard for a thousand years, her language. He smiled.

She did not return the smile. "Your largesse is unwanted."

"Is it? Surely you'll want to partake of some of the delicacies I have had prepared for you." He strolled over to a bowl heaped with grapes, selected one, and popped it into his mouth. "Delicious. And straight from the vineyards surrounding your father's villa. Surely you remember the flavor, the burst of sweet juice upon the tongue, the yield of soft flesh beneath the skin?"

She *did* remember stealing grapes from the vineyards when she was very small, crouching down in the dirt and devouring the fruit by the handful, alert should any of the servants catch her and go telling tales to the master, her father.

She had been so young then, free of the ambition and avarice that had driven her thousands of miles from home. Her greed then had not been for power or magic, but grapes. A child's covetousness.

"And surely whatever food Bram has been able to provide for you cannot match any of this." The Dark One gestured to the arrayed feast. "Of a certain, you must be hungry and thirsty. A millennium without a proper meal." He tsked. "That must be remedied."

Her mouth watered, yet she would not touch any of the food. She knew the dangers of the Dark One's munificence. A single bite could enslave her for eternity.

"You brought me to this place for a reason," she snapped.

"Your manners have always been appalling," he answered, shaking his head. "It was always, *I want this* or *Give me that*. Never a *please*. Never any humility."

"Yet you came when I summoned you."

His smile was indulgent. "Such conceit from a mortal amused me. And I knew that the ambitious ones were the easiest to sway. Simply dangle the prospect of a little power, and they fell into my grasp like overripe fruit." The moment the words left his mouth, an orange appeared in his hand. "You, my dear, were too delicious to forgo. Seldom in my ancient life had I encountered another mortal as hungry for power as you. Now look at the wonders you have brought to pass."

He waved his empty hand, and scenes appeared in the spray of the fountain. She saw herself as she stood in the underground temple, a room carved from rock. She watched herself summoning the Dark One. The bound Druid priestess and Indian slave lay upon the ground as she used a draining spell to rip magic from them. Alight with their power, Livia spilled ewe's blood on an altar. She chanted as smoke billowed up from the altar, smoke dark as oblivion, and the temple shook. Her captives' eyes were wide with horror as a door of black stone appeared, then, with an awful groan, swung open. The Dark One emerged, dressed as he was now, and laughing. Her triumphant laughter had joined his. She had done it—summoned the ultimate evil.

The scene shifted, and now Livia beheld the terror that harried Londinium. Brawls, fires, chaos, human depravity. She felt sick to witness the destruction all over again.

The images changed once more, revealing the Hellraisers in the temple ruins as they unwittingly opened the Devil's prison. Images of horror followed—a demon attack on a band of Gypsies, a riot within a theater that spilled out into the street, Edmund lying dead in the street. Madness and death.

Her cheeks burned. She knew full well her culpability, but to see it played out before her in these garish shadows felt like swallowing molten lead.

"I will undo it all," she said, tipping up her chin.

The Dark One snapped his fingers, and the scenes vanished. "The fight against me is impossible."

"I defeated you once before."

He scowled, but he smoothed out his expression to elegant blandness. "It was a mere temporary holding. No one can truly best me. Certainly not some Roman sorceress and her pack of dissolute rakes."

"If you have brought me to this place simply to taunt me," she answered, "then your efforts are wasted. I'll not give up. Nothing you say or do will alter my resolve." She moved to leave.

"I could offer you more," he said, smooth as a polished gem.

She turned back, wary. "More?"

He was all consideration, his smile convivial. "Power, of course."

"I already have power." She lifted her hands, and shimmering magic surrounded her.

The Dark One scoffed. "Parlor tricks and mountebanks' artifice. That is not *true* power. A single snap of my fingers, and I could give you magic far beyond your reckoning. The means to reign over millions of mortals. You would have only to think of something you desire, anything at all, from wealth to the might of legions, and it would be yours."

"None of that entices me."

Yet he smirked. Neither of them believed her. "Is that not what you pursued for countless years? The acquisition of still greater magic, the means by which you could possess more and still more? Your hindrance had been yourself, the bounds of your own mortal capabilities. With my influence, all your aspirations will come to pass. The whole of the world's magic would belong to you alone."

Her mouth dried and her heart pounded. Oh, when he spoke like that, offering precisely what she had coveted, her every dark hunger roared back to life. Strength and power could be hers. So many spells, so much magic—hers.

She forced herself to shake her head, though her neck felt made of rusted iron. "Spare me your persuasion. You cannot offer anything I want."

"Again you speak untruths." He snapped his fingers, and suddenly they stood in the villa chamber where she had awakened.

Bram continued to sleep on the couch. He had rolled onto his back, one arm flung above his head, so the lamplight gleamed along the contours of his muscles. The flame markings seemed to dance down his torso.

"Threaten him," she growled at the Devil, "and I vow your destruction."

"Threaten?" He pressed a slim white hand to his chest, the gems upon his fingers giving sly winks in the flickering light. "My dearest girl, I offer you not a threat but a promise of pleasure. You have tasted the joys of mortal life with your lover. But mortal life is a fragile thing, and brief. I could give you both eternity, together."

She stared at him, too stunned to speak. He could not possibly be offering . . . ?

"So I do," he answered, smiling. "Everlasting life for yourself and Bram. You shall not suffer the privations of age, but remain young and beautiful forever. Neither will watch the other wither and die. No sword will be able to pierce your flesh and spill your blood. You will have each other just as you are now. And with the power I will bestow upon you, there is nothing you both cannot have. You shall be as gods."

Livia squeezed her eyes shut, a futile protection against the Dark One's beguiling words. How could she possibly resist his offer? When he proffered precisely what she wanted most? Power—and Bram—forever. Everything she had suffered these thousand years, all the loss, and the wisdom she had gained, it all fell away like ash.

The pleasure she and Bram had shared was unlike any other she had experienced. Far more than two people creating sensation, more than simply taking him within her body, she had taken him within her heart. It made her feel godlike in her power, it made her feel vulnerable. Like a fortress surrounded by thick walls, yet a single, well-aimed mortar could turn everything to crumbling dust.

She forced her eyes open. "If I refuse?"

The Devil's smile persisted, yet it had the bite of frost. "You shall be crushed." He held up the orange still gripped in one hand, and, without any effort, squeezed it into pulp. Juice ran down his fingers to spatter on the floor.

"Consider it, child," he said mildly, wiping his hand on

a cloth. "Life eternal with your lover, unlimited power. Everything your heart covets. Or assured death. Agony. Watching Bram suffer abominably before he is killed. And the certainty that, after your own death, you will never see one another again."

He dropped the cloth onto the floor. "Do not forget, I still possess this." With another wave of his hand, the gleaming orb of Bram's soul appeared, clutched in the Dark One's thin fingers.

Sickness clogged Livia's throat to see him holding the precious object.

"Should he die whilst I am the owner of his soul, which he assuredly shall, he spends eternity suffering the torments of the underworld. There are so many lovely punishments. Being flayed over and over, and the regrowing of the skin is just as painful as its removal. Or he may suffer constant, excruciating thirst, but his only means of relief to drink liquid fire. I have had a very long while to invent new means of suffering. Of a certain, I shall find something particularly novel for your lover."

She wrapped her arms around her stomach but could not stop the wave of nausea churning through her. The Dark One spoke literally. Any of these torments awaited Bram. Simply thinking of them filled her with fury and despair.

The Devil stared at the radiant glow of Bram's soul. "A clever woman like you—the choice should be obvious."

She swallowed hard, then barely whispered the word, "No."

The Dark One tapped his finger to his chin. "Shall I wake Bram? I think I ought. Give your lover an opportunity to hear you condemn him to eternal suffering."

Having only recently rediscovered what it felt like to breathe, she lost her breath. She stared with burning eyes at Bram, slumbering and unaware. Would he revile her? Hate her?

She knew him, knew what he would want.

"No," she said again, and then louder, "No. I'll not succumb to your temptation."

Rather than look angry, or storm and scream in rage, the Dark One continued to smile. "Take all the time you need to consider my proposition. Nothing needs to be hastily spoken."

"My answer will be the same."

"When you have decided to accept," he went on, as if she hadn't spoken, "summon me. Ordinarily, I do not look favorably upon those who do bid me to attend upon them. I shall make an exception for you, my dear."

"How gratifying," she said flatly.

He laughed, the sound as ice upon bare branches. "I always thought highly of you, Valeria Livia Corva. You hold such marvelous promise. I can make all of that come to pass. Merely a few words from you: *Veni, Maleficus.* Both you and Bram will have everything. Or you will die in anguish as the world burns around you. Followed by eternal separation and Bram's everlasting suffering. The choice is yours."

A wave of his hand, and he and Bram's soul vanished. At that same moment, flames erupted at the edges of the couch. Yet Bram continued to slumber, unaware that in moments the fire would cover the bed and he would be burned.

Livia tried to run to him, but her feet were rooted to the ground. She could not move. Could not open her mouth to shout a warning or lift her hands to cast a spell that would smother the fire. All she could do was watch as the fire crept nearer to Bram.

She had to do something, but she was helpless—and her helplessness fueled her rage.

Suddenly, her arms were free. Her body was no longer immobile, and she leapt forward with a shout.

"Livia?"

She blinked, then glanced down to see Bram propped up on his elbow, frowning with concern. There was no fire. The villa had been replaced by the warehouse. She wore no tunic, but stood naked beside the couch, her hands upraised as though on the verge of casting a spell.

"Livia?" Bram reached for her.

Anger and tension continued to blaze through her. She stepped out of his reach, mistrustful of herself. Riled as she was, she might accidentally hit him with a killing curse. "He came to me. The Devil."

Bram was immediately out of bed, sword in hand, glaring into the darkness.

"He wasn't here," Livia said.

"You said he came to you."

"We were in my villa. In Londinium."

Lowering his sword, Bram said, "A dream. Nothing real."

She shook her head. "Dreams are real. They exist in the boundary realm of the *Ambitus*. Through a dream, I gave Leo's wife her magic. Upon waking, the power was truly hers. The Dark One visited me, Bram. He . . . tempted me."

Bram sheathed his sword, yet kept it close. "Tempted you, how?"

"Power without limitation. The world's magic would belong to me. Anything I desired could be mine." Anger blistered her—she hated the Dark One for tempting her, his threats, and reminding her of her own fallibility.

"You wanted that once," he said, "but no longer."

"I was enticed." The confession burned, though she would not look away from Bram's incisive gaze. "It seems I am not as reformed as I'd believed."

"Who of us is wholly good or wholly sinful?" He stared out as ashen dawn light sifted into the warehouse, transforming darkness into shades of gray. "Greed, rage—I feel them, still. And damn anyone who stands in my way."

In the smoke-colored light, he was hard angles and brutal

purpose, the same man with whom she'd created fathomless pleasure, and yet starkly different.

"Yet you won't yield to that need," she said, and she did not miss the caution in her words.

"Every moment's a fight. For you, it's the same." He turned his gaze to hers. "The struggle won't stop. So it will ever be. That bastard Devil offers you everything your wicked heart desires. Small surprise you're tempted. It's the way of villains like us." He stepped close and pressed a kiss to the crown of her head. "We'll keep each other on the path of virtue—dull as that might be. Us on our very best behavior is still more exciting than a pair of straying saints."

"He made threats, as well." Her hands curled, as if she clutched the Dark One's throat in her hands.

Bram tensed. "Threatened you?"

"Both of us." Her heart pounded as she thought of all the torments Bram would suffer after death. "They weren't baseless. He's still in possession of your soul." They each knew what this meant, the eternal agony that awaited Bram.

He was silent for a long while. Finally, he said, "To hell with him." His eyes were blue diamonds. "He must be pissing himself with fear if he's cajoling and threatening you. It's an old tactical maneuver. Undermine the enemy. Let them do the work for you. The battle is won before it's ever fought. If we weren't dangerous, he wouldn't bother. But he is. Meaning, he's frightened."

"He tried to frighten me, too."

"It didn't work. Look at you." His gaze moved over her, admiring. "Naked as the morning but ready to fight."

"He threatened you," she said.

Bram stared at her for a moment, then lowered his head and put his lips to hers with a kiss so sweet her heart shattered.

He broke away, frowning, his head tilted as if to catch a faint sound. She heard it, too, a scrabbling—the sound of claws belonging to large animals. And the sound was growing closer.

Without speaking, she and Bram threw on their clothing. As they did so, the scratching reverberated up the walls. Something climbed up the sides of the warehouse. The ceiling shook from the weight of heavy bodies, and the scratching of claws.

"He found us," Livia said, grim. "Through my dream, the Dark One found us."

Bram already held his sword. He grabbed her hand, and together they ran for the small side door.

The warehouse shuddered. With a crash and shower of splintered wood, the ceiling broke apart. Massive black-furred bodies fell from above, landing in front of Bram and Livia.

Rats. Three gigantic rats, each the size of ponies. Their eyes glowed yellow, and they hissed at Livia and Bram, revealing fangs and tongues of flame. Both their claws and metallic tails gouged trenches in the stone floor.

The creatures blocked the only way out.

As Bram raised his sword, Livia reached for her magic—an Etruscan fire spell—yet when she grasped at the power, it guttered and died like a candle caught in a gust. She strained for her power, again and again, trying different spells. Every time, her magic dwindled to nothing. She was still too weakened from her journey back from the dead.

Leaving her without any means to fight these Hell-sent beasts.

The monsters attacked.

Chapter 14

Bram lunged the same time that one of the giant rats leapt forward. He aimed for the creature's heart, but it dodged his strike, and his sword plunged into the creature's shoulder. It squealed in rage and pain. He pulled out his blade and jumped aside, narrowly missing its whipping tail.

A second rat attacked, fangs first. He vaulted backward before it could tear a chunk out of his leg.

Glancing over at Livia, he saw her backing slowly away from the third beast, as the rat growled in its advance. Though she held her hands up, no glow of magic encircled them. She'd always been quick to summon her power.

"Use your magic," he shouted.

"I cannot," she yelled back. "I am still not strong enough."

"Damn it," he growled. She had no way of defending herself. Not even a mortal weapon.

He sprinted toward Livia, determined to protect her. But the two other monstrous rats blocked him. Both creatures attacked, keeping him from coming to her aid. He leapt and dodged, striking the beasts wherever he could. The damned things took far more damage than any normal animal might, their black fur glistening with patches of blood drawn by his blade.

One dragged a claw across his thigh, and pain followed in a burning line. He hardly noticed. He had to kill these things and get to Livia, safeguard her.

Peach silk flashed in the corner of his eye.

"Don't run!" he shouted. Running meant turning one's back, inviting attack. But she didn't listen. She ran straight toward the couch.

As he held back two rats, he saw her tearing off the blanket. She put the couch between herself and the creature stalking her, twisting the blanket into a rope as she did so. The beast clambered up onto the couch, its lips curled in a snarl, the fur on its back raised up in spikes.

It would tear her apart.

To his shock, she didn't run. Instead, she allowed the rat to attack, and shoved the twisted blanket into its mouth. The beast choked on the fabric. Its flaming tongue set the blanket alight. Fire spread quickly along the clot. The creature couldn't drop the blanket in time before flames jumped onto its fur. In seconds the monster was engulfed. It careened around the interior of the warehouse, shrieking, then collapsed in a heap of charred fur.

As one of the rats made another feint at Bram, he slammed his foot down on its muzzle, pinning its head to the floor. He stabbed the beast directly behind its left shoulder, skewering its heart. It shuddered then stilled, blood spreading across the ground.

The second rat lunged, and Bram kicked it so the thing flew back. It collided with the desk. He darted forward and attacked, thrusting his blade between the creature's ribs. He pushed hard, until the sword's tip hit the wood of the desk. The beast squealed, thrashing and scraping at the air with its claws. He wouldn't relent. Not until it went motionless, and the glow of its eyes dimmed, bereft of life.

He pulled his blade free and turned back to help Livia.

She stood beside the couch, her hands on her knees, gasping for breath. The rat still had the blanket twisted around its neck, but it splayed upon the couch. Dead.

He strode to her. "No magic, no weapons, and still you find a way."

"I've never cared for being powerless." She straightened and glanced at the trio of dead monsters. "The Dark One will send more."

"Then we make sure he doesn't find us." He ran a hand along her shoulder, down her arm, a quick confirmation that she was sound.

"Where can we go? It must be someplace John doesn't know of."

He gathered up their few belongings. "There's never a shortage of hiding places in London."

Bram and Livia rode his horse beside the river, past ships at anchor and smaller boats tied to piers. The river embankment was heavily shadowed, and the figures picking their way along the muddy shore seemed distant, lost recollections. Fog crept up from the water, heavy and dank. A girl passed by, selling oyster pies, and Bram purchased two, which Livia and Bram bolted as they walked. A few hoarse and muttering watermen lingered nearby, stamping their feet and complaining of the lack of business, but otherwise there was only tense suspension.

They moved away from the river, into an old and crumbling part of town.

"Here," he said, nodding toward a tavern. A sign swinging from its shingle announced, BEDS BY THE HOUR OR FOR THE NIGHT.

She eyed the tavern dubiously, and well she might. The two-story structure looked as though it had been built in the time of Henry VIII, and no repairs or maintenance had been done since the reign of Elizabeth. What windows weren't broken were coated in grime.

Yet Livia seemed to understand that this was the kind of place John would never look, and, as such, was far safer than one of the more elegant inns. So, after Bram paid a boy to tend to his horse, she followed him inside.

Half a dozen men cradled tankards as they sat in chairs and settles, and suspicion glinted in their eyes when Bram and Livia entered. More than suspicion shone in their gazes when they looked at Livia. Bram stepped so that he stood in front of her, blocking her from their leers.

"What do you want?" a haggard woman in an apron asked.

"A room for the night." Bram coarsened his accent. An aristocrat in Whitechapel would only attract unwanted attention. "Got to have a lock on the door."

One of the patrons stood and swaggered over. Gin seemed to ooze from his pores. A knife with a worn handle was tucked into the waistband of his breeches. Puffing out his chest, he sneered, "Don't talk like a nob, but you dress like one, an' got a sword like them fancy gents, too. Maybe you is a nob, and you got a nice fat purse with you."

Bram met his gaze without blinking. "Try taking it. You'll wind up as dead as the toff I stole this gear from." His grip tightened on the pommel of his sword.

The gin-soaked man blanched. He scuttled back to his seat and paid particular attention to the bottom of his tankard.

"No trouble," the tavern keeper said sharply.

"Don't want trouble," Bram answered. "Just a room."

The woman led him and Livia up the rickety stairs, then unlocked a room at the end of a hallway. He peered inside. The room held minimal furnishings, and the walls were bowed with age, but the bed appeared clean, at least. He held out his hand, until the tavern keeper relented and gave him the key.

She stepped out into the hallway. "Food's extra."

"We won't be eating." He shut the door in her face, then locked it. Turning back, he faced Livia, who stood in the middle of the room wearing a wry expression.

"From an abandoned house to a dockside warehouse to a dilapidated inn," she murmured. "No woman has ever been so overindulged."

"I'd take you to a goddamn palace if I could." He glowered at the warped floorboards.

She crossed to him and cupped a hand to his cheek. "There are no palaces for fugitives."

He leaned into her touch. Even in this shabby place, his need for her roused easily. But he could not give in to that need when peril loomed close on every side.

By force of will, he turned away. "We'll abide here. The other Hellraisers are making their way back to London, and you need to regain your strength."

She scowled. "Curse this helplessness . . ."

"Not so helpless. You did manage to kill a giant demonic rat."

She waved her hand in dismissal. "One creature is nothing. We'll face far more than that in the coming battle."

The small window looked out onto the street, but hardly anyone was out. "In the Colonies, we had scouts keeping watch on the French. They'd warn us in advance of hostile action. What I wouldn't give for those Rangers now."

"Spiders use their webs much the same," she said, thoughtful.

He turned and leaned against the wall. "As we've neither Rangers nor giant spiders, we're at a disadvantage."

"Perhaps not." She studied her hands. "I can spin a web of magic, cast it over the city. Should John or the Dark One disturb the web, I'll know."

He moved to her and took her hands in his, palms upward. "You were unable to use magic against the creatures in the warehouse."

Bands of angry color stained her cheeks. He realized too late that she didn't like being reminded of her perceived shortcomings. "Summoning the Hellraisers taxed my power." Her words turned husky. "But I know of a way to replenish my strength."

His breath caught as she grasped his hands and walked backward toward the bed.

"Ancient and powerful, this magic," she continued, her eyes growing heavy-lidded. "The first acts of creation were the joining of male and female."

"Tempting," he rasped. "So bloody tempting. But we'll be vulnerable."

She shook her head. "It makes us stronger."

Brutal hunger gripped him, knowing now what it could be like between them. "Then let us be strong." He kissed her with a need as fierce as madness.

Light threw bands of watery sun through gaps in the walls upon the floor as Livia and Bram made love. The need they had for each other couldn't be sated, and the day's tension sharpened their desire rather than dulled it. Her power responded to his nearness, drawing strength from him, from the passion they created. Together, they were unleashed, fearless.

They each possessed a wealth of experience, and neither could begrudge the other's past profligacy when it meant hour upon hour of pleasure, of strength.

Livia felt herself borne upon waves of sensation, every part of her learning every part of Bram. Were she not half so worldly, she might have blushed at their activity. Yet she was no girl, but a woman grown, and felt no shame when she beheld the red markings she left on Bram's back, his buttocks, the indentation of her teeth upon his neck.

He marked her, too. In every way. On and within her. They took turns having each other, and sometimes it was a battle to see who would win. He was indefatigable, bold, sly, inventive. And he devoured her demonstrations of power. He stretched out across the bed and she used him as she pleased while he rasped rough words of encouragement.

With each touch, each moan of pleasure and shivered response, she felt her magic strengthen, as though feeding kindling to a fire. She'd previously used sex to create power—yet she'd never had a lover like Bram before. Not merely his experience, but the bond they shared. His caresses held more import than merely the sensation of flesh to flesh.

They took and gave with equal measure, her magic growing more potent. It fair glowed around her like a corona. He saw this, and it seemed to stimulate him further, his gaze and hands and mouth devouring her.

The web of magic spun out from her with each touch and release. She felt herself at the center of an invisible yet gleaming net, attuned to everything.

"I can feel it," he murmured against her damp skin. "The web. How it grows. You've done it."

"*We* have," she answered, "but it isn't strong enough." Then she took him in her mouth, and he stopped speaking.

Later, she pressed a hand to his chest, holding him back when he moved to cover her with his body once more. "Power is a delicate thing. Too much, and we risk collapse."

"But what a spectacular collapse," he said, lying back with one arm flung above his head. He stroked her bared flesh with his other hand, and she had to smile at the self-satisfaction on his face. Here was a man who had not only ravished her, but who had been ravished in return.

She allowed herself a momentary fantasy—that she and

Bram could spend their days and nights in just this way, discovering new and favored ways to give each other pleasure, that they had no concerns save for sleeping and occasionally eating, that this shabby room served as the demarcation of their world and nothing else existed beyond it. Not the Dark One. Not John. Not the looming war.

Yet, as she and Bram entwined, drowsing and sated, it came upon her suddenly, and she sat up, gasping.

"What is it?" Bram was instantly alert, all traces of languid satisfaction gone.

Her brow lowered. "I can feel him. The web shudders."

"The Devil."

"John." She closed her eyes, homing in on his presence. "He's using a transporting spell. The beginning and ending of the passage are marked. I feel him working to bore through."

Bram was already standing. "You can take us to where he'll transport himself."

She nodded. Though the remaining Hellraisers had not yet returned, if John was using new, dangerous magic, something had changed, the balance tipping. "If I were to attempt the same spell, John could find *us* as well."

"Horseback it is."

As she and Bram struggled into their clothing, she took in the details of their room, from the streaked windows to the single chair in the corner. This was no dream palace of silk and gold, built for loving. And yet she would clutch these memories close.

They hurried downstairs. None of the patrons remained, and the woman who kept the tavern scurried out.

"You said you'd take the room for the whole night," she complained.

Bram said nothing, only tossed her a coin. The woman's mouth clapped shut and her eyes widened when she beheld the coin's denomination.

Outside, they mounted Bram's horse, with Livia sitting behind Bram, her arms wrapped around him. She concentrated on the strain in the web. "Head west."

Bram kicked his horse into a canter, and they pushed deeper into the city as night fell. Livia was not sorry to leave behind the tavern and ramshackle buildings.

As she and Bram wove through the city, some of the windows they passed were illuminated, candles and lamps lit as early darkness descended and people attempted to conduct their lives with a semblance of normalcy. Others remained dim, shapes and shadows moving within. A bitter wind scoured the streets.

She guided Bram through sense, feeling the pull of John's magic on the web she'd spun. Until they stopped outside a large home.

"This is Walcote's place." Bram dismounted and helped Livia down.

"A dangerous man, this Walcote?"

"A Parliamentarian. One of Maxwell's set."

They hurried up the steps. Before Bram could pound his fist on the door, it opened, revealing a servant.

"My lord, madam," he said with a bow. "Alas, my master is not at home to visitors."

Bram shouldered past the servant. "He'll see us. Where is he? Is he by himself?"

The servant opened his mouth to object, but a single glance from Bram stopped his protestations. "My master attends to matters of business in the Green Drawing Room. Alone."

No relief there. John could easily appear without the servant knowing.

"Take us to him," Livia said.

Without another word, the servant led her and Bram down a corridor, and paused outside a tall, carved door. The servant paused to tap on the door, but Bram had already opened it and strode inside.

A man of middle age sat at a table, sifting through stacks of paper. He stood, frowning, when Bram and Livia entered the chamber.

John was nowhere to be seen.

"I wasn't to be disturbed by anyone," Walcote snapped at the servant. He glared at his visitors. "What is this about?"

"Your life is in jeopardy," Livia said.

Walcote approached. "In the name of God? Who threatens me?"

"John Godfrey." Bram paced through the chamber, studying the corners, peering behind curtains. He was a commanding presence in the room, radiating purpose.

Walcote laughed. "Godfrey? He's no threat. The past ugliness of assassins and schemes is over. As of today, John Godfrey has been ousted from Parliament."

Livia's heart stuttered, and Bram swore under his breath.

Walcote glanced back and forth between them, clearly anticipating a more enthusiastic response to his intelligence. "We've nothing to fear from him now."

"You bloody idiot," Bram growled. "Now you've *everything* to fear."

Livia neared Bram and spoke lowly. "He won't be held back anymore. Not by the rules of your government or society." John was free, the chain around his neck loosed.

"You need to flee this place," Bram said to Walcote.

"The man is a pariah," Walcote protested. "He has no friends, no allies."

"He has a very powerful ally," said Livia

Walcote smirked. "Not in London, he doesn't. Do I know you, madam?"

"London is not the final word in power," Bram said darkly.

"John Godfrey can do nothing," responded Walcote. "He is stripped of authority. He—"

"Is here," said a muffled voice from the doorway.

Everyone turned to see a lanky figure standing at the entrance to the chamber. Only through his voice did Livia recognize John, for he wore a broad-brimmed hat pulled down, and a scarf obscured the lower half of his face. Leather gloves covered his hands. Save for a narrow band around his eyes, his skin was entirely concealed.

The servant who had let Livia and the others into the house now slumped at John's feet, unconscious. Blood seeped from a wound on the servant's head. Though John carried no mortal weapon, Livia saw the energy crackling around him in a dark nimbus, the lingering traces of having used magic to hurt the footman. She murmured a shielding incantation, yet left off the final words—keeping her own magic ready for whatever should happen next.

"Godfrey," Walcote exclaimed. "What in God's name?"

"Not God's name." John stepped over the prostrate servant, his gaze locked on Bram.

The two men faced each other, both alert, wary. Bram was tense as an arrow, confronting his erstwhile friend. He drew his sword.

The lines of battle were drawn, Bram on one side, John standing on the other.

"This is how friendship is rewarded?" John spat. "With basest treachery?"

"You know nothing of friendship," Bram said. "Nothing of loyalty or honor."

The scarf around John's mouth could not stifle his harsh laugh. "Abraham Stirling, Baron Rothwell speaking of honor. Next, I'll hear a woman talk of learning." His gaze turned to Livia, and she tensed. "And here is the Roman slut who challenges me."

She held Bram back with a warning glare, though he plainly wanted to ram his fist in John's face.

"Who will defeat you," she answered.

"No longer a ghost, madam? That makes it all the easier to destroy you. I shall delight in that. Never killed a woman before."

This time, Livia could not restrain Bram. He feinted with his sword, and John dodged the blow. But as John reacted, Bram's other fist collided with John's jaw. John staggered back. As he did, his hat tumbled off, and his scarf slipped, revealing his face.

She pressed her hand to her mouth, whilst Bram cursed and Walcote gasped.

The markings of flame covered John's face. Across his cheeks and forehead, surrounding his eyes. He was entirely enveloped in the Dark One's mark, with only his burning eyes left clear.

Sneering, John tugged off his gloves and threw them onto the ground. The markings covered him there, as well, the backs of his hands, his palms. Every inch of exposed skin proclaimed him to be the Devil's possession. If ever there'd been a shred of humanity left in him, it was gone now. With such fertile ground as his covetous ambition, the markings had spread quickly.

"Oh, John," Bram said, mournful. "You poor bastard."

Yet John only laughed again. "I'll remember your pity, when your throat is beneath my heel."

"What does all this mean?" Walcote cried.

"It means," said John with an icy smile, "that you are nothing but a buzzing fly. One I will easily swat." He lifted his marked hands.

Both Livia and Bram acted instantly. Bram stepped in front of Walcote, taking up a defensive position with his upraised sword. Livia spoke the final words of her shielding spell. Power rose like a current of light as she wielded the defensive magic at the same moment John hurled a bolt of dark power at the stunned Walcote.

John's spell bounced off the defense Livia had flung up,

then slammed into a wall. It punched a hole into the plaster. A killing blow, had it struck its intended target.

Walcote fell to his knees, furiously praying.

Livia would concern herself with this mortal later. She readied another incantation as Bram advanced toward John.

"This is but a skirmish." John took several steps backward glancing cautiously between Livia and Bram. He muttered the beginnings of an incantation under his breath, then spoke aloud. "The final battle is on the horizon. Nothing will endure. Not you, nor your Roman whore, nor all the traitorous Hellraisers will survive."

Bram struck. Yet before his sword pierced John's chest, John vanished in a pall of acrid smoke.

In the stillness that followed, punctuated only by Walcote's fevered prayer, Livia and Bram stared at each other.

"What devilry?" Walcote exclaimed, ashen-faced.

Sheathing his sword, Bram said, "The greatest devilry. Now get you far from here. Gather your family, your weapons, and go as quickly as you can to your country estate. Do not leave there until I give you explicit permission to do so."

"Tell me what is happening," Walcote pleaded. "I cannot understand any of this."

"It is all very simple," answered Livia. "Bram and I must stop hell on earth."

Since turning renegade, Bram had abandoned the luxury that had been his birthright. He'd slept in a crumbling, abandoned house and an empty warehouse, and spent half the day in a decrepit Whitechapel inn. He had eaten the coarse, filling food of the lower orders. His meticulously tailored Parisian clothing had been swapped for his father's musty castoffs. He'd had neither rest nor comfort. In truth, these past days he had lived more as he'd once done in the Colonies, a hardscrabble existence that pared away superfluity.

It felt more true than anything he had experienced since returning home, years ago.

As he and Livia briskly mounted the steps to his sprawling home, he felt a curious remove, as though stepping into someone else's life.

The doors opened in welcome, spilling light out onto the street. Dalby, his steward, stood waiting at the top of the stairs, his polite disinterest barely disguising his curiosity. After several nights' absence, the master had returned.

"Dalby," said Bram, his arm around Livia's waist as he guided her into the echoing foyer.

"A bath, my lord?"

"Two baths. And a hot meal for myself and Mrs. Corva. She'll need fresh clothing, too."

"None of the modistes will be open at this hour," Dalby said.

"Then buy a gown from a neighbor. The key to my coffer is in a secret compartment beneath the second drawer in my desk. Lively, now."

The steward bowed and hurried away—showing only a trace of surprise that his indolent master now spoke like an officer commanding one of his troops.

There would be talk, of course. How could there not? The master of the house had returned, looking like a brigand, talking like a soldier, with a strange woman in a secondhand gown on his arm. Whenever Bram had brought women home, they had been the polished jewels plucked from theater boxes, artfully beguiling, full of laughter.

Livia's face was solemn as a graveside angel, her mien irreproachably regal despite her shabby clothing. Left alone with Bram in the foyer of his home, she gazed at everything—from the polished floor to the crystals hanging from sconces—assessing and astute.

"A new perspective," she murmured. "Seeing your home through mortal eyes."

"It seemed smaller to me when I came back from the Colonies."

She gave him a distracted nod, her gaze still in motion.

Restlessness gnawed at him. He wanted to run training drills, review strategies. Yet he knew they both needed refortification before the coming battle.

He offered her his arm. "Let us go up."

It startled him, how the light pressure of her fingers on his arm could make his heart beat faster. He ought to be sated, ought to be inured to her touch—especially after the hours they had spent making love this very day. Yet it was as if those hours had never happened. He still burned for her, craved her.

They ascended the stairs together in silence. Here again was a new experience. He'd never brought a woman home with the intent to have her stay.

His home boasted several bedrooms, all of them ready to receive guests. Instead, he led her into his private chambers. An industrious, fast-moving servant had already lit the fire to dispel the chill.

She sank down into a wing-backed chair drawn beside the fire, her gaze lingering on the flames. Though he knew she was weary, she did not lean back or slump in the chair. Her back remained straight, her hands folded elegantly in her lap.

He wanted to stare at her, to see her bathed in the fire's glow as she sat in his bedchamber. Trace the noble line of her profile, her unmistakably Roman features, and read the thoughts behind her dark eyes.

Instead, he pulled out fresh garments from the clothes press. Everywhere he moved, he saw the familiar furnishings with an outsider's gaze. For all the sumptuousness of this room—the bed's silk canopy, the warm smell of beeswax candles, the rosewood writing desk—it was cold.

Or it had been. Turning back to Livia, he revised his opinion. She warmed it by her presence alone.

"You'd prefer the field of battle." She continued to stare at the fire.

"It's looming," he answered. "Yet we wait here for baths and roast partridge."

"We're filthy and hungry."

"And idle. I cannot like it." He paced to the windows and stared out at the night. The stars burned like ice.

Her gown rustled as she stood and crossed to him. They both watched the evening sky, their bodies close, but not touching.

"See there?" She pointed at the sickle moon, rising above the rooftops. "How it gleams red?"

Indeed, as the moon climbed higher, he did mark the color—a febrile crimson staining its surface.

"John opens the gate between the Underworld and this realm," she said. "He hasn't enough power to open it completely, not yet. Had he killed his enemy, that man Walcote, his power would have grown. He could have forced the gate sooner. By thwarting him, we've bought ourselves a small measure of time. Not much time, though. He'll find other means of gaining power, and when he has the gate wide enough, he will summon his army of demons."

Bram swore, swinging away from the window. "Sod the baths and the food. We have to stop him."

"Confronting him now would surely be our doom." She tapped her fingers against the glass.

"You're damned serene," he growled, "considering that a demonic army is whetting their swords as we speak."

Livia's eyes blazed, and she whirled away. "Serene? How very mistaken you are. It's taking my very last measure of control to keep from tearing this chamber apart."

He did not feel assuaged. He was edge and temper and a furious, hungry energy. And all the while, a voice at the back of his mind dripped its acid whisper. *It isn't enough. Nothing you do will stop the coming doom. Even if she wanted your protection, you cannot keep her safe.*

It was better when he cared for nothing and no one.

A scratch sounded at the door, and at his command, servants came trooping in. They carried a bathing tub and pitchers of steaming water. Bram directed them to place the tub by the fire, and fill both it and the tub in the closet adjoining the chamber. A footman and a maid also set trays of food upon a table. The room filled with the scents of sandalwood soap and roast meat.

"Very domestic," Livia noted once the servants departed.

"Strange—that's certain." Bram stepped forward and helped remove her gown. He turned her around once the dress slipped to the ground, loosening the laces of her stays. Yet he was already at the door to the closet by the time she wriggled free of her remaining clothing.

He needed her too much. The sight of her nude body would push him past the limits of his discipline.

The scalding bathwater came as a welcome distraction, and he washed himself roughly, scrubbing at his skin as though he could wash off this new self. Too much was at stake. He could ill afford to allow himself to truly feel when he had so much to lose. Yet it could not be undone. For all her hauteur, her commanding ways and pride, the Roman sorceress had stripped him bare and bleeding.

He had died for her. Would do so again. The loss of his own life was nothing. But if the Devil's threats came to pass, if he were to see her struck down—there would be no recovering. Even in death he would carry that loss with him, and the memory of her pain. And that would be his true agony.

Stepping from the tub, he dried himself and dressed in a

shirt, breeches, and boots. When he returned to the bed-chamber, he found her with her hair curling damply down her back, clothed in a slightly faded cotton *robe à la française*. Dalby must have found a neighbor willing to part with some garments for ample compensation.

His breath caught. *Mine,* he thought, gazing at her as she contemplated the trays of food. This possessiveness came from nowhere and had no precedent. Yet he wanted her to be his, in every way. Just as he wanted to be hers.

A fine time for revelations. At the very moment when I could lose everything.

"My first bath in a thousand years," she said as he approached. "I nearly wept."

He bent close to her and inhaled. "Laurel oil and sandal-wood. An Aleppo soap I've specially made for me." And now she carried his scent—the most primal marking. Yet beneath was the warm spice of her own fragrance, combining with his to create something wholly new, the joining of them together.

"There was a bay laurel grove at my family's summer estate in Tusculum." Her gaze held his. "It was always a relief to escape the heat of the day and lie in the shade, listen to the leaves whisper their secrets."

"And what did they tell you?"

"That the world was far larger than I could imagine. That there was power beyond my sight." Memories flickered behind her eyes, people and places Bram would never know, and he found himself greedy for even these pieces of her. "I stopped traveling to Tusculum once I became a votary, but I'd think of those laurel trees whenever the summer heat lay heavy in the temple."

"We've a country estate in Sussex, my family. There's a forest on the estate—hazel trees, alder and silver birch—but I wasn't much for laying in the shade."

"Too busy running wild." She smiled.

Though spoke lightly, tension glinted like a buried sword beneath their words, and a sure knowledge that evil gathered and strengthened with every passing moment. She kept glancing at the moon, monitoring it.

They helped themselves to the excellent food—he took some gratification in that, to provide her at last with meals worth eating—and dined in silence. Officers did this, dining well in the hours leading up to the first shots of battle, as though determined to wring experience out of life right up to the end.

After their supper had been consumed, the trays and tub removed by the servants. They sat at the edge of the bed, expectant, silent.

He thought, the moment he had her truly in his bed-chamber, he would be on her in a moment. Every part of him hungered for her.

Yet he did nothing more than take her hand, her fingers weaving with his.

"Love is a sickness," she whispered. "It robs you of your strength, hollows you out."

"Yes." He laughed once, bleak and wry. "And here I thought I was immune."

As Livia slept, laying atop the blankets, Bram went down to the music room and selected his tomahawk and favorite sword. He returned to his chamber and sat by the fire, sharpening the blades of both, all the while aware of the moon turning red. He considered his sword in the flickering firelight. All the battles he'd fought in the Colonies were nothing compared to what awaited him and his weapons now, his reasons for fighting so much greater.

Soft footsteps in the hallway alerted him. He leapt to his feet and pulled open the door.

A footman stood there, hand upraised as if about to

knock. The servant's clothing was rumpled. He must have been roused from sleep, and he blinked at Bram—and his unsheathed sword.

"What is it?" Bram demanded.

The servant lowered his hand. "Forgive me, my lord. There are a number of people below. I said they should return on the morrow, but they were most insistent. Lord Whitney, Mr. Bailey, and two ladies. Well, one is a lady. The other is . . ." He coughed, embarrassed. "A Gypsy."

"Put them in my practice room, and tell them I'll be down presently."

Clearly, the servant had not expected this response. He stared at Bram in confusion.

"Go!" And with that, Bram closed the door.

He turned to find Livia awake and already out of bed. In the half light, in her pale gown and with her expression so grave, he nearly mistook her for a spirit once more.

"They've come," he said.

She nodded, grim. "It begins."

A thought scraped at the back of his mind. Once they set foot outside of his bedchamber, their time alone would be at an end. The tempest would grab hold of them. No stopping until the storm burned itself out, at which point, they would either remain standing or be razed like trees.

They met each other in the middle of the chamber. She stared up at him, full knowledge of what was to come in her night-dark eyes. When he cupped the back of her head, her hands gripped the fabric of his shirt, her fingers digging into the flesh beneath, gaining purchase.

His mouth found hers, her hunger matching his own. They were not gentle or tentative. This might be the end, an awareness that gave their kiss its desperation.

It could not last. The world would not stop in its inexorable rotation. They had to break apart, and so they did, as the fire muttered.

Bram strapped on his sword and tucked the tomahawk into his belt. It had seen considerable use. Soon, its blade would be red—or whatever color demons bled. For all his experience on the battlefield and in the blood-soaked forests of the Colonies, he realized he had no idea what to anticipate in this upcoming confrontation. Such a challenge once excited him.

He glanced over toward Livia, stepping into her slippers. No, he did not fear what lay ahead. He wanted it here, now, and done.

They walked out into the corridor together, putting behind them the idyll of seclusion. Neither he nor Livia faltered in their steps and they went down the stairs, her on his arm. She moved with confidence, as if clad in Caesar's armor.

He and Livia entered the practice room. The Hellraisers waited for them.

Four pairs of eyes turned to him and Livia as they stepped into the chamber. Even though he had seen Whit a short while ago, it still gave Bram pause to behold his old friend here again in his home. They had spent many a midnight here, carousing or in companionable drink. Yet they were not the same boyhood friends as they had been. They weren't even the men they had been half a year ago. They—and the world—had irreversibly changed.

Zora hovered close, her gaze chary as she eyed the walls and ceiling as if they might collapse.

Leo stepped from the darker edges of the chamber. Less than a month had passed since last Bram had seen the youngest member of the Hellraisers, but, like Whit, he was profoundly altered. Leo's gaze had always been incisive, yet now there was a new clarity in his gray eyes, a precision more cutting than the sharpest blade. He was no gentleman of noble or distinguished birth, his vast fortune having been earned through the Exchange, and never did his rougher origins show as they did now. The elegant town fashions he favored had been abandoned for plain, serviceable clothes more suited to a working man. He, too, seemed leaner, tougher—a brawler rather than a man of business.

Bram barely recognized the woman beside Leo. It took him a moment to realize she was Anne, Leo's wife. The first time Bram met her had been on her wedding day. She had been a slight creature, possessing a quiet prettiness that she had buried beneath reticence. At the time of her marriage to Leo, Bram had wondered what, besides her aristocratic lineage, she could bring to the union. To himself, Bram thought such a diffident woman would be a lackluster bed partner.

It seemed that the experience of being married to a Hellraiser had also transformed Anne. No longer did she shyly avoid his gaze or stand meekly to the side of the room. Her shoulders were straight, her expression self-assured, an abundance of maturity in her hazel eyes. This was no genteel girl, but a woman of experience.

Both Anne and Leo Bailey eyed him guardedly. As well they should. They had not seen one another since Edmund's death.

"The Devil still owns my soul," Bram said, "but I'm your ally."

"He has my espousal," added Whit.

"I'm merely to take your word?" Leo demanded of Whit.

Scowling, Whit said, "We fought side by side not a month past. You trusted my judgment then."

Leo narrowed his eyes. "Treacherous times make for inconstant allies."

"*I* have remained constant," Livia said before Whit could snap a retort. "You cannot question my integrity, and I swear upon the magic that runs through my veins that Bram is not your enemy. He's as true as any of you. More."

All four visitors gaped at Livia. Cautiously, Zora approached Livia, her coin-decked necklaces jingling with each step. She reached out with one ring-adorned hand. When her finger brushed across Livia's arm, the Gypsy woman cursed softly in Romani.

"But this cannot be so," she murmured. "A ghost made flesh?"

Eternally the regal empress, Livia tilted up her chin. "You cannot fathom the extent of what is possible." With a wave of her hand, glowing spheres appeared overhead like stars, bathing the chamber in celestial blue light. Another wave and the spheres combined to form a second, pale sun.

"Fireworks may impress the crowds at Vauxhall." Leo, as usual, appeared skeptical. "They'll not be so effective against the Devil."

"Or John," Whit noted.

Livia flung out her hand. A sound like thunder shook the chamber as a shaft of light shot from her palm. It slammed into the practice dummy at the far end of the room. Ash drifted to the floor—all that remained of the figure.

Whit, Zora, Leo, and Anne looked back and forth between the destruction and a smirking Livia, their expressions identically shocked.

"Welcome back to London, Hellraisers," Bram said. "You're just in time for the end of the world."

Chapter 15

Rows of dispassionate faces stared down, ageless, untouchable. The faces would never age, know want or fear. They did not care that a great evil was massing, or that soon, very soon, that same wickedness would lay waste to everything.

Bram looked at the portrait of himself in the Red Drawing Room, hung between the rows of past men to wear the title Lord Rothwell. Gazing at his painted image, he felt neither disgust nor anger, but a dim kind of pity. The poor bastard in the painting had no idea what awaited him, the horrors he would see, and yet for all the agony he would endure, ultimately he emerged, if not better, then stronger. Everything brought him to this place, this moment: leading a counsel of war, his friendships in the process of being repaired, and an extraordinary woman by his side.

His dreams of the future had been facile. Honor. Glory. Unformed concepts that hadn't been tested. Not once did he envision himself as he was now.

As it must be. The process of maturation took us far from all preconceptions. One could either bemoan the fact, curling in on oneself in a misery of stasis, or move forward.

Forward, then.

"John leading an army of demons?" This from Leo, arms crossed as he stood behind his seated wife. "A militia of books, perhaps, or an infantry of Parliamentary bills—but demons? I can't see it."

"He's a scholar not a soldier." Whit stood by the mantel, his arms also crossed.

Bram glanced down to see that he, too, had folded his arms across his chest. He smiled wryly to himself. Men were much the same when it came to preparing for combat, from the Colonies to a London mansion.

"His old identities have gone up in flames." Livia sat in a throne-like Tudor chair. Her words were abstracted as she continued to maintain the web of magic over the city. "The Dark One has worked his alchemy on him. Nothing of his old self remains."

"Nothing?" Zora stood next to Whit, hands on her hips.

"Not an inch of his skin is without the Devil's mark," Bram said.

Anne shuddered, and Leo and Whit swore.

"There's no hope for him," Whit said.

"None." Bram gazed at his friends. "No redemption, no clemency. I need to know that when the time comes, I can rely on all of you to do what must be done."

"Kill him." Leo's expression hardened. "Edmund died in the street like an animal. I'll gladly wipe John from the face of the earth."

Rather than rebuke her husband for his bloodthirstiness, Anne nodded in agreement.

"A fight it must be." Bram glanced at Zora and Anne. "This shall be hard warfare. Harder than any battles you've yet fought. Are you equipped for the challenge?"

Whit and Leo chuckled, while Zora and Anne exchanged speaking glances. Zora stepped back from the mantel, as did Whit. Suddenly, her hand was gloved in flame. The flames stretched, becoming longer, until she held what looked like a whip made of fire. She snapped the whip. The burning logs inside the fireplace shattered. She smiled as she turned back to Bram, the flames around her hand shrinking until they went out.

Anne rose from her chair. She, too, faced the fireplace, then lifted her hands. A biting gust of air seemed to spring from her palms, knocking over a small table in her path. The wind scoured the hearth, dousing the flames just as all the candles in the room were extinguished.

Darkness filled the drawing room.

Livia snapped her fingers, and the fire and candles all relit. Both Zora and Anne gazed at Bram, wearing matching expressions of challenge.

"You'll make for excellent artillery," said Bram.

"Better than any cannon or firearm." Whit curved an arm around Zora's shoulders.

"More accurate, too," added Leo, taking his wife's hand.

"The women are our most powerful weapons." Livia raised a brow. "The men may prove the greater liability, for they've no magic."

"True." Whit rested his hand on the hilt of his sword. "Yet Zora can turn this ordinary saber into a weapon of exceptional power."

"She might do the same for you," Livia said to Leo.

His mouth twisted. "Swords are forbidden to commoners. I'd say hang the rules, but I never learned the art of swordplay. But I'm a damned good shot, and can fight with my fists."

"You can persuade the demons to turn back," Whit said to Bram, "or fight amongst themselves."

Bram hadn't made use of his Devil-given gift in a long while. It could prove useful in the coming fight. He turned to Leo. "Let me kiss your wife."

Whit and Zora exclaimed, Anne gasped, and Leo snarled, "Like hell."

From her position near the fire, Livia remained still, her expression opaque.

"I'm going to kiss your wife," Bram said, "and you are going to permit me." He focused his will on Leo, exerting pressure through thought. *You'll allow me to do as I want.*

Bram took a step toward Anne. She immediately brought her hands up, a swirl of cold air churning around her. Yet before she could push Bram back with her magic, Leo planted his fist solidly in Bram's jaw. Bram stumbled back, his head ringing, but he kept his feet.

"You don't bloody touch my wife," Leo said with a rumble.

"We just proved two hypotheses," said Bram.

"That you're the same damned libertine you've always been?"

"That my gift of persuasion no longer exists. I'd never attempted to use it on you before, so it ought to work. Clearly, it didn't."

"And the other theory?" Anne asked, slowly lowering her hands. The icy wind abated, so the only sounds came from the fire and Leo's enraged growls.

Bram lightly touched his jaw and winced. By morning, he'd have a large bruise adorning his face. "Master Bailey does indeed throw a very powerful left hook."

"You could have tried to persuade him to do something else," Whit objected.

"Such as?" asked Bram.

"Punch you."

Though it hurt like a bastard, Bram grinned. "He'd want to do that anyway, magic or no."

By minute degrees, the strain in the chamber eased, yet it did not entirely dissolve. They were not the same band of friends they had been months earlier, affable and reckless, unconcerned with anything but their own pleasure. A metamorphosis had transpired. Bram saw it in Whit and Leo's gazes, in the set of their shoulders and the way they both stood as though ready to brawl. Nothing was certain, no outcome was a given. If they had once been confident that the world would bend to their desires with nary a consequence, that confidence had been replaced by a hard-edged understanding—they must fight for what they wanted.

Bram did not regret the difference.

"You're like us, then," Leo said. "No magic."

Livia rose and moved to stand in front of him. She was older than the other two women in the room, and she wore her experience like an empress wore her ermine. He had always preferred his lovers to be worldly—it made for a more stimulating time in bed, and it also ensured that there would be no misunderstandings as to the transitory nature of their relationship.

But all those were fatuous reasons. Gazing at Livia, at the hard-won wisdom in her eyes, he understood that there were facets of her he would never entirely grasp, and that he could spend the rest of his days searching them out with only the promise of knowing her fully.

How many days he had left . . . that was a duration no one knew, least of all himself.

"There's magic still within him," she said quietly. She placed her palm against his chest.

He covered her hand with his own and closed his eyes. Following the means she had taught him, he delved into himself, down through the shadowed labyrinth of his consciousness. Something shone in that darkness, still. The golden key shimmering in the gloom. It hadn't the same bright edge as when she had been a spirit, but even diminished, the power continued.

Opening his eyes, he smiled at her, and she smiled back. They were part of each other. Now and for eternity.

Feeling the Hellraisers' gazes upon him, he returned their stares. If there had been any doubt that he and Livia were lovers, that doubt now vanished. Yet they were more than lovers, and Bram let the Hellraisers know this with a meaningful look. In silent communication and solidarity, Leo glanced at Anne as Whit gazed at Zora, then both men looked back to Bram. Men needed few words to converse, and so they did now.

These are our women, and we are theirs.

Only months prior he, Whit and Leo shared in everything, bound together by friendship more powerful than any female could ever provide. They might not have unburdened their deepest selves to one another, but each man had been stalwart in his loyalty to the others.

That had changed. Three women had altered the terrain, reshaping whole continents. Livia, Zora, and Anne were the keepers of their hearts now. And though the Hellraisers might repair the fractures between them, they were no longer everything to one another.

"Your hand," Whit said.

Everyone's gaze fell on Bram's hand resting atop Livia's. The Devil's mark curled over his skin, flames dancing up to his knuckles.

"*Wafodu guero* still has your soul," said Zora.

Bram remained silent.

"If that's so," Leo said, "then if anything happened to you during the battle—"

"I'll be trapped. In Hell." He did not miss Livia's flinch. "Already been considered."

"Perhaps you ought to remain safely behind," Anne said.

"I realize that you do not know me, Mrs. Bailey," said Bram, "but you've only to look at me to realize that I'd rather suffer eternal torment than sit out this battle."

"No matter the cost?" Anne pressed.

His gaze solely on Livia, Bram said, "I do this *because* of all I have to lose."

* * *

Livia studied the assembled company, ringed close around the fire, everyone wearing matching expressions of grim determination. An odd gathering, this. Noblemen and commoners, well-bred ladies and windblown wanderers. Soldiers and sorceresses.

Had she planned to assemble an army, one capable of defeating the Dark One, this would not be it. She needed a whole battalion of warriors, trained not only in martial combat but the use of magic. These mortals had only recently walked the paths of magic, imperfectly learning its ways. Of all of them, she alone knew all of magic's depths, its uses and dangers. And of all of them, she alone knew how great their enemy truly was, how the odds against them were so steep as to be impossible.

She looked at them now, these Hellraisers and their women, understanding that they might all be marching to their deaths. Commanders of armies did the same. They would review their troops and issue orders, knowing full well that within hours or minutes, the living men would be reduced to inanimate collections of cold muscle and blood.

She had seen Bram's memories, learned the contours of his mind. He had looked into men's eyes, understanding that, on his orders, the men would die.

Once, not very long ago, Livia had been comfortable with her role as general, rallying her patchwork battalion and prepared to sacrifice anyone and everyone to vanquish the Dark One. That had been before. Before Bram. With his touch and his words, his gaze and his will, he had altered the landscape of her heart. He'd died to bring her back to the realm of the living.

Which was precisely why she could not allow thoughts of failure to poison her resolve. This was the time of determination, confidence. If she did not genuinely feel these things, she must believe her own lie, else everything was lost.

"Waiting for John to act first will only see us scrambling to defend ourselves," she said to the others.

"Aggression is the position of power," said Bram with a nod.

"His is to be an army of demons." Whit planted his hands on his hips. "We've no scouts to tell us where they are massing, which means we've no way to stop their advance."

"The Rom always have their ears to the ground," Zora said. "We trade information even more than we trade horses. I could try to contact my band, see if they've heard anything."

"There isn't time," Bram said. "I saw the madness in John's eyes, the flames on his skin. He tried to kill Lord Walcote in order to gain more dark power. The moon turns the color of blood—a sign, Livia tells me, of the gate opening between Hell and this world. He'll act, and soon."

"This very night." Livia moved to the window and stared out at the moon she and Bram had seen earlier. The web she'd spun shook as if in a wind, but she couldn't quite pinpoint a specific origin. She turned her thoughts over and over in her mind, gnawing on them like a wolf with a bone.

"Hell." Leo growled. "They could appear right in the middle of Covent Garden, but we wouldn't know until it's too late."

"If we went out in pairs," Anne suggested, "we might comb the city and report back should we find anything."

Bram shook his head. "We'd still lag behind. Livia's right—we need an aggressive approach. Find him before he brings out his army."

Turning away from the group, Whit picked up the fire iron. He jabbed it moodily into the logs burning in the hearth. "He's got the Devil on his side. If John doesn't want to be found, he won't be."

Livia straightened. "The Dark One hasn't much power of his own. He's a manipulator. When he wants something accomplished, he influences others to do his deeds."

"Including give the Hellraisers magic," noted Leo.

"A puller of strings," Livia said. "With John as his puppet."

"Where the Devil is," Bram said, his feet braced wide, his hands on his hips, "that's where we find John."

A sound of frustration from Zora. "*Wafodu guero* isn't forthcoming with his whereabouts. Tracking him will be just as difficult as finding that murderous *gorgio*."

"He has something in his possession," Livia said. "Something too valuable to risk to another vault, thus he keeps on his person." She turned to Bram. "Your soul."

His expression was sharp and fierce. "You're capable of this."

She nodded. "We'll need silence, and seclusion, but it can be done."

"*What* can be done?" Leo demanded.

"We must find John," she said. "To do that, we have to track the Dark One. To do that, we must hunt him down—"

"With my soul as a beacon," Bram finished.

Leo's brows rose. "Damn—it's possible to do that?"

"I've seen his soul a handful of times, and it guided us from the darkness of the other realm," Livia said. "I know it as well as I know my own." She felt Bram's heated gaze on her, and she returned the look.

"Find Bram's soul, find the Devil." Whit gave the fire another jab, sparks rising up, then tossed the iron to the ground. "If it's seclusion you need, we'll give it." He herded everyone toward the door. They swiftly moved out of the chamber, until she and Bram were alone.

He stood his ground as she approached him, his eyes fevered blue beneath his lowered lids. The other Hellraisers were prime specimens of masculinity. She recognized this, but from a distance. It was him, Bram, who ensnared her, whose presence she felt at all times. She sensed him, awake or asleep, alive or dead, and as she closed the distance between them now, she felt anew the twist in her heart.

"Convenient," he murmured, his voice low. "That tracking my soul demands privacy."

"It doesn't." She slid her hands up his chest. "Yet I don't want an audience when I do this." Raising up on her toes, she pressed her lips to his.

He growled into her mouth, and drank of her deeply. And briefly. A groan resounded in his chest as he pulled back. "I want nothing more than to kiss you for hours. But, damn it, we haven't the time."

"This *is* the spell." She wove her fingers into his hair and pulled him down again.

He did not resist her. He brought his arms up to wrap around her, one hand pressed low on her back, the other curved against her throat.

She sank into the kiss, savoring him, feeling him. His heat and taste. His tongue stroked like velvet in her mouth, and she responded in kind with her own hunger.

Beyond the sensations, the sensual pull between them, she submerged herself in the essence of him. His unrelenting strength, and the core of darkness that would always be part of him. She had seen his memories, had felt his experiences, and though some of the threads connecting them had been severed, their silver echoes lingered, binding them together. From hellion child to Hellraiser man, she knew every part of who he once was and who he continued to be.

That essence of him never diminished, even when his actual soul had been torn from him. She felt its resonance within him, in the hot and demanding sensation of his mouth joined with hers.

Where are you? Where is your missing self?

And as they kissed, as desire rose up in her and the need

for him, for all of him, words tumbled through her mind, summoning her power.

In her own language, long dead, she called out with her thoughts and with her innermost self. *Let me find you, my heart, my love. From the shadows to the light, let me find you.*

Here.

She jolted. The answer had come clear as a song.

Reaching out again, she searched.

Here.

She broke the kiss. Features drawn with desire, Bram gazed down at her. His hands were like hot iron as they held her close.

"I have found it." She spoke in a husky murmur, her body alight with need. Need that could not be sated. Not now.

He did not look surprised that the spell had worked. Only nodded. Yet before he let her go, he tipped his forehead down to touch hers, and his breath was rough and labored over her skin.

"I wonder that I ever felt alive," he said, voice a smoke-tinged rumble. "Until you."

By slow degrees, he released her. With the fire blazing close, she still missed his heat, and fought the impulse to cling. She did not cling. She was whole and entire without him—yet so much better with him.

She went to the door to summon the other Hellraisers back into the chamber. Casting a glance over her shoulder, she saw that Bram had moved away from the fireplace, and now faced the windows, hands braced on the sill. His shoulders rose and fell, as if he still fought to regain his breath.

Whit, Zora, Leo, and Anne all drifted into the chamber. Each of them looked expectantly at her.

"The time to act is now," she said without preamble. "The gate is open, the army of demons assembling."

"Where?" Whit demanded.

"I know the place but not the name."

"So long as you can lead us there," Leo said, "names aren't important."

Bram at last turned away from the window, fully in command. "My armory is plentiful. We each equip ourselves—swords, guns, knives. Anything you can use to fight, take it."

"Will they be enough?" Zora asked.

"No." Livia gazed at her, and at each mortal in turn. "It's not the weapons, but those who wield them."

The city streets stood oddly empty, even for so late an hour. From her experience with Bram's memories, she knew that no matter the time, London's streets swarmed with life—exhausted chairmen waiting to take home a reveler, link boys carrying torches, whores, thieves, farmers, drunkards, beggars. That the avenues were nearly pitch black and treacherous with refuse served as no obstacle. At any hour, humanity abounded.

Tonight proved the exception.

Livia rode beside Bram, the head of their caravan of six. Zora and Whit each had their own horses—the Romani woman sat upon her steed as though she had been born in the saddle—and Leo rode with Anne sitting behind him, her arms around his waist. The five horses' hooves clattered loudly in the stillness, the sound echoing off impassive façades.

A thick miasma clung to the cobblestones, and the sky formed an ash-colored canopy that the moon could not breach. And everywhere was heavy choking silence.

"We've not been in London for weeks," Whit said lowly. "Has it been thus the whole time?"

"This night sees a new malevolence," Livia answered.

Bram murmured, "Even the criminals are in hiding."

"There's a greater evil out tonight," said Livia.

Whit gave a soft snort. "Used to be that the Hellraisers kept people cowering at home."

"Now Hell itself is the threat," Bram replied. He frowned as the broad, black stretch of Hyde Park appeared ahead of them. Beneath the leaden sky, the Serpentine gleamed dully, and appeared as still as the frozen lake of Cocytus. There was no sign of the water demon they had beheld several days prior. The trees stood in mute sentry. What, during daylight hours, was a place of leisure, seemed at that moment a blighted wasteland.

"John's coming here?" asked Anne.

Livia nodded toward the expanse of parkland. "Not here, but this is where we'll find more strength for our fight."

Though it was clear that the others in the company wanted more explanation, they remained silent as they followed.

Livia did not know this place well, yet she understood precisely where she needed to be. She urged her mount faster, heading toward the northeast corner of the park. As she neared, it became clear what drew her.

"Damn and hell," Leo muttered.

The mist thickened here, swirling and clotting. It glowed with a terrible light. Then gathered—into human shapes. They were hollow-eyed, gaunt, and collected like flies over a corpse. The figures jostled one another, mouths open as if to speak, but no sound emerging.

"Demons?" Anne whispered.

"Our allies," said Livia. "Perhaps."

"Must be a thousand of them," Zora whispered.

"More," said Livia. "This has been a place of execution for centuries."

"Oh, God." Anne gulped. "Their necks."

All of the apparitions bore dark bruises around their throats. Some had their necks twisted at unnatural angles.

"The fruit of Tyburn Tree," Bram said, stone-faced.

As Livia and the others neared the throng, the specters turned to face them. The vastness of their numbers formed an icy stone in the pit of Livia's stomach. She had seen heretics thrown to lions and enslaved gladiators battle unto death, yet never had she witnessed the assembly of the dead, hundreds of years of executions gathered together as ruined testimonial to the demand for blood. All sanctioned under the auspices of the law.

Men, women. Even some children.

"I thought Romans enjoyed their executions," Livia said.

"Beer, beef, and hangings," answered Bram. "It's the English way. The cost of freedom." The grimness of his expression belied his flippancy.

"The Dark One's presence rouses them." Livia eyed the multitude as they drew closer.

"You said they're our allies," said Whit. "They can fight alongside us. Even our numbers."

"Poor fools—they've no flesh. They can touch nothing, move nothing—as it was with me. But they aren't without power."

"The hell are you doing?" Bram demanded when she dismounted.

She leveled him a glance over the neck of her horse. "Attempting to level the odds."

By the time she had turned around to face the throng of chalk-faced specters, Bram stood beside her. "Whatever you mean to try," he growled, "you aren't doing it alone."

She drew yet more strength, knowing he was with her, and stepped closer to the horde of ghosts. Four reached out—three men and one woman—their hands open and searching. Bram tensed, poised to strike back, but Livia held him back. The spirits' hands all moved through Livia's body, just as insubstantial as she had once been. They opened their mouths to speak, yet no sound emerged.

"I know your frustration," she said. Indeed, a restive energy moved through the crowd, its discontent and anger palpable. "No mercy shown to you. Your lives stolen. And to what end? To satisfy a feeble sense of justice? To deter others from repeating your folly? Those were the platitudes mouthed at you, but we all know they meant nothing."

As she spoke, her words carrying across the field and through the mob of ghosts, they grew more restless and agitated.

Behind her, Whit, Zora, Leo, and Anne made sounds of concern, and their horses snorted in anxiety, tugging on their bridles and hooves pawing at the ground.

"Riling them is injudicious," Bram muttered.

"We need them angry," she answered under her breath.

At the least, he didn't ask her why. He said, louder, "I've seen a hanging. 'Tis a holiday for the crowd. They don't care if justice is being served. They don't concern themselves with right or wrong, or the law. All they want is a good death. No blubbering. No begging for mercy. The people of London wouldn't know mercy if it had its hands wrapped around their necks."

The assembled specters grew yet more uneasy, their images flickering, expressions shifting from bafflement to anger.

Livia pressed, "How many of you died for a theft no greater than a loaf of bread? Or on the basis of hearsay or circumstance? Who amongst you were killed because it was easier for the law to end your lives than admit it was wrong?"

As she talked, and the horde of ghosts became more roused, the air above them began to shimmer. It crackled with hot red energy, bright and sharp. The rage of the dead taking shape.

"In life, you were denied vengeance," she continued. "Those who wronged you, who profited or enjoyed your death—they never faced retribution. Their wickedness lived on. But this night," she said, staring into a thousand faces, a thousand abbreviated lives, "we can take back what was stolen."

She pointed toward the south. "A great evil masses. The greatest evil known. *This* is the wickedness in men's hearts that robbed you of life. *This* is what denied you compassion, for the enemy I and my friends face tonight is the source of that darkness. And so I ask of you, will you aid in our fight?"

Though the crowd could not speak, the red light sizzling above the mob turned volatile, its glare blinding. She had her answer.

"Leo," she threw over her shoulder. "Make haste. To my side, and take the leather bindings from my saddlebag."

In a moment, Leo handed her the strips of leather as he stood on her other side. She cradled the material in her cupped hands. "I need you," she said to Bram.

"Whatever you require."

Quickly, she outlined her plan. Both Leo and Bram raised their eyebrows as she described what she intended to do, but neither argued. This was her realm, and she ruled it well. When she was certain that the two men knew their parts, she began to chant in the tongue of Egypt—her words shaping a spell of gathering. She envisioned it as a net, vast and inescapable, ancient language fashioning the web she cast out over the ghosts' fury.

It taxed her, the creation of the spell, as she struggled to subdue the enraged energy. Twice, the red force threw off the net, but on the third attempt, she covered it with her sorcery.

At once, the energy fought back, trying to break free.

"Now," she said through gritted teeth.

Bram stepped forward and took the straps from her hands. Muttering words in the long-dead tongue, he wrapped the straps around one edge of the net. He pulled hard on the straps, drawing the net toward him. As he hauled the energy nearer, he dug his feet into the ground and his body strained. The glare of red light covered him, casting a long shadow behind him so he appeared as a god of creation. Yet she kept her attention fixed on maintaining the net, continually repairing tears, re-knotting it when the strain threatened to rip it open.

By slow, painful degrees, she and Bram brought the energy closer, closer. And then, at last, with a groan, she pulled all of that seething force into the leather bindings held in Bram's hands. The straps glowed with power.

Leo stepped forward. As he took the strips of leather, he hissed softly. He quickly wrapped the straps around his hands, binding them as a pugilist would wrap his hands in preparation for a fight. Clearly, he had ample experience doing precisely that. He flexed his hands experimentally, testing the straps to ensure their give. Bright red energy gleamed up from the leather, spreading up his arms.

He strode toward a nearby tree, then threw a punch right into the tree's thick trunk. A splintering, shattering sound cracked through the silence. The tree shuddered and fell, its branches snapping, its roots torn up from the ground.

Leo stared down at his wrapped hands. When he glanced up at Livia and Bram, he wore a brutal smile.

"Fitting," he said. "These spirits of Tyburn, they're *my* people. We're of the same low birth, the same status. And now the strength of their righteous anger is mine."

"Nothing for me?" muttered Bram.

She slanted him a look. "You've power of your own. None needs to be borrowed."

"Having more is always better."

Turning back to the assembled ghosts, Livia said, "Be at peace now. Your fight is now ours."

The spirits uttered soundless thanks. A moment later,

they faded back into mist. The stillness that followed felt absolute, a thousand grasping hands had let go of their clinging hold, and the welcome oblivion that ensued.

Leo strode back toward the others, with a cautious Anne meeting him halfway. She lightly touched his wrapped hands, then stared at Livia.

"I think there is nothing you cannot do," she breathed in wonder.

"You're right," Bram answered. He gazed at Livia with heat and pride.

Her heart expanded, growing to fill the vast, shadowed park, yet she dared not voice the truth—she could not guarantee them a victory. That lay beyond the compass of her power. All she could do was arm herself and her allies, and hope it would be enough.

Chapter 16

Bram had led columns of troops through the forests of the New World. They had marched through ancient, unexplored woods, surrounded on all sides by cool arboreal shadow and unseen enemies. Crimson coats had made for bright targets in those green places, and the convoy of hundreds of men made an irresistible lure to their foes. Yet he and his fellow soldiers marched on in a show of force, unbowed by an enemy that conducted war in a most un-English fashion.

He and his brother soldiers had been proud, confident. They fought for king and country. Even when hungry, wet and exhausted, they marched on, knowing with the certainty of children that they—with their training and numbers—would prevail.

Bram now rode at the head of an army consisting of six. He had no idea the size of the enemy's forces. He did not know how they conducted battle. He understood only that he must fight, and command his troops. He had to believe they would conquer their foe. No other alternative.

He did know that they would be badly outnumbered. Six against a horde of demons. And John, the possessor of tremendous power, and the Devil, himself. There couldn't be greater adversaries.

Yet Bram wasn't helpless, nor alone. Anne and Zora had impressive magic, Whit and Leo both wielded powerful weapons. Bram felt the quick energy of magic within himself. He felt the purpose and determination of his own heart.

Nothing, however, had the strength of Livia.

He glanced over his shoulder to see her riding just behind him, her shoulders back, eyes ahead. A warrior queen. The magical energy within him caught the resonance of hers, and hummed with life, as though hearing the call of its own mate.

Every muscle tightened in readiness. He wanted this battle. Needed it. Staggering odds be damned. It must happen.

The unnatural silence continued as Bram led everyone south. Every street stood empty, windows shuttered. London retreated into itself, sensing somehow the battle to come.

Following Livia's instruction, he rode over Westminster Bridge. As he did, he felt himself breach a film of sinister power that sizzled across his skin. More heat danced across his chest, his arm, his abdomen. All the places where the Devil's mark writhed over his flesh. As if anticipating the flames of Hell that would greet him after death, and eager to burn the meat from his bones.

He felt, too, the pitch in his stomach. The enemy was just ahead—so his soldiering sense declared, and it had never guided him astray.

The bridge came and went, and they rode to the very edge of a wide, dark field ringed with trees. He knew this place, as did the other Hellraisers. They brought their horses to a stop and looked out over the empty expanse.

"St. George's Fields," Bram murmured.

"Where everything began," Livia said.

"Not the underground temple?" asked Whit.

Bram shook his head. "The breach between us—it was here it first happened. Here the Hellraisers took up arms against each other, and the Devil's snare broke us apart."

An ugly night. Whit had been the first of the Hellraisers to see the Devil's gifts for what they truly were. They had brawled here, in this liminal place at the edge of London, raised swords and fists. Bram had been deep in his sins' thrall. He'd wanted pleasure at any cost—even the loss of his closest friend. That night, in this place, they had become enemies.

"I see no one." Leo scanned the field. The moon broke through the clouds, glazing the plain with pale, cold light. Not a single soul waited for them. Not John, nor the Devil. No armies of demons. An empty expanse, an ordinary field at the southern edge of London.

"They're coming," Bram answered. Tension knotted along his shoulders and in his gut, as it always did before a battle. Presaging what was in store.

"This is where Bram's soul led us." Livia studied the field like a general.

Zora said, "Perhaps we ought to—"

The ground shook, the air filled with a sound like rock being torn apart, and bestial screams. It rattled in Bram's bones. The horse beneath him danced and shied, its eyes rolled back in fear. He fought to keep his mount under control, pulling tight on the reins. His focus wasn't on the animal, however.

At the furthest edge of the field, the ground cleaved open. It shuddered and splintered as if a massive pair of hands ripped the earth asunder. A visible darkness poured forth from the fracture, bleeding outward, seeping poison into the night. Talons and clawed hands appeared at the edge of the widening crevice. They clutched at the dirt, dragging themselves up.

"Exalted gods." Livia's curse barely rose above the din.

Bram joined her in swearing. No other words came to him.

Demons clambered out of the torn earth, each one more vile and terrible than the last. They swarmed like pestilence, creatures wrought in the depths of nightmares. Some were formed in human shape, massive in size, with blister-red skin and claws the length of a man's forearm. Others slid upon the ground, serpent-like, dragging themselves forward on stunted arms as their gaping fanged mouths gulped at the air. Winged creatures spilled out like flies from a rotting carcass, and though they had huge bodies and wings like beetles, they had men's distorted faces.

Bram lost count of variety of demons that crawled and flew from the depths of Hell. He never suspected such an abundance, and the tension within him ratcheted higher as the foulest beasts he'd ever seen gathered at the edge of St. George's Fields.

Some of the demons carried weapons—jagged blades that devoured light, ancient-looking pikes and short swords seemingly made from sharpened dragon teeth.

The creatures were massing at the other end of the field, shrieking in rage, seething with readiness to fight, yet held back as though waiting for something. More creatures were crawling up from the rift.

A thunderclap shook the plain once more, and there was John, mounted atop a beast that appeared half horse, half lizard. Its eyes of flame nearly matched the madness burning in John's gaze. Even from the other side of the field, Bram saw the deranged fury blazing in his erstwhile friend. Moonlight gleamed over the flames writhing across John's skin and on the blade of the sword he carried.

The demons that had managed to free themselves from the rift milled in disordered groups. John positioned himself in front of them, patrolling the line and chanting loudly. Summoning more creatures up from Hell.

His words broke off when he saw Bram and the other Hellraisers. A brief look of confusion crossed his face. He hadn't been expecting them.

He schooled his features quickly. From the back of his cloven-hoofed mount, he stared at the Hellraisers and laughed. "Once I thought the Hellraisers invincible," he shouted across the field. "Now I see them for what they truly are: a pathetic collection of reprobates. And their women," he added with a sneer. "How did I ever count myself as one of your number?"

"Because we took pity on you," Bram called back.

A snarl twisted John's face. "I'm gathering Hell's might behind me. A handful of dissolute libertines and their sluts cannot keep me from my fate."

"Nor shall we." Livia looked scornful. "Your destiny is to burn in the flames of the Underworld for eternity. I'm eager to escort you to your fate."

Snarling, John flung out a hand. A bolt of black fire leapt from his palm. It shot across the field. Bram and Livia pulled their horses sharply to the side, narrowly missing the bolt. It tore into the ground, scorching the grass and flinging rocks.

Bringing his horse back under control, Bram allowed himself the fullness of his rage. It filled him with a cold, deliberate purpose. He dismounted and handed the reins to Livia, who watched him cautiously.

He drew his sword. A trusted weapon. It had saved his life more times than he could recall, had tasted the blood of his enemies and hungered for more. The feel of it in his hand was natural, right.

"I've need of your strength," he said to Livia.

"It is yours. Always."

He turned to face John and his growing demon army. Despite every soldierly instinct telling him not to, he closed his eyes. Yet he could not allow any distractions. Within himself, he felt the sharp edge of his magic. He drew on it, drew on the anger and darkness and demand for combat. Livia's magic surged in him, as well, hot and bright as an unforgiving sun, and he welcomed her ruthless power.

There were lives to avenge. Lives to save—especially Livia's. The task fell to him. He could not falter, nor fail.

The magic within him rose up. He did not know incantations and spells as Livia did. Instinct alone led him. He opened his eyes. Blue energy crackled around him, the sky overhead suddenly filling with jagged streaks of lightning.

A sharp, loud snap. Lightning struck his sword. Its current traveled through the metal, through his veins, filling him with power. He embraced it, pulling it deep, illuminating the darkest corners of his fury.

Livia was there, beside him. "Your eyes . . ."

He studied his reflection in the blade of his sword. Though the blade itself seethed with energy, he could see that his eyes themselves blazed with light, pure blue. Like a demon he looked. Like a demon he felt.

He felt his mouth curl into a savage grin. Livia's answering smile was equally wicked.

Oh, they were a fine pair.

Bram raised his sword once more. With John watching from the other side of the field, Bram stuck the tip of his blade into the dirt, as though stabbing an adversary. Lightning crackled up from his sword. He dragged the weapon through the soil, trailing electricity. Shimmering blue light radiated up from the gouge in the earth.

"Here and no farther," he shouted to John. "You will never cross this line."

The demons screamed and John scowled.

A grinning figure suddenly appeared, twenty feet from where Bram had drawn a line in the earth. Rage choked Bram's throat when he saw that the Devil wore a parody of a general's uniform, the fabric black instead of scarlet, adorned all over with silver braid and the marks of his rank.

An insult.

Bram barely held himself back from striding to Mr. Holliday and thrusting his blade into the bastard's chest. Of a certain the Devil would strike him down before he could so much as cut off one of his silver buttons.

"These displays are enthralling." The Devil eyed the shimmering demarcation, a mocking smile on his lips. He turned his gaze to Livia, making Bram tense, and then looked beyond her at Whit, Zora, Leo, and Anne. "A superior fighting force you've assembled here. Shall we negotiate the terms of surrender?"

"I won't accept your surrender." Bram kept his feet planted firmly, his sword in hand. "Only your destruction."

Mr. Holliday chuckled. "Never lose your sense of idealism, Bram. It will make your torment that much greater." He raised his hand, and Bram's heart contracted. In the Devil's hand was Bram's soul, gleaming far more brightly than ever before.

Bram thought he'd grown inured to seeing it, his soul. It could no longer move him, or so he believed. Yet to see it again, see its radiance and promise, made him ache with loss. He glanced over at Livia. He hadn't known what he was missing. Now he did.

Under her breath, Livia cursed in her own tongue.

"I am so used to entrusting these things to my subordinates," the Devil murmured, conversational. "It never occurred to me how delightful it is to keep them close. Perhaps I shall revise my policy. Besides, there is nowhere safer than in my grasp." His face twisted into a grotesque sneer, illuminated by the glow from Bram's soul. "This shall always be mine. You will fight, you will die. And still this will belong to me. The consequences of which you are fully aware."

"I've felt Hell's fire at my back," Bram said.

"You will feel it everywhere." The Devil tapped the center of his chest. "Most especially here—knowing that you fought and died for nothing."

Bram said, "Not nothing."

The Devil swore. His smooth countenance distorted with anger and confusion as the soul he held slipped from his fingers. He snatched at it, trying to steal it back, yet it kept sliding from his grasp. As Bram stared, his soul drifted toward him, breaching the distance. Mr. Holliday flung nets of shadowed energy, but no sooner had the net closed around Bram's soul than it glided free again. It floated resolutely toward him.

"How are you doing this?" Bram demanded of Livia.

Eyes wide, she shook her head. "This is not my work. I believe . . . it is entirely you."

"I haven't enough magic—"

"No magic. *You.* Your fight is for me, for your friends, and untold thousands. But not for yourself." She gazed with wonder as Bram's soul neared. "He cannot hold you, not when you have become . . . complete."

Bram stood, stunned. For so long, he'd felt a part of himself missing, an empty expanse inside. Searching for that emptiness now, he discovered it gone, filled as he was with purpose, with Livia.

Not a perfect man, not by a considerable amount, but striving.

Hissing, the Devil made a last desperate lunge for Bram's soul. The shining object moved faster. Eluding his grasp, it shot forward. Straight into Bram's chest.

Radiance suffused him, a warmth unlike anything he'd experienced. Not merely a physical warmth, but a sense of rightness, a unification. The manifold facets of himself aligned. A thousand emotions beset him—sorrow, joy, relief, rage—as though the barrier holding them at bay shattered. He saw the face of his father, his brother, fallen soldiers, Edmund.

It was too much. He could not withstand the onslaught. He could bear a hundred wounds and not falter, but this . . . this threatened to raze him to ashes.

A hand, slim and steady, clasped his. He knew her touch by deepest instinct. It shored him, strengthened him. She would not let him fall.

Bram shuddered once, and then came back into himself. Beside him, her hand in his, stood Livia. Pride shone in her eyes, and a gleam of tears he knew she would deny.

"All your own doing," she whispered.

"Useless distraction," the Devil spat. He tugged on his coat, righting his appearance. "It signifies nothing. There's one outcome to this battle. My army will cross that line"— he pointed to the boundary in the dirt—"and transform London into my kingdom on earth. The streets will run with blood. It will be a banquet of suffering."

"The Devil has no gift of prophecy," Bram answered. "There are no certainties."

John snarled. "I'll enjoy grinding your bones to powder—*that* is certain."

"Six against over a hundred." Mr. Holliday tutted. "If your friend Whit still gambled, I'd stake everything on us. The odds don't favor you."

Livia released Bram's hand as she stepped forward. "Even probability can be altered."

"It does not matter," John cried. "None of this matters." He wheeled his mount around and resumed his chanting. More demons clambered up from the rift to join the assembled others.

After a final sneering glance, the Devil snapped his fingers and vanished. He would be back—of that, Bram was certain.

Bram now turned to Livia.

She nodded toward the Hellraisers. "Your troops await your orders."

Livia had seen Bram as a soldier and officer—in his memories. Now, she saw him assume that role once more. The mantle of authority settled easily across his wide shoulders. He swung back up into the saddle, fluid, and brought his skittish horse around so that he faced the Hellraisers.

His expression was steely, betraying nothing.

"Leo, you'll take the slithering demons, the things that crawl. Anne, use your command of air to beat back the winged creatures. Throw them to the ground and Leo can finish them." He turned to Whit and Zora. "The demons with hooves and those that walk on two feet, they're your responsibility. Cut them down."

Livia could not tear her gaze from him as he gestured with his sword. It was clear he expected obedience, assured in his judgment. His friends nodded, accepting his directives without question.

This is what Bram was always meant to do. If he held any trepidation, any uncertainty, he did not reveal it. The sharp angles of his face held confidence, and his long, muscled body seemed coiled to strike.

All the while, the enemy across the field snarled in readiness. John shouted orders to the demons.

Every part of Livia tensed. All of this had come to pass because of her greed for power. Now the war to end everything awaited.

Never before had she been in actual battle, moments away from plunging headlong into full combat. She had come to the aid of Leo and Anne as they fought a band of attacking demons, but this—over a hundred hellspawn beasts waiting to bring down the wrath of the Dark One, creatures growling and rattling their weapons, eager for blood—this was an unknown realm.

One that might well see her and Bram dead, and the world horribly transformed.

She watched him now, a man not only at the height of his physical strength but also the strength of his heart, his will. He had changed utterly from the dissipated rogue she once knew, yet the core of him, shadowed and edged, that remained constant.

And she loved him for it.

The thought struck her like a blade of fire.

A fine time for revelations.

She gave an inward, mocking smile. Yet she fooled no one, least of all herself.

All her years, all the knowledge she possessed, the cynical wisdom that sheltered her, all of it fell away. Watching Bram now prepare his army of six, she felt herself engulfed in emotion. He had won her, in every way.

She could not speak of this. Not now. So she kept the knowledge of her love close, a hoarded, feared treasure, as dangerous as it was valuable.

"What of you and Livia?" Whit asked.

"We head the charge." His gaze held hers, and her heart stuttered. "I need you at my side."

"The only place I want," she answered.

He brought his horse alongside hers so the flanks nearly touched. With a single, direct movement, he leaned close, cupping the back of her head. Then kissed her. A greedy, demanding kiss, his mouth hot, his need like flame. She gave as she received, just as eager, just as ravenous. This kiss might have to last the rest of her life, however short that might be, and into eternity.

For all her vows to keep her newly discovered love to herself, he must have felt it in her kiss, for he pulled back enough to stare into her eyes.

"This is not the end," he said, low and fierce.

"We shall prevail," she whispered back. Even if she did not truly believe they could defeat the Dark One and his army, she had to cling to hope.

The blue fire in his gaze flared. He kissed her once more, and she clutched at his shoulders, holding him as tightly as these last moments would allow.

They broke apart. It felt as though the world itself had been torn in two.

Needing something to stop the pain, she glanced over at their fellow Hellraisers. Her heart contracted once more as she saw both couples—Whit and Zora, Leo and Anne—locked in their own passionate, fraught kisses. The final communion before battle. With equal shows of reluctance, the couples broke apart.

At last, there could be no further delay. The moment had arrived.

Everyone took up their positions. Across the field, John broke off from his chanting to order the demons into rough groups. As though they were indeed an army.

Time slowed to mark each second, each breath and heartbeat. She had dwelled in a state of endless time, believing it would stretch on without cessation, that one moment was no different from the next.

That had changed. An entire kingdom resided within every inhalation. The world shifted with every exhalation.

She knew love. Recognized it just in time to have it ripped away. Perhaps. They might yet survive, she and Bram. They might win.

Yet she strongly doubted it.

"Charge!" screamed John.

"For the world's souls!" Bram shouted.

The battle had begun.

* * *

The Hellraisers and demons thundered toward one another. The ground shook, and the sky itself seemed to tremble.

Closer and closer drew the enemy. Moonlight glinted on their weapons, their claws and fangs and wings.

Livia did not feel fear. Only quiet, deadly purpose.

A sound like Armageddon crashed over the field as the two sides met. Demon and Hellraisers clashed. Everything became chaos. Movement and noise.

Livia pulled fire from herself, summoning the magic of every warrior goddess she knew. Minerva, Morrigan, Artemis. She felt their power suffuse her, her body alight with energy, as though flame had replaced muscle and bone. As demons advanced, she lashed out, fiery bolts of power coursing from her free hand, the other hand holding her mount's reins. Beasts screamed and fell, their limbs severed, holes blasted into their bodies, whilst others pushed in.

She fought to keep her horse controlled, thick swarms of foul creatures on every side. The air stank of sulfur and carrion.

She caught brief glimpses of the other Hellraisers locked in combat. Zora lashed out with a whip of fire, turning long-legged bloated demons to ash. Whit's sword was likewise engulfed in flame, and he used it to hack down centaur-like beasts. The force of Leo's blows sent the slithering demons scattering like leaves, and Anne used her power over air to batter at the winged beasts. She dashed them to the ground, where they lay unmoving, or else Leo would rush up and pummel the creatures until they went still.

All of the Hellraisers fought well, their faces hard with fierce determination. But none possessed Bram's skill and art. Atop his horse, he never broke stride as his lightning-swathed blade tore through clawed demons. He cut the heads off two leather-skinned creatures and kicked away a third, then slammed the pommel of his sword into another's temple. But his goal was clear—he fought his way toward John.

Bram was straight from the legends and myths of her time, one of the fabled warriors who founded dynasties and remade the world. He fought with brutality and purpose, and only by force was she able to turn her gaze away from him to battle back more of the demons.

A scream sounded overhead. She ducked as one of the flying demons dove for her, its grasping claws attempting to pull her from the saddle. Red pain blossomed. Using her fingers, she felt a long gouge stretching from her shoulders to the middle of her back. Her fingertips came away stained with blood.

The demon made another dive. She called for Minerva's Shield, and the creature slammed into it before careening away. The impact unbalanced her. A dizzying, tilting moment, and she found herself on the ground. Panicked, her horse galloped away, pushing through the clashing armies.

"Livia!" Bram's roar rose above the din.

She stood. Without her horse to raise her up, she was in the thick of the battle, demons surging around her. She crouched low to avoid a demon's swinging blade. As she did, she cut its legs out from underneath with a flare of ancient Akkadian magic. The beast toppled to the ground, and she leapt onto it and slammed the blade of energy into the center of its chest. It screamed, then went still, eyes glassy as it stared up at the night sky.

With Minerva's shield on one arm and the edged Akkadian spell in her other hand, she fought off more demons, wave after wave of the awful beasts.

"Livia!" Bram shouted again. As she battled back more demons, she looked for him.

He pushed his horse through the throng toward her, his brows drawn down in a savage scowl. Baring his teeth, he hacked down any demon standing between her and him. Resolute, ferocious, he carved a path to her.

Then he was in front of Livia, one broad hand reaching for her. She took his offered hand, and he lifted her up in a swift motion. Seating herself behind him, she saw the field of battle from a better vantage. The Hellraisers had managed to carve paths of destruction out of the demons' ranks.

Bram glanced down and saw the beasts she had felled on her own. He gave her a vicious smile. "Lucky we're on the same side."

She struck out with a spell just as a demon charged. At the same time, Bram stabbed the creature through the throat. Hardly anything was left of the beast as it fell to the ground. "We didn't start out that way, but it was meant to be. Besides," she added with her own cutting grin, "no one of sense will have us."

There was no further opportunity for conversation. Though a goodly number of the demons in this arena of the battle had fallen, many still stood.

John, too distracted by the battle to summon more demons up from Hell, hoarsely shouted orders at the creatures that had made it above ground. He kept casting alarmed glances at Bram.

"There's my target," Bram growled. He urged his horse toward John, but more demons blocked the way. He hacked at scaled arms that tried to pull him from the saddle, and she drove her own magic blade into the throats of two-headed, four-legged monsters.

The Hellraisers briefly converged.

"Report," Bram commanded.

"Took out two dozen of those slithering bastards." A trickle of blood dripped in the corner of Leo's mouth, and he wiped it onto the sleeve of his torn coat.

"A third of those flying things have been thrown halfway to Portugal," Anne added, looking windblown.

"Zora's turned a score of demons to ash," Whit said. A rip along the sleeve of his coat revealed a long, shallow cut.

"And Whit's carved twenty into nothing but meat," said Zora. Ash streaked the hem of her skirts.

Something was missing. Some*one*. Livia scanned the ranks of the demons. Chaos reigned, yet she finally grasped the crucial element.

"Where is John?"

Bram gazed at the ongoing battle. He cursed.

John was nowhere to be seen. Rather than be comforted by this, panic gnawed at Livia. An unseen enemy was even more dangerous than a visible one.

"There." Bram pointed to the tree line, where the woods abutted the field. John, on foot, ran into the forest.

Livia knew better than to mistake it for a retreat. A regrouping, perhaps, but not a retreat. Whatever he intended, it meant certain disaster.

She wrapped her arms tightly around his narrow waist. "You know what we must do."

"Aye," he answered, grim. "And I'm eager for it."

"Go," said Whit. "We'll hold this end."

Pressing his heels into his horse's sides, Bram urged the animal to give chase. Livia and Bram raced away from the demon-choked field of combat. Death and danger were everywhere. Yet the true threat lay not on the battlefield but up ahead in the trees. The sounds of combat faded as she and Bram plunged into the dark forest in pursuit of their enemy.

Chapter 17

Trouble, almost at once. The trees grew too thick and close to pursue on horseback. Only a moment earlier, there had been more than enough room for a horse and riders. Now they crowded in on every side. It had to be John's doing. No choice but to dismount and follow on foot.

Bram kept ahead of Livia, the stride of his long legs twice the length of her own. And she was not as accustomed to running as he. She cursed herself as she fell behind, her body already weary and taxed from the battle.

Seeing that she lagged, Bram slowed.

"No, keep with him," she said.

"I stay with you," Bram growled.

"He cannot have an opportunity to collect himself or summon reinforcements. Go," she added, when still Bram lingered. "Don't insult me by thinking you need to protect me."

He sent her a glance that clearly indicated his displeasure with this arrangement, but, seeing that John was indeed disappearing further into the woods, he seemed to understand there was no choice. With a final, searching look, Bram sped off.

She allowed herself a moment to gather her breath,

summoning reserves of energy. This was not the time to let mortal weakness hinder her. Surrounded as she was by the woods, she drew on the true strength of the trees, their primal living strength, green and nourishing. This was not the trickery used by John to slow their advance. The Druids had worshiped these forests and the spirits within them. Once, Livia had stolen magic from a Druid priestess for her own avaricious purpose. Now, she called upon that ancient force once more, in service to a higher cause.

It flooded her in warm verdant waves—renewing strength, lifting her heart. She felt alight with primeval strength. With reawakened energy, she picked up her skirts and ran after Bram.

Noises of struggle sounded just ahead. She emerged from a thick stand of trees and skidded to a stop. Bram grappled with a giant beast, its skin rough and brown as bark, its long, clawed fingers gnarled like branches. It had a vaguely lupine face, and serrated yellow teeth. Bram swung his sword at the creature, hacking into its limbs and torso, but the blows hardly slowed its assault.

Just beyond where Bram and this monster fought, John stood, his lips moving silently as he spun out the spell that controlled the beast. Livia darted toward him. But she only took a step when another of the tree-like monsters emerged from the darker shadows and attacked.

Thus distracted, she could do nothing as John turned and fled deeper into the forest.

She bit back an oath. Then shouted, *"Incendia!"*

Flames leapt from her hands. Fire caught on the beast's limbs, spreading up, until the whole of the monster burned. It thrashed around, nearly striking her and Bram. Roaring, it collapsed, turning to smoldering carbon.

Bram followed her example. He ducked past the beast's limbs, then stuck his sword into its chest. As Bram pulled his blade free, the creature's woody flesh ignited. It flailed for several moments, but the fire crept inside, and glowing red appeared in cracks in its body. Bram struck with his sword again. The monster shattered in an explosion of charred debris.

Ash dusted Bram's shoulders and streaked his face, and there were rips in his coat, yet he appeared largely unhurt.

"Bastard doesn't fight fair," he muttered.

"Neither should we."

They took up their chase. For a man more familiar with books and the corridors of power, John proved himself remarkably fleet. He kept ahead of them. Energy gathered between his hands. She knew the words his lips formed, recognizing the spell. But not in time. He wildly flung bolts of violent energy from his hands. Livia and Bram dodged as they ran, trees and earth exploding all around them.

"Damned tired of this," Bram said through gritted teeth.

"This must stop." Fury coursed through her. "It can only end where it truly began."

Bram kept John in his sights, but he was a wily bastard, weaving between the trees and holding them back with a mad barrage of dark, jagged flame.

As he and Livia ran, he felt the change before he saw it. The trees turned white, the rough texture of their bark becoming fluted as their trunks straightened. Branches disappeared. The wood turned to marble. The trees were now pillars. Roman pillars.

Dread scraped down his back. They looked distinctly familiar. He realized where he had seen them before: at the ruined temple, the place where he and the other Hellraisers had freed the Devil.

He glanced at Livia. She murmured words in Latin, and she glowed with power. This was her doing.

"You couldn't bring us to the temple. So you brought the temple to us."

And that's precisely where they were. The forest that bordered St. George's Field had become a Roman ruin. Some of the columns stood upright, whilst others had toppled. Weeds choked what had once been a tiled floor, and everywhere hung a low mist, just as it had on that night months before. The ruin itself stood atop a steep knoll. Its solidity was deceptive, however. The true temple was *within* the hill. On that fateful night, Bram, Whit and the others had discovered a heavy stone door leading beneath the hill's surface. Like starving wolves lured by a fresh kill, they had followed. Straight toward their doom.

It would have been their doom, had not a headstrong Roman priestess not intervened.

In an eerie echo of that night, Bram saw John at the entrance to the underground temple. Unlike the first time he and John had been here, though, there was no hesitation in John's step as he hurried below, disappearing beneath the hill's surface.

They had to pursue.

Voices stopped him and Livia before they could give chase.

"We gather again." Whit led Zora, Leo, and Anne up the hill. Blood crusted along Whit's temple, Zora walked with a slight limp, Anne's once-tidy hair was wild, and half of Leo's coat was missing. Yet they were here.

"Courtesy of our sorceress," Whit added.

Livia tilted her head, regal, though she swayed with weariness.

"He's down there?" Leo nodded toward the entrance to the subterranean temple. "Why corner himself?"

"Desperation," Bram said.

"There's yet more power he can summon." Livia looked grim.

"Enough chatter." Bram strode toward the entrance to the temple. "This fight ends now."

No sooner had he taken a step, however, than the hill began to shudder. The marble columns shook like the trees they had once been, and pieces of stone rained down as the pillars cracked.

Demons clambered up the hillside. Each of them stood as tall as a man, with long bodies and stinging tails like scorpions, but having human torsos and heads covered in an insect's glinting armor. Pincers rather than hands snapped at the ends of their arms.

The monsters appeared on all sides of the temple, scuttling up, their legs making clicking sounds and shaking the ground with every step.

At once, Bram, Livia, and the others faced this new threat. They formed a ring, weapons and magic at the ready.

Seeing the Hellraisers positioned to make a stand, the demons shrieked and brandished their claws. One snapped at a nearby column, and the stone pillar shattered. Venom dripped from the creatures' stingers. One sting, Bram knew, meant death.

He glanced quickly at the entrance to the temple. It had been dark below, but now an unholy light glowed. John had to be the source, summoning more demons—or worse.

Looking back to the massive, crawling demons encircling the Hellraisers, Bram cursed, and Livia echoed his sentiment. Costly time slipped away.

"Go."

Bram scowled at Whit's directive. "A damned poor friend I'd be, to abandon you to this."

"It's not abandonment, but strategy. A veteran like you knows that." Whit jerked his head toward the entrance to the temple. "You and Livia. Send that bastard to his deserving reward."

"Most eagerly." Bright streaks of magical energy danced along Livia's fingertips.

"And you?" Bram asked.

Leo grinned like a fiend. "Fighting is the only vice left to us."

"No more carousing," said Anne.

"Or wenching," Zora added.

"Don't deny us our final pleasure," Whit said.

Bram gave a clipped nod. If this was how the Hellraisers were to meet their end, so be it. All of them fighting to their very last exhalation, without regret.

"Time to redeem the Hellraiser name," he said. He turned and, with Livia beside him, sprinted toward the temple entrance.

Carved stone steps led from the surface to the underground chamber. Bram took the lead, his sword drawn, whilst Livia kept sharp vigil at his back. They cautiously descended the stairs, and he was struck with a sense of symmetry, time folding in on itself. When last he'd walked down these steps, he'd no awareness of what awaited him. He had been driven by a compulsion he hadn't understood, a force outside of his will, and a dark, grasping hunger.

The Devil's pawn. It maddened him now—how easily he and his friends had been manipulated, how ripe they had been for the plucking. For all their claims of jaded sophistication, they had been no better than rustics at a fair, gaping in wonderment at a magician's tricks as an accomplice lifted their purses.

He'd grown wiser since then. Humbler. Yet more certain. This was the moment he needed all of his wisdom and confidence.

Livia's hand pressed between his shoulder blades, anchoring him.

They delved further down the stairs until they stood in the underground chamber. It looked precisely as it had months past. A large room had been carved out of the rock—walls, floor, and ceiling all made of stone. Torches set into the walls threw shuddering light. At one end of the chamber rested the skeletal remains of a Roman soldier still in his armor. The intervening months and exposure to air had hastened the skeleton's decay. Bones had turned chalky, and the once-pristine armor had dulled, the leather rotting. Whoever that soldier had been, he'd given his life to guard the Devil's prison.

The skeleton rested near a stone altar, and Bram heard Livia's shaky inhalation as she beheld the place where she had performed her greatest sin.

They had both done much sinning in their lives. Here, ultimately, they must undo their wrongs.

John had no such intention. He stood before the altar, arms flung out with his back to Bram and Livia. Seething red light eddied around him. The chamber itself felt like an inferno, the air sizzling in Bram's lungs and sweat dampening his back. John chanted in a foreign tongue, but his words stopped abruptly and he whirled to face Livia and Bram.

Any semblance John once shared with the man he'd been was gone. The shrewd scholar, who preferred long, arid discussions about politics to wine-soaked merriment, who never lost at chess and always held the box for the other Hellraisers at the theater—that man had vanished. He had always been a lean man. Now he appeared gaunt, as if the Devil's power fed upon his very essence. His sunken eyes were glazed and hectic. And everywhere upon him twisted the marks of flame. Grotesque.

"You poor, sodding bastard," Bram muttered.

Hate burned in John's gaze. "It's inexorable. The world you know will fall."

"Spoken with the certainty of the doomed," Livia answered.

John sneered. "How quick you are to decide who will emerge victorious." The chamber shook and the sound of human shouts comingled with demon screams tumbled down the stairs. John smiled. "A lovely tune in three-part harmony. I'd never dabbled in music before, but perhaps I ought to take up composing. I call this melody, *The Slaughter of the Hellraisers.* Ah," he added at the unmistakable sound of Whit yelling in pain, "what a perfect note."

Bram no longer felt the wound of betrayal, for this thing standing before him bore only the slightest resemblance to his old friend. All he felt now was cold fury.

He lunged at John. At the same moment, Livia threw a bright bolt of energy toward the enemy. John cut the air with his hand. Livia's killing spell and Bram were thrown back. The ricocheting spell punched a deep indentation into the wall, whilst Bram stumbled backward, struggling to gain his footing.

All the while, the red light whirling around John grew larger and more frenzied.

"He means to pull more demons up from the underworld." Livia spoke under her breath, just loud enough for only Bram to hear when he stood beside her. "Our forces aren't strong enough to repel anymore."

"Then we stop him before he goes any further." He charged John once more.

John made a fist. He muttered an incantation. A sword of black flame appeared in John's hand, and he narrowly blocked Bram's strike. They crossed blades again. Heat burst from both swords, coursing up Bram's arm, bathing his face. Sweat ran into his eyes. He knew he was the better swordsman, yet somehow John continued to parry his blows with an inhuman speed. John's attack was equally fast, a blur of movement, and Bram grappled with keeping pace.

Bram hissed as the edge of John's sword cut him across the thigh. A searing pain, unlike any wound he'd ever received.

"All those hours," John said, derision seeping from his voice, "spent in that grim practice chamber of yours with those dummies and targets. Wasting time."

"Won't be a waste when I run this through your heart." Bram feinted, a move that always drew blood from his opponent when they'd attempt to counterattack. But John seemed to know the gambit, even though Bram had never dueled with him before this moment. With a burst of unnatural swiftness, John evaded the feint and made his own attack, cutting Bram again. This time, the wound crossed his arm.

Bram and John circled one another.

"Besting me is hopeless," John taunted. "Not so long as the Devil's power courses through me." He shook his head. "Simple Bram—led by your cock, not your brain. You'd never understand."

"Fortunate, then," said Livia, "that I do not have a cock." Her gaze turned hard as obsidian as she spoke. "*Veni, Maleficus.*"

A tolling like thunder, and then there stood the Devil himself.

And he looked furious.

The first time Livia had summoned the Dark One, she'd had to steal the power of a Druid priestess and an Indian slave. The ritual itself had taken careful planning, the spilling of blood—and wicked intent. She had not realized her mistake until far too late, the world turned to fire. But at the moment when she first beheld the Dark One stepping through the gate between realms, triumph had filled her, all her labors rewarded.

Appallingly simple, summoning the Devil now. Merely two words, and he appeared before her, his face contorted with rage.

Making the Dark One angry was never wise. This wasn't the moment for wisdom. At the least, she now understood the significance of her actions.

"I should have slaughtered you," the Devil spat, "all those years ago. Saved myself an infinite amount of trouble."

"That would have been the intelligent thing to do." Her mouth curled. "You do make some spectacularly poor decisions."

"Impudent slut," John hissed from where he and Bram fought on the other side of the temple.

Bram's answering grin was vicious. "One of the many reasons I love her."

The Devil smiled icily. "How pleased I am to hear that. It will only heighten your suffering when I paint these walls with her blood."

Bram darkened, but before he could speak or act, Livia ran to the altar. She drew the Akkadian blade she held down her bare arms and across her palms, ignoring the answering pain. Crimson welled and dropped in thick splatters upon the stone. She smeared her blood, drawing her fingers through it to inscribe symbols on the altar. Symbols of eternity, and death, and the great immeasurable beyond.

It came so much easier now. She had learned a great deal, having paid a terrible price. Yet she did not need the Druid priestess, nor the Indian slave. Her own power was enough—fed by Bram's revelation of his love for her. And she spoke the words, words from the very beginning of time, when a single utterance could call entire worlds into being. No one had taught her these words—she had discovered them herself, delving into the mists of eternity.

She continued to speak them now, painting the altar with her own blood.

Heat, unendurable heat, filled the chamber. A thunderous shaking. Livia staggered back as light poured from the wall just beside the altar. A massive door appeared, as though hewn from the rock itself. Images of serpents and horned beasts were carved into the door. There came a dreadful, shattering groan.

The door opened.

Hell lay just beyond.

It was the sound that struck her first. The screams of the damned. Fraught with unrelenting anguish. Souls without hope. It made her want to fling up her hands, cover her ears, yet nothing could block the noise of eternal suffering. The Dark One was inventive in his punishments.

Beyond the door lay a blighted, smoke-swathed plain, charred and lifeless. Plumes of yellow vapor drifted up from rifts in the ground. The sky was made of fire, and huge creatures swung through the air on leathery wings. And everywhere, everywhere, were the souls of the damned, naked, and bound. Demons presided over them, inflicting such tortures that Livia sickened to see them.

She turned away from this. Fixed her gaze on Bram. He stared back, and he looked so sternly beautiful she thought her heart might simply crumble away to dust.

The blue light in his eyes blazed. "Livia—"

"I love you," she said, then stepped through the door and into Hell.

She heard Bram's shout, but could not turn or stop herself. This must be done, and she could not allow herself to falter.

The underground temple had been hot, but stepping through the door and into Hell itself, she was assaulted by a conflagration. It was a crushing force that made every breath a punishment, as though inhaling fire. Decay scented the thick air, the smell of untold corpses forever rotting, and she fought to keep from gagging. On this side of the door, the sounds of misery were louder, unhindered, and if the heat and smell did not assault her, the cries and screams surely did. Staying on her feet taxed her to the depths of her soul.

She faced the door. From this side of the portal, it appeared to be torn right into the air, without a wall to support it. Though smoke and heat filmed her eyes, she could just see Bram and John within the temple. Bram leapt forward, intending to follow her. John blocked his path. The two men launched into furious combat, their blades striking sparks.

The Devil, with a malicious smile, watched the one-time friends combat each other.

"The opportunity has arrived," Livia shouted to the Dark One. "You want to spill my blood? Here it is." She spread her arms wide.

When the Devil hesitated, she called, "The greatest evil ever known, afraid of one mortal. How unbearably sad."

Snarling, the Dark One plunged through the door. They faced one another on the blasted, charred plain.

His elegant human façade flaked away, revealing the twisted, monstrous face beneath. Pieces of his disguise still remained, so that his visage was a patchwork of man and monster. One half of his mouth was full of jagged fangs, the other still had the graceful curve of a courtier's lips. Rotted flesh appeared beside smooth skin. But his eyes, white and burning, those were the same.

He stared at her with those blazing diamond eyes. "A valuable lesson you've taught me, Valeria Livia Corva. Never again will I allow any mortal to attain so much power. Their nuisance far outweighs their usefulness."

Through the portal, she saw Bram and John, locked in battle, their blades crashing together in a torrent of flame.

"As though you've a say in the matter." She circled him, all the while silently, frantically working to build a spell. Taken from Vulcan's forge. The incantation formed links, hammered with the force of her will. She prayed she lasted long enough to complete the spell. "When you've no true power of your own. All you can do is ride upon the backs of others, like a child being carried through the marketplace, his legs too short and weak to hold himself."

Bellowing in rage, the Dark One swept his arm into the air. Burning rocks tore up from the ground and flung themselves at her. Livia could not build her forging spell and also shield herself from the attack. All she could do was crouch down, covering her head with her arms, as red hot stones showered down on her.

Pain blanketed her in searing profusion. Her gown offered no protection, and she caught the smell of burning silk and flesh—both her own.

The bombardment finally stopped. Raising her head, she saw angry, blistering burns all over her body. If she thought she might survive this, she'd be permanently scarred. But she knew she wouldn't survive.

Rising up, she glanced toward Bram and saw him continuing to fight toward her. Seeing him, she found a small pocket of unused magic within herself, as the rest worked to shape a chain of power. With a shout, she pulled fire from the sky. Tongues of flame spun down and engulfed the Dark One, covering him with flames.

The conflagration solidified, as though frozen, and shattered apart. The Devil laughed as he shed the effects of her spell like a man dusting snow off his shoulders.

"This is *my* kingdom." He chuckled. "You may as well try to drown a shark."

He flicked his fingers. Knotted vines emerged from

the ground and snaked up her legs, pinning her in place. Before she could attempt another spell, the vines wrapped around her chest and arms, binding her. She hissed in pain as the vines dug into the burns covering her body, then lost her breath as the vines tightened, squeezing her like bands of iron.

The Dark One ambled toward her. He shook his head. "All of that knowledge, the years of study. None of it served you."

Livia fought for consciousness. She needed to remain alive long enough to complete her spell. "Able to . . . command you like . . . a dog."

When the Devil snarled, more of his human disguise peeled away, revealing further his hideous face. "Had you paid greater attention in your studies, you would have learned that *no one* defeats me. It cannot be achieved."

"Done it . . . three times."

"Temporary impediments." With one clawed hand and one human hand, he tore at the remaining pieces of mortal flesh clinging to his visage. A monster stood before her. "Too much evil exists in the world. The ground is fertile. So long as mankind persists, so do I. Even in your own heart, I'm there. In your greed, your pride. I am always part of you. Part of every mortal. And I will never. Be. Vanquished."

With each of these final words, the vines around her tightened. Her vision dimmed and she felt something crack. *No!* If only she had a little more time. The spell was nearly finished.

The living cage around her abruptly loosened, and she fell to the ground. Body screaming with effort, she looked up, and nearly wept.

Bram was here. He'd blindsided the Dark One and thrust his sword through the Devil's shoulder. It had been enough to break off the attacking vines.

He'd never looked more glorious, more deadly. The Dark One turned, and the sword tore from his putrid flesh. He slashed with his claws, and Bram used his blade to parry. Bram's sword gleamed bright in the thick waves of heat. The Devil struggled to hold him back, flinging wave after wave of burning debris and conjured blades.

John stood on the other side of the portal, watching, clearly torn between staying in the mortal realm and going to the assistance of his master.

Bram countered the Dark One's deadly attacks, but he couldn't block them all. He bore each wound with grim endurance. Fury tightened his face, an anger she had never seen. Even the rage he had felt when fighting in the war, witnessing the wanton death and ruin—that was nothing compared to the wrath he showed now.

For all his strength and skill, his opponent was powerful, and he took wounds over his face and body. Yet he never relented, continuing his attack, sweeping and stabbing with his blade even as blood dripped from his face, his hands.

As she lay sprawled across the smoldering ground, Livia gathered the last of her magic. She hammered together the final link in the chain. With the last piece completed, the chain glowed to life, becoming visible. It coiled beside her, heavy and solid, forged from the strength of the blacksmith god. Thick shackles the width of an ankle were attached at each end of the chain.

She focused all her power, and the chain rose up like a serpent. Muttering a Gallaecian incantation, she guided the chain toward the Dark One. But her intended target kept moving, avoiding Bram's attacks. She hadn't the strength to chase the Devil, and the chain began to lower closer to the ground.

Bram saw her struggle, and renewed his assault. He backed the Dark One toward her.

Too occupied by Bram's assault, the Devil did not notice

the binding until it was too late. She fastened the shackle around his ankle.

Screaming in anger, the Devil clawed at the fetter. Yet she had done her work well, and the binding would not come off.

John hovered, hesitating, at the portal. He moved to cross the portal to help the Dark One.

As the Dark One struggled, Bram crouched beside her. Concern dug deep lines into his face as he carefully gathered her up. Her wounds must have been terrible, for as Bram gazed at her, his eyes took on a wet sheen.

"Tell me what I can do to help," he said, hoarse.

She had reached the limit of her strength. "Take the other manacle. Fasten it to my ankle."

His brows drew down in a sharp scowl. "Binding you to him."

"Has to be. Need a mortal to bind him. Keep him imprisoned. In Hell."

"Then I'll do it." He reached for the shackle.

"No." She struggled to stop him, yet her arms refused to move.

"I goddamn *love you*, Livia," he snarled. "So don't tell me to trap you here in Hell. It won't happen."

"Someone has to anchor him." The effort it took to speak made her dizzy. "Cannot let it be you."

For a moment, he only frowned at her. Then his eyes narrowed, his expression turning shrewd.

"What—?"

He pressed a soft kiss to her forehead, then gently laid her down. She levered herself up, watching him as he stood and cupped his hands around his mouth.

"Know why the other Hellraisers turned against you, John?" he called toward the portal. "Because you were never one of us. Not truly. We pitied you. No one else would have you. Skulking around Whitehall like a beggar. An outcast."

John remained at the doorway, though he still did not cross the threshold. "The four of you were privileged to have my company!"

Bram gave an ugly laugh. "Tell yourself whatever lies you require. But the truth persists. Without the Hellraisers, you would have been another forgettable man, scrounging for crumbs of recognition. Forgotten. Hell," he sneered, "you always had to pay for your quim. No woman would willingly spread her legs for you. Only your coin could make them endure your rutting."

With a jackal's snarl, John plunged through the portal, sword upraised. Bram stood ready for the attack. Their swords clashed, the sound ringing over the screams of the damned. Bram's fury seemed renewed as he attacked. He and John fought, their bodies blurring with speed, the combat furious. Their fight circled the Dark One, who continued to tear at the shackle binding him.

Bram lunged and knocked away John's blade. Yet John continued to fight, grappling for control of Bram's sword. They each planted their feet in the ground, pushing against each other.

Bram held John steady, and threw her a glance. *Now.*

Shaking, exhausted and riddled with pain, Livia pushed herself up, onto her knees. She mustered the dim filaments of her strength. Wrapped her magic around the other shackle, and sent it straight to John.

It snapped around his ankle. Binding him.

Like the Dark One, he screamed and pulled at the binding. It would not open.

Livia felt herself topple. Before she hit the ground, strong arms wrapped around her and lifted her up. She did not care how much it hurt, all that mattered was being held by Bram, feeling the solidity of his chest and pound of his heart against her cheek.

He sprinted toward the portal. The Dark One screamed as he saw them running. More fire poured from the Devil's hands. Bram dodged this attack, and kept his body between her and the flames.

Then they were on the other side, back in the underground temple, the coolness of the air a fresh torment.

"The door," she whispered. It needed to be closed for the binding to work, yet she had no strength left. Even breathing cost too much. She turned her head to see John running toward the portal. If he made it back to the realm of the living, her spell would be rendered useless, John and the Dark One free to wreak devastation.

A whip of fire lashed out. It snapped past her and Bram, flicking through the gateway to Hell. The whip pushed John back, keeping him on the other side of the portal.

Livia stirred and looked over Bram's shoulder. The Hellraisers all stood within the underground chamber. Each of them were battered, their faces and clothes covered in grime and blood. Yet they were all there. Zora wielded her lash of fire, using it to prevent John from crossing back. The whip carved patterns of light as it snapped, and Zora bared her teeth with the effort.

Anne stepped forward, raising her hands. A powerful, chill wind blasted through the chamber. The tempest roared toward the open portal. It gathered around the door itself and began to push the heavy stone shut. Whit and Leo pushed on the door, aiding Anne's wind.

John and the Dark One both stared with wide, disbelieving eyes as the door swung closed. Horror blanched John's face—and understanding. He stretched out, reaching for the door. But not in time. Just before the door shut, a look of utter despair crossed his face. He had lost.

The chamber shook as the door slammed shut.

"Must be . . . bolted," Livia gasped. She held out her hands to Anne and Zora.

The women hurried forward and clasped her hands. Drawing on Anne's cold, Livia employed it to create metal, which she forged using Zora's fire. She shaped the magic into a substantial lock, which appeared hovering in the middle of the chamber. The Dark One's new prison. This she fastened to the door's bolt. It made a heavy clang as the tumblers slid into place.

Like dissipating smoke, the door vanished. The lock remained, and fell to the ground, but it and the chamber itself dissolved soundlessly. A scent of dry stone filled the air as the ruined temple also evaporated. Until everyone stood at the very edge of St. George's Fields once more.

Chapter 18

The giant rift in the ground had closed. Heaps of demon bodies lay across the field, yet already they rotted. Within hours, they would likely be nothing more than stains upon the grass.

Bram didn't care. All that mattered was the woman in his arms. Her breathing was too shallow, her skin too pale. Burns covered her, angry and red.

"A physician," he snapped, laying her down gently upon a patch of clean grass. "A surgeon. Fetch someone. *Now.*"

He did not see the exchanged glances between the others.

"There isn't time," Whit said, and Bram hated the pity in his friend's voice.

"Then I'll doctor her." He tore off his coat and wadded it beneath her head. Glowering up at Anne and Zora, he snarled, "Tear your petticoats. I need to bind her wounds. Stop *looking* at me like that, damn it, and get to work."

He poured through all he knew of field surgery. One could pull out a bullet, sew up a wound, and hope the injured soldier survived. But this . . . Horrible burns, and her breath rattled, as though a broken rib had punctured a lung. What could he do to help? He was no damned sawbones with an Edinburgh education. At best, all he knew was how to keep someone alive long enough to reach a surgeon. Yet even he knew she wouldn't last that long.

He started when someone lightly touched his shoulder. Zora.

"There may be a way."

"Anything."

Zora knelt beside Livia. She motioned for Anne to sit at Livia's head.

"And us?" asked Leo.

"Hope." She turned to Bram. "Once I was poisoned by demons, and verged on death. Livia used her power to help Whit heal me. Partially. They gave me strength enough to see the job done, myself."

He clung to her offer of tenuous optimism. "What do we do?"

A rueful shrug from Zora. "Let our instinct direct us. Lend her back the power she gave us, that she may find the rest of the way herself."

Bram took Livia's hand, careful to keep from pressing against her burns. Zora took Livia's other hand, and Anne pressed the very tips of her fingers to Livia's forehead.

There were more hands on his shoulders. Bram glanced up and saw Whit and Leo standing close. They wore similar looks of empathy, and he saw in their eyes, their faces, that they too had seen their women imperiled, and knew what Bram suffered.

Of all the deeds the Hellraisers had ever done together, all their revelry, the dissolution, even their moments of camaraderie—this was their truest moment. It bound them together in a way simple friendship never could.

His throat, already raw and tight, closed even further. He could manage only a nod, then turned back to Livia, lying too still upon the grass.

As Zora had suggested, he let instinct guide him. He

closed his eyes. The magic remaining in him hadn't the same potency as it possessed when Livia had been a spirit. But it had to be enough. And he wasn't alone.

As he drew upon the glow of power within him, he felt it—the fresh surges of strength from Zora and Anne. For a moment, he rebelled. It was wrong to join his power with anyone other than Livia. Yet he knew this remained his one hope, and so he permitted their magic to unite with his. It formed a gold and silver radiance. He channeled this light into her, into all the recesses of her damaged, broken body. He sensed the raw pain of her wounds from within as the energy moved through her. This was a kind of intimacy he'd never known—and prayed to never experience again.

Faintly, faintly, the damaged tissues began to repair themselves, healing minutely.

It wasn't enough. She could not survive, not at this sluggish rate of mending.

Magic alone couldn't heal her. But he had nothing more.

No—that wasn't true. He had love.

Once, they had shared thoughts, the ability to communicate without voicing a single word aloud. Even if he spoke now, he doubted she could hear him, sunk too deeply into the twilight between life and death. So he poured his thoughts into her.

You think I'll allow you to slip away from me? That I won't go chasing after you?

He snarled. If anyone thought him a madman for growling beside the terribly still form of his lover, he did not care.

I rose high in the army, and quickly. Know why? Because I never let anything go. I ran my prey into the ground. A fort that needed capturing? I took it. A supply chain to be cut off? I severed it.

It'll be the same with you, love. I went to the realm of the dead for you. I shall do it again. And again. As many times as I must. I won't let you go.

Stubborn witch, understand this—before you tore into my life, I was . . . I was more of a ghost than you. A shade of a man. Haunting this world but without sense enough to realize I wasn't truly alive.

Then . . . you.

He searched through her body, the broken parts of her, feeling her suffering as though it was his own. No wounds he'd ever received ever pained him as much.

You gave me more life than I'd ever possessed. Domineering, imperious, proud. Foolish ghost that I was, I believed you were my punishment for a life of sin.

No man had such sweet punishment. No man was less deserving of redemption. And yet, you fought for me. When I had abandoned hope, you continued to believe.

I cannot . . . He struggled, for merely thinking these thoughts was an agony. *I cannot live without you. I won't. I love you. And to have you with me, I will tear this world and the next apart.*

"Please." He did not know he spoke aloud until he opened his eyes to see Anne and Zora watching him with pity. His voice was a broken whisper as he bent low, laying his head lightly upon her breast. The fabric of her gown grew damp, and he knew he was the cause. "As you fought for me, fight for yourself. For us."

Beneath his cheek, her heart slowed. Stopped.

His own stopped with it. Pain the likes of which he'd never known tore through him. An animal sound ripped from his chest. Hazily, he felt the hands of his friends on his shoulders, trying to offer comfort. He shook them off, and clutched handfuls of her gown as he kept his head buried against her breast.

A faint beat under his cheek. It came again, stronger this time. Then once more. With each successive throb, her heartbeat strengthened. Until, at last, it came steadily.

Lifting his head, he stared down at her, but her eyes

remained closed. The rattling in her lungs disappeared, and her breathing cleared.

"You've never yielded," he rasped. "Not once. And you won't tonight."

Livia continued to lie motionless. Yet he peered closely at her exposed skin. The burns were mending, the skin fresh and undamaged.

"Light," he demanded of Zora.

Flames appeared around the Romani woman's hands, and she held them up to provide illumination. Bram allowed himself a shuddering exhale. Livia was healing.

He cradled her hand in both of his, watching, waiting.

The first streaks of pink and crimson appeared in the sky as she opened her eyes.

Her gaze immediately searched for, and found, Bram. "Is it . . ." Her voice was barely a whisper. "The door has closed?"

"Trapping the Devil and John together." He brushed his mouth against hers, savoring the feel of her breath on his lips. "It's done."

She said in a thready voice, "Help me up."

With infinite care, he curved an arm around her shoulders and eased her up to sitting, resting her back against his chest. The feel of her . . . he'd never tire of it.

She looked at the other Hellraisers, each in turn, and gave them a soft, exhausted smile. "All of you. No better allies."

Whit said, "None of us had a better champion."

Leo, Anne, and Zora nodded their agreement.

"The threat is gone, then?" Anne asked.

"Hell is John's home now," Livia said.

Frowning, Zora lifted her hands. "My magic . . . it's gone."

Anne's gaze turned inward, then she looked at Leo. "Mine, as well."

"The price of healing me," Livia said.

Yet Anne and Zora appeared untroubled by this loss. "Seems a fair exchange," Zora said. "You gave us our power, and we returned it when you needed it."

"And we've fought and defeated the Devil," Anne said. "That is why you gave us our powers in the first place."

Zora murmured, "With *Wafodu guero* imprisoned again, there's no need for our magic."

"We're ordinary women, now." Anne smiled, rueful.

"Not ordinary," Leo said.

At the same time, Whit said, "Never."

Bram gazed at his friends. They formed dark shapes against the paling sky, a fragile, deep blue. The sun was rising higher. Soon, morning would arrive.

"We wore the name of Hellraiser once," he said. "And it was a shameful thing. But we can bear that name again—with pride."

Both Leo and Whit grinned, and though they bore passing resemblance to the pleasure-seeking scoundrels they once were, all of them had transformed. Honed by purpose into something sharper, better than they had been. And as Anne rose to stand beside Leo, and Zora with Whit, Bram understood that their true metamorphosis had come with the arrival of three extraordinary women.

Bram's gaze moved back down to the woman he held. She looked bruised, weary, yet never more beautiful. She returned his look, her own dark and replete. Her fingers trailed along his jaw, down the length of his scar, and he minded her touch not at all. He soaked up the sensation.

She moved her hand lower and began to pluck at the buttons of his waistcoat. At his curious look, she murmured, "Let me see you. Whole and unmarked."

It took some careful wrangling, with her still resting against him, but he managed to undo the top of his waistcoat and pull at the laces of his shirt. The first gilding rays of sunlight touched him, revealing the flesh across his chest to be free of any markings. Only a few old scars, and those had been honestly earned.

Her smile created a new sunrise within him. She leaned forward and pressed a kiss to his chest.

He was vaguely aware that Whit, Zora, Leo, and Anne had all drifted away, leaving him and Livia some small measure of privacy.

Cradling Livia close, he brought his mouth to hers in a kiss that pierced him with its tenderness.

"A punishment?" she murmured against his lips. "That is what I am?"

"A sweet punishment," he corrected.

"One you justly deserve."

"Two inveterate sinners. We deserve each other." They held each other, and he felt the sunlight warming them.

A small frown appeared between her brows. "I hope this doesn't mean that from this moment on, we must be *good*."

"If anyone can find a way to make being good wicked," he said before taking her mouth once more, "it's you and I."

Epilogue

Sussex, 1765

The morning rain had burned off, leaving the ground glimmering in the afternoon sunlight as though someone had scattered handfuls of diamonds. After the initial downpour, the day itself had turned fair, a crisp spring sky arching overhead, dazzling in its clarity.

Six riders cantered across the fields. Three men, three women. With the weather so fine, they wanted to take advantage, and so an outing had been proposed. By tacit agreement, they knew precisely where they wanted to go. They had been to that particular spot before, and surely there were better, more picturesque views on the ancestral property, but this location held significance for everyone in the party, and so there they headed.

Their destination appeared no different from the rolling green fields surrounding them. Save for a small stand of elms, nothing distinguished this place. Anyone else would have passed it without further thought.

Yet the riders dismounted here. After hobbling their horses, they drifted around, picking their way through overgrown grasses and studying the ground as if it held long-kept secrets. Indeed, the ground *did* hold secrets.

"I still cannot fathom," Leo said, "how a whole Roman temple and the hill it stood upon, vanished."

Bram shrugged, looking out across the field. "Its purpose had been served."

"The place is empty, yet we keep coming here," noted Whit.

"We keep our memories close even as the land changes," Zora said.

A shared, silent concurrence. This was where their transformation had begun. It was an ongoing process, every day revealing new truths, new discoveries.

One of Bram's discoveries: love was not a finite thing. It could grow with each hour.

He watched Livia as she paced what had once been the perimeter of the temple. She had never grown acclimated to wearing stays, and in her gown of spice-hued sateen, her dark curls wind-tumbled, and golden light upon her skin, she looked both sensuously pagan and indisputably regal. No one moved like her, or carried herself as she did—confident, aware of her power, yet continually intrigued by her surroundings. Hers was an insatiable greed for knowledge, for experience, and he was at all times eager to gratify her.

As if feeling his gaze upon her, she turned and gave him one of her slow, heated smiles. They had been to this place on their own, many times. It was on his property after all. What the other Hellraisers did not know was that Bram and Livia had ridden out in the middle of the night and made love here, beneath the canopy of stars. A re-consecration of the site. Great evil had been done here. They reclaimed it, changed from a place of wickedness to a place of love.

He strode to her and took her hand. At all times he liked to touch her. A quick glance revealed that Leo and Anne walked together with their arms around each other's waists. Whit and Zora strolled shoulder-to-shoulder, their fingers brushing in quick, eloquent meetings.

The marriage between a nobleman and a Gypsy had caused a scandal, but Whit cared naught for society's opinion—after all that had been seen and done, the battles waged against true evil, gossip meant nothing. The temperate months were spent with Zora's band, and when frost lay upon the ground, he and his wife found warmth at his estates. An unusual arrangement, but one that seemed to suit them.

He'd heard that Rosalind had been traveling the Continent, and that she was writing a philosophical discourse about the complex nature of love. Since being made a widow a second time, she'd taken lovers but refused all offers of marriage. Bram supposed that if any woman deserved her freedom, it would be she.

Now all of the remaining Hellraisers lingered at what had once been the site of the ruin, until the sun dipped and shadows lengthened. A chill threaded through the air and the new green leaves upon the tree branches shivered.

"Come, let us for home." Livia's voice was husky and low as she wrapped her arm around his.

He thought of the warmth of the fire, surrounded by friends, and the heat of the bed he and Livia shared. That he, who had sinned so grievously, could receive such gifts never ceased to astonish him. More proof that the world held mysteries he could never understand.

"Your humble servant, madam," he murmured with a kiss.

"Never humble." She cupped his face with her hands and returned the kiss. "Not my warrior."

Once, Zora had spoken a Romani adage, and the words had embroidered themselves upon his mind. As he and Livia walked back to their horses, with the other Hellraisers trailing behind them, he recalled the proverb.

We are all wanderers on this earth. Our hearts are full of wonder, and our souls are deep with dreams.

Two years ago, he would have scoffed at such sentiment. Now, he held the words close, a man transformed.

With Livia beside him, he rode for home, and the brilliance of the sun upon the horizon could not match the light within his heart.

Have you read the other books
in Zoë's HELLRAISERS series?

Devil's Kiss

A Handsome Devil

1762. James Sherbourne, Earl of Whitney, is a gambling man. Not for the money. But for the thrill, the danger—and the company: Whit has become one of the infamous Hellraisers, losing himself in the chase for adventure and pleasure with his four closest friends.

Which was how Whit found himself in a gypsy encampment, betting against a lovely Romani girl. Zora Grey's smoky voice and sharp tongue entrance Whit nearly as much as her clever hands—watching them handle cards inspires thoughts of another kind . . .

Zora can't explain her attraction to the careless blue-eyed Whit. She also can't stop him and his Hellraisers from a fiendish curse: the power to grant their own hearts' desires, to chase their pleasures from the merely debauched to the truly diabolical. And if Zora can't save Whit, she still has to escape him . . .

Demon's Bride

Hell to Pay

Leo Bailey may have been born to poverty, but ruthless business sense and sparkling intelligence have made money worries a thing of his past. It doesn't hurt that the Devil himself has granted Leo the ability to read the future.

But even infallible predictions are a déclassé commoner's trick to some members of the ton. They'll never see Leo as their equal—one good reason to prove himself their better. And a noble marriage is an obvious start.

Bookish Anne Hartfield, daughter of a baron, is hardly the flashiest miss on the marriage market. But her thoughtful reserve complements Leo's brash boldness in an attraction neither can deny. A whirlwind courtship sweeps Anne and Leo into a smoldering marriage before either can believe their luck. But happiness built on Leo's dark powers can't last. Soon, Anne will have to save her husband . . . or lose her heart . . .

Romantic Suspense from
Lisa Jackson

Books by Bestselling Author
Fern Michaels

___The Jury	0-8217-7878-1	$6.99US/$9.99CAN
___Sweet Revenge	0-8217-7879-X	$6.99US/$9.99CAN
___Lethal Justice	0-8217-7880-3	$6.99US/$9.99CAN
___Free Fall	0-8217-7881-1	$6.99US/$9.99CAN
___Fool Me Once	0-8217-8071-9	$7.99US/$10.99CAN
___Vegas Rich	0-8217-8112-X	$7.99US/$10.99CAN
___Hide and Seek	1-4201-0184-6	$6.99US/$9.99CAN
___Hokus Pokus	1-4201-0185-4	$6.99US/$9.99CAN
___Fast Track	1-4201-0186-2	$6.99US/$9.99CAN
___Collateral Damage	1-4201-0187-0	$6.99US/$9.99CAN
___Final Justice	1-4201-0188-9	$6.99US/$9.99CAN
___Up Close and Personal	0-8217-7956-7	$7.99US/$9.99CAN
___Under the Radar	1-4201-0683-X	$6.99US/$9.99CAN
___Razor Sharp	1-4201-0684-8	$7.99US/$10.99CAN
___Yesterday	1-4201-1494-8	$5.99US/$6.99CAN
___Vanishing Act	1-4201-0685-6	$7.99US/$10.99CAN
___Sara's Song	1-4201-1493-X	$5.99US/$6.99CAN
___Deadly Deals	1-4201-0686-4	$7.99US/$10.99CAN
___Game Over	1-4201-0687-2	$7.99US/$10.99CAN
___Sins of Omission	1-4201-1153-1	$7.99US/$10.99CAN
___Sins of the Flesh	1-4201-1154-X	$7.99US/$10.99CAN
___Cross Roads	1-4201-1192-2	$7.99US/$10.99CAN

DISCARD

Available Wherever Books Are Sold!
Check out our website at **www.kensingtonbooks.com**